By England's Aid Or The Freeing of the Netherlands 1585 to 1604

By England's Aid: or The Freeing

Table of Contents

By England's Aid: or The Freeing

G.A. Henty

PREFACE.

MY DEAR LADS,

In my preface to By Pike and Dyke I promised in a future story to deal with the closing events of the War of Independence in Holland. The period over which that war extended was so long, and the incidents were so numerous and varied, that it was impossible to include the whole within the limit of a single book. The former volume brought the story of the struggle down to the death of the Prince of Orange and the capture of Antwerp; the present gives the second phase of the war, when England, who had long unofficially assisted Holland, threw herself openly into the struggle, and by her aid mainly contributed to the successful issue of the war. In the first part of the struggle the scene lay wholly among the low lands and cities of Holland and Zeeland, and the war was strictly a defensive one, waged against overpowering odds. After England threw herself into the strife it assumed far wider proportions, and the independence of the Netherlands was mainly secured by the defeat and destruction of the great Armada, by the capture of Cadiz and the fatal blow thereby struck at the mercantile prosperity of Spain, and by the defeat of the Holy League by Henry of Navarre, aided by English soldiers and English gold. For the facts connected with the doings of Sir Francis Vere and the British contingent in Holland, I have depended much upon the excellent work by Mr. Clement Markham entitled the Fighting Veres. In this full justice is done to the great English general and his followers, and it is conclusively shown that some statements to the disparagement of Sir Francis Vere by Mr. Motley are founded upon a misconception of the facts. Sir Francis Vere was, in the general opinion of the time, one of the greatest commanders of the age, and more, perhaps, than any other man with the exception of the Prince of Orange contributed to the successful issue of the struggle of Holland to throw off the yoke of Spain.

Yours sincerely,

G.A. HENTY

CHAPTER I. AN EXCURSION

"And we beseech Thee, 0 Lord, to give help and succour to Thy servants the people of Holland, and to deliver them from the cruelties and persecutions of their wicked oppressors; and grant Thy blessing, we pray Thee, upon the arms of our soldiers now embarking to aid them in their extremity."

These were the words with which the Rev. John Vickars, rector of Hedingham, concluded the family prayers on the morning of December 6th, 1585.

For twenty years the first portion of this prayer had been repeated daily by him, as it had been in tens of thousands of English households; for since the people of the Netherlands first rose against the Spanish yoke the hearts of the Protestants of England had beat warmly in their cause, and they had by turns been moved to admiration at the indomitable courage with which the Dutch struggled for independence against the might of the greatest power in Europe, and to horror and indignation at the pitiless cruelty and wholesale massacres by which the Spaniards had striven to stamp out resistance.

From the first the people of England would gladly have joined in the fray, and made common cause with their co-religionists; but the queen and her counsellors had been restrained by weighty considerations from embarking in such a struggle. At the commencement of the war the power of Spain overshadowed all Europe. Her infantry were regarded as irresistible. Italy and Germany were virtually her dependencies, and England was but a petty power beside her. Since Agincourt was fought we had taken but little part in wars on the Continent. The feudal system was extinct; we had neither army nor military system; and the only Englishmen with the slightest experience of war were those who had gone abroad to seek their fortunes, and had fought in the armies of one or other of the continental powers. Nor were we yet aware of our naval strength. Drake and Hawkins and the other buccaneers had not yet commenced their private war with Spain, on what was known as the Spanish Main — the waters of the West Indian Islands — and no one dreamed that the time was approaching when England would be able to hold her own against the strength of Spain on the seas.

Thus, then, whatever the private sentiments of Elizabeth and her counsellors, they shrank from engaging England in a life and death struggle with the greatest power of the time;

3

though as the struggle went on the queen's sympathy with the people of the Netherlands was more and more openly shown. In 1572 she was present at a parade of three hundred volunteers who mustered at Greenwich under Thomas Morgan and Roger Williams for service in the Netherlands. Sir Humphrey Gilbert, half brother of Sir Walter Raleigh, went out a few months later with 1500 men, and from that time numbers of English volunteers continued to cross the seas and join in the struggle against the Spaniards. Nor were the sympathies of the queen confined to allowing her subjects to take part in the fighting; for she sent out large sums of money to the Dutch, and as far as she could, without openly joining them, gave them her aid.

Spain remonstrated continually against these breaches of neutrality, while the Dutch on their part constantly implored her to join them openly; but she continued to give evasive answers to both parties until the assassination of William of Orange on 10th July, 1584, sent a thrill of horror through England, and determined the queen and her advisers to take a more decisive part in the struggle. In the following June envoys from the States arrived in London, and were received with great honour, and a treaty between the two countries was agreed upon. Three months later the queen published a declaration to her people and to Europe at large, setting forth the terrible persecutions and cruelties to which "our next neighbours, the people of the Low Countries," the special allies and friends of England, had been exposed, and stating her determination to aid them to recover their liberty. The proclamation concluded: "We mean not hereby to make particular profit to ourself and our people, only desiring to obtain, by God's favour, for the Countries, a deliverance of them from war by the Spaniards and foreigners, with a restitution of their ancient liberties and government.

Sir Thomas Cecil was sent out at once as governor of Brill, and Sir Philip Sidney as governor of Flushing, these towns being handed over to England as guarantees by the Dutch. These two officers, with bodies of troops to serve as garrisons, took charge of their respective fortresses in November. Orders were issued for the raising of an army for service in the Low Countries, and Dudley, Earl of Leicester, was appointed by the queen to its command. The decision of the queen was received with enthusiasm in England as well as in Holland, and although the Earl of Leicester was not personally popular, volunteers flocked to his standard.

Breakfast at Hedingham Rectory had been set at an earlier hour than usual on the 6th of December, 1585. There was an unusual stir and excitement in the village, for young Mr.

By England's Aid: or The Freeing

Francis Vere, cousin of the Earl of Oxford, lord of Hedingham and of all the surrounding country, was to start that morning to ride to Colchester, there to join the Earl of Leicester and his following as a volunteer. As soon as breakfast was over young Geoffrey and Lionel Vickars, boys of fourteen and thirteen years old, proceeded to the castle close by, and there mounted the horses provided for them, and rode with Francis Vere to Colchester.

Francis, who was at this time twenty−five years old, was accompanied by his elder brother, John, and his two younger brothers, Robert and Horace, and by many other friends; and it was a gay train that cantered down the valley of the Colne to Colchester. That ancient town was all astir. Gentlemen had ridden in from all the country seats and manors for many miles round, and the quiet streets were alive with people. At two o'clock in the afternoon news arrived that the earl was approaching, and, headed by the bailiffs of the town in scarlet gowns, the multitude moved out to meet the earl on the Lexden road. Presently a long train was seen approaching; for with Leicester were the Earl of Essex, Lords North and Audley, Sir William Russell, Sir Thomas Shirley, and other volunteers, to the number of five hundred horse. All were gaily attired and caparisoned, and the cortege presented a most brilliant appearance. The multitude cheered lustily, the bailiffs presented an address, and followed by his own train and by the gentlemen who had assembled to meet him, the earl rode into the town. He himself took up his abode at the house of Sir Thomas Lucas, while his followers were distributed among the houses of the townsfolk. Two hours after the arrival of the earl, the party from Hedingham took leave of Mr. Francis Vere.

"Goodbye, lads," he said to the young Vickars, "I will keep my promise, never fear; and if the struggle goes on till you are old enough to carry arms, I will, if I am still alive, take you under my leading and teach you the art of war."

Upon the following day the Earl of Leicester and his following rode to Manningtree, and took boat down the Stour to Harwich, where the fleet, under Admiral William Borough, was lying. Here they embarked, and on the 9th of December sailed for Flushing, where they were joined by another fleet of sixty ships from the Thames.

More than a year passed. The English had fought sturdily in Holland. Mr. Francis Vere had been with his cousin, Lord Willoughby, who was in command of Bergen op Zoom, and had taken part in the first brush with the enemy, when a party of the garrison marched out and attacked a great convoy of four hundred and fifty wagons going to Antwerp, killed three hundred of the enemy, took eighty prisoners, and destroyed all their wagons except twenty–seven, which they carried into the town. Leicester provisioned the town of Grave, which was besieged by the Duke of Parma, the Spanish commander in chief. Axel was captured by surprise, the volunteers swimming across the moat at night, and throwing open the gates. Doesburg was captured, and Zutphen besieged.

Parma marched to its relief, and, under cover of a thick fog, succeeded in getting close at hand before it was known that he was near. Then the English knights and volunteers, 200 in number, mounted in hot haste and charged a great Spanish column of 5000 horse and foot. They were led by Sir William Russell, under whom were Lord Essex, North, Audley, and Willoughby, behind the last of whom rode Francis Vere. For two hours this little band of horse fought desperately in the midst of the Spanish cavalry, and forced them at last to fall back, but were themselves obliged to retreat when the Spanish infantry came up and opened fire upon them. The English loss was 34 killed and wounded, while 250 of the Spaniards were slain, and three of their colours captured. Among the wounded on the English side was the very noble knight Sir Philip Sidney, who was shot by a musket ball, and died three weeks afterwards.

The successes of the English during these two years were counterbalanced by the cowardly surrender of Grave by its governor, and by the treachery of Sir William Stanley, governor of Deventer, and of Roland Yorke, who commanded the garrisons of the two forts known as the Zutphen Sconces. Both these officers turned traitors and delivered up the posts they commanded to the Spaniards. Their conduct not only caused great material loss to the allies, but it gave rise to much bad feeling between the English and Dutch, the latter complaining that they received but half hearted assistance from the English.

It was not surprising, however, that Leicester was unable to effect more with the little force under his command, for it was necessary not only to raise soldiers, but to invent regulations and discipline. The Spanish system was adopted, and this, the first English regular army, was trained and appointed precisely upon the system of the foe with whom they were fighting. It was no easy task to convert a body of brave knights and gentlemen and sturdy countrymen into regular troops, and to give them the advantages conferred by discipline and order. But the work was rendered the less difficult by the admixture of the volunteers who had been bravely fighting for ten years under Morgan, Rowland Williams, John Norris, and others. These had had a similar experience on their first

6

arrival in Holland. Several times in their early encounters with the Spaniards the undisciplined young troops had behaved badly; but they had gained experience from their reverses, and had proved themselves fully capable of standing in line even against the splendid pikemen of Spain.

While the English had been drilling and fighting in Holland things had gone on quietly at Hedingham. The village stands near the headwaters of the Colne and Stour, in a rich and beautiful country. On a rising ground behind it stood the castle of the Veres, which was approached from the village by a drawbridge across the moat. There were few more stately piles in England than the seat of the Earl of Oxford. On one side of the great quadrangle was the gatehouse and a lofty tower, on another the great hall and chapel and the kitchens, on a third the suites of apartments of the officials and retinue. In rear were the stables and granaries, the butts and tennis court, beyond which was the court of the tournaments.

In the centre of the quadrangle rose the great keep, which still stands, the finest relic of Norman civil architecture in England. It possessed great strength, and at the same time was richly ornamented with carving. The windows, arches, and fireplaces were decorated with chevron carvings. A beautiful spiral pattern enriched the doorway and pillars of the staircase leading to galleries cut in the thickness of the wall, with arched openings looking into the hall below. The outlook from the keep extended over the parishes of Castle Hedingham, Sybil Hedingham, Kirby, and Tilbury, all belonging to the Veres — whose property extended far down the pretty valley of the Stour — with the stately Hall of Long Melford, the Priory of Clare, and the little town of Lavenham; indeed, the whole country was dotted with the farm houses and manors of the Veres. Seven miles down the valley of the Colne lies the village of Earl's Colne, with the priory, where ten of the earls of Oxford lie buried with their wives.

The parish church of Castle Hedingham stood at the end of the little village street, and the rectory of Mr. Vickars was close by. The party gathered at morning prayers consisted of Mr. Vickars and his wife, their two sons, Geoffrey and Lionel, and the maidservants, Ruth and Alice. The boys, now fourteen and fifteen years old respectively, were strong grown and sturdy lads, and their father had long since owned with a sigh that neither of them was likely to follow his profession and fill the pulpit at Hedingham Church when he was gone. Nor was this to be wondered at, for lying as it did at the entrance to the great castle of the Veres, the street of the little village was constantly full of armed men, and resounded with the tramp of the horses of richly dressed knights and gay ladies.

Here came great politicians, who sought the friendship and support of the powerful earls of Oxford, nobles and knights, their kinsmen and allies, gentlemen from the wide spreading manors of the family, stout fighting men who wished to enlist under their banner. At night the sound of music from the castle told of gay entertainments and festive dances, while by day parties of knights and ladies with dogs and falcons sallied out to seek sport over the wide domains. It could hardly be expected, then, that lads of spirit, brought up in the midst of sights and sounds like these, should entertain a thought of settling down to the tranquil life of the church. As long as they could remember, their minds had been fixed upon being soldiers, and fighting some day under the banner of the Veres. They had been a good deal in the castle; for Mr. Vickars had assisted Arthur Golding, the learned instructor to young Edward Vere, the 17th earl, who was born in 1550, and had succeeded to the title at the age of twelve, and he had afterwards been tutor to the earl's cousins, John, Francis, Robert, and Horace, the sons of Geoffrey, fourth son of the 15th earl. These boys were born in 1558, 1560, 1562, and 1565, and lived with their mother at Kirby Hall, a mile from the Castle of Hedingham.

The earl was much attached to his old instructor, and when he was at the castle there was scarce a day but an invitation came down for Mr. Vickars and his wife to be present either at banquet or entertainment. The boys were free to come and go as they chose, and the earl's men−at−arms had orders to afford them all necessary teaching in the use of weapons.

Mr. Vickars considered it his duty to accept the invitations of his friend and patron, but he sorely grudged the time so abstracted from his favourite books. It was, indeed, a relief to him when the earl, whose love of profusion and luxury made serious inroads even into the splendid possessions of the Veres, went up to court, and peace and quietness reigned in the castle. The rector was fonder of going to Kirby, where John, Geoffrey's eldest son, lived quietly and soberly, his three younger brothers having, when mere boys, embraced the profession of arms, placing themselves under the care of the good soldier Sir William Brownie, who had served for many years in the Low Countries. They occasionally returned home for a time, and were pleased to take notice of the sons of their old tutor, although Geoffrey was six years junior to Horace, the youngest of the brothers.

By England's Aid: or The Freeing

The young Vickars had much time to themselves, much more, indeed, than their mother considered to be good for them. After their breakfast, which was finished by eight o'clock, their father took them for an hour and heard the lessons they had prepared the day before, and gave them instruction in the Latin tongue. Then they were supposed to study till the bell rang for dinner at twelve; but there was no one to see that they did so, for their father seldom came outside his library door, and their mother was busy with her domestic duties and in dispensing simples to the poor people, who, now that the monasteries were closed, had no medical aid save that which they got from the wives of the gentry or ministers, or from the wise women, of whom there was generally one in every village.

Therefore, after half an hour, or at most an hour, spent in getting up their tasks, the books would be thrown aside, and the boys be off, either to the river or up to the castle to practice sword play with the men—at—arms, or to the butts with their bows, or to the rabbit warren, where they had leave from the earl to go with their dogs whenever they pleased. Their long excursions were, however, generally deferred until after dinner, as they were then free until suppertime — and even if they did not return after that hour Mrs. Vickars did not chide them unduly, being an easygoing woman, and always ready to make excuses for them.

There were plenty of fish in the river; and the boys knew the pools they loved best, and often returned with their baskets well filled. There were otters on its banks, too; but, though they sometimes chased these pretty creatures, Tan and Turk, their two dogs, knew as well as their masters that they had but small chance of catching them. Sometimes they would take a boat at the bridge and drop down the stream for miles, and once or twice had even gone down to Bricklesey at the mouth of the river. This, however, was an expedition that they never performed alone, making it each time in charge of Master Lirriper, who owned a flat barge, and took produce down to Bricklesey, there to be transhipped into coasters bound for London. He had a married daughter there, and it was at her house the boys had slept when they went there; for the journey down and up again was too long to be performed in a single day.

But this was not the only distant expedition they had made, for they had once gone down the Stour as far as Harwich with their father when he was called thither on business. To them Harwich with its old walls and the houses crowned up within them, and its busy port with vessels coming in and going out, was most delightful, and they always talked about that expedition as one of the most pleasant recollections of their lives.

After breakfast was over on the 1st of May, 1587, and they had done their lessons with their father, and had worked for an hour by themselves, the boys put by their books and strolled down the village to the bridge. There as usual stood their friend Master Lirriper with his hands deep in his pockets, a place and position in which he was sure to be found when not away in his barge.

"Good morning, Master Lirriper."

"Good morning, Master Geoffrey and Master Lionel."

"So you are not down the river today?"

"No, sir. I am going tomorrow, and this time I shall be away four or five days — maybe even a week."

"Shall you?" the boys exclaimed in surprise. "Why, what are you going to do?"

"I am going round to London in my nephew Joe Chambers' craft."

"Are you really?" Geoffrey exclaimed. "I wish we were going with you. Don't you think you could take us, Master Lirriper?"

The bargeman looked down into the water and frowned. He was slow of speech, but as the minutes went on and he did not absolutely refuse the boys exchanged glances of excitement and hope.

"I dunno how that might be, young sirs," John Lirriper said slowly, after long cogitation. "I dussay my nephew would have no objection, but what would parson say about it?"

"Oh, I don't think he would object," Geoffrey said. "If you go up and ask him, Master Lirriper, and say that you will take care of us, you know, I don't see why he should say no."

"Like enough you would be ill," John Lirriper said after another long pause. "It's pretty rough sometimes.

"Oh, we shouldn't mind that," Lionel protested. "We should like to see the waves and to be in a real ship."

"It's nothing much of a ship," the boatman said. "She is a ketch of about ten tons and carries three hands."

"Oh, we don't care how small she is if we can only go in her; and you would be able to show us London, and we might even see the queen. Oh, do come up with us and ask father, Master Lirriper."

"Perhaps parson wouldn't be pleased, young sirs, and, might say I was putting wandering thoughts into your heads; and Mistress Vickars might think it a great liberty on my part."

"Oh, no, she wouldn't, Master Lirriper. Besides, we will say we asked you."

"But suppose any harm comes to you, what would they say to me then?"

"Oh, there's no fear of any harm coming to us. Besides, in another year or two we mean to go over to the Low Countries and fight the Spaniards, and what's a voyage to London to that?"

"Well, I will think about it," John Lirriper said cautiously.

"No, no, Master Lirriper; if you get thinking about it it will never be done. Do come up with us at once," and each of them got hold of one of the boatman's arms.

"Well, the parson can but say no," he said, as he suffered himself to be dragged away. "And I don't say as it isn't reasonable that you should like to see something of the world, young sirs; but I don't know how the parson will take it."

Mr. Vickars looked up irritably from his books when the servant came in and said that Master Lirriper wished to see him.

"What does he want at this hour?" he said. "You know, Ruth, I never see people before dinner. Any time between that and supper I am at their service, but it's too bad being disturbed now."

"I told him so, sir; but Master Geoffrey and Master Lionel were with him, and they said he wanted particular to see you, and they wanted particular too."

The clergyman sighed as he put his book down.

"If Geoffrey and Lionel have concerned themselves in the matter, Ruth, I suppose I must see the man; but it's very hard being disturbed like this. Well, Master Lirriper, what is it?" he asked, as the boatman accompanied by Geoffrey and Lionel entered the room. Master Lirriper twirled his hat in his hand. Words did not come easily to him at the best of times, and this was a business that demanded thought and care. Long before he had time to fix upon an appropriate form of words Geoffrey broke in:

"This is what it is, father. Master Lirriper is going down the river to Bricklesey tomorrow, and then he is going on board his nephew's ship. She is a ketch, and she carries ten tons, though I don't know what it is she carries; and she's going to London, and he is going in her, and he says if you will let him he will take us with him, and will show us London, and take great care of us. It will be glorious, father, if you will only let us go."

Mr. Vickars looked blankly as Geoffrey poured out his torrent of words. His mind was still full of the book he had been reading, and he hardly took in the meaning of Geoffrey's words.

"Going in a ketch!" he repeated. "Going to catch something, I suppose you mean? Do you mean he is going fishing?"

"No, father, — going in a ketch. A ketch is a sort of ship, father, though I don't quite know what sort of ship. What sort of ship is a ketch, Master Lirriper?"

"A ketch is a two masted craft, Master Geoffrey," John Lirriper said. "She carries a big mizzen sail."

"There, you see, father," Geoffrey said triumphantly; "she carries a big mizzen sail. That's what she is, you see; and he is going to show us London, and will take great care of us if you will let us go with him."

"Do you mean, Master Lirriper," Mr. Vickars asked slowly, "that you are going to London in some sort of ship, and want to take my sons with you?"

"Well, sir, I am going to London, and the young masters seemed to think that they would like to go with me, if so be you would have no objection."

"I don't know," Mr. Vickars said, "It is a long passage, Master Lirriper; and, as I have heard, often a stormy one. I don't think my wife —"

"Oh, yes, father," Lionel broke in. "If you say yes, mother is sure to say yes; she always does, you know. And, you see, it will be a great thing for us to see London. Every one else seems to have seen London, and I am sure that it would do us good. And we might even see the queen."

"I think that they would be comfortable, sir," John Lirriper put in. "You see, my nephew's wife is daughter of a citizen, one Master Swindon, a ship's chandler, and he said there would be a room there for me, and they would make me heartily welcome. Now, you see, sir, the young masters could have that room, and I could very well sleep on board the ketch; and they would be out of all sort of mischief there."

"That would be a very good plan certainly, Master Lirriper. Well, well, I don't know what to say."

"Say yes, father," Geoffrey said as he saw Mr. Vickars glance anxiously at the book he had left open. "If you say yes, you see it will be a grand thing for you, our being away for a week with nothing to disturb you."

"Well, well," Mr. Vickars said, "you must ask your mother. If she makes no objection, then I suppose you can go," and Mr. Vickars hastily took up his book again.

The boys ran off to the kitchen, where their mother was superintending the brewing of some broth for a sick woman down the village.

By England's Aid: or The Freeing

"Mother!" Geoffrey exclaimed, "Master Lirriper's going to London in a ketch — a ship with a big mizzen sail, you know — and he has offered to take us with him and show us London. And father has said yes, and it's all settled if you have no objection; and of course you haven't."

"Going to London, Geoffrey!" Mrs. Vickars exclaimed aghast. "I never heard of such a thing. Why, like enough you will be drowned on the way and never come back again. Your father must be mad to think of such a thing."

"Oh, no, mother; I am sure it will do us a lot of good. And we may see the queen, mother. And as for drowning, why, we can both swim ever so far. Besides, people don't get drowned going to London. Do they, Master Lirriper?"

John was standing bashfully at the door of the kitchen. "Well, not as a rule, Master Geoffrey," he replied. "They comes and they goes, them that are used to it, maybe a hundred times without anything happening to them."

"There! You hear that, mother? They come and go hundreds of times. Oh, I am sure you are not going to say no. That would be too bad when father has agreed to it. Now, mother, please tell Ruth to run away at once and get a wallet packed with our things. Of course we shall want our best clothes; because people dress finely in London, and it would never do if we saw the queen and we hadn't our best doublets on, for she would think that we didn't know what was seemly down at Hedingham."

"Well, my dears, of course if it is all settled —"

"Oh, yes, mother, it is quite all settled."

"Then it's no use my saying anything more about it, but I think your father might have consulted me before he gave his consent to your going on such a hazardous journey as this."

"He did want to consult you, mother. But then, you see, he wanted to consult his books even more, and he knew very well that you would agree with him; and you know you would too. So please don't say anything more about it, but let Ruth run upstairs and see to our things at once.

14

By England's Aid: or The Freeing

"There, you see, Master Lirriper, it is all settled. And what time do you start tomorrow? We will be there half an hour before, anyhow."

"I shall go at seven from the bridge. Then I shall just catch the turn of the tide and get to Bricklesey in good time."

"I never did see such boys," Mrs. Vickars said when John Lirriper had gone on his way. "As for your father, I am surprised at him in countenancing you. You will be running all sorts of risks. You may be drowned on the way, or killed in a street brawl, or get mixed up in a plot. There is no saying what may not happen. And here it is all settled before I have even time to think about it, which is most inconsiderate of your father."

"Oh, we shall get back again without any harm, mother. And as to getting killed in a street brawl, Lionel and I can use our hangers as well as most of them. Besides, nothing of that sort is going to happen to us. Now, mother, please let Ruth go at once, and tell her to put up our puce doublets that we had for the jousting at the castle, and our red hose and our dark green cloth slashed trunks."

"There is plenty of time for that, Geoffrey, as you are not going until tomorrow. Besides, I can't spare Ruth now, but she shall see about it after dinner."

There was little sleep for the boys that night. A visit to London had long been one of their wildest ambitions, and they could scarcely believe that thus suddenly and without preparation it was about to take place. Their father had some time before promised that he would someday make request to one or other of the young Veres to allow them to ride to London in his suite, but the present seemed to them an even more delightful plan. There would be the pleasure of the voyage, and moreover it would be much more lively for them to be able to see London under the charge of John Lirriper than to be subject to the ceremonial and restraint that would be enforced in the household of the Veres. They were, then, at the appointed place a full hour before the time named, with wallets containing their clothes, and a basket of provisions that their mother had prepared for them. Having stowed these away in the little cabin, they walked up and down impatiently until Master Lirriper himself appeared.

"You are up betimes, my young masters," the boatman said. "The church has not yet struck seven o'clock."

By England's Aid: or The Freeing

"We have been here ever so long, Master Lirriper. We could not sleep much last night, and got up when it chimed five, being afraid that we might drop off to sleep and be late."

"Well, we shall not be long before we are off. Here comes my man Dick, and the tide is just on the turn. The sky looks bright, and the weather promises well. I will just go round to the cottage and fetch up my things, and then we shall be ready."

In ten minutes they pushed off from the shore. John and his man got out long poles shod with iron, and with these set to work to punt the barge along. Now that they were fairly on their way the boys quieted down, and took their seats on the sacks of flour with which the boat was laden, and watched the objects on the bank as the boat made her way quietly along.

Halstead was the first place passed. This was the largest town near Hedingham, and was a place of much importance in their eyes. Then they passed Stanstead Hall and Earl's Colne on their right, Colne Wake on their left, and Chapel Parish on their right. Then there was a long stretch without any large villages, until they came in sight of the bridge above Colchester. A few miles below the town the river began to widen. The banks were low and flat, and they were now entering an arm of the sea. Half an hour later the houses and church of Bricklesey came in sight. Tide was almost low when they ran on to the mud abreast of the village, but John put on a pair of high boots and carried the boys ashore one after the other on his back, and then went up with them to the house where they were to stop for the night.

Here, although not expected, they were heartily welcomed by John's daughter.

"If father had told me that you had been coming, Masters Vickars, I would have had a proper dinner for you; but though he sent word yesterday morning that he should be over today, he did not say a word about your coming with them."

"He did not know himself," Geoffrey said; "it was only settled at ten o'clock yesterday. But do not trouble yourself about the dinner. In the first place, we are so pleased at going that we don't care a bit what we eat, and in the second place we had breakfast on board the boat, and we were both so hungry that I am sure we could go till supper time without eating if necessary."

By England's Aid: or The Freeing

"Where are you going, father?" the young woman asked.

"I am going to set about unloading the flour."

"Why, it's only a quarter to twelve, and dinner just ready. The fish went into the frying pan as you came up from the boat. You know we generally dine at half past eleven, but we saw you coming at a distance and put it off. It's no use your starting now."

"Well, I suppose it isn't. And I don't know what the young masters' appetite may be, but mine is pretty good, I can tell you."

"I never knew it otherwise, father," the woman laughed. "Ah, here is my Sam. Sam, here's father brought these two young gentlemen. They are the sons of Mr. Vickars, the parson at Hedingham. They are going to stop here tonight, and are going with him in the Susan tomorrow to London."

"Glad to see you, young masters," Sam said. "I have often heard Ann talk of your good father. I have just been on board the Susan, for I am sending up a couple of score sides of bacon in her, and have been giving Joe Chambers, her master, a list of things he is to get there and bring down for me.

"Now then, girl, bustle about and get dinner on as soon as you can. We are half an hour late. I am sure the young gentlemen here must be hungry. There's nothing like being on the water for getting an appetite."

A few minutes later a great dish of fish, a loaf of bread and some wooden platters, were placed on the table, and all set to at once. Forks had not yet come into use, and tablecloths were unknown, except among the upper classes. The boys found that in spite of their hearty breakfast their appetites were excellent. The fish were delicious, the bread was home baked, and the beer from Colchester, which was already famous for its brewing. When they had finished, John Lirriper asked them if they would rather see what there was to be seen in the village, or go off to the ketch. They at once chose the latter alternative. On going down to the water's edge they found that the tide had risen sufficiently to enable Dick to bring the barge alongside the jetty. They were soon on board.

"Which is the Susan, Master Lirriper?"

"That's her lying out there with two others. She is the one lowest down the stream. We shall just fetch her comfortably."

CHAPTER II. A MEETING IN CHEPE

A row of ten minutes took the boat with Master Lirriper and the two boys alongside the ketch.

"How are you, Joe Chambers?" Master Lirriper hailed the skipper as he appeared on the deck of the Susan. "I have brought you two more passengers for London. They are going there under my charge."

"The more the merrier, Uncle John," the young skipper replied. "There are none others going this journey, so though our accommodation is not very extensive, we can put them up comfortably enough if they don't mind roughing it."

"Oh, we don't mind that," Geoffrey said, as they climbed on board; "besides, there seems lots of room."

"Not so much as you think," the skipper replied. "She is a roomy craft is the Susan; but she is pretty nigh all hold, and we are cramped a little in the fo'castle. Still we can sleep six, and that's just the number we shall have, for we carry a man and a boy besides myself. I think your flour will about fill her up, Master Lirriper. We have a pretty full cargo this time."

"Well, we shall soon see," John Lirriper said. "Are you ready to take the flour on board at once? Because, if so, we will begin to discharge."

"Yes, I am quite ready. You told me you were going to bring forty sacks, and I have left the middle part of the hold empty for them. Sam Hunter's bacon will stow in on the top of your sacks, and just fill her up to the beams there, as I reckon. I'll go below and stow them away as you hand them across."

In an hour the sacks of flour were transferred from the barge to the hold of the Susan, and the sides of bacon then placed upon them.

"It's a pity we haven't all the rest of the things on board," the skipper said, "and then we could have started by this evening's tide instead of waiting till the morning. The wind is fair, and I hate throwing away a fair wind. There is no saying where it may blow tomorrow, but I shouldn't be at all surprised if it isn't round to the south, and that will be foul for us till we get pretty nigh up into the mouth of the river. However, I gave them till tonight for getting all their things on board and must therefore wait."

To the boys the Susan appeared quite a large craft, for there was not water up at Hedingham for vessels of her size; and though they had seen ships at Harwich, they had never before put foot on anything larger than Master Lirriper's barge. The Susan was about forty feet long by twelve feet beam, and drew, as her skipper informed them, near five feet of water. She was entirely decked. The cabin in the bows occupied some fourteen feet in length. The rest was devoted to cargo. They descended into the cabin, which seemed to them very dark, there being no light save what came down through the small hatchway. Still it looked snug and comfortable. There was a fireplace on one side of the ladder by which they had descended, and on this side there were two bunks, one above the other. On the other side there were lockers running along the entire length of the cabin. Two could sleep on these and two on the bunks above them.

"Now, young masters, you will take those two bunks on the top there. John Lirriper and I will sleep on the lockers underneath you. The man and the boy have the two on the other side. I put you on the top because there is a side board, and you can't fall out if she rolls, and besides, the bunks are rather wider than the lockers below. If the wind is fair you won't have much of our company, because we shall hold on till we moor alongside the wharves of London; but if it's foul, or there is not enough of it to take us against tide, we have to anchor on the ebb, and then of course we turn in."

"How long do you take getting from here to London?"

"Ah, that I can tell you more about when I see what the weather is like in the morning. With a strong fair wind I have done it in twenty–four hours, and again with the wind foul it has taken me nigh a week. Taking one trip with another I should put it at three days."

"Well, now we will be going ashore," John Lirriper said. "I will leave my barge alongside till tide turns, for I could not get her back again to the jetty so long as it is running in strong, so I will be off again in a couple of hours."

So saying he hauled up the dinghy that was towing behind the barge, and he and Dick rowed the two boys ashore. Then he walked along with them to a spot where several craft were hauled up, pointing out to them the differences in their rig and build, and explained their purpose, and gave them the names of the principal ropes and stays.

"Now," he said, "it's getting on for supper time, and it won't do to keep them waiting, for Ann is sure to have got some cakes made, and there's nothing puts a woman out more than people not being in to meals when they have something special ready. After that I shall go out with Dick and bring the barge ashore. He will load up her tomorrow, and take her back single handed; which can be done easy enough in such weather as this, but it is too much for one man if there is a strong wind blowing and driving her over to the one side or other of the river."

As John Lirriper had expected, his daughter had prepared a pile of hot cakes for supper, and her face brightened up when she saw the party return punctually. The boys had been up early, and had slept but little the night before, and were not sorry at eight o'clock to lie down on the bed of freshly cut rushes covered with home spun sheets, for regular beds of feathers were still but little used in England. At five o'clock they were astir again, and their hostess insisted on their eating a manchet of bread with some cheese, washed down by a stoup of ale, before starting. Dick had the boat at the jetty ready to row them off, and as soon as they were on board the Susan preparations were made for a start.

The mainsail was first hoisted, its size greatly surprising the boys; then the foresail and jib were got up, and lastly the mizzen. Then the capstan was manned, and the anchor slowly brought on board, and the sails being sheeted home, the craft began to steal through the water. The tide was still draining up, and she had not as yet swung. The wind was light, and, as the skipper had predicted, was nearly due south. As the ketch made its way out from the mouth of the river, and the wide expanse of water opened before them, the boys were filled with delight. They had taken their seats, one on each side of the skipper, who was at the tiller.

"I suppose you steer by the compass, Master Chambers?" Geoffrey said. "Which is the compass? I have heard about it, always pointing to the north."

"It's down below, young sir; I will show it you presently. We steer by that at night, or when it's foggy; but on a fine day like this there is no need for it. There are marks put up on all the sands, and we steer by them. You see, the way the wind is now we can lay our course for the Whittaker. That's a cruel sand, that is, and stretches out a long way from a point lying away on the right there. Once past that we bear away to the southwest, for we are then, so to speak, fairly in the course of the river. There is many a ship has been cast away on the Whittaker. Not that it is worse than other sands. There are scores of them lying in the mouth of the river, and if it wasn't for the marks there would be no sailing in or out."

"Who put up the marks?" Lionel asked.

"They are put up by men who make a business of it. There is one boat of them sails backwards and forwards where the river begins to narrow above Sheerness, and every ship that goes up or down pays them something according to her size. Others cruise about with long poles, putting them in the sands wherever one gets washed away. They have got different marks on them. A single cross piece, or two cross pieces, or a circle, or a diamond; so that each sand has got its own particular mark. These are known to the masters of all ships that go up and down the river, and so they can tell exactly where they are, and what course to take. At night they anchor, for there would be no possibility of finding the way up or down in the dark. I have heard tell from mariners who have sailed abroad that there ain't a place anywhere with such dangerous sands as those we have got here at the mouth of the Thames."

In the first three or four hours' sail Geoffrey and Lionel acquired much nautical knowledge. They learned the difference between the mainmast and the mizzen, found that all the strong ropes that kept the masts erect and stiff were called stays, that the ropes that hoist sails are called halliards, and that sheets is the name given to the ropes that restrain the sails at the lower corner, and are used to haul them in more tightly when sailing close to the wind, or to ease them off when the wind is favourable. They also learned that the yards at the head of the main and mizzen sails are called gaffs, and those at the bottom, booms.

"I think that's about enough for you to remember in one day, young masters," John Lirriper said. "You bear all that in your mind, and remember that each halliard and sheet has the name of the sail to which it is attached, and you will have learnt enough to make yourself useful, and can lend a hand when the skipper calls out, `Haul in the jib sheet,' or `Let go the fore halliards.' Now sit yourselves down again and see what is doing. That beacon you can just see right ahead marks the end of the Whittaker Spit. When we get there we shall drop anchor till the tide turns. You see we are going across it now, but when we round that beacon we shall have it dead against us, and the wind would be too light to take us against it even if it were not from the quarter it is. You see there are two or three other craft brought up there."

"Where have they come from, do you think, Master Lirriper?"

"Well, they may have come out from Burnham, or they may have come down from London and be going up to Burnham or to Bricklesey when the tide turns. There is a large ship anchored in the channel beyond the Whittaker. Of course she is going up when tide begins to flow. And there are the masts of two vessels right over there. They are in another channel. Between us and them there is a line of sands that you will see will show above the water when it gets a bit lower. That is the main channel, that is; and vessels coming from the south with a large draught of water generally use that, while this is the one that is handiest for ships from the north. Small vessels from the south come in by a channel a good bit beyond those ships. That is the narrowest of the three; and even light draught vessels don't use it much unless the wind is favourable, for there is not much room for them to beat up if the wind is against them."

"What is to beat up, Master Lirriper?"

"Well, you will see about that presently. I don't think we shall be able to lay our course beyond the Whittaker. To lay our course means to steer the way we want to go; and if we can't do that we shall have to beat, and that is tedious work with a light wind like this."

They dropped anchor off the beacon, and the captain said that this was the time to take breakfast. The lads already smelt an agreeable odour arising from the cabin forward, where the boy had been for some time busily engaged, and soon the whole party were seated on the lockers in the cabin devouring fried fish.

"Master Chambers," Geoffrey said, "we have got two boiled pullets in our basket. Had we not better have them for dinner? They were cooked the evening before we came away, and I should think they had better be eaten now."

"You had better keep them for yourselves, Master Geoffrey," the skipper said. "We are accustomed to living on fish, but like enough you would get tired of it before we got to London."

But this the boys would not hear of, and it was accordingly arranged that the dinner should be furnished from the contents of the basket.

As soon as tide turned the anchor was hove up and the Susan got under way again. The boys soon learnt the meaning of the word beating, and found that it meant sailing backwards and forwards across the channel, with the wind sometimes on one side of the boat and sometimes on the other. Geoffrey wanted very much to learn why, when the wind was so nearly ahead, the boat advanced instead of drifting backwards or sideways. But this was altogether beyond the power of either Master Lirriper or Joe Chambers to explain. They said every one knew that when the sails were full a vessel went in the direction in which her head pointed. "It's just the same way with yourself, Master Geoffrey. You see, when you look one way that's the way you go. When you turn your head and point another way, of course you go off that way; and it's just the same thing with the ship."

"I don't think it's the same thing, Master Lirriper," Geoffrey said puzzled. "In one case the power that makes one go comes from the inside, and so one can go in any direction one likes; in the other it comes from outside, and you would think the ship would have to go any way the wind pushes her. If you stand up and I give you a push, I push you straight away from me. You don't go sideways or come forward in the direction of my shoulder, which is what the ship does."

John Lirriper took off his cap and scratched his head.

"I suppose it is as you say, Master Geoffrey, though I never thought of it before. There is some reason, no doubt, why the craft moves up against the wind so long as the sails are full, instead of drifting away to leeward; though I never heard tell of it, and never heard anyone ask before. I dare say a learned man could tell why it is; and if you ask your good father when you go back I would wager he can explain it. It always seems to me as if a boat have got some sort of sense, just like a human being or a horse, and when she knows which way you wants her to go she goes. That's how it seems to me — ain't it, Joe?"

"Something like that, uncle. Every one knows that a boat's got her humours, and sometimes she sails better than she does others; and each boat's got her own fancies. Some does their best when they are beating, and some are lively in a heavy sea, and seem as if they enjoy it; and others get sulky, and don't seem to take the trouble to lift their bows up when a wave meets them; and they groans and complains if the wind is too hard for them, just like a human being. When you goes to a new vessel you have got to learn her tricks and her ways and what she will do, and what she won't do, and just to humour her as you would a child. I don't say as I think she is actually alive; but every sailor will tell you that there is something about her that her builders never put there."

"That's so," John Lirriper agreed. "Look at a boat that is hove up when her work's done and going to be broke up. Why, anyone can tell her with half an eye. She looks that forlorn and melancholy that one's inclined to blubber at the sight of her. She don't look like that at any other time. When she is hove up she is going to die, and she knows it."

"But perhaps that's because the paint's off her sides and the ropes all worn and loose," Geoffrey suggested.

But Master Lirriper waved the suggestion aside as unworthy even of an answer, and repeated, "She knows it. Anyone can see that with half an eye."

Geoffrey and Lionel talked the matter over when they were sitting together on deck apart from the others. It was an age when there were still many superstitions current in the land. Even the upper classes believed in witches and warlocks, in charms and spells, in lucky and unlucky days, in the arts of magic, in the power of the evil eye; and although to the boys it seemed absurd that a vessel should have life, they were not prepared altogether to discredit an idea that was evidently thoroughly believed by those who had been on board ships all their lives. After talking it over for some time they determined to submit the question to their father on their return.

It took them two more tides before they were off Sheerness. The wind was now more favourable, and having increased somewhat in strength, the Susan made her way briskly along, heeling over till the water ran along her scuppers. There was plenty to see now, for there were many fishing boats at work, some belonging, as Master Chambers told them, to the Medway, others to the little village of Leigh, whose church they saw at the top of the hill to their right. They met, too, several large craft coming down the river, and passed more than one, for the Susan was a fast boat.

"They would beat us," the skipper said when the boys expressed their surprise at their passing such large vessels, "if the wind were stronger or the water rough. We are doing our best, and if the wind rises I shall have to take in sail; while they could carry all theirs if it blew twice as hard. Then in a sea, weight and power tell; a wave that would knock the way almost out of us would hardly affect them at all."

So well did the Susan go along, that before the tide was much more than half done they passed the little village of Gravesend on their left, with the strong fort of Tilbury on the opposite shore, with its guns pointing on the river, and ready to give a good account of any Spaniard who should venture to sail up the Thames. Then at the end of the next reach the hamlet of Grays was passed on the right; a mile further Greenhithe on the left. Tide was getting slack now, but the Susan managed to get as far as Purfleet, and then dropped her anchor.

"This is our last stopping place," Joe Chambers said. "The morning tide will carry us up to London Bridge."

"Then you will not go on with tonight's tide?" Geoffrey asked.

"No; the river gets narrower every mile, and I do not care to take the risk of navigating it after dark, especially as there is always a great deal of shipping moored above Greenwich. Tide will begin to run up at about five o'clock, and by ten we ought to be safely moored alongside near London Bridge. So we should not gain a great deal by going on this evening instead of tomorrow morning, and I don't suppose you are in a particular hurry."

"Oh, no," Lionel said. "We would much rather go on in the morning, otherwise we should miss everything by the way; and there is the Queen's Palace at Greenwich that I want to see above all things."

By England's Aid: or The Freeing

Within a few minutes of the hour the skipper had named for their arrival, the Susan was moored alongside some vessels lying off one of the wharves above the Tower. The boys' astonishment had risen with every mile of their approach to the city, and they were perfectly astounded at the amount of shipping that they now beheld. The great proportion were of course coasters, like themselves, but there were many large vessels among them, and of these fully half were flying foreign colours. Here were traders from the Netherlands, with the flag that the Spaniards had in vain endeavoured to lower, flying at their mastheads. Here were caravels from Venice and Genoa, laden with goods from the East. Among the rest Master Chambers pointed out to the lads the ship in which Sir Francis Drake had circumnavigated the world, and that in which Captain Stevens had sailed to India, round the Cape of Good Hope. There were many French vessels also in the Pool, and indeed almost every flag save that of Spain was represented. Innumerable wherries darted about among the shipping, and heavier cargo boats dropped along in more leisurely fashion. Across the river, a quarter of a mile above the point at which they were lying, stretched London Bridge, with its narrow arches and the houses projecting beyond it on their supports of stout timbers. Beyond, on the right, rising high above the crowded roofs, was the lofty spire of St. Paul's. The boys were almost awed by this vast assemblage of buildings. That London was a great city they had known, but they were not prepared for so immense a difference between it and the place where they had lived all their lives. Only with the Tower were they somewhat disappointed. It was very grand and very extensive, but not so much grander than the stately abode of the Veres as they had looked for.

"I wouldn't change, if I were the earl, with the queen's majesty," Geoffrey said. "Of course it is larger than Hedingham, but not so beautiful, and it is crowded in by the houses, and has not like our castle a fair lookout on all sides. Why, there can be no hunting or hawking near here, and I can't think what the nobles can find to do all day."

"Now, young sirs," Master Lirriper said, "if you will get your wallets we will go ashore at once."

The boys were quite bewildered as they stepped ashore by the bustle and confusion. Brawny porters carrying heavy packages on their backs pushed along unceremoniously, saying from time to time in a mechanical sort of way, "By your leave, sir!" but pushing on and shouldering passersby into the gutter without the smallest compunction. The narrowness and dinginess of the streets greatly surprised and disappointed the boys, who found that in these respects even Harwich compared favourably with the region they were traversing. Presently, however, after passing through several lanes and alleys, they emerged into a much broader street, alive with shops. The people who were walking here were for the most part well dressed and of quiet demeanour, and there was none of the rough bustle that had prevailed in the riverside lanes.

"This is Eastchepe," their conductor said; "we have not far to go now. The street in which my friend dwells lies to the right, between this and Tower Street. I could have taken you a shorter way there, but I thought that your impressions of London would not be favourable did I take you all the way through those ill smelling lanes."

In a quarter of an hour they arrived at their destination, and entered the shop, which smelt strongly of tar; coils of rope of all sizes were piled up one upon another by the walls, while on shelves above them were blocks, lanterns, compasses, and a great variety of gear of whose use the boys were ignorant. The chandler was standing at his door.

"I am right glad to see you, Master Lirriper," he said, "and have been expecting you for the last two or three days. My wife would have it that some evil must have befallen you; but you know what women are. They make little allowance for time or tide or distance, but expect that every one can so arrange his journeys as to arrive at the very moment when they begin to expect him. But who have you here with you?"

"These are the sons of the worshipful Mr. Vickars, the rector of our parish and tutor to the Earl of Oxford and several of the young Veres, his cousins — a wise gentleman and a kind one, and much loved among us. He has entrusted his two sons to me that I might show them somewhat of this city of yours. I said that I was right sure that you and your good dame would let them occupy the chamber you intended for me, while I can make good shift on board the Susan."

"Nay, nay, Master Lirriper; our house is big enough to take in you and these two young masters, and Dorothy would deem it a slight indeed upon her hospitality were you not to take up your abode here too.

"You will be heartily welcome, young sirs, and though such accommodation as we can give you will not be equal to that which you are accustomed to, I warrant me that you will find it a pleasant change after that poky little cabin on board the Susan. I know it

27

well, for I supply her with stores, and have often wondered how men could accustom themselves to pass their lives in places where there is scarce room to turn, to say nothing of the smell of fish that always hangs about it. But if you will follow me I will take you up to my good dame, to whose care I must commit you for the present, as my foreman, John Watkins, is down by the riverside seeing to the proper delivery of divers stores on board a ship which sails with the next tide for Holland. My apprentices, too, are both out, as I must own is their wont. They always make excuses to slip down to the riverside when there is aught doing, and I am far too easy with the varlets. So at present, you see, I cannot long leave my shop."

So saying the chandler preceded them up a wide staircase that led from a passage behind the shop, and the boys perceived that the house was far more roomy and comfortable than they had judged from its outward appearance. Turning to the left when he reached the top of the stairs the chandler opened a door.

"Dorothy," he said, "here is your kinsman, Master Lirriper, who has suffered none of the misadventures you have been picturing to yourself for the last two days, and he has brought with him these young gentlemen, sons of the rector of Hedingham, to show them something of London."

"You are welcome, young gentlemen," Dame Dorothy said, "though why anyone should come to London when he can stay away from it I know not."

"Why, Dorothy, you are always running down our city, though I know right well that were I to move down with you to your native Essex again you would very soon cry out for the pleasures of the town."

"That would I not," she said. "I would be well contented to live in fresh country air all the rest of my life, though I do not say that London has not its share of pleasures also, though I care but little for them."

"Ah, Master Lirriper," her husband said laughing, "you would not think, to hear her talk, that there is not a feast or a show that Dorothy would stay away from. She never misses an opportunity, I warrant you, of showing herself off in her last new kirtle and gown. But I must be going down; there is no one below, and if a customer comes and finds the shop empty he will have but a poor idea of me, and will think that I am away gossiping instead of attending to my business."

"Are you hungry, young sirs?" the dame asked. "Because if so the maid shall bring up a manchet of bread and a cup of sack; if not, our evening meal will be served in the course of an hour."

The boys both said that they were perfectly able to wait until the meal came; and Geoffrey added, "If you will allow us, mistress, as doubtless you have private matters to talk of with Master Lirriper, my brother and I will walk out for an hour to see something of the town."

"Mind that you lose not your way," Master Lirriper said. "Do not go beyond Eastchepe, I beg you. There are the shops to look at there, and the fashions of dress and other matters that will occupy your attention well enough for that short time. Tomorrow morning I will myself go with you, and we can then wander further abroad. I have promised your good father to look after you, you know; and it will be but a bad beginning if you meet with any untoward adventure upon this the first day of your arrival here."

"We will not go beyond the limits of Eastchepe; and as to adventures, I can't see very well how any can befall us."

"Oh, there are plenty of adventures to be met with in London, young sir; and I shall be well content if on the day when we again embark on board the Susan none of them have fallen to your share."

The two lads accordingly sallied out and amused themselves greatly by staring at the goods exhibited in the open shops. They were less surprised at the richness and variety of the silver work, at the silks from the East, the costly satins, and other stuffs, than most boys from the country would have been, for they were accustomed to the splendour and magnificence displayed by the various noble guests at the castle, and saw nothing here that surpassed the brilliant shows made at the jousting and entertainments at Hedingham.

It was the scene that was novel to them: the shouts of the apprentices inviting attention to their employers' wares, the crowd that filled the street, consisting for the most part of the citizens themselves, but varied by nobles and knights of the court, by foreigners from many lands, by soldiers and men−at−arms from the Tower, by countrymen and sailors.

Their amusement was sometimes turned into anger by the flippant remarks of the apprentices; these varlets, perceiving easily enough by the manner of their attire that they were from the country, were not slow, if their master happened for the moment to be absent, in indulging in remarks that set Geoffrey and Lionel into a fever to commit a breach of the peace. The "What do you lack, masters?" with which they generally addressed passersby would be exchanged for remarks such as, "Do not trouble the young gentlemen, Nat. Do you not see they are up in the town looking for some of their master's calves?" or, "Look you, Philip, here are two rustics who have come up to town to learn manners."

"I quite see, Geoffrey," Lionel said, taking his brother by the arm and half dragging him away as he saw that he was clenching his fist and preparing to avenge summarily one of these insults even more pointed than usual, "that Master Lirriper was not very far out, and there is no difficulty in meeting with adventures in the streets of London. However, we must not give him occasion on this our first stroll in the streets to say that we cannot be trusted out of his sight. If we were to try to punish these insolent varlets we should have them on us like a swarm of bees, and should doubtless get worsted in the encounter, and might even find ourselves hauled off to the lockup, and that would be a nice tale for Master Lirriper to carry back to Hedingham."

"That is true enough, Lionel; but it is not easy to keep one's temper when one is thus tried. I know not how it is they see so readily that we are strangers, for surely we have mixed enough with the earl's family and friends to have rubbed off the awkwardness that they say is common to country folk; and as to our dress, I do not see much difference between its fashion and that of other people. I suppose it is because we look interested in what is going on, instead of strolling along like those two youths opposite with our noses in the air, as if we regarded the city and its belongings as infinitely below our regard. Well, I think we had best be turning back to Master Swindon's; it will not do to be late for our meal."

"Well, young sirs, what do you think of our shops?" Dame Swindon asked as they entered.

"The shops are well enough," Geoffrey replied; "but your apprentices seem to me to be an insolent set of jackanapes, who take strange liberties with passersby, and who would be all the better for chastisement. If it hadn't been that Lionel and I did not wish to become engaged in a brawl, we should have given some of them lessons in manners."

"They are free in speech," Dame Swindon said, "and are an impudent set of varlets. They have quick eyes and ready tongues, and are no respecters of persons save of their masters and of citizens in a position to lay complaints against them and to secure them punishment. They hold together greatly, and it is as well that you should not become engaged in a quarrel with them. At times they have raised serious tumults, and have even set not only the watch but the citizens at large at defiance. Strong measures have been several times taken against them; but they are a powerful body, seeing that in every shop there are one or more of them, and they can turn out with their clubs many thousand strong. They have what they call their privileges, and are as ready to defend them as are the citizens of London to uphold their liberties. Ordinances have been passed many times by the fathers of the city, regulating their conduct and the hours at which they may be abroad and the carrying of clubs and matters of this kind, but the apprentices seldom regard them, and if the watch arrest one for a breach of regulations, he raises a cry, and in two or three minutes a swarm of them collect and rescue the offender from his hands. Therefore it is seldom that the watch interferes with them."

"It would almost seem then that the apprentices are in fact the masters," Geoffrey said.

"Not quite as bad as that," Master Swindon replied. "There are the rules which they have to obey when at home, and if not they get a whipping; but it is difficult to keep a hand over them when they are abroad. After the shops are closed and the supper over they have from time immemorial the right to go out for two hours' exercise. They are supposed to go and shoot at the butts; but archery, I grieve to say, is falling into disrepute, and although many still go to the butts the practice is no longer universal. But here is supper."

Few words were spoken during the meal. The foreman and the two apprentices came up and sat down with the family, and it was not until these had retired that the conversation was again resumed.

"Where are you going to take them tomorrow, Master Lirriper?"

"Tomorrow we will see the city, the shops in Chepe, the Guildhall, and St. Paul's, then we shall issue out from Temple Bar and walk along the Strand through the country to Westminster and see the great abbey, then perhaps take a boat back. The next day, if the weather be fine, we will row up to Richmond and see the palace there, and I hope you will go with us, Mistress Dorothy; it is a pleasant promenade and a fashionable one, and methinks the river with its boats is after all the prettiest sight in London."

"Ah, you think there can be nothing pretty without water. That is all very well for one who is ever afloat, Master Lirriper; but give me Chepe at high noon with all its bravery of dress, and the bright shops, and the gallants of the court, and our own citizens too, who if not quite so gay in colour are proper men, better looking to my mind than some of the fops with their silver and satins."

"That's right, Dorothy," her husband said; "spoken like the wife of a citizen."

All these plans were destined to be frustrated. As soon as breakfast was over the next morning Master Lirriper started with the two boys, and they had but just entered Chepeside when they saw two young men approaching.

"Why, Lionel, here is Francis Vere!" Geoffrey exclaimed. "I thought he was across in Holland with the Earl of Leicester." They doffed their caps. Captain Vere, for such was now his rank, looked at them in surprise.

"Why!" he exclaimed, "here are Mr. Vickars' two sons. How came you here, lads? Have you run away from home to see the wonders of London, or to list as volunteers for the campaigns against the Dons?"

"I wish we were, Mr. Francis," Geoffrey said. "You promised when you were at Hedingham a year and a half since that you would some day take us to the wars with you, and our father, seeing that neither of us have a mind to enter the church, has quite consented that we shall become soldiers, the more so as there is a prospect of fighting for the persecuted Protestants of Holland. And oh, Mr. Francis, could it be now? You know we daily exercise with arms at the castle, and we are both strong and sturdy for our age, and believe me you should not see us flinch before the Spaniards however many of them there were."

"Tut, tut!" Captain Vere laughed. "Here are young cockerels, Allen; what think you of these for soldiers to stand against the Spanish pikemen?"

32

"There are many of the volunteers who are not very much older than they are," Captain Allen replied.

"There are two in my company who must be between seventeen and eighteen."

"Ah! but these boys are three years younger than that."

"Would you not take us as your pages, Mr. Francis?" Lionel urged. "We would do faithful service, and then when we come of age that you could enter us as volunteers we should already have learnt a little of war."

"Well, well, I cannot stop to talk to you now, for I am on my way to the Tower on business. I am only over from Holland for a day or two with despatches from the Earl to Her Majesty's Council, and am lodging at Westminster in a house that faces the abbey. It is one of my cousin Edward's houses, and you will see the Vere cognizance over the door. Call there at one hour after noon, and I will have a talk with you; but do not buoy yourselves up with hopes as to your going with me." So saying, with a friendly nod of his head Francis Vere continued his way eastward.

"What think you, Allen?" he asked his comrade as they went along. "I should like to take the lads with me if I could. Their father, who is the rector of Hedingham, taught my cousin Edward as well as my brothers and myself. I saw a good deal of the boys when I was at home. They are sturdy young fellows, and used to practise daily, as we did at their age, with the men–at–arms at the castle, and can use their weapons. A couple of years of apprenticeship would be good schooling for them. One cannot begin to learn the art of war too young, and it is because we have all been so ignorant of it that our volunteers in Holland have not done better."

"I think, Vere, that they are too young yet to be enlisted as volunteers, although in another two years, perhaps, you might admit the elder of the two; but I see no reason why, if you are so inclined, you should not take them with you as pages. Each company has its pages and boys, and you might take these two for the special service of yourself and your officers. They would then be on pretty well the same footing as the five gentlemen volunteers you have already with you, and would be distinct from the lads who have entered as pages to the company. I suppose that you have not yet your full number of boys?"

"No; there are fifteen boys allowed, one to each ten men, and I am several short of this number, and have already written my brother John to get six sturdy lads from among our own tenantry and to send them over in the first ship from Harwich. Yes, I will take these lads with me. I like their spirit, and we are all fond of their father, who is a very kindly as well as a learned man."

"I don't suppose he will thank you greatly, Francis," Captain Allen laughed.

"His goodwife is more likely to be vexed than he is," Captain Vere said, "for it will give him all the more time for the studies in which he is wrapped up. Besides, it will be a real service to the boys. It will shorten their probation as volunteers, and they may get commissions much earlier than they otherwise would do. We are all mere children in the art of war; for truly before Roger Morgan first took out his volunteers to fight for the Dutch there was scarce a man in England who knew how to range a company in order. You and I learned somewhat of our business in Poland, and some of our leaders have also had a few lessons in the art of war in foreign countries, but most of our officers are altogether new to the work. However, we have good masters, and I trust these Spaniards may teach us how to beat them in time; but at present, as I said, we are all going to school, and the earlier one begins at school the sooner one learns its lessons. Besides, we must have pages, and it will be more pleasant for me having lads who belong in a sort of way of our family, and to whom, if I am disposed, I can talk of people at home. They are high spirited and full of fun, and I should like to have them about me. But here we are at the Tower. We shall not be long, I hope, over the list of arms and munitions that the earl has sent for. When we have done we will take boat back to Westminster. Half an hour will take us there, as the tide will be with us."

CHAPTER III. IN THE LOW COUNTRY

Master Lirriper had stood apart while the boys were conversing with Francis Vere.

"What do you think, Master Lirriper?" Geoffrey exclaimed as they joined him. "We have asked Mr. Vere to take us with him as pages to the war in the Low Country, and though he said we were not to be hopeful about his reply, I do think he will take us. We are to go round to Westminster at one o'clock to see him again. What do you think of that?"

"I don't know what to think, Master Geoffrey. It takes me all by surprise, and I don't know how I stand in the matter. You see, your father gave you into my charge, and what could I say to him if I went back empty handed?"

"But, you see, it is with Francis Vere," Geoffrey said. "If it had been with anyone else it would be different. But the Veres are his patrons, and he looks upon the earl, and Mr. Francis and his brothers, almost as he does on us; and, you know, he has already consented to our entering the army some day. Besides, he can't blame you; because, of course, Mr. Vere will write to him himself and say that he has taken us, and so you can't be blamed in the matter. My father would know well enough that you could not withstand the wishes of one of the Veres, who are lords of Hedingham and all the country round."

"I should withstand them if I thought they were wrong," the boatman said sturdily, "and if I were sure that your father would object to your going; but that is what I am not sure. He may think it the best thing for you to begin early under the protection of Master Francis, and again he may think you a great deal too young for such wild work. He has certainly always let you have pretty much your own way, and has allowed you to come and go as you like, but this is a different business altogether. I am sorely bested as to what I ought to do."

"Well, nothing is settled yet, Master Lirriper; and, besides, I don't see that you can help yourself in the matter, and if Mr. Vere says he will take us I suppose you can't carry us off by force."

"It is Mistress Vickars that I am thinking of more than your father. The vicar is an easygoing gentleman, but Mistress Vickars speaks her mind, and I expect she will be in a terrible taking over it, and will rate me soundly; though, as you say, I do not see how I can help myself in the matter. Well now, let us look at the shops and at the Guildhall, and then we will make our way down to Westminster as we had proposed to do and see the abbey; by that time it will be near the hour at which you are to call upon Mr. Vere."

But the sights that the boys had been so longing to see had for the time lost their interest in their eyes. The idea that it was possible that Mr. Vere would take them with him to fight against the cruel oppressors of the Low Country was so absorbing that they could think of nothing else. Even the wonders of the Guildhall and St. Paul's received but scant attention, and the armourers' shops, in which they had a new and lively interest, alone sufficed to detain them. Even the gibes of the apprentices fell dead upon their ears. These varlets might laugh, but what would they say if they knew that they were going to fight the Spaniards? The thought so altered them that they felt almost a feeling of pity for these lads, condemned to stay at home and mind their masters' shops.

As to John Lirriper, he was sorely troubled in his mind, and divided between what he considered his duty to the vicar and his life long respect and reverence towards the lords of Hedingham. The feudal system was extinct, but feudal ideas still lingered among the people. Their lords could no longer summon them to take the field, had no longer power almost of life and death over them, but they were still their lords, and regarded with the highest respect and reverence. The earls of Oxford were, in the eyes of the people of those parts of Essex where their estates lay, personages of greater importance than the queen herself, of whose power and attributes they had but a very dim notion. It was not so very long since people had risen in rebellion against the queen, but such an idea as that of rising against their lords had never entered the mind of a single inhabitant of Hedingham.

However, Master Lirriper came to the conclusion that he was, as Geoffrey had said, powerless to interfere. If Mr. Francis Vere decided to take the boys with him, what could he do to prevent it? He could hardly take them forcibly down to the boat against their will, and even could he do so their father might not approve, and doubtless the earl, when he came to hear of it, would be seriously angry at this act of defiance of his kinsman. Still, he was sure that he should have a very unpleasant time with Mistress Vickars. But, as he reassured himself, it was, after all, better to put up with a woman's scolding than to bear the displeasure of the Earl of Oxford, who could turn him out of his house, ruin his business, and drive him from Hedingham. After all, it was natural that these lads should like to embark on this adventure with Mr. Francis Vere, and it would doubtless be to their interest to be thus closely connected with him. At any rate, if it was to be it was, and he, John Lirriper, could do nothing to prevent it. Having arrived at this conclusion he decided to make the best of it, and began to chat cheerfully with the boys.

Precisely at the appointed hour John Lirriper arrived with the two lads at the entrance to the house facing the abbey. Two or three servitors, whose doublets were embroidered with the cognizance of the Veres, were standing in front of the door.

By England's Aid: or The Freeing

"Why, it is Master Lirriper!" one of them said. "Why, what has brought you here? I did not know that your trips often extended to London."

"Nor do they," John Lirriper said. "It was the wind and my nephew's craft the Susan that brought me to London, and it is the will of Mr. Francis that these two young gentlemen should meet him here at one o'clock that has brought me to this door."

"Captain Francis is in; for, you know, he is a captain now, having been lately appointed to a company in the Earl of Leicester's army. He returned an hour since, and has but now finished his meal. Do you wish to go up with these young masters, or shall I conduct them to him?"

"You had best do that," John Lirriper answered. "I will remain here below if Captain Francis desires to see me or has any missive to intrust to me."

The boys followed the servant upstairs, and were shown into a room where Francis Vere, his cousin the Earl of Oxford, and Captain Allen were seated at table.

"Well, lads," the earl said, "so you want to follow my cousin Francis to the wars?"

"That is our wish, my lord, if Captain Francis will be so good as to take us with him."

"And what will my good tutor your father say to it?" the earl asked smiling.

"I think, my lord," Geoffrey said boldly, "that if you yourself will tell my father you think it is for our good, he will say naught against it."

"Oh, you want to throw the responsibility upon me, and to embroil me with your father and Mistress Vickars as an abettor of my cousin Francis in the kidnapping of children? Well, Francis, you had better explain to them what their duties will be if they go with you.

"You will be my pages," Francis Vere said, "and will perform the usual duties of pages in good families when in the field. It is the duty of pages to aid in collecting firewood and forage, and in all other ways to make themselves useful. You will bear the same sort of relation to the gentlemen volunteers as they do towards the officers. They are aspirants for commissions as officers as you will be to become gentlemen volunteers. You must not think that your duties will be light, for they will not, and you will have to bear many discomforts and hardships. But you will be in an altogether different position from that of the boys who are the pages of the company. You will, apart from your duties, and bearing in mind the difference of your age, associate with the officers and the gentlemen volunteers on terms of equality when nor engaged upon duty. On duty you will have to render the same strict and unquestionable obedience that all soldiers pay to those of superior rank. What say you? Are you still anxious to go? Because, if so, I have decided to take you."

Geoffrey and Lionel both expressed their thanks in proper terms, and their earnest desire to accompany Captain Vere, and to behave in all ways conformably to his orders and instructions.

"Very well, that is settled," Francis Vere said. "The earl is journeying down to Hedingham tomorrow, and has kindly promised to take charge of a letter from me to your father, and personally to assure him that this early embarkation upon military life would prove greatly to your advantage."

"Supposing that you are not killed by the Spaniards or carried off by fever," the earl put in; "for although possibly that might be an advantage to humanity in general, it could scarcely be considered one to you personally."

"We are ready to take our risk of that, my lord," Geoffrey said; "and are indeed greatly beholden both to Captain Francis for his goodness in taking us with him, and to yourself in kindly undertaking the mission of reconciling our father to our departure."

"You have not told me yet how it is that I find you in London?" Francis Vere said.

"We only came up for a week, sir, to see the town. We are in charge of Master Lirriper, who owns a barge on the river, and plies between Hedingham and Bricklesey, but who was coming up to London in a craft belonging to his nephew, and who took charge of us. We are staying at the house of Master Swindon, a citizen and ship chandler."

"Is Master Lirriper below?"

By England's Aid: or The Freeing

"He is, sir."

"Then in that case he had better go back to the house and bring your mails here. I shall sail from Deptford the day after tomorrow with the turn of tide. You had best remain here now. There will be many things necessary for you to get before you start. I will give instructions to one of my men—at—arms to go with you to purchase them."

"I will take their outfit upon myself, Francis," the earl said. "My steward shall go out with them and see to it. It is the least I can do when I am abetting you in depriving my old tutor of his sons."

He touched a bell and a servitor entered. "See that these young gentlemen are fed and attended to. They will remain here for the night. Tell Master Dotterell to come hither to me."

The boys bowed deeply and retired.

"It is all settled, Master Lirriper," they said when they reached the hall below. "We are to sail with Captain Francis the day after tomorrow, and you will be pleased to hear that the earl himself has taken charge of the matter, and will see our father and communicate the news to him."

"That is a comfort indeed," John Lirriper said fervently; "for I would most as soon have had to tell him that the Susan had gone down and that you were both drowned, as that I had let you both slip away to the wars when he had given you into my charge. But if the earl takes the matter in hand I do not think that even your lady mother can bear very heavily on me. And now, what is going to be done?"

"We are to remain here in order that suitable clothes may be obtained for us by the time we sail. Will you bring down tomorrow morning our wallets from Master Swindon's, and thank him and his good dame for their hospitality, and say that we are sorry to leave them thus suddenly without having an opportunity of thanking them ourselves? We will write letters tonight to our father and mother, and give them to you to take with you when you return."

By England's Aid: or The Freeing

John Lirriper at once took his departure, greatly relieved in mind to find that the earl himself had taken the responsibility upon his shoulders, and would break the news long before he himself reached Hedingham. A few minutes later a servitor conducted the boys to an apartment where a meal was laid for them; and as soon as this was over they were joined by the steward, who requested them to set out with him at once, as there were many things to be done and but short time for doing them. No difficulty in the way of time was, however, thrown in the way by the various tradesmen they visited, these being all perfectly ready to put themselves to inconvenience to do pleasure to so valuable a patron as the powerful Earl of Oxford.

Three suits of clothes were ordered for each of them: the one such as that worn by pages in noble families upon ordinary occasions, another of a much richer kind for special ceremonies and gaieties, the third a strong, serviceable suit for use when actually in the field. Then they were taken to an armourer's where each was provided with a light morion or head piece, breast plate and back piece, sword and dagger. A sufficient supply of under garments, boots, and other necessaries were also purchased; and when all was complete they returned highly delighted to the house. It was still scarce five o'clock, and they went across to the abbey and wandered for some time through its aisles, greatly impressed with its dignity and beauty now that their own affairs were off their mind.

They returned to the house again, and after supper wrote their letters to their father and mother, saying that they hoped they would not be displeased at the step they had taken, and which they would not have ventured upon had they not already obtained their father's consent to their entering the army. They knew, of course, that he had not contemplated their doing so for some little time; but as so excellent an opportunity had offered, and above all, as they were going out to fight against the Spaniards for the oppressed people of the Low Countries, they hoped their parents would approve of the steps they had taken, not having had time or opportunity to consult them.

At noon two days later Francis Vere with Captain Allen and the two boys took their seats in the stern of a skiff manned by six rowers. In the bow were the servitors of the two officers, and the luggage was stowed in the extreme stern.

"The tide is getting slack, is it not?" Captain Vere asked the boatmen.

"Yes, sir; it will not run up much longer. It will be pretty well slack water by the time we get to the bridge."

Keeping close to the bank the boat proceeded at a rapid pace. Several times the two young officers stood up and exchanged salutations with ladies or gentlemen of their acquaintance. As the boatman had anticipated, tide was slack by the time they arrived at London Bridge, and they now steered out into the middle of the river.

"Give way, lads," Captain Allen said. "We told the captain we would not keep him waiting long after high water, and he will be getting impatient if he does not see us before long."

As they shot past the Susan the boys waved their hands to Master Lirriper, who, after coming down in the morning and receiving their letters for their parents, had returned at once to the city and had taken his place on board the Susan, so as to be able to tell their father that he had seen the last of them. The distance between London Bridge and Deptford was traversed in a very short time. A vessel with her flags flying and her canvas already loosened was hanging to a buoy some distance out in the stream, and as the boat came near enough for the captain to distinguish those on board, the mooring rope was slipped, the head sails flattened in, and the vessel began to swing round. Before her head was down stream the boat was alongside. The two officers followed by the boys ascended the ladder by the side. The luggage was quickly handed up, and the servitors followed. The sails were sheeted home, and the vessel began to move rapidly through the water.

The boys had thought the Susan an imposing craft, but they were surprised, indeed, at the space on board the Dover Castle. In the stern there was a lofty poop with spacious cabins. Six guns were ranged along on each side of the deck, and when the sails were got up they seemed so vast to the boys that they felt a sense of littleness on board the great craft. They had been relieved to find that Captain Vere had his own servitor with him; for in talking it over they had mutually expressed their doubt as to their ability to render such service as Captain Vere would be accustomed to.

The wind was from the southwest, and the vessel was off Sheerness before the tide turned. There was, however, no occasion to anchor, for the wind was strong enough to take them against the flood.

By England's Aid: or The Freeing

During the voyage they had no duties to perform. The ship's cook prepared the meals, and the officers' servants waited on them, the lads taking their meals with the two officers. Their destination was Bergen op Zoom, a town at the mouth of the Scheldt, of the garrison of which the companies of both Francis Vere and Captain Allen formed a part.

As soon as the low coasts of Holland came in sight the boys watched them with the most lively interest.

"We are passing Sluys now," Captain Vere said. "The land almost ahead of us is Walcheren; and that spire belongs to Flushing. We could go outside and up the channel between the island and Beveland, and then up the Eastern Scheldt to Bergen op Zoom; but instead of that we shall follow the western channel, which is more direct."

"It is as flat as our Essex coast," Geoffrey remarked.

"Aye, and flatter; for the greater part of the land lies below the level of the sea, which is only kept out by great dams and dykes. At times when the rivers are high and the wind keeps back their waters they burst the dams and spread over a vast extent of country. The Zuider Zee was so formed in 1170 and 1395, and covers a tract as large as the whole county of Essex. Twenty–six years later the river Maas broke its banks and flooded a wide district. Seventy–two villages were destroyed and 100,000 people lost their life. The lands have never been recovered; and where a fertile country once stood is now a mere swamp."

"I shouldn't like living there," Lionel said. "It would be terrible, every time the rivers are full and the wind blows, to think that at any moment the banks may burst and the flood come rushing over you."

"It is all habit," Captain Vere replied; "I don't suppose they trouble themselves about it. But they are very particular in keeping their dykes in good repair. The water is one of the great defences of their country. In the first place there are innumerable streams to be crossed by an invader, and in the second, they can as a last resource cut the dykes and flood the country. These Dutchmen, as far as I have seen of them, are hard working and industrious people, steady and patient, and resolved to defend their independence to the last. This they have indeed proved by the wonderful resistance they have made against the power of Spain. There, you see the ship's head has been turned and we shall before

42

long be in the channel. Sluys lies up that channel on the right. It is an important place. Large vessels can go no further, but are unloaded there and the cargoes taken to Bruges and thence distributed to many other towns. They say that in 1468 as many as a hundred and fifty ships a day arrived at Sluys. That gives you an idea of the trade that the Netherlands carry on. The commerce of this one town was as great as is that of London at the present time. But since the troubles the trade of Sluys has fallen off a good deal."

The ship had to anchor here for two or three hours until the tide turned, for the wind had fallen very light and they could not make head against the ebb. As soon as it turned they again proceeded on their way, dropping quietly up with the tide. The boys climbed up into the tops, and thence could see a wide extent of country dotted with villages stretching beyond the banks, which restricted their view from the decks. In five hours Bergen op Zoom came in sight, and they presently dropped anchor opposite the town. The boat was lowered, and the two officers with the lads were rowed ashore. They were met as they landed by several young officers.

"Welcome back, Vere; welcome, Allen. You have been lucky indeed in having a few days in England, and getting a view of something besides this dreary flat country and its sluggish rivers. What is the last news from London?"

"There is little news enough," Vere replied. "We were only four days in London, and were busy all the time. And how are things here? Now that summer is at hand and the country drying the Dons ought to be bestirring themselves."

"They say that they are doing so," the officer replied. "We have news that the Duke of Parma is assembling his army at Bruges, where he is collecting the pick of the Spanish infantry with a number of Italian regiments which have joined him. He sent off the Marquess Del Vasto with the Sieur De Hautepenne towards Bois le Duc. General Count Hohenlohe, who, as you know, we English always call Count Holland, went off with a large force to meet him, and we heard only this morning that a battle has been fought, Hautepenne killed, and the fort of Crevecoeur on the Maas captured. From what I hear, some of our leaders think that it was a mistake so to scatter our forces, and if Parma moves forward from Bruges against Sluys, which is likely enough, we shall be sorely put to it to save the place."

As they were talking they proceeded into the town, and presently reached the house where Francis Vere had his quarters. The officers and gentlemen volunteers of his company soon assembled, and Captain Vere introduced the two boys to them.

"They are young gentlemen of good family," he said, "who will act as my pages until they are old enough to be enrolled as gentlemen volunteers. I commend them to your good offices. Their father is a learned and reverend gentleman who was my tutor, and also tutor to my cousin, the Earl of Oxford, by whom he is greatly valued. They are lads of spirit, and have been instructed in the use of arms at Hedingham as if they had been members of our family. I am sure, gentlemen volunteers, that you will receive them as friends. I propose that they shall take their meals with you, but of course they will lodge here with me and my officers; but as you are in the next house this will cause no inconvenience. I trust that we shall not remain here long, but shall soon be on the move. We have now been here seven months, and it is high time we were doing something. We didn't bargain to come over here and settle down for life in a dull Dutch town."

In a few hours the boys found themselves quite at home in their new quarters. The gentlemen volunteers received them cordially, and they found that for the present their duties would be extremely light, consisting chiefly in carrying messages and orders; for as the officers had all servants of their own, Captain Vere dispensed with their attendance at meals. There was much to amuse and interest them in Bergen op Zoom. It reminded them to some extent of Harwich, with its narrow streets and quaint houses; but the fortifications were far stronger, and the number of churches struck them as prodigious. The population differed in no very large degree in dress from that of England, but the people struck them as being slower and more deliberate in their motion. The women's costumes differed much more widely from those to which they were accustomed, and their strange and varied headdresses, their bright coloured handkerchiefs, and the amount of gold necklaces and bracelets that they wore, struck them with surprise.

Their stay in Bergen op Zoom was even shorter than they had anticipated, for three days after their arrival a boat came with a letter from Sir William Russell, the governor at Flushing. He said that he had just received an urgent letter from the Dutch governor of Sluys, saying that Patina's army was advancing from Bruges towards the city, and had seized and garrisoned the fort of Blankenburg on the sea coast to prevent reinforcements arriving from Ostend; he therefore prayed the governor of Flushing to send off troops and provisions with all haste to enable him to resist the attack. Sir William requested that the governor of Bergen op Zoom would at once embark the greater portion of his force on board ship and send them to Sluys. He himself was having a vessel filled with grain for the use of the inhabitants, and was also sending every man he could spare from Flushing.

In a few minutes all was bustle in the town. The trumpets of the various companies called the soldiers to arms, and in a very short time the troops were on their way towards the river. Here several ships had been requisitioned for the service; and as the companies marched down they were conducted to the ships to which they were allotted by the quartermasters.

Geoffrey and Lionel felt no small pride as they marched down with their troop. They had for the first time donned their steel caps, breast and back pieces; but this was rather for convenience of carriage than for any present utility. They had at Captain Vere's orders left their ordinary clothes behind them, and were now attired in thick serviceable jerkins, with skirts coming down nearly to the knee, like those worn by the troops. They marched at the rear of the company, the other pages, similarly attired, following them.

As soon as the troops were on board ship, sail was made, and the vessels dropped down the stream. The wind was very light, and it was not until thirty hours after starting that the little fleet arrived off Sluys. The town, which was nearly egg shaped, lay close to the river, which was called the Zwin. At the eastern end, in the centre of a detached piece of water, stood the castle, connected with the town by a bridge of boats. The Zwin formed the defence on the north side while the south and west were covered by a very wide moat, along the centre of which ran a dyke, dividing it into two channels. On the west side this moat extended to the Zwin, and was crossed at the point of junction by the bridge leading to the west gate.

The walls inclosed a considerable space, containing fields and gardens. Seven windmills stood on the ramparts. The tower of the town hall, and those of the churches of Our Lady, St. John, and the Grey Friars rose high above the town.

The ships from Flushing and Bergen op Zoom sailed up together, and the 800 men who landed were received with immense enthusiasm by the inhabitants, who were Protestants, and devoted to the cause of independence. The English were under the command of Sir Roger Williams, who had already seen so many years of service in the Low Countries; and under him were Morgan, Thomas Baskerville, and Huntley, who had long served with him.

Roger Williams was an admirable man for service of this kind. He had distinguished himself by many deeds of reckless bravery. He possessed an inexhaustible fund of confidence and high spirits, and in his company it was impossible to feel despondent, however desperate the situation.

The citizens placed their houses at the disposal of their new allies, handsome quarters were allotted to the officers, and the soldiers were all housed in private dwellings or the warehouses of the merchants. The inhabitants had already for some days been working hard at their defences, and the English at once joined them in their labours, strengthening the weak portions of the walls, mounting cannon upon the towers, and preparing in all ways to give a warm reception to the Spaniards.

Captain Vere, his lieutenant and ensign and his two pages, were quartered in the house of a wealthy merchant, whose family did all in their power to make them comfortable. It was a grand old house, and the boys, accustomed as they were to the splendours of Hedingham Castle, agreed that the simple merchants of the Low Countries were far in advance of English nobles in the comforts and conveniences of their dwellings. The walls of the rooms were all heavily panelled; rich curtains hung before the casements. The furniture was not only richly carved, but comfortable. Heavy hangings before the doors excluded draughts, and in the principal apartments Eastern carpets covered the floors. The meals were served on spotless white linen. Rich plates stood on the sideboard, and gold and silver vessels of rare carved work from Italy glittered in the armoires.

Above all, from top to bottom, the house was scrupulously clean. Nor a particle of dust dimmed the brightness of the furniture, and even now, when the city was threatened with siege, the merchant's wife never relaxed her vigilance over the doings of her maids, who seemed to the boys to be perpetually engaged in scrubbing, dusting, and polishing.

"Our mother prides herself on the neatness of her house," Geoffrey said; "but what would she say, I wonder, were she to see one of these Dutch households? I fear that the maids would have a hard time of it afterwards, and our father would be fairly driven out of his library."

"It is all very well to be clean," Lionel said; "but I think they carry it too far here. Peace and quietness count for something, and it doesn't seem to me that Dutchmen, fond of it as they say they are, know even the meaning of the words as far as their homes are concerned. Why, it always seems to be cleaning day, and they must be afraid of going into their own houses with their boots on!"

"Yes, I felt quite like a criminal today," Geoffrey laughed, "when I came in muddy up to the waist, after working down there by the sluices. I believe when the Spaniards open fire these people will be more distracted by the dust caused by falling tiles and chimneys than by any danger of their lives."

Great difficulties beset the Duke of Parma at the commencement of the siege. Sluys was built upon the only piece of solid ground in the district, and it was surrounded by such a labyrinth of canals, ditches, and swamps, that it was said that it was almost as difficult to find Sluys as it was to capture it. Consequently, it was impossible to find ground solid enough for a camp to be pitched upon, and the first labour was the erection of wooden huts for the troops upon piles driven into the ground. These huts were protected from the fire of the defenders by bags of earth brought in boats from a long distance. The main point selected for the attack was the western gate; but batteries were also placed to play upon the castle and the bridge of boats connecting it with the town.

"There is one advantage in their determining to attack us at the western extremity of the town," John Menyn, the merchant at whose house Captain Vere and his party were lodging, remarked when his guest informed him there was no longer any doubt as to the point at which the Spaniards intended to attack, "for they will not be able to blow up our walls with mines in that quarter."

"How is that?" Francis Vere asked.

"If you can spare half an hour of your time I will show you," the merchant said.

"I can spare it now, Von Menyn," Vere replied; "for the information is important, whatever it may be."

"I will conduct you there at once. There is no time like the present."

47

By England's Aid: or The Freeing

"Shall we follow you, sir?" Geoffrey asked his captain.

"Yes, come along," Vere replied. "The matter is of interest, and for the life of me I cannot make out what this obstacle can be of which our host speaks."

They at once set out.

John Menyn led them to a warehouse close to the western wall, and spoke a few words to its owner, who at once took three lanterns from the wall and lighted them, handing one to Vere, another to John Menyn, and taking the other himself; he then unlocked a massive door. A flight of steps leading apparently to a cellar were visible. He led the way down, the two men following, and the boys bringing up the rear. The descent was far deeper than they had expected, and when they reached the bottom they found themselves in a vast arched cellar filled with barrels. From this they proceeded into another, and again into a third.

"What are these great magazines?" Francis Vere asked in surprise.

"They are wine cellars, and there are scores similar to those you see. Sluys is the centre of the wine trade of Flanders and Holland, and cellars like these extend right under the wall. All the warehouses along here have similar cellars. This end of the town was the driest, and the soil most easily excavated. That is why the magazines for wines are all clustered here. There is not a foot of ground behind and under the walls at this end that is not similarly occupied, and if the Spaniards try to drive mines to blow up the walls, they will simply break their way into these cellars, where we can meet them and drive them back again."

"Excellent!" Francis Vere said. "This will relieve us of the work of countermining, which is always tiresome and dangerous, and would be specially so here, where we should have to dive under that deep moat outside your walls. Now we shall only have to keep a few men on watch in these cellars. They would hear the sound of the Spanish approaching, and we shall be ready to give them a warm reception by the time they break in. Are there communications between these cellars?"

"Yes, for the most part," the wine merchant said. "The cellars are not entirely the property of us dealers in wine. They are constructed by men who let them, just as they would let houses. A merchant in a small way would need but one cellar, while some of us occupy twenty or more; therefore, there are for the most part communications, with doors, between the various cellars, so that they can be let off in accordance with the needs of the hirers."

"Well, I am much obliged to you for telling me of this," Captain Vere said. "Williams and Morgan will be glad enough to hear that there is no fear of their being blown suddenly into the air while defending the walls, and they will see the importance of keeping a few trusty men on watch in the cellars nearest to the Spaniards. I shall report the matter to them at once. The difficulty," he added smiling, "will be to keep the men wakeful, for it seems to me that the very air is heavy with the fumes of wine."

CHAPTER IV. THE SIEGE OF SLUYS

Until the Spaniards had established their camp, and planted some of their batteries, there was but little firing. Occasionally the wall pieces opened upon parties of officers reconnoitring, and a few shots were fired from time to time to harass the workmen in the enemy's batteries; but this was done rather to animate the townsmen, and as a signal to distant friends that so far matters were going on quietly, than with any hopes of arresting the progress of the enemy's works. Many sorties were made by the garrison, and fierce fighting took place, but only a score or two of men from each company were taken upon these occasions, and the boys were compelled to remain inactive spectators of the fight.

In these sorties the Spanish works were frequently held for a few minutes, gabions thrown down, and guns overturned, but after doing as much damage as they could the assailants had to fall back again to the town, being unable to resist the masses of pikemen brought up against them. The boldness of these sorties, and the bravery displayed by their English allies, greatly raised the spirits of the townsfolk, who now organized themselves into companies, and undertook the work of guarding the less exposed portion of the wall, thus enabling the garrison to keep their whole strength at the points attacked. The townsmen also laboured steadily in adding to the defenses; and two companies of women were formed, under female captains, who took the names of May in the Heart and Catherine the Rose. These did good service by building a strong fort at one of the threatened points, and this work was in their honour christened Fort Venus.

By England's Aid: or The Freeing

"It is scarcely a compliment to Venus," Geoffrey laughed to his brother. "These square shouldered and heavily built women do not at all correspond with my idea of the goddess of love."

"They are strong enough for men," Lionel said. "I shouldn't like one of those big fat arms to come down upon my head. No, they are not pretty; but they look jolly and good tempered, and if they were to fight as hard as they work they ought to do good service."

"There is a good deal of difference between them," Geoffrey said. "Look at those three dark haired women with neat trim figures. They do not look as if they belonged to the same race as the others."

"They are not of the same race, lad," Captain Vere, who was standing close by, said. "The big heavy women are Flemish, the others come, no doubt, from the Walloon provinces bordering on France. The Walloons broke off from the rest of the states and joined the Spanish almost from the first. They were for the most part Catholics, and had little in common with the people of the Low Country; but there were, of course, many Protestants among them, and these were forced to emigrate, for the Spanish allow no Protestants in the country under their rule. Alva adopted the short and easy plan of murdering all the Protestants in the towns he took; but the war is now conducted on rather more humane principles, and the Protestants have the option given them of changing their faith or leaving the country.

"In this way, without intending it, the Spaniards have done good service to Holland, for hundreds of thousands of industrious people have flocked there for shelter from Antwerp, Ghent, Bruges, and other cities that have fallen into the hands of the Spaniards, thus greatly raising the population of Holland, and adding to its power of defence. Besides this, the presence of these exiles, and the knowledge that a similar fate awaits themselves if they fall again under the yoke of Spain, nerves the people to resist to the utmost. Had it not been for the bigotry of the Spanish, and the abominable cruelties practised by the Inquisition, the States would never have rebelled; and even after they did so, terms might easily have been made with them had they not been maddened by the wholesale massacres perpetrated by Alva. There, do you hear those women speaking? Their language is French rather than Flemish."

50

Just as they were speaking a heavy roar of cannon broke out from the eastern end of the town.

"They have opened fire on the castle!" Vere exclaimed. "Run, lads, quick! and summon the company to form in the marketplace in front of our house. We are told off to reinforce the garrison of the castle in case of attack."

The boys hurried away at the top of their speed. They had the list of all the houses in which the men of the company were quartered; and as the heavy roar of cannon had brought every one to their doors to hear what was going on, the company were in a very short time assembled.

Francis Vere placed himself at their head, and marched them through the long streets of the town and out through the wall on to the bridge of boats. It was the first time the boys had been under fire; and although they kept a good countenance, they acknowledged to each other afterwards that they had felt extremely uncomfortable as they traversed the bridge with the balls whistling over their heads, and sometimes striking the water close by and sending a shower of spray over the troops.

They felt easier when they entered the castle and were protected by its walls. Upon these the men took their station. Those with guns discharged their pieces against the Spanish artillerymen, the pikemen assisted the bombardiers to work the cannon, and the officers went to and fro encouraging the men. The pages of the company had little to do beyond from time to time carrying cans of wine and water to the men engaged. Geoffrey and Lionel, finding that their services were not required by Captain Vere, mounted on to the wall, and sheltering themselves as well as they could behind the battlements, looked out at what was going on.

"It doesn't seem to me," Geoffrey said, "that these walls will long withstand the balls of the Spanish. The battlements are already knocked down in several places, and I can hear after each shot strikes the walls the splashing of the brickwork as it falls into the water. See! there is Tom Carroll struck down with a ball. It's our duty to carry him away."

They ran along the wall to the fallen soldier. Two other pages came up, and the four carried him to the top of the steps and then down into the courtyard, where a Dutch surgeon took charge of him. His shoulder had been struck by the ball, and the arm hung only by a shred of flesh. The surgeon shook his head.

"I can do nothing for him," he said. "He cannot live many hours."

Lionel had done his share in carrying the man down but he now turned sick and faint.

Geoffrey caught him by the arm. "Steady, old boy," he said; "it is trying at first, but we shall soon get accustomed to it. Here, take a draught of wine from this flask."

"I am better now," Lionel said, after taking a draught of wine. "I felt as if I was going to faint, Geoffrey. I don't know why I should, for I did not feel frightened when we were on the wall."

"Oh, it has nothing to do with fear; it is just the sight of that poor fellow's blood. There is nothing to be ashamed of in that. Why, I saw Will Atkins, who was one of the best fighters and singlestick players in Hedingham, go off in a dead swoon because a man he was working with crushed his thumb between two heavy stones. Look, Lionel, what cracks there are in the wall here. I don't think it will stand long. We had better run up and tell Captain Vere, for it may come toppling down with some of the men on it."

Captain Vere on hearing the news ran down and examined the wall.

"Yes," he said, "it is evidently going. A good earthwork is worth a dozen of these walls. They will soon have the castle about our ears. However, it is of no great importance to us. I saw you lads just now on the wall; I did not care about ordering you down at the time; but don't go up again except to help to carry down the wounded. Make it a rule, my boys, never to shirk your duty, however great the risk to life may be; but, on the other hand, never risk your lives unless it is your duty to do so. What is gallantry in the one case is foolishness in the other. Although you are but pages, yet it may well be that in such a siege as this you will have many opportunities of showing that you are of good English stock; but while I would have you shrink from no danger when there is a need for you to expose yourselves, I say also that you should in no way run into danger wantonly."

Several times in the course of the afternoon the boys took their turn in going up and helping to bring down wounded men. As the time went on several yawning gaps appeared in the walls. The courtyard was strewn with fragments of masonry, and the pages were ordered to keep under shelter of the wall of the castle unless summoned on duty. Indeed, the courtyard had now become a more dangerous station than the wall itself; for not only did the cannon shot fly through the breaches, but fragments of bricks, mortar, and rubbish flew along with a force that would have been fatal to anything struck.

Some of the pages were big fellows of seventeen or eighteen years old, who had been serving for some years under Morgan and Williams, and would soon be transferred into the ranks.

"I like not this sort of fighting," one of them said. "It is all very well when it comes to push of pike with the Spaniards, but to remain here like chickens in a coop while they batter away at us is a game for which I have no fancy. What say you, Master Vickars?"

"Well, it is my first experience, Somers, and I cannot say that it is agreeable. I do not know whether I should like hand to hand fighting better; but it seems to me at present that it would be certainly more agreeable to be doing something than to be sitting here and listening to the falls of the pieces of masonry and the whistling of the balls. I don't see that they will be any nearer when they have knocked this place to pieces. They have no boats, and if they had, the guns on the city wall would prevent their using them; besides, when the bridge of boats is removed they could do nothing if they got here."

Towards evening a council was held, all the principal officers being present, and it was decided to evacuate the castle. It could indeed have been held for some days longer, but it was plain it would at length become untenable; the bridge of boats had already been struck in several places, and some of the barges composing it had sunk level with the water. Were it destroyed, the garrison of the castle would be completely cut off; and as no great advantage was to be gained by holding the position, for it was evident that it was upon the other end of the town the main attack was to be made, it was decided to evacuate it under cover of night. As soon as it became dark this decision was carried into effect, and for hours the troops worked steadily, transporting the guns, ammunition, and stores of all kinds across from the castle to the town.

Already communication with their friends outside had almost ceased, for the first operation of the enemy had been to block the approach to Sluys from the sea. Floats had been moored head and stern right across Zwin, and a battery erected upon each shore to protect them; but Captains Hart and Allen twice swam down to communicate with friendly vessels below the obstacle, carrying despatches with them from the governor to the States General, and from Roger Williams to the English commanders, urging that no time should be lost in assembling an army to march to the relief of the town.

Both contained assurances that the garrison would defend the place to the last extremity, but pointed out that it was only a question of time, and that the town must fall unless relieved. The Dutch garrison were 800 strong, and had been joined by as many English. Parma had at first marched with but 6000 men against the city, but had very speedily drawn much larger bodies of men towards him, and had, as Roger Williams states in a letter to the queen sent from Sluys at an early period of the siege, four regiments of Walloons, four of Germans, one of Italians, one of Burgundians, fifty–two companies of Spaniards, twenty–four troops of horse, and forty–eight guns. This would give a total of at least 17,000 men, and further reinforcements afterwards arrived.

Against so overwhelming a force as this, it could not be hoped that the garrison, outnumbered by more than ten to one, could long maintain themselves, and the Duke of Parma looked for an easy conquest of the place. By both parties the possession of Sluys was regarded as a matter of importance out of all proportion to the size and population of the town; for at that time it was known in England that the King of Spain was preparing a vast fleet for the invasion of Britain, and Sluys was the nearest point to our shores at which a fleet could gather and the forces of Parma embark to join those coming direct from Spain. The English, therefore, were determined to maintain the place to the last extremity; and while Parma had considered its capture as an affair of a few days only, the little garrison were determined that for weeks at any rate they would be able to prolong the resistance, feeling sure that before that time could elapse both the States and England, knowing the importance of the struggle, would send forces to their relief.

The view taken as to the uselessness of defending the castle was fully justified, as the Spaniards on the following day removed the guns that they had employed in battering it, to their works facing the western gate, and fire was opened next morning. Under cover of this the Spanish engineers pushed their trenches up to the very edge of the moat, in spite of several desperate sorties by the garrison. The boys had been forbidden by Captain Vere to take their place with the company on the walls.

"In time," he said, "as our force decreases, we shall want every one capable of handling arms to man the breaches, but at present we are not in any extremity; and none save those whom duty compels to be there must come under the fire of the Spaniards, for to do so would be risking life without gain."

They had, however, made friends with the wine merchant whose cellars they had visited, and obtained permission from him to visit the upper storey of his warehouse whenever they chose. From a window here they were enabled to watch all that was taking place, for the warehouse was much higher than the walls. It was not in the direct line of fire of the Spanish batteries, for these were chiefly concentrated against the wall a little to their right. After heavy fighting the Spaniards one night, by means of boats from the Zwin, landed upon the dyke which divided the moat into two channels, and thus established themselves so close under the ramparts that the guns could not be brought to bear upon them. They proceeded to intrench themselves at once upon the dyke.

The governor, Arnold Groenvelt, consulted with the English leaders, and decided that the enemy must be driven off this dyke immediately, or that the safety of the city would be gravely imperilled. They therefore assembled a force of four hundred men, sallied out of the south gate, where two bastions were erected on the dyke itself, and then advanced along it to the assault of the Spaniards. The battle was a desperate one, the English and Dutch were aided by their comrades on the wall, who shot with guns and arquebuses against the Spaniards, while the later were similarly assisted by their friends along the outer edge of the moat, and received constant reinforcements by boats from their ships.

The odds were too great for the assailants, who were forced at last to fall back along the dyke to the south gate and to re−enter the town. It was already five weeks since the English had arrived to take part in the defence, and the struggle now began upon a great scale — thirty cannon and eight culverins opening fire upon the walls. The heaviest fire was on St. James' day, the 25th of July, when 4000 shots were fired between three in the morning and five in the afternoon. While this tremendous cannonade was going on, the boys could not but admire the calmness shown by the population. Many of the shots, flying over the top of the walls, struck the houses in the city, and the chimneys, tiles, and masses of masonry fell in the streets. Nevertheless the people continued their usual avocations. The shops were all open, though the men employed served their customers with breast and back pieces buckled on, and their arms close at hand, so that they could run to the walls at once to take part in their defence did the Spaniards attempt an assault upon them. The women stood knitting at their doors, Frau Menyn looked as sharply after her maids as ever, and washing and scouring went on without interruption.

55

"I believe that woman will keep those girls at work after the Spaniards have entered the city, and until they are thundering at the door," Lionel said. "Who but a Dutch woman would give a thought to a few particles of dust on her furniture when an enemy was cannonading the town?"

"I think she acts wisely after all, Lionel. The fact that everything goes on as usual here and in other houses takes people's thoughts off the dangers of the position, and prevents anything like panic being felt."

The lads spent the greater part of the day at their lookout, and could see that the wall against which the Spanish fire was directed was fast crumbling. Looking down upon it, it seemed deserted of troops, for it would be needlessly exposing the soldiers to death to place them there while the cannonade continued; but behind the wall, and in the street leading to it, companies of English and Dutch soldiers could be seen seated or lying on the ground.

They were leaning our of the dormer window in the high roof watching the Spanish soldiers in the batteries working their guns, when, happening to look round, they saw a crossbow protruded from a window of the warehouse to their right, and a moment afterwards the sharp twang of the bow was heard. There was nothing unusual in this; for although firearms were now generally in use the longbow and the crossbow had not been entirely abandoned, and there were still archers in the English army, and many still held that the bow was a far better weapon than the arquebus, sending its shafts well nigh as far and with a truer aim.

"If that fellow is noticed," Geoffrey said, "we shall have the Spanish musketeers sending their balls in this direction. The governor has, I heard Captain Vere say, forbidden shooting from the warehouses, because he does not wish to attract the Spanish fire against them. Of course when the wall yields and the breach has to be defended the warehouses will be held, and as the windows will command the breach they will be great aids to us then, and it would be a great disadvantage to us if the Spaniards now were to throw shells and fireballs into these houses, and so to destroy them before they make their attack. Nor can much good be gained, for at this distance a crossbow would scarce carry its bolts beyond the moat."

"Most likely the man is using the crossbow on purpose to avoid attracting the attention of the Spaniards, Geoffrey. At this distance they could not see the crossbow, while a puff of smoke would be sure to catch their eye."

"There, he has shot again. I did not see the quarrel fall in the moat. See, one of the Spanish soldiers from that battery is coming forward. There, he has stooped and picked something up. Hallo! do you see that? He has just raised his arm; that is a signal, surely."

"It certainly looked like it," Lionel agreed. "It was a sort of half wave of the hand. That is very strange!"

"Very, Lionel; it looks to me very suspicious. It is quite possible that a piece of paper may have been tied round the bolt, and that someone is sending information to the enemy. This ought to be looked to."

"But what are we to do, Geoffrey? Merely seeing a Spanish soldier wave his arm is scarcely reason enough for bringing an accusation against anyone. We are not even sure that he picked up the bolt; and even if he did, the action might have been a sort of mocking wave of the hand at the failure of the shooter to send it as far as the battery."

"It might be, of course, Lionel. No, we have certainly nothing to go upon that would justify our making a report on the subject, but quite enough to induce us to keep a watch on this fellow, whoever he may be. Let us see, to begin with, if he shoots again."

They waited for an hour, but the head of the crossbow was not again thrust out of the window.

"He may have ceased shooting for either of two reasons," Geoffrey said. "If he is a true man, because he sees that his bolts do nor carry far enough to be of any use. If he is a traitor, because he has gained his object, and knows that his communication has reached his friends outside. We will go down now and inquire who is the occupier of the next warehouse."

The merchant himself was not below, for as he did business with other towns he had had nothing to do since Sluys was cut off from the surrounded country; but one of his clerks was at work, making out bills and accounts in his office as if the thunder of the guns outside was unheard by him. The boys had often spoken to him as they passed in and out.

"Who occupies the warehouse on the right?" Geoffrey asked him carelessly.

"William Arnig," he replied. "He is a leading citizen, and one of the greatest merchants in our trade. His cellars are the most extensive we have, and he does a great trade in times of peace with Bruges, Ghent, Antwerp, and other towns."

"I suppose he is a Protestant like most of the townspeople?" Geoffrey remarked.

"No, he is a Catholic; but he is not one who pushes his opinions strongly, and, he is well disposed to the cause, and a captain in one of the city bands. The Catholics and Protestants always dwell quietly together throughout the Low Countries, and would have no animosities against each other were it nor for the Spaniards. Formerly, at least, this was the case; but since the persecutions we have Protestant towns and Catholic towns, the one holding to the States cause, the other siding with the Spaniards. Why do you ask?"

"Oh, I hadn't heard the name of your next neighbour, and, was wondering who he might be."

The boys had now been nearly two months in Holland, and were beginning to understand the language, which is not difficult to acquire, and differed then even less than now from the dialect spoken in the eastern counties of England, between whom and Holland there had been for many generations much trade and intimate relations.

"What had we better do next, Geoffrey?" Lionel asked as they left the warehouse.

"I think that in the first place, Lionel, we will take our post at the window tomorrow, and keep a close watch all day to see whether this shooting is repeated. If it is, we had better report the matter to Captain Vere, and leave him to decide what should be done. I do not see that we could undertake anything alone, and in any case, you see, it would be a serious matter to lay an accusation against a prominent citizen who is actually a captain of one of the bands."

Upon the following day they took their post again at the window, and after some hours watching saw three bolts fired from the next window. Watching intently, they saw the two first fall into the moat. They could not see where the other fell; but as there was no splash in the water, they concluded that it had fallen beyond it, and in a minute they saw a soldier again advance from the battery, pick up something at the edge of the water, raise his arm, and retire. That evening when Captain Vere returned from the ramparts they informed him of what they had observed.

"Doubtless it is an act of treachery," he said, "and this merchant is communicating with the enemy. At the same time what you have seen, although convincing evidence to me, is scarce enough for me to denounce him. Doubtless he does not write these letters until he is ready to fire them off, and were he arrested in his house or on his way to the warehouse we might fail to find proofs of his guilt, and naught but ill feeling would be caused among his friends. No, whatever we do we must do cautiously. Have you thought of any plan by which we might catch him in the act?"

"If two or three men could be introduced into his warehouse, and concealed in the room from which he fires, they might succeed in catching him in the act, Captain Vere; but the room may be an empty one without any place whatever where they could be hidden, and unless they were actually in the room they would be of little good, for he would have time, if he heard footsteps, to thrust any letter he may have written into his mouth, and so destroy it before it could be seized."

"That is so," Captain Vere agreed. "The matter seems a difficult one, and yet it is of the greatest importance to hinder communications with the Spaniards. Tonight all the soldiers who can be spared, aided by all the citizens able to use mattock and pick, are to set to work to begin to raise a half moon round the windmill behind the point they are attacking, so as to have a second line to fall back upon when the wall gives way, which it will do ere long, for it is sorely shaken and battered. It is most important to keep this from the knowledge of the Spaniards. Now, lads, you have shown your keenness by taking notice of what is going on, see if you cannot go further, and hit upon some plan of catching this traitor at his work. If before night we can think of no scheme, I must go to the governor and tell him frankly that we have suspicions of treachery, though we cannot prove them, and ask him, in order to prevent the possibility of our plans being communicated to the enemy, to place some troops in all the warehouses along that line, so that none can shoot there from any message to the Spaniards."

Just as Captain Vere finished his supper, the boys came into the room again.

"We have thought of a plan, sir, that might succeed, although it would be somewhat difficult. The dormer window from which these bolts have been fired lies thirty or forty feet away from that from which we were looking. The roof is so steep that no one could hold a footing upon it for a moment, nor could a plank be placed upon which he could walk. The window is about twelve feet from the top of the roof. We think that one standing on the ledge of our window might climb on to its top, and once there swing a rope with a stout grapnel attached to catch on the ridge of the roof; then two or three men might climb up there and work themselves along, and then lower themselves down with a rope on to the top of the next window. They would need to have ropes fastened round their bodies, for the height is great, and a slip would mean death.

"The one farthest out on the window could lean over when he hears a noise below him, and when he saw the crossbow thrust from the window, could by a sudden blow knock it from the fellow's hand, when it would slide down the roof and fall into the narrow yard between the warehouse and the walls. Of course some men would be placed there in readiness to seize it, and others at the door of the warehouse to arrest the traitor if he ran down."

"I think the plan is a good one, though somewhat difficult of execution," Captain Vere said. "But this enterprise on the roof would be a difficult one and dangerous, since as you say a slip would mean death."

"Lionel and myself, sir, would undertake that with the aid of two active men to hold the ropes for us. We have both done plenty of bird nesting in the woods of Hedingham, and are nor likely to turn giddy."

"I don't think it is necessary for more than one to get down on to that window," Captain Vere said. "Only one could so place himself as to look down upon the crossbow. However, you shall divide the honour of the enterprise between you. You, as the eldest and strongest, Geoffrey, shall carry out your plan on the roof, while you, Lionel, shall take post at the door with four men to arrest the traitor when he leaves. I will select two strong and active men to accompany you, Geoffrey, and aid you in your attempt; but mind, before you try to get out of the window and to climb on to its roof, have a strong rope fastened round your body and held by the others; then in case of a slip, they can haul you in again. I will see that the ropes and grapnels are in readiness."

By England's Aid: or The Freeing

The next morning early Geoffrey proceeded with the two men who had been selected to accompany him to his usual lookout. Both were active, wiry men, and entered fully into the spirit of the undertaking when Geoffrey explained its nature to them. They looked out of the dormer window at the sharp roof slanting away in front of them and up to the ridge above.

"I think, Master Vickars," one of them, Roger Browne by name, said, "that I had best go up first. I served for some years at sea, and am used to climbing about in dizzy places. It is no easy matter to get from this window sill astride the roof above us, and moreover I am more like to heave the grapnel so that it will hook firmly on to the ridge than you are."

"Very well, Roger. I should be willing to try, but doubtless you would manage it far better than I should. But before you start we will fasten the other rope round your body, as Captain Vere directed me to do. Then in case you slip, or anything gives way with your weight, we can check you before you slide far down below us."

A rope was accordingly tied round the man's body under his arms. Taking the grapnel, to which the other rope was attached, he got out on to the sill. It was not an easy task to climb up on to the ridge of the dormer window, and it needed all his strength and activity to accomplish the feat. Once astride of the ridge the rest was easy. At the first cast he threw the grapnel so that it caught securely on the top of the roof. After testing it with two or three pulls he clambered up, leaving the lower end of the rope hanging by the side of the window. As soon as he had gained this position Geoffrey, who was to follow him, prepared to start.

According to the instructions Browne had given him he fastened the end of the rope which was round Browne's body under his own shoulders, then leaning over and taking a firm hold of the rope to which the grapnel was attached, he let himself out of the window. Browne hauled from above at the rope round his body, and he pulled himself with his hands by that attached to the grapnel, and presently reached the top.

"I am glad you came first, Roger," he said. "I do not think I could have ever pulled myself up if you had not assisted me."

He unfastened the rope, and the end was thrown down to the window, and Job Tredgold, the other man, fastened it round him and was hauled up as Geoffrey had been.

"We will move along now to that stack of chimneys coming through the roof four feet below the ridge on the town side," Geoffrey said. "We can stand down there out of sight of the Spaniards. We shall be sure to attract attention sitting up here, and might have some bullets flying round our ears, besides which this fellow's friends might suspect our object and signal to him in some way. It is two hours yet to the time when we have twice seen him send his bolts across the moat."

This was accordingly done, and for an hour and a half they sat down on the roof with their feet against the stack of chimneys.

"It is time to be moving now," Geoffrey said at last. "I think the best way will be for me to get by the side of the dormer window instead of above it. It would be very awkward leaning over there, and I should not have strength to strike a blow; whereas with the rope under my arms and my foot on the edge of the sill, which projects a few inches beyond the side of the window, I could stand upright and strike a downright blow on the crossbow."

"That would be the best way, I think," Roger Browne agreed; "and I will come down on to the top of the window and lean over. In the first place your foot might slip, and as you dangle there by the rope he might cut it and let you shoot over, or he might lean out and shoot you as you climb up the roof again; but if I am above with my pistol in readiness there will be no fear of accidents."

CHAPTER V. AN HEROIC DEFENCE

The plan Roger Browne suggested was carried out. Geoffrey was first lowered to his place by the side of the window, and bracing himself against its side with a foot on the sill he managed to stand upright, leaning against the rope that Job Tredgold held from above. Job had instructions when Geoffrey lifted his arm to ease the rope a few inches so as to enable the lad to lean forward. After two or three attempts Geoffrey got the rope to the exact length which would enable him to look round the corner and to strike a blow with his right hand, in which he held a stout club. Roger Browne then descended by the aid of the other rope, and fastening it round his body lay down astride of the roof of the window with his head and shoulders over the end, and his pistol held in readiness.

It seemed an age to Geoffrey before he heard the sound of a footstep in the loft beside him. He grasped his cudgel firmly and leaned slightly forward. For ten minutes there was quiet within, and Geoffrey guessed that the traitor was writing the missive he was about to send to the enemy; then the footstep approached the window, and a moment later a crossbow was thrust out. A glance at it sufficed to show that the bolt was enveloped in a piece of paper wound round it and secured with a string. Steadying himself as well as he could Geoffrey struck with all his force down upon the crossbow. The weapon, loosely held, went clattering down the tiles. There was an exclamation of surprise and fury from within the window, and at the same moment Job Tredgold, seeing that Geoffrey's attempt had been successful, hauled away at the rope and began to drag him backward up the tiles.

The lad saw a man lean out of the window and look up at him, then a pistol was levelled; but the report came from above the window, and not from the threatening weapon. A sharp cry of pain was heard, as the pistol fell from the man's hand and followed the crossbow down the roof. A few seconds later Geoffrey was hauled up to the ridge, where he was at once joined by Roger Browne. Shifting the ropes they moved along till above the window from which they had issued. Geoffrey was first lowered down. As soon as he had got in at the window he undid the rope and Job Tredgold followed him, while Roger Browne slid down by the rope attached to the grapnel; then they ran downstairs.

As soon as they sallied out below they saw that Lionel and the men with him had captured a prisoner; and just as they joined the party the guard came round from the other side of the warehouse, bringing with them the crossbow, its bolt, and the pistol. The prisoner, whose shoulder was broken by Roger Browne's shot, was at once taken to Captain Vere's quarters. That officer had just arrived from the walls, knowing the time at which the capture would probably be made.

"So you have succeeded," he said. "Well done, lads; you have earned the thanks of all. We will take this man at once to the governor, who is at present at the town hall."

By the time they issued out quite a crowd had assembled, for the news that William Von Arnig had been brought a prisoner and wounded to Captain Vere's quarters had spread rapidly. The crowd increased as they went along, and Captain Vere and his party had difficulty in making their way to the town hall, many of the people exclaiming loudly against this treatment of one of the leading citizens. The governor was, when they entered, holding council with the English leader, Sir Roger Williams.

"Why, what is this, Captain Vere?" he asked in surprise as that officer, accompanied by the two boys and followed by Roger Browne and Job Tredgold guarding the prisoner, entered.

"I have to accuse this man of treacherously communicating with the enemy," Francis Vere said.

"What?" Arnold de Groenvelt exclaimed in surprise. "Why, this is Mynheer Von Arnig, one of our most worshipful citizens! Surely, Captain Vere, there must be some error here?"

"I will place my evidence before you," Captain Vere said; "and it will be for you to decide upon it. Master Geoffrey Vickars, please to inform the governor what you know about this matter."

Geoffrey then stated how he and his brother, being at the upper window of the warehouse, had on two days in succession seen a crossbow discharged from a neighbouring window, and had noticed a Spanish soldier come out of a battery and pick up something which they believed to be the bolt, and how he and his brother had reported the circumstances to Captain Vere. That officer then took up the story, and stated that seeing the evidence was not conclusive, and it was probable that if an attempt was made to arrest the person, whomsoever he might be, who had used the crossbow, any evidence of treasonable design might be destroyed before he was seized, he had accepted the offer of Master Vickars to climb the roof, lower himself to the window from which the bolt would be shot, and, if possible, strike it from the man's hands, so that it would fall down the roof to the courtyard below, where men were placed to seize it.

Geoffrey then related how he, with the two soldiers guarding the prisoner, had scaled the roof and taken a position by the window; how he had seen the crossbow thrust out, and had struck it from the hands of the man holding it; how the latter had leaned out, and would have shot him had not Roger Browne from his post above the window shot him in the shoulder.

"Here are the crossbow and pistol," Captain Vere said; "and this is the bolt as it was picked up by my men. You see, sir, there is a paper fastened round it. I know not its contents, for I judged it best to leave it as it was found until I placed it in your hands."

The governor cut the string, unrolled the paper and examined it. It contained a statement as to the state of the wall, with remarks where it was yielding, and where the enemy had best shoot against it. It said that the defenders had in the night begun to form a half moon behind it, and contained a sketch showing the exact position of the new work.

"Gentlemen, what think you of this?" the governor asked the English officers.

"There can be no doubt that it is a foul act of treachery," Williams said, "and the traitor merits death."

"We will not decide upon it ourselves," the governor said. "I will summon six of the leading citizens, who shall sir as a jury with us. This is a grave matter, and touches the honour of the citizens as well as the safety of the town."

In a few minutes the six citizens summoned arrived. The evidence was again given, and then the prisoner was asked what he had to say in his defence.

"It is useless for me to deny it," he replied. "I am caught in the act, and must suffer for it. I have done my duty to the King of Spain, my sovereign; and I warn you he will take vengeance for my blood."

"That we must risk," the governor said. "Now, gentlemen, you citizens of this town now attacked by the Spaniards, and you, sir, who are in command of the soldiers of the queen of England, have heard the evidence and the answer the prisoner has made. What is your opinion thereon? Do you, Sir Roger Williams, being highest in rank and authority, first give your opinion."

"I find that he is guilty of an act of gross treason and treachery. For such there is but one punishment — death." And the six citizens all gave the same decision.

65

By England's Aid: or The Freeing

"You are found guilty of this foul crime," the governor said, "and are sentenced to death. In half an hour you will be hung in the marketplace, as a punishment to yourself and a warning to other traitors, if such there be in this town of Sluys. As to you, young sirs, you have rendered a great service to the town, and have shown a discernment beyond your years. I thank you in the name of the city and of its garrison, and also in that of the States, whose servant I am."

A guard of armed citizens were now called in, the prisoner was handed to them, and orders given to their officer to carry the sentence into effect. A statement of the crime of the prisoner, with the names of those who had acted as his judges, and the sentence, was then drawn out, signed by the governor, and, ordered by him to be affixed to the door of the town hall. The two lads, finding that they were no longer required, hastened back to their quarters, having no wish to be present at the execution of the unhappy wretch whose crime they had been the means of detecting.

A few days later considerable portions of the battered wall fell, and shortly afterwards a breach of two hundred and fifty paces long was effected, and a bridge of large boats constructed by the enemy from the dyke to the foot of the rampart.

This was not effected without terrible loss. Hundreds of the bravest Spanish soldiers and sailors were killed, and three officers who succeeded each other in command of the attack were badly wounded. The Spanish had laboured under great difficulties owing to the lack of earth to push their trenches forward to the edge of the moat, arising from the surrounding country being flooded. They only succeeded at last by building wooden machines of bullet proof planks on wheels, behind each of which four men could work. When all was prepared the Spaniards advanced to the attack, rushing up the breach with splendid valour, headed by three of their bravest leaders; but they were met by the English and Dutch, and again and again hurled back.

Day and night the fighting continued, the Spaniards occasionally retiring to allow their artillery to open fire again upon the shattered ruins. But stoutly as the defenders fought, step by step the Spaniards won their way forward until they had captured the breach and the west gate adjoining it, there being nothing now beyond the hastily constructed inner work between them and the town. The finest regiment of the whole of the Spanish infantry now advanced to the assault, but they were met by the defenders — already sadly diminished in numbers, but firm and undaunted as ever, — and their pikes and their axes well supplied the place of the fallen walls.

Assault after assault was met and repulsed, Sir Roger Williams, Thomas Baskerville, and Francis Vere being always in the thick of the fight. Baskerville was distinguished by the white plumes of his helmet, Vere by his crimson mantle; and the valour of these leaders attracted the admiration of the Duke of Parma himself, who watched the fight from the summit of the tower of the western gate. Francis Vere was twice wounded, but not disabled. Sir Roger Williams urged him to retire, but he replied that he would rather be killed ten times in a breach than once in a house.

Day by day the terrible struggle continued. The Spaniards were able constantly to bring up fresh troops, but the defenders had no relief. They were reduced in numbers from 1600 to 700 men, and yet for eighteen days they maintained the struggle, never once leaving the breach.

The pages brought their food to them, and when the attacks were fiercest joined in the defence, fighting as boldly and manfully as the soldiers themselves. Geoffrey and Lionel kept in close attendance upon Francis Vere, only leaving him to run back to their quarters and bring up the meals cooked for him and his two officers by Frau Menyn and her handmaids. Both kept close to him during the fighting. They knew that they were no match in strength for the Spanish pikemen; but they had obtained pistols from the armoury, and with these they did good service, several times freeing him from some of his assailants when he was sorely pressed. On one occasion when Francis Vere was smitten down by a blow from an axe, the boys rushed forward and kept back his assailants until some of the men of the company came to his aid.

"You have done me brave service indeed," Captain Vere said to them when he recovered; for his helmet had defended him from serious injury, though the force of the blow had felled him. "It was a happy thought of mine when I decided to bring you with me. This is not the first time that you have rendered me good service, and I am sure you will turn our brave and valiant soldiers of the queen."

When each assault ceased the weary soldiers threw themselves down behind the earthen embankment, and obtained such sleep as they could before the Spaniards mustered for fresh attack. When, after eighteen days' terrible fighting, the Duke of Parma saw that even his best troops were unable to break through the wall of steel, he desisted from the assault and began the slower process of mining. The garrison from their lookout beheld the soldiers crossing the bridge with picks and shovels, and prepared to meet them in this new style of warfare. Captain Uvedale was appointed to command the men told off for this duty, and galleries were run from several of the cellars to meet those of the enemy.

As every man was employed either on the rampart or in mining, many of the pages were told off to act as watchers in the cellars, and to listen for the faint sounds that told of the approach of the enemy's miners. As the young Vickars were in attendance on the officers, they were exempted from this work; but they frequently went down into the cellars, both to watch the process of mining by their own men and to listen to the faint sounds made by the enemy's workmen. One day they were sitting on two wine kegs, watching four soldiers at work at the end of a short gallery that had been driven towards the Spaniards. Suddenly there was an explosion, the miners were blown backwards, the end of the gallery disappeared, and a crowd of Walloon soldiers almost immediately afterwards rushed in.

The boys sprang to their feet and were about to fly, when an idea occurred to Geoffrey. He seized a torch, and, standing by the side of a barrel placed on end by a large tier, shouted in Dutch, "Another step forward and I fire the magazine!"

The men in front paused. Through the fumes of smoke they saw dimly the pile of barrels and a figure standing with a lighted torch close to one of them. A panic seized them, and believing they had made their way into a powder magazine, and that in another instant there would be a terrible explosion, they turned with shouts of "A magazine! a magazine! Fly, or we are all dead men!"

"Run, Lionel, and get help," Geoffrey said, and in two or three minutes a number of soldiers ran down into the cellar. The Walloons were not long before they recovered from their panic. Their officers knew that the wine cellars of the city were in front of them, and reassured them as to the character of the barrels they had seen. They were, however, too late, and a furious conflict took place at the entrance into the cellar, but the enemy, able only to advance two or three abreast, failed to force their way in.

Captain Uvedale and Francis Vere were soon on the spot, and when at last the enemy, unable to force an entrance, fell back, the former said, "This is just as I feared. You see, the Spaniards drove this gallery, and ceased to work immediately they heard us approaching them. We had no idea that they were in front of us, and so they only had to put a barrel of powder there and fire it as soon as there was but a foot or two of earth between us and them."

"But how was it," Francis Vere asked, "that when they fired it they did not at once rush forward? They could have captured the whole building before we knew what had happened."

"That I cannot tell," Captain Uvedale replied. "The four men at work must have been either killed or knocked senseless. We shall know better another time, and will have a strong guard in each cellar from which our mines are being driven."

"If it please you, Captain Uvedale," Lionel said, "it was my brother Geoffrey who prevented them from advancing; for indeed several of them had already entered the cellar, and the gallery behind was full of them."

"But how did he do that?" Captain Uvedale asked in surprise.

Lionel related the ruse by which Geoffrey had created a panic in the minds of the Spaniards.

"That was well thought of indeed, and promptly carried out!" Captain Uvedale exclaimed. "Francis, these pages of yours are truly promising young fellows. They detected that rascally Dutchman who was betraying us. I noticed them several times in the thick of the fray at the breach; and now they have saved the city by their quickness and presence of mind; for had these Spaniards once got possession of this warehouse they would have speedily broken a way along through the whole tier, and could then have poured in upon us with all their strength."

"That is so, indeed," Francis Vere agreed. "They have assuredly saved the town, and there is the greatest credit due to them. I shall be glad, Uvedale, if you will report the matter to our leader. You are in command of the mining works, and it will come better from you than from me who is their captain."

Captain Uvedale made his report, and both Sir Roger Williams and the governor thanked the boys, and especially Geoffrey, for the great service they had rendered.

Very shortly the galleries were broken into in several other places, and the battle became now as fierce and continuous down in the cellars as it had before been on the breach. By the light of torches, in an atmosphere heavy with the fumes of gunpowder, surrounded by piled up barrels of wine, the defenders and assailants maintained a terrible conflict, men staggering up exhausted by their exertion and by the stifling atmosphere while others took their places below, and so, night and day, the desperate struggle continued.

All these weeks no serious effort had been made for the relief of the beleaguered town. Captains Hall and Allen had several times swum down at night through the bridge of boats with letters from the governor entreating a speedy succour. The States had sent a fleet which sailed some distance up the Zwin, but returned without making the slightest effort to break through the bridge of boats. The Earl of Leicester had advanced with a considerable force from Ostend against the fortress of Blankenburg, but had retreated hastily as soon as Parma despatched a portion of his army against him; and so the town was left to its fate.

The last letter that the governor despatched said that longer resistance was impossible. The garrison were reduced to a mere remnant, and these utterly worn out by constant fighting and the want of rest. He should ask for fair and honourable terms, but if these were refused the garrison and the whole male inhabitants in the city, putting the women and children in the centre, would sally out and cut their way through, or die fighting in the midst of the Spaniards. The swimmer who took the letter was drowned, but his body was washed ashore and the letter taken to the Duke of Parma.

Three days afterwards a fresh force of the enemy embarked in forty large boats, and were about to land on an unprotected wharf by the riverside when Arnold de Groenvelt hung out the white flag. His powder was exhausted and his guns disabled, and the garrison so reduced that the greater portion of the walls were left wholly undefended. The Duke of Parma, who was full of admiration at the extraordinary gallantry of the defenders, and was doubtless also influenced by the resolution expressed in his letter by the governor, granted them most honourable terms. The garrison were to march out with all their baggage and arms, with matches lighted and colours displayed. They were to proceed to Breskans, and there to embark for Flushing. The life and property of the inhabitants were to be respected, and all who did not choose to embrace the Catholic faith were to be allowed to leave the town peaceably, taking with them their belongings, and to go wheresoever they pleased.

When the gates were opened the garrison sallied out. The Duke of Parma had an interview with several of the leaders, and expressed his high admiration of the valour with which they had fought, and said that the siege of Sluys had cost him more men than he had lost in the four principal sieges he had undertaken in the Low Country put together. On the 4th of August the duke entered Sluys in triumph, and at once began to make preparations to take part in the great invasion of England for which Spain was preparing.

After their arrival at Flushing Captains Vere, Uvedale, and others, who had brought their companies from Bergen op Zoom to aid in the defence of Sluys, returned to that town.

The Earl of Leicester shortly afterwards resigned his appointment as general of the army. He had got on but badly with the States General, and there was from the first no cordial cooperation between the two armies. The force at his disposal was never strong enough to do anything against the vastly superior armies of the Duke of Parma, who was one of the most brilliant generals of his age, while he was hampered and thwarted by the intrigues and duplicity of Elizabeth, who was constantly engaged in half hearted negotiations now with France and now with Spain, and whose capricious temper was continually overthrowing the best laid plans of her councillors and paralysing the actions of her commanders. It was nor until she saw her kingdom threatened by invasion that she placed herself fairly at the head of the national movement, and inspired her subjects with her energy and determination.

Geoffrey Vickars had been somewhat severely wounded upon the last day of the struggle in the cellar, a Spanish officer having beaten down his guard and cleft through his morion. Lionel was unwounded, but the fatigue and excitement had told upon him greatly, and soon after they arrived at Bergen Captain Vere advised both of them to return home for a few months.

"There is nothing likely to be doing here until the spring. Parma has a more serious matter in hand. They talk, you know, of invading England, and after his experience at Sluys I do not think he will be wasting his force by knocking their head against stone walls. I should be glad if I could return too, but I have my company to look after and must remain where I am ordered; but as you are but volunteers and giving your service at your pleasure, and are not regularly upon the list of the pages of the company, I can undertake to grant you leave, and indeed I can see that you both greatly need rest. You have begun well and have both done good service, and have been twice thanked by the governor of Sluys and Sir Roger Williams.

"You will do yourselves no good by being shut up through the winter in this dull town, and as there is a vessel lying by the quay which is to set sail tomorrow, I think you cannot do better than go in her. I will give you letters to my cousin and your father saying how well you have borne yourselves, and how mightily Sir Roger Williams was pleased with you. In the spring you can rejoin, unless indeed the Spaniards should land in England, which Heaven forfend, in which case you will probably prefer to ride under my cousin's banner at home."

The boys gladly accepted Francis Vere's proposal. It was but three months since they had set foot in Holland, but they had gone through a tremendous experience, and the thought of being shut up for eight or nine months at Bergen op Zoom was by no means a pleasant one. Both felt worn out and exhausted, and longed for the fresh keen air of the eastern coast. Therefore the next morning they embarked on board ship. Captain Vere presented them each with a handsome brace of pistols in token of his regard, and Captains Uvedale, Baskerville, and other officers who were intimate friends of Vere's, and had met them at his quarters, gave them handsome presents in recognition of the services they had rendered at Sluys.

The ship was bound for Harwich, which was the nearest English port. Landing there, they took passage by boat to Manningtree and thence by horse home, where they astounded their father and mother by their sudden appearance.

"And this is what comes of your soldiering," Mrs. Vickars said when the first greeting was over. "Here is Geoffrey with plasters all over the side of his head, and you, Lionel, looking as pale and thin as if you had gone through a long illness. I told your father when we heard of your going that you ought to be brought back and whipped; but the earl talked him over into writing to Captain Francis to tell him that he approved of this mad brained business, and a nice affair it has turned out."

"You will not have to complain of our looks, mother, at the end of a week or two," Geoffrey said. "My wound is healing fast, and Lionel only needs an extra amount of sleep for a time. You see, for nearly a month we were never in bed, but just lay down to sleep by the side of Captain Vere on the top of the ramparts, where we had been fighting

By England's Aid: or The Freeing

all day.

"It was a gallant defence," Mr. Vickars said, "and all England is talking of it. It was wonderful that 800 English and as many Dutchmen should hold a weak place for two months against full twelve times their number of Spaniards, led by the Duke of Parma himself, and there is great honour for all who took part in the defence. The governor and Sir Roger Williams especially mentioned Francis Vere as among the bravest and best of their captains, and although you as pages can have had nought to do with the fighting, you will have credit as serving under his banner."

"I think, father," Geoffrey said, touching the plasters on his head, "this looks somewhat as if we had had something to do with the fighting, and here is a letter for you from Captain Vere which will give you some information about it."

Mr. Vickars adjusted his horn spectacles on his face and opened the letter. It began: "My dear Master and Friend, — I have had no means of writing to you since your letter came to me, having had other matters in mind, and being cut off from all communication with England. I was glad to find that you did not take amiss my carrying off of your sons. Indeed that action has turned out more happily than might have been expected, for I own that they were but young for such rough service.

"However, they have proved themselves valiant young gentlemen. They fought stoutly by my side during our long tussle with the Spaniards, and more than once saved my life by ridding me of foes who would have taken me at a disadvantage. Once, indeed, when I was down from a blow on the pate from a Spanish axe, they rushed forward and kept my assailants at bay until rescue came. They discovered a plot between a traitor in the town and the Spaniards, and succeeded in defeating his plans and bringing him to justice.

"They were also the means of preventing the Spaniards from breaking into the great wine cellars and capturing the warehouses, and for each of these services they received the thanks of the Dutch governor and of Sir Roger Williams, our leader. Thus, you see, although so young they have distinguished themselves mightily, and should aught befall me, there are many among my friends who will gladly take them under their protection and push them forward. I have sent them home for a time to have quiet and rest, which they need after their exertions, and have done this the more willingly since there is no chance of fighting for many months to come. I hope that before the Spaniards again

73

advance against us I may have them by my side."

"Well, well, this is wonderful," Mrs. Vickars said when her husband had finished reading the letter. "If they had told me themselves I should not have believed them, although they have never been given to the sin of lying; but since it is writ in Master Vere's own hand it cannot be doubted. And now tell us all about it, boys."

"We will tell you when we have had dinner, mother. This brisk Essex air has given us both an appetite, and until that is satisfied you must excuse us telling a long story. Is the earl at the castle, father? because we have two letters to him from Captain Francis — one, I believe, touching our affairs, and the other on private matters. We have also letters from him to his mother and his brother John, and these we had better send off at once by a messenger, as also the private letters to the earl."

"That I will take myself," Mr. Vickars said. "I was just going up to him to speak about my parish affairs when you arrived."

"You had better have your dinner first," Mrs. Vickars said decidedly. "When you once get with the earl and begin talking you lose all account of the time, and only last week kept dinner waiting for two hours. It is half past eleven now, and I will hurry it on so that it will be ready a few minutes before noon."

"Very well, my dear; but I will go out into the village at once and find a messenger to despatch to Crepping Hall with the letters to Dame Elizabeth and John Vere."

The boys' story was not told until after supper, for as soon as dinner was over Mr. Vickars went up to the castle with the letters for the earl. The latter, after reading them, told him that his cousin spoke most highly of his two sons, and said they had been of great service, even as far as the saving of his life. The earl told Mr. Vickars to bring the boys up next day to see him in order that he might learn a full account of the fighting at Sluys, and that he hoped they would very often come in, and would, while they were at home, practise daily with his master of arms at the castle.

"I know, Mr. Vickars, that you had hoped that one of them would enter the church; but you see that their tastes lie not in that direction, and it is evident that, as in the case of my cousin Francis, they are cut out for soldiers."

"I am afraid so," Mr. Vickars said; "and must let them have their own way, for I hold, that none should be forced to follow the ministry save those whose natural bent lies that way."

"I don't think they have chosen badly," the earl said. "My cousin Francis bids fair to make a great soldier, and as they start in life as his pages they will have every chance of getting on, and I warrant me that Francis will push their fortunes. Perhaps I may be able to aid them somewhat myself. If aught comes of this vapouring of the Spaniards, before the boys return to Holland, they shall ride with me. I am already arming all the tenantry and having them practised in warlike exercises, and in the spring I shall fit out two ships at Harwich to join the fleet that will put to sea should the Spaniards carry out their threats of invading us."

CHAPTER VI. THE LOSS OF THE SUSAN

There were few people in Hedingham more pleased to see the two lads on their return than John Lirriper, to whom they paid a visit on the first day they went out.

"I am glad to see you back, young masters; though, to say the truth, you are not looking nigh so strong and well as you did when I last parted from you."

"We shall soon be all right again, John. We have had rather a rough time of it over there in Sluys."

"Ah, so I have heard tell, Master Geoffrey. Your father read out from the pulpit a letter the earl had received from Captain Francis telling about the fighting, and it mentioned that you were both alive and well and had done good service; but it was only a short letter sent off in haste the day after he and the others had got out of the town. I was right glad when I heard it, I can tell you, for there had been nought talked of here but the siege; and though your lady mother has not said much to me, I always held myself ready to slip round the corner or into a house when I saw her come down the street, for I knew well enough what was in her mind. She was just saying to herself, `John Lirriper, if it hadn't been for you my two boys would not be in peril now. If aught comes to them, it will be your doing.' And though it was not my fault, as far as I could see, for Captain Francis took you off my hands, as it were, and I had no more to say in the matter than a child, still, there it was, and right glad was I when I heard that the siege was over and you were both alive.

"I had a bad time of it, I can tell you, when I first got back, young sirs, for your mother rated me finely; and though your father said it was not my fault in any way, she would not listen to him, but said she had given you into my charge, and that I had no right to hand you over to any others save with your father's permission — not if it were to the earl himself, — and for a long time after she would make as if she didn't see me if she met me in the street. When my wife was ill about that time she sent down broths and simples to her, but she sent them by one of the maids, and never came herself save when she knew I was away in my boat.

"However, the day after the reading of that letter she came in and said she was sorry she had treated me hardly, and that she had known at heart all along that it was not altogether my fault, and asked my pardon as nice as if I had been the earl. Of course I said there was nothing to ask pardon for, and indeed that I thought it was only natural she should have blamed me, for that I had often blamed myself, though not seeing how I could have done otherwise. However, I was right glad when the matter was made up, for it is not pleasant for a man when the parson's wife sets herself against him."

"It was certainly hard upon you, John," Geoffrey said; "but I am sure our mother does not in any way blame you now. You see, we brought home letters from Captain Vere, or rather Sir Francis, for he has been knighted now, and he was good enough to speak very kindly of what we were able to do in the siege. Mother did not say much, but I am sure that at heart she is very grateful, for the earl himself came down to the Rectory and spoke warmly about us, and said that he should always be our fast friend, because we had given his cousin some help when he was roughly pressed by the Spaniards. I hope we shall have another sail with you in a short time, for we are not going back to the Netherlands at present, as things are likely to be quiet there now. Although he did not say so, I think Sir Francis thought that we were over young for such rough work, and would be more useful in a year's time; for, you see, in these sieges even pages have to take their share in the fighting, and when it comes to push of pike with the Spaniards more strength and vigour are needed than we possess at present. So we are to continue our practice at arms at the castle, and to take part in the drilling of the companies the earl is raising in case the Spaniards carry out their threat of invading England."

By England's Aid: or The Freeing

Mrs. Vickars offered no objection whatever the first time Geoffrey asked permission to go down to Bricklesey with John Lirriper.

"I have no objection, Geoffrey; and, indeed, now that you have chosen your own lives and are pages to Sir Francis Vere, it seems to me that in matters of this kind you can judge for yourself. Now that you have taken to soldiering and have borne your part in a great siege, and have even yourselves fought with the Spaniards, I deem it that you have got beyond my wing, and must now act in all small matters as it pleases you; and that since you have already run great danger of your lives, and may do so again ere long, it would be folly of me to try to keep you at my apron strings and to treat you as if you were still children."

So the two lads often accompanied John Lirriper to Bricklesey, and twice sailed up the river to London and back in Joe Chambers' smack, these jaunts furnishing a pleasant change to their work of practising with pike and sword with the men–at–arms at the castle, or learning the words of command and the work of officers in drilling the newly raised corps. One day John Lirriper told them that his nephew was this time going to sail up the Medway to Rochester, and would be glad to take them with him if they liked it; for they were by this time prime favourites with the master of the Susan. Although their mother had told them that they were at liberty to go as they pleased, they nevertheless always made a point of asking permission before they went away.

"If the wind is fair we shall not be long away on this trip, mother. Two days will take us up to Rochester; we shall be a day loading there, and shall therefore be back on Saturday if the wind serves, and may even be sooner if the weather is fine and we sail with the night tides, as likely enough we shall, for the moon is nearly full, and there will be plenty of light to keep our course free of the sands."

The permission was readily given. Mrs. Vickars had come to see that it was useless to worry over small matters, and therefore nodded cheerfully, and said she would give orders at once for a couple of chickens to be killed and other provision prepared for their voyage.

"I do not doubt you are going to have a rougher voyage than usual this time, young masters," John Lirriper said when the boat was approaching Bricklesey. "The sky looks wild, and I think there is going to be a break in the weather. However, the Susan is a stout boat, and my nephew a careful navigator."

"I should like a rough voyage for a change, John," Geoffrey said. "We have always had still water and light winds on our trips, and I should like a good blow."

"Well, I think you will have one; though may be it will only come on thick and wet. Still I think there is wind in those clouds, and that if it does come it will be from the southeast, in which case you will have a sharp buffeting. But you will make good passage enough down to the Nore once you are fairly round the Whittaker."

"Glad to see you, young masters," Joe Chambers said, as the boat came alongside his craft. "You often grumbled at the light winds, but unless I am mistaken we shall be carrying double reefs this journey. What do you think, Uncle John?"

"I have been saying the same, lad; still there is no saying. You will know more about it in a few hours' time."

It was evening when the boys went on board the Susan, and as soon as supper was over they lay down, as she was to start at daybreak the next morning. As soon as they were roused by the creaking of the blocks and the sound of trampling of feet overhead they went up on deck. Day had just broken; the sky was overspread by dark clouds.

"There is not much wind after all," Geoffrey said as he looked round.

"No, it has fallen light during the last two hours," the skipper replied, "but I expect we shall have plenty before long. However, we could do with a little more now."

Tide was half out when they started. Joe Chambers had said the night before that he intended to drop down to the edge of the sands and there anchor, and to make across them past the Whittaker Beacon into the channel as soon as there was sufficient water to enable him to do so. The wind was light, sometimes scarcely sufficient to belly out the sails and give the boat steerage way, at others coming in short puffs which heeled her over and made her spring forward merrily.

Before long the wind fell lighter and lighter, and at last Joe Chambers ordered the oars to be got out.

78

"We must get down to the edge of the Buxey," he said, "before the tide turns, or we shall have it against us, and with this wind we should never be able to stem it, but should be swept up the Crouch. At present it is helping us, and with a couple of hours' rowing we may save it to the Buxey."

The boys helped at the sweeps, and for two hours the creaking of the oars and the dull flapping of the sail alone broke the silence of the calm; and the lads were by no means sorry when the skipper gave the order for the anchor to be dropped.

"I should like to have got about half a mile further," he said; "but I can see by the landmarks that we are making no way now. The tide is beginning to suck in."

"How long will it be before we have water enough to cross the Spit?" Lionel asked as they laid in the oars.

"Well nigh four hours, Master Lionel. Then, even if it keeps a stark calm like this, we shall be able to get across the sands and a mile or two up the channel before we meet the tide. There we must anchor again till the first strength is past, and then if the wind springs up we can work along at the edge of the sands against it. There is no tide close in to the sands after the first two hours. But I still think this is going to turn into wind presently; and if it does it will be sharp and heavy, I warrant. It's either that or rain."

The sky grew darker and darker until the water looked almost black under a leaden canopy.

"I wish we were back into Bricklesey," Joe Chambers said. "I have been well nigh fifteen years going backwards and forwards here, and I do not know that ever I saw an awkwarder look about the sky. It reminds me of what I have heard men who have sailed to the Indies say they have seen there before a hurricane breaks. If it was not that we saw the clouds flying fast overhead when we started, I should have said it was a thick sea fog that had rolled in upon us. Ah, there is the first drop. I don't care how hard it comes down so that there is not wind at the tail of it. A squall of wind before rain is soon over; but when it follows rain you will soon have your sails close reefed. You had best go below or you will be wet through in a minute."

The great drops were pattering down on the deck and causing splashes as of ink on the surface of the oily looking water. Another half minute it was pouring with such a mighty roar on the deck that the boys below needed to shout to make each other heard. It lasted but five minutes, and then stopped as suddenly as it began. The lads at once returned to the deck.

"So it is all over, Master Chambers."

"Well the first part is over, but that is only a sort of a beginning. Look at that light under the clouds away to the south of east. That is where it is coming from, unless I am mistaken. Turn to and get the mainsail down, lads," for although after dropping anchor the head sails had been lowered, the main and mizzen were still on her.

The men set to work, and the boys helped to stow the sail and fasten it with the tiers. Suddenly there was a sharp puff of wind. It lasted a few seconds only, then Joe Chambers pointed towards the spot whence a hazy light seemed to come.

"Here it comes," he said. "Do you see that line of white water? That is a squall and no mistake. I am glad we are not under sail."

There was a sharp, hissing sound as the line of white water approached them, and then the squall struck them with such force and fury that the lads instinctively grasped at the shrouds. The mizzen had brought the craft in a moment head to wind, and Joe Chambers and the two sailors at once lowered it and stowed it away.

"Only put a couple of tiers on," the skipper shouted. "We may have to upsail again if this goes on."

The sea got up with great rapidity, and a few minutes after the squall had struck them the Susan was beginning to pitch heavily. The wind increased in force, and seemed to scream rather than whistle in the rigging.

"The sea is getting up fast!" Geoffrey shouted in the skipper's ear as he took his place close to him.

"It won't be very heavy yet," Joe Chambers replied; "the sands break its force. But the tide has turned now, and as it makes over the sand there will be a tremendous sea here in no time; that is if this wind holds, and it seems to me that it is going to be an unusual gale altogether."

"How long will it be before we can cross the Spit?"

"We are nor going to cross today, that's certain," the skipper said. "There will be a sea over those sands that would knock the life out of the strongest craft that ever floated. No, I shall wait here for another hour or two if I can, and then slip my cable and run for the Crouch. It is a narrow channel, and I never care about going into it after dark until there is water enough for a craft of our draught over the sands. It ain't night now, but it is well nigh as dark. There is no making out the bearings of the land, and we have got to trust to the perches the fishermen put up at the bends of the channel. However, we have got to try it. Our anchors would never hold here when the sea gets over the sands, and if they did they would pull her head under water."

In half an hour a sea had got up that seemed to the boys tremendous. Dark as it was they could see in various directions tracts of white water where the waves broke wildly over the sands. The second anchor had been let go some time before. The two cables were as taut as iron bars, and the boat was pulling her bow under every sea. Joe Chambers dropped a lead line overboard and watched it closely.

"We are dragging our anchors," he said. "There is nothing for it but to run."

He went to the bow, fastened two logs of wood by long lines to the cables outside the bow, so that he could find and recover the anchors on his return, then a very small jib was hoisted, and as it filled two blows with an axe severed the cables inboard. The logs attached to them were thrown over, and the skipper ran aft and put up the helm as the boat's head payed off before the wind. As she did so a wave struck her and threw tons of water on board, filling her deck nearly up to the rails. It was well Joe had shouted to the boys to hold on, for had they not done so they would have been swept overboard.

Another wave struck them before they were fairly round, smashing in the bulwark and sweeping everything before it, and the boys both thought that the Susan was sinking under their feet. However she recovered herself. The water poured our through the broken bulwark, and the boat rose again on the waves as they swept one after another down upon her stern. The channel was well marked now, for the sands on either side were covered with breaking water. Joe Chambers shouted to the sailors to close reef the mizzen and hoist it, so that he might have the boat better under control. The wind was not directly astern but somewhat on the quarter; and small as was the amount of sail shown, the boat lay over till her lee rail was at times under water; the following waves yawing her about so much that it needed the most careful steering to prevent her from broaching to.

"It seems to me as the wind is northering!" one of the men shouted.

The skipper nodded and slackened out the sheet a bit as the wind came more astern. He kept his eyes fixed ahead of him, and the men kept gazing through the gloom.

"There is the perch," one of them shouted presently, "just on her weather bow!"

The skipper nodded and held on the same course until abreast of the perch, which was only a forked stick. The men came aft and hauled in the mizzen sheer. Chambers put up the helm. The mizzen came across with a jerk, and the sheet was again allowed to run out. The jib came over with a report like the shot of a cannon, and at the same moment split into streamers.

"Hoist the foresail!" the skipper shouted, and the men sprang forward and seized the halliards; but at this moment the wind seemed to blow with a double fury, and the moment the sail was set it too split into ribbons.

"Get up another jib!" Joe Chambers shouted, and one of the men sprang below. In half a minute he reappeared with another sail.

"Up with it quick, Bill. We are drifting bodily down on the sand."

Bill hurried forward. The other hand had hauled in the traveller, to which the bolt rope of the jib was still attached, and hauling on this had got the block down and in readiness for fastening on the new jib. The sheets were hooked on, and then while one hand ran the sail out with the out haul to the bowsprit end, the other hoisted with the halliards. By this time the boat was close to the broken water. As the sail filled her head payed off towards it.

By England's Aid: or The Freeing

The wind lay her right over, and before she could gather way there was a tremendous crash. The Susan had struck on the sands. The next wave lifted her, but as it passed on she came down with a crash that seemed to shake her in pieces. Joe Chambers relaxed his grasp of the now useless tiller.

"It is all over," he said to the boys. "Nothing can save her now. If she had been her own length farther off the sands she would have gathered way in time. As it is another ten minutes and she will be in splinters."

She was now lying over until her masthead was but a few feet above water. The seas were striking her with tremendous force, pouring a deluge of water over her.

"There is but one chance for you," he went on. "The wind is dead on the shore, and Foulness lies scarce three miles to leeward."

He went into the cabin and fetched out a small axe fastened in the companion where it was within reach of the helmsman. Two blows cut the shrouds of the mizzen, a few vigorous strokes were given to the foot of the mast, and, as the boat lifted and crashed down again on the sand, it broke off a few inches above the deck.

"Now, lads, I will lash you loosely to this. You can both swim, and with what aid it will give you may well reach the shore. There are scarce three feet of water here, and except where one or two deeps pass across it there is no more anywhere between this and the land. It will not be rough very far. Now, be off at once; the boat will go to pieces before many minutes. I and the two men will take to the mainmast, but I want to see you off first."

Without hesitation the boys pushed off with the mast. As they did so a cataract of water poured over the smack upon them, knocking them for a moment under the surface with its force.

For the next few minutes it was a wild struggle for life. They found at once that they were powerless to swim in the broken water, which, as it rushed across the sand, impelled alike by the rising tide behind it and the force of the wind, hurried them along at a rapid pace, breaking in short steep waves. They could only cling to the mast and snatch a breath of air from time to time as it rolled over and over. Had they not been able to swim they would very speedily have been drowned; but, accustomed as they were to diving, they kept their presence of mind, holding their breath when under water and breathing whenever they were above it with their faces to the land. It was only so that they could breathe, for the air was thick with spray, which was swept along with such force by the wind that it would have drowned the best swimmer who tried to face it as speedily as if he had been under water.

After what seemed to them an age the waves became somewhat less violent, though still breaking in a mass of foam. Geoffrey loosed his hold of the spar and tried to get to his feet. He was knocked down several times before he succeeded, but when he did so found that the water was little more than two feet deep, although the waves rose to his shoulders. The soft mud under his feet rendered it extremely difficult to stand, and the rope which attached him to the spar, which was driving before him, added to the difficulty. He could not overtake the mast, and threw himself down again and swam to it.

"Get up, Lionel!" he shouted; "we can stand here." But Lionel was too exhausted to be capable of making the effort. With the greatest difficulty Geoffrey raised him to his feet and supported him with his back to the wind.

"Get your breath again!" he shouted. "We are over the worse now and shall soon be in calmer water. Get your feet well out in front of you, if you can, and dig your heels into the mud, then you will act as a buttress to me and help me to keep my feet."

It was two or three minutes before Lionel was able to speak. Even during this short time they had been carried some distance forward, for the ground on which they stood seemed to be moving, and the force of the waves carried them constantly forward.

"Feel better, old fellow?" Geoffrey asked, as he felt Lionel making an effort to resist the pressure of the water.

"Yes, I am better now," Lionel said.

"Well, we will go on as we are as long as we can; let us just try to keep our feet and give way to the sea as it rakes us along. The quicker we go the sooner we shall be in shallower water; but the tide is rising fast, and unless we go on it will speedily be as bad here as it was where we started."

As soon as Lionel had sufficiently recovered they again took to the spar; but now, instead of clasping it with their arms and legs, they lay with their chest upon it, and used their efforts only to keep it going before the wind and ride. Once they came to a point where the sand was but a few inches under water. Here they stood up for some minutes, and then again proceeded on foot until the water deepened to their waists.

Their progress was now much more easy, for the high bank had broken the run of the surf. The water beyond it was much smoother, and they were able to swim, pushing the spar before them.

"We are in deep water," Geoffrey said presently, dropping his feet. "It is out of my depth. Chambers said there was a deep channel across the sands nor far from the island; so in that case the shore cannot be far away."

In another quarter of an hour the water was again waist deep. Geoffrey stood up.

"I think I see a dark line ahead, Lionel; we shall soon be there."

Another ten minutes and the water was not above their knees. They could see the low shore now at a distance of but a few hundred yards ahead, and untying the ropes under their arms they let the spar drift on, and waded forward until they reached the land. There was a long mud bank yet to cross, and exhausted as they were it took them a long time to do this; but at last they came to a sandy bank rising sharply some ten feet above the flat. They threw themselves down on this and lay for half an hour without a word being spoken.

"Now, Lionel," Geoffrey said at last, raising himself to a sitting position, "we must make an effort to get on and find a shelter. There are people living in the island. I have heard that they are a wild set, making their living by the wrecks on these sands and by smuggling goods without paying dues to the queen. Still, they will nor refuse us shelter and food, and assuredly there is nothing on us to tempt them to plunder us."

He rose to his feet and helped Lionel up. Once on the top of the bank a level country stretched before them. The wind aided their footsteps, sweeping along with such tremendous force that at times they had difficulty in keeping their feet. As they went on they came upon patches of cultivated land, with hedgerows and deep ditches. Half a mile further they perceived a house. On approaching it they saw that it was a low structure of some size with several out buildings. They made their way to it and knocked at the door. They knocked twice before it was opened, then some bolts were withdrawn. The door was opened a few inches. A man looked out, and seeing two lads opened it widely.

"Well, who are you, and what do you want?" he asked roughly.

"We have been wrecked in a storm on the sands. We were sailing from Bricklesey for Sheerness when the storm caught us."

The man looked at them closely. Their pale faces and evidently exhausted condition vouched for the truth of their story.

"The house is full," he said gruffly, "and I cannot take in strangers. You will find some dry hay in that out house, and I will bring you some food there. When you have eaten and drunk you had best journey on."

So saying he shut the door in their faces.

"This is strange treatment," Geoffrey said. "I should not have thought a man would have refused shelter to a dog such a day as this. What do you say, Lionel, shall we go on?"

"I don't think I can go any further until I have rested, Geoffrey," Lionel replied faintly. "Let us lie down in shelter if it is only for half an hour. After that, if the man brings us some food as he says, we can go on again."

They went into the shed the man had pointed out. It was half full of hay.

"Let us take our things off and wring them, Lionel, and give ourselves a roll in the hay to dry ourselves. We shall soon get warm after that."

They stripped, wrung the water from their clothes, rolled themselves in the hay until they felt a glow of returning warmth, and then put on their clothes again. Scarcely had they done so when the man came in with a large tankard and two hunks of bread.

"Here," he said, "drink this and then be off. We want no strangers hanging round here."

At any other time the boys would have refused hospitality so cheerlessly offered, but they were too weak to resist the temptation. The tankard contained hot spiced ale, and a sensation of warmth and comfort stole over them as soon as they had drunk its contents and eaten a few mouthfuls of bread. The man stood by them while they ate.

"Are you the only ones saved from the wreck?" he asked.

"I trust that we are not," Geoffrey replied. "The master of the boat tied us to a mast as soon as she struck, and he and the two men with him were going to try to get to shore in the same way."

As soon as they had finished they stood up and handed the tankard to the man.

"I am sorry I must turn you out," he said, as if somewhat ashamed of his want of courtesy. "Any other day it would be different, but today I cannot take anyone in."

"I thank you for what you have given us," Geoffrey said. "Can you tell us which is the way to the ferry?"

"Follow the road and it will take you there. About a couple of miles. You cannot mistake the way."

Feeling greatly strengthened and refreshed the lads again started.

"This is a curious affair," Geoffrey said, "and I cannot make out why they should not let us in. However, it does not matter much. I feel warm all over now, in spite of my wet clothes."

"So do I," Lionel agreed. "Perhaps there were smugglers inside, or some fugitives from justice hiding there. Anyhow, I am thankful for that warm ale; it seems to have given me new life altogether."

They had walked a quarter of a mile, when they saw four horsemen coming on the road. They were closely wrapped up in cloaks, and as they passed, with their heads bent down to meet the force of the gale and their broad brimmed hats pulled low down over their eyes, the boys did nor get even a glimpse of their features.

"I wonder who they can be," Geoffrey said, looking after them. "They are very well mounted, and look like persons of some degree. What on earth can they be doing in such a wretched place as this? They must be going to that house we left, for I noticed the road stopped there."

"It is curious, Geoffrey, but it is no business of ours."

"I don't know that, Lionel. You know there are all sorts of rumours about of Papist plots, and conspirators could hardly choose a more out of the way spot than this to hold their meetings. I should not be at all surprised if there is some mischief on foot."

Half a mile further three men on foot met them, and these, like the others, were closely wrapped up to the eyes.

"They have ridden here," Geoffrey said after they had passed. "They have all high riding boots on; they must have left their horses on the other side of the ferry. See, there is a village a short distance ahead. We will go in there and dry our clothes, and have a substantial meal if we can get it. Then we will talk this business over."

The village consisted of a dozen houses only, but among them was a small public house. Several men were sitting by the fire with pots of ale before them.

"We have been wrecked on the coast, landlord, and have barely escaped with our lives. We want to dry our clothes and to have what food you can give us."

"I have plenty of eggs," the landlord said, "and my wife will fry them for you; but we have no meat in the house. Fish and eggs are the chief food here. You are lucky in getting ashore, for it is a terrible gale. It is years since we have had one like it. As to drying your clothes, that can be managed easy enough. You can go up into my room and take them off, and I will lend you a couple of blankets to wrap yourselves in, and you can sit by the fire here until your things are dry."

A hearty meal of fried eggs and another drink of hot ale completed the restoration of the boys. Their clothes were speedily dried, for the landlady had just finished baking her week's batch of bread, and half an hour in the oven completely dried the clothes. They were ready almost as soon as the meal was finished. Many questions were asked them as to the wreck, and the point at which they had been cast ashore.

"It was but a short distance from a house at the end of this road," Geoffrey said. "We went there for shelter, but they would not take us in, though they gave us some bread and hot ale."

Exclamations of indignation were heard among the men sitting round.

"Ralph Hawker has the name of being a surly man," one said, "but I should not have thought that he would have turned a shipwrecked man from his door on such a day as this. They say he is a Papist, though whether he be or not I cannot say; but he has strange ways, and there is many a stranger passes the ferry and asks for his house. However, that is no affair of mine, though I hold there is no good in secret ways."

"That is so," another said; "but it goes beyond all reason for a man to refuse shelter to those the sea has cast ashore on such a day as this."

As soon as they had finished their meal and again dressed themselves, the lads paid their reckoning and went out. Scarcely had they done so when two horsemen rode up, and, drawing rein, inquired if they were going right for the house of one Ralph Hawker.

"It lies about a mile on," Geoffrey said. "You cannot miss the way; the road ends there."

As he spoke a gust of wind of extra fury blew off one of the riders' hats. It was stopped by the wall of a house a few yards away. Geoffrey caught it and handed it to the horseman. With a word of thanks he pressed it firmly on his head, and the two men rode on.

"Did you notice that?" Geoffrey asked his brother. "He has a shaven spot on the top of his head. The man is a Papist priest in disguise. There is something afoot, Lionel. I vote that we try and get to the bottom of it."

"I am ready if you think so, Geoffrey. But it is a hazardous business, you know; for we are unarmed, and there are, we know, seven or eight of them at any rate.

"We must risk that," Geoffrey said; "besides, we can run if we cannot fight. Let us have a try whatever comes of it."

CHAPTER VII. A POPISH PLOT

There was no one about, for the wind was blowing with such fury that few cared to venture out of doors, and the boys therefore started back along the road by which they had come, without being observed.

"We had better strike off from the road," Geoffrey said, "for some more of these men may be coming along. Like enough someone will be on the watch at the house, so we had best make a long detour, and when we get near it come down on it from the other side. You know we saw no windows there."

"That is all well enough," Lionel agreed; "but the question is, how are we to hear what they are saying inside? We are obliged to shout to catch each others' words now, and there is not the least chance of our hearing anything through the closed shutters."

"We must wait till we get there, and then see what is to be done, Lionel. We managed to detect a plot at Sluys, and we may have the same luck here."

After half an hour's brisk walking they again approached the house from the side at which they had before come upon it, and where, as Geoffrey observed, there were no windows; they made their way cautiously up to it, and then moved quietly round to the side. Here there were two windows on the ground floor. The shutters were closed, for glass was unknown except in the houses of the comparatively wealthy. Its place was taken by oiled paper, and this in bad weather was protected by outer shutters. Geoffrey stole out a few paces to look at the window above.

"It is evidently a loft," he said as he rejoined Lionel. "You can see by the roof that the rooms they live in are entirely upon the ground floor. If we can get in there we might possibly hear what is going on below. The rooms are not likely to be ceiled, and there are sure to be cracks between the planks through which we can see what is going on below. The noise of the wind is so great there is little chance of their hearing us. Now, let us look about for something to help us to climb up."

By England's Aid: or The Freeing

Lying by an out house close by they found a rough ladder, composed of a single pole with bits of wood nailed on to it a foot apart. This they placed up against the door of the loft. They could see that this was fastened only by a hasp, with a piece of wood put through the staple. It had been arranged that Geoffrey only should go up, Lionel removing the pole when he entered, and keeping watch behind the out house lest anyone should come round the house. Both had cut heavy sticks as they came along to give them some means of defence. Lionel stood at the pole, while Geoffrey climbed up, removed the piece of wood from the staple, and then holding the hasp to prevent the wind blowing in the door with a crash, entered the loft. A glance showed him that it extended over the whole of the house, and that it was entirely empty.

He closed the door behind him, and jammed it with a couple of wedges of wood he had cut before mounting; then he lay down on the rough planks and began to crawl along. He saw a gleam of light at the further end, and felt sure that it proceeded from the room in which the party were assembled. Although he had little fear of being heard owing to the din kept up by the wind, he moved along with extreme care until he reached the spot whence the light proceeded. As he had anticipated, it was caused by lights in a room below streaming through the cracks between the rough planking.

Rising on to his knees he looked round, and then crawled to a crack that appeared much wider than the rest, the boards being more than half an inch apart. Lying down over it, he was able to obtain a view of a portion of the room below. He could see a part of a long table, and looked down upon the heads of five men sitting on one side of it. He now applied his ear to the crevice. A man was speaking, and in the intervals between the gusts of wind which shook the house to its foundation, he could hear what was said.

"It is no use hesitating any longer, the time for action has arrived — Jezebel must be removed — interests of our holy religion — little danger in carrying out the plan that has been proposed. Next time — Windsor — road passes through wood near Datchet — a weak guard overpowered — two told off to execute — free England from tyranny — glory and honour throughout Catholic world. England disorganized and without a head could offer no resistance — as soon as day fixed — meet at Staines at house of — final details and share each man is to — done, scatter through country, readiness for rising — Philip of Spain —"

This was the last sentence Geoffrey caught, for when the speaker ceased a confused and general talk took place, and he could only catch a word here and there without meaning or connection. He therefore drew quietly back to the door of the loft and opened it. He thought first of jumping straight down, but in that case he could not have fastened the door behind him. He therefore made a sign to Lionel, who was anxiously peering round the corner of the out house. The pole was placed into position, and pulling the door after him and refastening the latch he made his way down to the ground, replaced the pole at the place from which they had taken it, and then retired in the direction from which they had come.

"Well, what have you heard, Geoffrey?" Lionel asked. "Was it worth the risk you have run?"

"Well worth it, Lionel. I could only hear a little of what was said, but that was quite enough to show that a plot is on foot to attack and kill the queen the next time she journeys to Windsor. The conspirators are to hide in a wood near Datchet."

"You don't say so, Geoffrey. That is important news indeed. What are we to do next?"

"I have not thought yet," Geoffrey replied. "I should say, though, our best plan would be to make our way back as quickly as we can by Burnham and Maldon round to Hedingham. The earl was going up to London one day this week, we may catch him before he starts; if not, we must, of course, follow him. But at any rate it is best to go home, for they will be in a terrible fright, especially if Joe Chambers or one of the men take the news to Bricklesey of the loss of the Susan, for it would be quickly carried up to Hedingham by John Lirriper or one or other of the boatmen. No day seems to be fixed, and the queen may not be going to Windsor for some little time, so the loss of a day will not make any difference. As we have money in our pockets we can hire horse at Burnham to take us to Maldon, and get others there to carry us home."

An hour's walking took them to the ferry. It was now getting dusk, and they had come to the conclusion as they walked that it would be too late to attempt to get on that night beyond Burnham. The storm was as wild as ever, and although the passage was a narrow one it was as much as the ferryman could do to row the boat across.

"How far is it from here to Burnham?"

"About four miles; but you won't get to Burnham tonight."

"How is that?" Geoffrey asked.

"You may get as far as the ferry, but you won't get taken over. There will be a big sea in the Crouch, for the wind is pretty nigh straight up it; but you will be able to sleep at the inn this side. In the morning, if the wind has gone down, you can cross; if not, you will have to go round by the bridge, nigh ten miles higher up."

This was unpleasant news. Not that it made any difference to them whether they slept on one side of the river or the other, but if the wind was too strong to admit of a passage in the morning, the necessity for making a detour would cost them many hours of valuable time. There was, however, no help for it, and they walked to Criksey Ferry. The little inn was crowded, for the ferry had been stopped all day, and many like themselves had been compelled to stop for a lull in the wind.

Scarcely had they entered when their names were joyously shouted out, "Ah, Masters Vickars, right glad am I to see you. We feared that surf had put an end to you. We asked at the ferry, but the man declared that no strange lads had crossed that day, and we were fearing we should have a sad tale to send to Hedingham by John Lirriper."

"We are truly glad to see you, Joe," Geoffrey said, as they warmly shook Joe Chambers and the two sailors by the hand. "How did you get ashore?"

"On the mainmast, and pretty nigh drowned we were before we got there. I suppose the tide must have taken us a bit further up than it did you. We got here well nigh two hours ago, though we got a good meal and dried our clothes at a farmhouse."

"We got a meal, too, soon after we landed," Geoffrey said; "but we did not dry our clothes till we got to a little village. I did not ask its name. I am awfully sorry, Joe, about the Susan."

"It is a bad job, but it cannot be helped, Master Geoffrey. I owned a third of her, and two traders at Bricklesey own the other shares. Still I have no cause to grumble. I have laid by more than enough in the last four years to buy a share in another boat as good as she was. You see, a trader ain't like a smack. A trader's got only hull and sails, while a smack has got her nets beside, and they cost well nigh as much as the boat. Thankful enough we are that we have all escaped with our lives; and now I find you are safe my mind feels at rest over it."

"Do you think it will be calm enough to cross in the morning, Joe?"

"Like enough," the sailor replied; "a gale like this is like to blow itself out in twenty–four hours. It has been the worst I ever saw. It is not blowing now quite so hard as it did, and by the morning I reckon, though there may be a fresh wind, the gale will be over."

The number of travellers were far too great for the accommodation of the inn; and with the exception of two or three of the first arrivals all slept on some hay in one of the barns.

The next morning, although the wind was still strong, the fury of the gale had abated. The ferryman, however, said the water was so rough he must wait for a time before they crossed. But when Geoffrey offered him a reward to put their party on shore at once, he consented to do so, Joe Chambers and the two sailors assisting with the oars; and as the ferry boat was large and strongly built, they crossed without further inconvenience than the wetting of their jackets.

Joe Chambers, who knew the town perfectly, at once took them to a place where they were able to hire a couple of horses, and on these rode to Maldon, some nine miles away. Here they procured other horses, and it was not long after midday when they arrived at Hedingham.

Mrs. Vickars held up her hands in astonishment at their shrunken garments; but her relief from the anxiety she had felt concerning what had befallen them during the gale was so great that she was unable to scold.

"We will tell you all about it, mother, afterwards," Geoffrey said, as he released himself from her embrace. "We have had a great adventure, and the Susan has been wrecked. But this is nor the most important matter. Father, has the earl started yet?"

"He was to have gone this morning, Geoffrey, but the floods are likely to be out, and the roads will be in such a state that I have no doubt he has put off his journey."

"It is important that we should see him at once, father. We have overheard some people plotting against the queen's life, and measures must be taken at once for her safety. We will run up and change our things if you will go with us to see him. If you are there he will see you whatever he is doing, while if we go alone there might be delay."

Without waiting for an answer the boys ran upstairs and quickly returned in fresh clothes. Mr. Vickars was waiting for them with his hat on.

"You are quite sure of what you are saying, Geoffrey?" he observed as they walked towards the castle. "Remember, that if it should turn out an error, you are likely to come to sore disgrace instead of receiving commendation for your interference. Every one has been talking of plots against the queen for some time, and you may well have mistaken the purport of what you have heard."

"There is no mistake, father, it is a real conspiracy, though who are those concerned in it I know not. Lionel and I are nor likely to raise a false alarm about anything, as you will say yourself when you hear the story I have to tell the earl."

They had by this time entered the gates of the castle. "The earl has just finished dinner," one of the attendants replied in answer to the question of Mr. Vickars.

"Will you tell him that I wish to see him on urgent business?"

In two or three minutes the servant returned and asked the clergyman to follow him. The earl received him in his private chamber, for the castle was full with guests.

"Well, dominie, what is it?" he asked. "You want some help, I will be bound, for somebody ill or in distress. I know pretty well by this time the meaning of your urgent business."

"It is nothing of that kind today," the clergyman replied; "it is, in fact, my sons who wish to see your lordship. I do not myself know the full purport of their story, save that it is something which touches the safety of the queen."

The earl's expression at once changed.

"Is that so, young sirs? This is a serious matter, you know; it is a grave thing to bring an accusation against anyone in matters touching the state."

"I am aware that it is, my lord, and assuredly my brother and I would not lightly meddle with such matters; but I think that you will say this is a business that should be attended to. It happened thus, sir." He then briefly told how, that being out in a ketch that traded from Bricklesey, they were caught in the gale; that the vessel was driven on the sands, and they were cast ashore on a mast.

He then related the inhospitable reception they had met with. "It seemed strange to us, sir, and contrary to nature, that anyone should refuse to allow two shipwrecked lads to enter the house for shelter on such a day; and it seemed well nigh impossible that his tale of the place being too full to hold us could be true. However, we started to walk. On our way we met four horsemen going towards the house, closely muffled up in cloaks."

"There was nothing very strange in that," the earl observed, "in such weather as we had yesterday."

"Nothing at all, sir; we should not have given the matter one thought had it not been that the four men were very well mounted, and, apparently, gentlemen; and it was strange that such should have business in an out of the way house in Foulness Island. A little further we met three men on foot. They were also wrapped up in cloaks; but they wore high riding boots, and had probably left their horses on the other side of the ferry so as nor to attract attention. A short time afterwards we met two more horsemen, one of whom asked us if he was going right for the house we had been at. As he was speaking a gust of wind blew off his hat. I fetched it and gave it to him, and as he stooped to put it on I saw that a tonsure was shaven on the top of his head. The matter had already seemed strange to us; but the fact that one of this number of men, all going to a lonely house, was a priest in disguise, seemed so suspicious that my brother and myself determined to try and get to the bottom of it."

Geoffrey then related how they had gone back to the house and effected an entrance into the loft extending over it; how he had through the cracks in the boards seen a party of men gathered in one of the lower rooms, and then repeated word for word the scraps of conversation that he had overheard.

The earl had listened with an expression of amused doubt to the early portion of the narrative; but when Geoffrey came to the part where accident had shown to him that one of these men proceeding towards the house was a disguised priest, his face became serious, and he listened with deep attention to the rest of the narrative.

"Faith," he said, "this is a serious matter, and you have done right well in following up your suspicions — and in risking your lives, for they would assuredly have killed you had they discovered you. Mr. Vickars, your sons must ride with me to London at once. The matter is too grave for a moment's delay. I must lay it before Burleigh at once. A day's delay might be fatal."

He rang a bell standing on the table. As soon as an attendant answered it he said, "Order three horses to be saddled at once; I must ride to London with these young gentlemen without delay. Order Parsons and Nichols to be ready in half an hour to set out with us.

"Have you had food, young sirs? for it seems you came hither directly you arrived." Finding that the boys had eaten nothing since they had left Maldon, he ordered food to be brought them, and begged them eat it while he explained to the countess and the guests that sudden business that could not be delayed called him away to London. Half an hour later he started with the boys, the two servants following behind. Late that evening they arrived in London. It was too late to call on Lord Burleigh that night; but early the next morning the earl took the boys with him to the house of the great statesman. Leaving them in the antechamber he went in to the inner apartment, where the minister was at breakfast. Ten minutes later he came out, and called the boys in.

"The Earl of Oxford has told me your story," Lord Burleigh said. "Tell it me again, and omit nothing; for things that seem small are often of consequence in a matter like this."

Geoffrey again repeated his story, giving full details of all that had taken place from the time of their first reaching the house.

Lord Burleigh then questioned him closely as to whether they had seen any of the faces of the men, and would recognize them again.

"I saw none from my spying place above, my lord," Geoffrey said. "I could see only the tops of their heads, and most of them still kept their hats on; nor did we see them as they passed, with the exception only of the man I supposed to be a priest. His face I saw plainly. It was smooth shaven; his complexion was dark, his eyebrows were thin and straight, his face narrow. I should take him for a foreigner — either a Spaniard or Italian."

Lord Burleigh made a note of this description.

"Thanks, young sirs," he said. "I shall, of course, take measures to prevent this plot being carried out, and shall inform her majesty how bravely you both risked your lives to discover this conspiracy against her person. The Earl of Oxford informs me that you are pages of his cousin, Captain Francis Vere, a very brave and valiant gentleman; and that you bore your part bravely in the siege of Sluys, but are at present at home to rest after your labours there, and have permission of Captain Vere to take part in any trouble that may arise here owing to the action of the Spaniards. I have now no further occasion for your services, and you can return with the earl to Hedingham, but your attendance in London will be needed when we lay hands upon these conspirators."

The same day they rode back to Hedingham, but ten days later were again summoned to London. The queen had the day before journeyed to Windsor. Half an hour before she arrived at the wood near Datchet a strong party of her guard had suddenly surrounded it, and had found twelve armed men lurking there. These had been arrested and lodged in the Tower. Three of them were foreigners, the rest members of Catholic families known to be favourable to the Spanish cause. Their trial was conducted privately, as it was deemed advisable that as little should be made as possible of this and other similar plots against the queen's life that were discovered about this time.

Geoffrey and Lionel gave their evidence before the council. As the only man they could have identified was not of the party captured, their evidence only went to show the motive of this gathering in the wood near Datchet. The prisoners stoutly maintained that Geoffrey had misunderstood the conversation he had partly overheard, and that their design was simply to make the queen a prisoner and force her to abdicate. Three of the prisoners, who had before been banished from the country and who had secretly returned, were sentenced to death; two of the others to imprisonment for a long term of years, the rest to banishment from England.

After the trial was over Lord Burleigh sent for the boys, and gave them a very gracious message in the queen's name, together with two rings in token of her majesty's gratitude. Highly delighted with these honours they returned to Hedingham, and devoted themselves even more assiduously than before to exercises in arms, in order that they might some day prove themselves valiant soldiers of the queen.

CHAPTER VIII. THE SPANISH ARMADA

The struggle that was at hand between Spain and England had long been foreseen as inevitable. The one power was the champion of Roman Catholicism, the other of Protestantism; and yet, although so much hung upon the result of the encounter, and all Europe looked on with the most intense interest, both parties entered upon the struggle without allies, and this entirely from the personal fault of the sovereigns of the two nations.

Queen Elizabeth, by her constant intrigues, her underhand dealings with France and Spain, her grasping policy in the Netherlands, her meanness and parsimony, and the fact that she was ready at any moment to sacrifice the Netherlands to her own policy, had wholly alienated the people of the Low Country; for while their own efforts for defence were paralysed by the constant interference of Elizabeth, no benefit was obtained from the English army, whose orders were to stand always on the defensive — the queen's only anxiety appearing to be to keep her grasp upon the towns that had been handed over to her as the price of her alliance.

Her own counsellors were driven to their wits' end by her constant changes of purpose. Her troops were starving and in rags from her parsimony, the fleet lay dismantled and useless from want of funds, and except such arming and drilling as took place at the expense of the nobles, counties, and cities, no preparation whatever was made to meet the coming storm. Upon the other hand, Philip of Spain, who might have been at the head of a great Catholic league against England, had isolated himself by his personal ambitions. Had he declared himself ready, in the event of his conquest of England, to place James of Scotland upon the throne, he would have had Scotland with him, together with the Catholics of England, still a powerful and important body.

France, too, would have joined him, and the combination against Elizabeth and the

Protestants of England would have been well nigh irresistible. But this he could not bring himself to do. His dream was the annexation of England to Spain; and smarting as the English Catholics were under the execution of Mary of Scotland, their English spirit revolted against the idea of the rule of Spain, and the great Catholic nobles hastened, when the moment of danger arrived, to join in the defence of their country, while Scotland, seeing no advantage to be gained in the struggle, stood sullenly aloof, and France gave no aid to a project which was to result, if successful, in the aggrandizement of her already dangerously formidable neighbour.

Thus England and Spain stood alone — Philip slowly but steadily preparing for the great expedition for the conquest of England, Elizabeth hesitating, doubtful; at one moment gathering seamen and arming her fleet, a month or two later discharging the sailors and laying up the ships.

In the spring of 1587 Drake, with six vessels belonging to the crown and twenty–four equipped by merchants of London and other places, had seized a moment when Elizabeth's fickle mind had inclined to warlike measures, and knowing that the mood might last but a day, had slipped out of Plymouth and sailed for Spain a few hours before a messenger arrived with a peremptory order from Elizabeth against entering any Spanish port or offering violence to any Spanish town or ships. Although caught in a gale in the Channel, Drake held on, and, reaching Gibraltar on the 16th April, ascertained that Cadiz was crowded with transports and store ships.

Vice Admiral Burroughs, controller of the navy, who had been specially appointed to thwart Drake's plans, opposed any action being taken; but Drake insisted upon attack, and on the 19th the fleet stood in to Cadiz harbour. Passing through the fire of the batteries, they sank the only great ship of war in the roads, drove off the Spanish galleys, and seized the vast fleet of store ships loaded with wine, corn, and provisions of all sorts for the use of the Armada. Everything of value that could be conveniently moved was transferred to the English ships, then the Spanish vessels were set on fire, their cables cut, and were left to drift in an entangled mass of flame. Drake took a number of prisoners, and sent a messenger on shore proposing to exchange them for such English seamen as were prisoners in Spain. The reply was there were no English prisoners in Spain; and as this notoriously untrue, it was agreed in the fleet that all the Spaniards they might take in the future should be sold to the Moors, and the money reserved for the redeeming of such Englishmen as might be in captivity there or elsewhere.

By England's Aid: or The Freeing

The English fleet then sailed for Cape St. Vincent, picking up on their way large convoys of store ships all bound for the Tagus, where the Armada was collecting. These were all burned, and Drake brought up at Cape St. Vincent, hoping to meet there a portion of the Armada expected from the Mediterranean. As a harbour was necessary, he landed, stormed the fort at Faro, and took possession of the harbour there. The expected enemy did not appear, and Drake sailed up to the mouth of the Tagus, intending to go into Lisbon and attack the great Spanish fleet lying there under its admiral, Santa Cruz. That the force gathered there was enormous Drake well knew, but relying as much on the goodness of his cause as on the valour of his sailors, and upon the fact that the enemy would be too crowded together to fight with advantage, he would have carried out his plan had not a ship arrived from England with orders forbidding him to enter the Tagus. However, he lay for some time at the mouth of the river, destroying every ship that entered its mouth, and sending in a challenge to Santa Cruz to come out and fight. The Spanish admiral did not accept it, and Drake then sailed to Corunna, and there, as at Cadiz, destroyed all the ships collected in the harbour and then returned to England, having in the course of a few months inflicted an enormous amount of damage upon Spain, and having taken the first step to prove that England was the mistress of the sea.

But while the little band of English had been defending Sluys against the army of the Duke of Parma, Philip had been continuing his preparations, filling up the void made by the destruction wrought by Drake, and preparing an Armada which he might well have considered to be invincible. Elizabeth was still continuing her negotiations. She was quite ready to abandon the Netherlands to Spain if she could but keep the towns she held there, but she could nor bring herself to hand these over either to the Netherlands or to Spain. She urged the States to make peace, to which they replied that they did not wish for peace on such terms as Spain would alone grant; they could defend themselves for ten years longer if left alone, they did not ask for further help, and only wanted their towns restored to them.

Had the Armada started as Philip intended in September, it would have found England entirely unprepared, for Elizabeth still obstinately refused to believe in danger, and the few ships that had been held in commission after Drake's return had been so long neglected that they could hardly keep the sea without repair; the rest lay unrigged in the Medway. But the delay gave England fresh time for preparation. Parma's army was lying in readiness for the invasion under canvas at Dunkirk, and their commander had received no information from Spain that the sailing of the Armada was delayed.

The cold, wet, and exposure told terribly upon them, and of the 30,000 who were ready to embark in September not 18,000 were fit for service at the commencement of the year. The expenses of this army and of the Armada were so great that Philip was at last driven to give orders to the Armada to start. But fortune again favoured England. Had the fleet sailed as ordered on the 30th of January they would again have found the Channel undefended, for Elizabeth, in one of her fits of economy, had again dismantled half the fleet that had been got ready for sea, and sent the sailors to their homes.

But the execution of Philip's orders was prevented by the sudden death of Santa Cruz. The Duke of Medina Sidonia was appointed his successor, but as he knew nothing of the state of the Armada fresh delays became necessary, and the time was occupied by Elizabeth, not in preparing for the defence of the country, but in fresh negotiations for peace. She was ready to make any concessions to Spain, but Philip was now only amusing himself by deceiving her. Everything was now prepared for the expedition, and just as the fleet was ready to start, the negotiations were broken off. But though Elizabeth's government had made no preparations for the defence of the country, England herself had not been idle. Throughout the whole country men had been mustered, officered, and armed, and 100,000 were ready to move as soon as the danger became imminent.

The musters of the Midland counties, 80,000 strong, were to form a separate army, and were to march at once to a spot between Windsor and Harrow. The rest were to gather at the point of danger. The coast companies were to fall back wherever the enemy landed, burning the corn and driving off the cattle, and avoiding a battle until the force of the neighbouring counties joined them. Should the landing take place as was expected in Suffolk, Kent, or Sussex, it was calculated that between 30,000 and 40,000 men would bar the way to the invaders before they reached London, while 20,000 men of the western counties would remain to encounter the Duke of Guise, who had engaged to bring across an army of Frenchmen to aid the Spaniards.

Spain, although well aware of the strength of England on the sea, believed that she would have no difficulty with the raw English levies; but Parma, who had met the English at Sluys, had learnt to respect their fighting qualities, and in a letter to Philip gave the opinion that even if the Armada brought him a reinforcement of 6000 men he would still have an insufficient force for the conquest of England. He said, "When I shall have landed I must fight battle after battle. I shall lose men by wounds and disease, I must leave detachments behind me to keep open my communications, and in a short time the body of my army will become so weak that not only I may be unable to advance in the face of the enemy, and time may be given to the heretics and your majesty's other enemies to interfere, but there may fall out some notable inconvenience, with the loss of everything, and I be unable to remedy it."

Unfortunately, the English fleet was far less prepared than the land forces. The militia had been easily and cheaply extemporized, but a fleet can only be prepared by long and painful sacrifices. The entire English navy contained but thirteen ships of over four hundred tons, and including small cutters and pinnaces there were but thirty– eight vessels of all sorts and sizes carrying the queen's flag. Fortunately, Sir John Hawkins was at the head of the naval administration, and in spite of the parsimony of Elizabeth had kept the fleet in a good state of repair and equipment. The merchant navy, although numerous, was equally deficient in vessels of any size.

Philip had encouraged ship building in Spain by grants from the crown, allowing four ducats a ton for every ship built of above three hundred tons burden, and six ducats a ton for every one above five hundred tons. Thus he had a large supply of great ships to draw upon in addition to those of the royal navy, while in England the largest vessels belonging to private owners did not exceed four hundred tons, and there were not more than two or three vessels of that size sailing from any port of the country. The total allowance by the queen for the repair of the whole of the royal navy, wages of shipwrights, clerks, carpenters, watchmen, cost of timber, and, all other necessary dockyard expenses, was but 4000 pounds a year.

In December the fleet was ready for sea, together with the contingent furnished by the liberality and patriotism of the merchants and citizens of the great ports. But as soon as it was got together half the crews collected and engaged at so great an expense were dismissed, the merchant ships released, and England open to invasion, and had Parma started in the vessels he had prepared, Lord Howard, who commanded the English navy, could not have fired a shot to have prevented his crossing.

Well might Sir John Hawkins in his despair at Elizabeth's caprices exclaim: "We are wasting money, wasting strength, dishonouring and discrediting ourselves by our uncertain dallying." But though daily reports came from Spain of the readiness of the Armada to set sail, Elizabeth, even when she again permitted the navy to be manned, fettered it by allowing it to be provided with rations for only a month at a time, and permitting no reserves to be provided in the victualling stores; while the largest vessels were supplied with ammunition for only a day and a half's service, and the rest of the fleet with but enough for one day's service. The council could do nothing, and Lord Howard's letters prove that the queen, and she only, was responsible for the miserable state of things that prevailed.

At last, in May, Lord Howard sailed with the fleet down Channel, leaving Lord Henry Seymour with three men of war and a squadron of privateers to watch Dunkirk. At Plymouth the admiral found Drake with forty ships, all except one raised and sent to sea at the expense of himself and the gentry and merchants of the west counties. The weather was wild, as it had been all the winter. Howard with the great ships lay at anchor in the Sound, rolling heavily, while the smaller craft went for shelter into the mouth of the river. There were but eighteen days' provisions on board; fresh supplies promised did not arrive, and the crews were put on half rations, and eked these out by catching fish. At last, when the supplies were just exhausted, the victualling ships arrived, with one month's fresh rations, and a message that no more would be sent. So villainous was the quality of the stores that fever broke out in the fleet.

It was not until the end of the month that Elizabeth would even permit any further preparations to be made, and the supplies took some time collecting. The crews would have been starved had not the officers so divided the rations as to make them last six weeks. The men died in scores from dysentery brought on by the sour and poisonous beer issued to them, and Howard and Drake ordered wine and arrow root from the town for the use of the sick, and had to pay for it from their own pockets.

But at last the Armada was ready for starting. Contingents of Spanish, Italians, and Portuguese were gathered together with the faithful from all countries — Jesuits from France; exiled priests, Irish and English; and many Catholic Scotch, English, and Irish noblemen and gentlemen. The six squadrons into which the fleet was divided contained sixty–five large war ships, the smallest of which was seven hundred tons. Seven were over one thousand, and the largest, an Italian ship, La Regazona, was thirteen hundred. All were built high like castles, their upper works musket proof, their main timbers four or five feet thick, and of a strength it was supposed no English cannon could pierce.

By England's Aid: or The Freeing

Next to the big ships, or galleons as they were called, were four galleasses, each carrying fifty guns and 450 soldiers and sailors, and rowed by 300 slaves. Besides these were four galleys, fifty–six great armed merchant ships, the finest Spain possessed, and twenty caravels or small vessels. Thus the fighting fleet amounted to 129 vessels, carrying in all 2430 cannon. On board was stored an enormous quantity of provisions for the use of the army after it landed in England, there being sufficient to feed 40,000 men for six months.

There were on board 8000 sailors, 19,000 soldiers, 1000 gentlemen volunteers, 600 priests, servants, and miscellaneous officers, and 2000 galley slaves. This was indeed a tremendous array to meet the fleet lying off Plymouth, consisting of 29 queen's ships of all sizes, 10 small vessels belonging to Lord Howard and members of his family, and 43 privateers between 40 and 400 tons under Drake, the united crews amounting to something over 9000 men.

The winter had passed pleasantly to Geoffrey and Lionel Vickars; the earl had taken a great fancy to them, and they had stayed for some time in London as members of his suite. When the spring came they had spoken about rejoining Francis Vere in Holland, but the earl had said that there was little doing there. The enmity excited by the conduct of Elizabeth prevented any cooperation between the Dutch and English; and indeed the English force was reduced to such straits by the refusal of the queen to furnish money for their pay, or to provide funds for even absolute necessaries, that it was wholly incapable of taking the field, and large numbers of the men returned to England.

Had this treatment of her soldiers and sailors at the time when such peril threatened their country been occasioned by want of funds, some excuse would have been possible for the conduct of Elizabeth; but at the time there were large sums lying in the treasury, and it was parsimony and not incapacity to pay that actuated Elizabeth in the course she pursued.

As the boys were still uneasy as to the opinion Francis Vere might form of their continued stay in England, they wrote to him, their letter being inclosed in one from the earl; but the reply set their minds at rest — "By all means stay in England," Captain Vere wrote, "since there is nothing doing here of any note or consequence, nor likely to be. We are simply idling our time in Bergen op Zoom, and not one of us but is longing to be at home to bear his part in the events pending there. It is hard, indeed, to be confined in this miserable Dutch town while England is in danger. Unfortunately we are soldiers and must obey orders; but as you are as yet only volunteers, free to act as you choose, it would be foolish in the extreme for you to come over to this dull place while there is so much going on in England. I have written to my cousin, asking him to introduce you to some of the country gentlemen who have fitted out a ship for service against the Spaniards, so that you may have a hand in what is going on."

This the earl had done, and early in May they had journeyed down to Plymouth on horseback with a party of other gentlemen who were going on board the Active, a vessel of two hundred and fifty tons belonging to a gentleman of Devonshire, one Master Audrey Drake, a relation of Sir Francis Drake. The earl himself was with the party. He did not intend to go on board, for he was a bad sailor; and though ready, as he said, to do his share of fighting upon land, would be only an encumbrance on board a ship.

He went down principally at the request of Cecil and other members of the council, who, knowing that he was a favourite of the queen, thought that his representations as to the state of the fleet might do more than they could do to influence her to send supplies to the distressed sailors. The earl visited the ships lying in the mouth of the Tamar, and three times started in a boat to go out to those in the Sound; but the sea was so rough, and he was so completely prostrated by sickness, that he had each time to put back. What he saw, however, on board the ships he visited, and heard from Lord Howard as to the state of those at sea, was quite sufficient. He at once expended a considerable amount of money in buying wine and fresh meat for the sick, and then hurried away to London to lay before the queen the result of his personal observations, and to implore her to order provisions to be immediately despatched to the fleet.

But even the description given by one of her favourites of the sufferings of the seamen was insufficient to induce the queen to open her purse strings, and the earl left her in great dudgeon; and although his private finances had been much straitened by his extravagance and love of display, he at once chartered a ship, filled her with provisions, and despatched her to Plymouth.

Mr. Drake and the gentlemen with him took up their abode in the town until there should be need for them to go on board the Active, where the accommodation was much cramped, and life by no means agreeable; and the Vickars therefore escaped sharing the sufferings of those on board ship.

By England's Aid: or The Freeing

At the end of May came the news that the Armada had sailed on the 19th, and high hopes were entertained that the period of waiting had terminated. A storm, however, scattered the great fleet, and it was not until the 12th of July that they sailed from the Bay of Ferrol, where they had collected after the storm.

Never was there known a season so boisterous as the summer of 1588, and when off Ushant, in a southwest gale, four galleys were wrecked on the French coast, and the Santa Anna, a galleon of 800 tons, went down, carrying with her ninety seamen, three hundred soldiers, and 50,000 ducats in gold.

After two days the storm abated, and the fleet again proceeded. At daybreak on the 20th the Lizard was in sight, and an English fishing boat was seen running along their line. Chase was given, but she soon out sailed her pursuers, and carried the news to Plymouth. The Armada had already been made out from the coast the night before, and beacon lights had flashed the news all over England. In every village and town men were arming and saddling and marching away to the rendezvous of the various corps.

In Plymouth the news was received with the greatest rejoicing. Thanks to the care with which the provisions had been husbanded, and to the manner in which the officers and volunteers had from their private means supplemented the scanty stores, there was still a week's provisions on board, and this, it was hoped, would suffice for their needs. The scanty supply of ammunition was a greater source of anxiety; but they hoped that fresh supplies would be forthcoming, now that even the queen could no longer close her eyes to the urgent necessity of the case.

As soon as the news arrived all the gentlemen in the town flocked on board the ships, and on the night of the 19th the queen's ships and some of the privateers went to moorings behind Ram Head, so that they could make clear to sea; and on the morning when the Spaniards sighted the Lizard, forty sail were lying ready for action under the headland.

At three o'clock in the afternoon the lookout men on the hill reported a line of sails on the western horizon. Two wings were at first visible, which were gradually united as the topsails of those in the centre rose above the line of sea. As they arose it could be seen that the great fleet was sailing, in the form of a huge crescent, before a gentle wind. A hundred and fifty ships, large and small, were counted, as a few store ships bound for Flanders had joined the Armada for protection.

By England's Aid: or The Freeing

The Active was one of the privateers that had late the evening before gone out to Ram Head, and just as it was growing dusk the anchors were got up, and the little fleet sailed out from the shelter of the land as the Armada swept along.

The Spanish admiral at once ordered the fleet to lie to for the night, and to prepare for a general action at daybreak, as he knew from a fisherman he had captured that the English fleet were at Plymouth. The wind was on shore, but all through the night Howard's and Drake's ships beat out from the Sound until they took their places behind the Spanish fleet, whose position they could perfectly make out by the light of the half moon that rose at two in the morning.

On board the English fleet all was confidence and hilarity. The sufferings of the last three months were forgotten. The numbers and magnitude of the Spanish ships counted as nothing. The sailors of the west country had met the Spaniards on the Indian seas and proved their masters, and doubted not for a moment that they should do so again.

There was scarce a breath of air when day broke, but at eight o'clock a breeze sprang up from the west, and the Armada made sail and attempted to close with the English; but the low, sharp English ships sailed two feet to the one of the floating castles of Spain, and could sail close to the wind, while the Spanish ships, if they attempted to close haul their sails, drifted bodily to leeward. Howard's flagship, the Ark Raleigh, with three other English ships, opened the engagement by running down along their rear line, firing into each galleon as they passed, then wearing round and repeating the manoeuvre. The great San Mateo luffed out from the rest of the fleet and challenged them to board, but they simply poured their second broadside into her and passed on.

The excellence of the manoeuvring of the English ships, and the rapidity and accuracy of their fire, astonished the Spaniards. Throughout the whole forenoon the action continued; the Spaniards making efforts to close, but in vain, the English ships keeping the weather gage and sailing continually backwards and forwards, pouring in their broadsides. The height and size of the Spanish ships were against them; and being to leeward they heeled over directly they came up to the wind to fire a broadside, and their shots for the most part went far over their assailants, while they themselves suffered severely from the English fire. Miquel de Oquendo, who commanded one of the six Spanish squadrons, distinguished himself by his attempts to close with the English, and by maintaining his position in the rear of the fleet engaged in constant conflict with them.

He was a young nobleman of great promise, distinguished alike for his bravery and chivalrous disposition; but he could do little while the wind remained in the west and the English held the weather gage. So far only the ships that had been anchored out under Ram Head had taken part in the fight, those lying higher up in the Sound being unable to make their way out. At noon the exertions of their crews, who had from the preceding evening worked incessantly, prevailed, and they were now seen coming out from behind the headland to take part in the struggle. Medina Sidonia signalled to his fleet to make sail up Channel, Martinez de Ricaldo covering the rear with the squadron of Biscay. He was vice admiral of the fleet, and considered to be the best seaman Spain possessed now that Santa Cruz was dead.

The wind was now rising. Lord Howard sent off a fast boat with letters to Lord Henry Seymour, telling him how things had gone so far, and bidding him be prepared for the arrival of the Spanish fleet in the Downs. As the afternoon went on the wind rose, and a rolling sea came in from the west. Howard still hung upon the Spanish rear, firing but seldom in order to save his powder. As evening fell, the Spanish vessels, huddled closely together, frequently came into collision with one another, and in one of these the Capitana, the flagship of the Andalusian division, commanded by Admiral Pedro de Valdez, had her bowsprit carried away, the foremast fell overboard, and the ship dropped out of her place.

Two of the galleasses came to her assistance and tried to take her in tow, but the waves were running so high that the cable broke. Pedro de Valdez had been commander of the Spanish fleet on the coast of Holland, and knew the English Channel and the northern shores of France and Holland well.

The duke therefore despatched boats to bring him off with his crew, but he refused to leave his charge. Howard, as with his ships he passed her, believed her to be deserted and went on after the fleet; but a London vessel kept close to her and exchanged shots with her all night, until Drake, who had turned aside to chase what he believed to be a portion of the Spanish fleet that had separated itself from the rest, but which turned out to be the merchant ships that had joined it for protection, came up, and the Capitana struck her flag. Drake took her into Torbay, and there left her in the care of the Brixham fishermen, and taking with him Valdez and the other officers sailed away to join Lord Howard. The fishermen, on searching the ship, found some tons of gunpowder on board her.

By England's Aid: or The Freeing

Knowing the scarcity of ammunition in the fleet they placed this on board the Roebuck, the fastest trawler in the harbour, and she started at once in pursuit of the fleet.

The misfortune to the Capitana was not the only one that befell the Spaniards. While Oquendo was absent from his galleon a quarrel arose among the officers, who were furious at the ill result of the day's fighting. The captain struck the master gunner with a stick; the latter, a German, rushed below in a rage, thrust a burning fuse into a powder barrel, and sprang through a porthole into the sea. The whole of the deck was blown up, with two hundred sailors and soldiers; but the ship was so strongly built that she survived the shock, and her mast still stood.

The duke sent boats to learn what had happened. These carried off the few who remained unhurt, but there was no means of taking off the wounded. These, however, were treated kindly and sent on shore when the ship was picked up at daylight by the English, who, on rifling her, found to their delight that there were still many powder barrels on board that had escaped the explosion.

The morning broke calm, and the wind, when it came, was from the east, which gave the Spaniards the advantage of position. The two fleets lay idle all day three or four miles apart, and the next morning, as the wind was still from the east, the Spaniards bore down upon Howard to offer battle.

The English, however, headed out to sea. Encouraged by seeing their assailants avoid a pitched battle the Spaniards gave chase. The San Marcos, the fastest sailer in the fleet, left the rest behind, and when the breeze headed round at noon she was several miles to windward of her consorts, and the English at once set upon her. She fought with extreme courage, and defended herself single handed for an hour and a half, when Oquendo came up to the rescue, and as the action off Plymouth had almost exhausted his stock of powder, and the Brixham sloop had not yet come up, Howard was obliged to draw off.

The action of this day was fought off Portland. During the three days the British fleet had been to sea they had received almost hourly reinforcements. From every harbour and fishing port along the coast from Plymouth to the Isle of Wight vessels of all sizes, smacks, and boats put off, crowded with noblemen and gentlemen anxious to take part in the action, and their enthusiasm added to that of the weary and ill fed sailors. At the end of the third day the English fleet had increased to a hundred sail, many of which, however, were of very small burden.

CHAPTER IX. THE ROUT OF THE ARMADA

The fight between the fleets had begun on Sunday morning, and at the end of the third day the strength of the Armada remained unbroken. The moral effect had no doubt been great, but the loss of two or three ships was a trifle to so large a force, and the spirit of the Spaniards had been raised by the gallant and successful defence the San Marcos had made on the Tuesday afternoon. Wednesday was again calm. The magazines of the English ships were empty. Though express after express had been sent off praying that ammunition might be sent, none had arrived, and the two fleets lay six miles apart without action, save that the galleasses came out and skirmished for a while with the English ships.

That evening, however, a supply of ammunition sufficient for another day's fighting arrived, and soon after daybreak the English fleet moved down towards the Armada, and for the first time engaged them at close quarters. The Ark Raleigh, the Bear, the Elizabeth Jones, the Lion, and the Victory bore on straight into the centre of the Spanish galleons, exchanging broadsides with each as they passed. Oquendo with his vessel was right in the course of the English flagship, and a collision took place, in which the Ark Raleigh's rudder was unshipped, and she became unmanageable.

The enemy's vessels closed round her, but she lowered her boats, and these, in spite of the fire of the enemy, brought her head round before the wind, and she made her way through her antagonists and got clear. For several hours the battle continued. The Spanish fire was so slow, and their ships so unwieldy, that it was rarely they succeeded in firing a shot into their active foes, while the English shot tore their way through the massive timbers of the Spanish vessels, scattering the splinters thickly among the soldiers, who had been sent below to be out of harm's way; but beyond this, and inflicting much damage upon masts and spars, the day's fighting had no actual results. No captures were made by the English.

The Spaniards suffered, but made no sign; nevertheless their confidence in their powers was shaken. Their ammunition was also running short, and they had no hope of refilling their magazines until they effected a junction with Parma. Their admiral that night wrote to him asking that two shiploads of shot and powder might be sent to him immediately.

"The enemy pursue me," he said; "they fire upon me most days from morning till nightfall, but they will not close and grapple. I have given them every opportunity. I have purposely left ships exposed to tempt them to board, but they decline to do it; and there is no remedy, for they are swift and we are slow. They have men and ammunition in abundance." The Spanish admiral was unaware that the English magazines were even more empty than his own.

On Friday morning Howard sailed for Dover to take in the supplies that were so sorely needed. The Earl of Sussex, who was in command of the castle, gave him all that he had, and the stores taken from the prizes came up in light vessels and were divided among the fleet, and in the evening the English fleet again sailed out and took up its place in the rear of the Armada. On Saturday morning the weather changed. After six days of calm and sunshine it began to blow hard from the west, with driving showers. The Spaniards, having no pilots who knew the coasts, anchored off Calais. The English fleet, closely watching their movements, brought up two miles astern.

The Spanish admiral sent off another urgent letter to Parma at Dunkirk, begging him to send immediately thirty or forty fast gunboats to keep the English at bay. Parma had received the admiral's letters, and was perfectly ready to embark his troops, but could not do this as the admiral expected he would, until the fleet came up to protect him. The lighters and barges he had constructed for the passage were only fit to keep the sea in calm weather, and would have been wholly at the mercy of even a single English ship of war. He could not, therefore, embark his troops until the duke arrived. As to the gunboats asked for, he had none with him.

But while the Spanish admiral had grave cause for uneasiness in the situation in which he found himself, Lord Howard had no greater reason for satisfaction. In spite of his efforts the enemy's fleet had arrived at their destination with their strength still unimpaired, and were in communication with the Duke of Parma's army. Lord Seymour had come up with a squadron from the mouth of the Thames, but his ships had but one day's provisions on board, while Drake and Howard's divisions had all but exhausted their supplies. The previous day's fighting had used up the ammunition obtained at Dover. Starvation would drive every English ship from the sea in another week at the latest. The Channel would then be open for the passage of Parma's army.

By England's Aid: or The Freeing

At five o'clock on Sunday evening a council of war was held in Lord Howard's cabin, and it was determined, that as it was impossible to attack the Spanish Fleet where they lay at the edge of shallow water, an attempt must be made to drive them out into the Channel with fireships. Eight of the private vessels were accordingly taken, and such combustibles as could be found — pitch, tar, old sails, empty casks, and other materials — were piled into them. At midnight the tide set directly from the English fleet towards the Spaniards, and the fireships, manned by their respective crews, hoisted sail and drove down towards them.

When near the Armada the crews set fire to the combustibles, and taking to their boats rowed back to the fleet. At the sight of the flames bursting up from the eight ships bearing down upon them, the Spaniards were seized with a panic. The admiral fired a gun as a signal, and all cut their cables and hoisted sail, and succeeded in getting out to sea before the fireships arrived. They lay to six miles from shore, intending to return in the morning and recover their anchors; but Drake with his division of the fleet, and Seymour with the squadron from the Thames, weighed their anchors and stood off after them, while Howard with his division remained off Calais, where, in the morning, the largest of the four galleasses was seen aground on Calais Bar. Lord Howard wasted many precious hours in capturing her before he set off to join Drake and Seymour, who were thundering against the Spanish fleet. The wind had got up during the night, and the Spaniards had drifted farther than they expected, and when morning dawned were scattered over the sea off Gravelines. Signals were made for them to collect, but before they could do so Drake and Seymour came up and opened fire within pistol shot. The English admiral saw at once that, with the wind rising from the south, if he could drive the unwieldy galleons north they would be cut off from Dunkirk, and would not be able to beat back again until there was a change of wind.

All through the morning the English ships poured a continuous shower of shot into the Spanish vessels, which, huddled together in a confused mass, were unable to make any return whatever. The duke and Oquendo, with some of the best sailors among the Fleet, tried to beat out from the crowd and get room to manoeuvre, but Drake's ships were too weatherly and too well handled to permit of this, and they were driven back again into the confused mass, which was being slowly forced towards the shoals and banks of the coasts.

Howard came up at noon with his division, and until sunset the fire was maintained, by which time almost the last cartridge was spent, and the crews worn our by their incessant labour. They took no prizes, for they never attempted to board. They saw three great galleons go down, and three more drift away towards the sands of Ostend, where they were captured either by the English garrisoned there or by three vessels sent by Lord Willoughby from Flushing, under the command of Francis Vere. Had the English ammunition lasted but a few more hours the whole of the Armada would have been either driven ashore or sunk; but when the last cartridge had been burned the assailants drew off to take on board the stores which had, while the fighting was going on, been brought up by some provision ships from the Thames.

But the Spaniards were in no condition to benefit by the cessation of the attack. In spite of the terrible disadvantages under which they laboured, they had fought with splendid courage. The sides of the galleons had been riddled with shot, and the splinters caused by the rending of the massive timbers had done even greater execution than the iron hail. Being always to leeward, and heeling over with the wind, the ships had been struck again and again below the waterline, and many were only kept from sinking by nailing sheets of lead over the shot holes.

Their guns were, for the most part, dismounted or knocked to pieces. Several had lost masts, the carnage among the crews was frightful, and yet not a single ship hauled down her colours. The San Mateo, which was one of those that grounded between Ostend and Sluys, fought to the last, and kept Francis Vere's three ships at bay for two hours, until she was at last carried by boarding.

Left to themselves at the end of the day, the Spaniards gathered in what order they could, and made sail for the north. On counting the losses they found that four thousand men had been killed or drowned, and the number of wounded must have been far greater. The crews were utterly worn out and exhausted. They had the day before been kept at work cleaning and refitting, and the fireships had disturbed them early in the night. During the engagement there had been no time to serve out food, and the labours of the long struggle had completely exhausted them. Worst of all, they were utterly disheartened by the day's fighting. They had been pounded by their active foes, who fired five shots to their one, and whose vessels sailed round and round them, while they themselves had inflicted no damage that they could perceive upon their assailants.

114

By England's Aid: or The Freeing

The English admirals had no idea of the extent of the victory they had won. Howard, who had only come up in the middle of the fight, believed that they "were still wonderful great and strong," while even Drake, who saw more clearly how much they had suffered, only ventured to hope that some days at least would elapse before they could join hands with Parma. In spite of the small store of ammunition that had arrived the night before, the English magazines were almost empty; but they determined to show a good front, and "give chase as though they wanted nothing."

When the morning dawned the English fleet were still to windward of the Armada, while to leeward were lines of white foam, where the sea was breaking on the shoals of Holland. It seemed that the Armada was lost. At this critical moment the wind suddenly shifted to the east. This threw the English fleet to leeward, and enabled the Spaniards to head out from the coast and make for the North Sea. The Spanish admiral held a council. The sea had gone down, and they had now a fair wind for Calais; and the question was put to the sailing masters and captains whether they should return into the Channel or sail north round Scotland and Ireland, and so return to Spain. The former was the courageous course, but the spirit of the Spaniards was broken, and the vote was in favour of what appeared a way of escape. Therefore, the shattered Fleet bore on its way north. On board the English fleet a similar council was being held, and it was determined that Lord Seymour's squadron should return to guard the Channel, lest Parma should take advantage of the absence of the fleet to cross from Dunkirk to England, and that Howard and Drake with their ninety ships should pursue the Spaniards; for it was not for a moment supposed that the latter had entirely abandoned their enterprise, and intended to return to Spain without making another effort to rejoin Parma.

During the week's fighting Geoffrey and Lionel Vickars had taken such part as they could in the contest; but as there had been no hand to hand fighting, the position of the volunteers on board the fleet had been little more than that of spectators. The crews worked the guns and manoeuvred the sails, and the most the lads could do was to relieve the ship boys in carrying up powder and shot, and to take round drink to men serving the guns. When not otherwise engaged they had watched with intense excitement the manoeuvres of their own ship and of those near them, as they swept down towards the great hulls, delivered their broadsides, and then shot off again before the Spaniards had had time to discharge more than a gun or two. The sails had been pierced in several places, but not a single shot had struck the hull of the vessel. In the last day's fighting, however, the Active became entangled among several of the Spanish galleons, and being almost becalmed by their lofty hulls, one of them ran full at her, and rolling heavily in the sea, seemed as if she would overwhelm her puny antagonist.

Geoffrey was standing at the end of the poop when the mizzen rigging became entangled in the stern gallery of the Spaniard, and a moment later the mast snapped off, and as it fell carried him overboard. For a moment he was half stunned, but caught hold of a piece of timber shot away from one of the enemy's ships, and clung to it mechanically. When he recovered and looked round, the Active had drawn out from between the Spaniards, and the great galleon which had so nearly sunk her was close beside him.

The sea was in a turmoil; the waves as they set in from the west being broken up by the rolling of the great ships, and torn by the hail of shot. The noise was prodigious, from the incessant cannonade kept up by the English ships and the return of the artillery on board the Armada, the rending of timber, the heavy crashes as the great galleons rolled against one another, the shouting on board the Spanish ships, the creaking of the masts and yards, and the flapping of the sails.

On trying to strike out, Geoffrey found that as he had been knocked overboard he had struck his right knee severely against the rail of the vessel, and was at present unable to use that leg. Fearful of being run down by one of the great ships, and still more of being caught between two of them as they rolled, he looked round to try to get sight of an English ship in the throng. Then, seeing that he was entirely surrounded by Spaniards, he left the spar and swam as well as he could to the bow of a great ship close beside him, and grasping a rope trailing from the bowsprit, managed by its aid to climb up until he reached the bobstay, across which he seated himself with his back to the stem. The position was a precarious one, and after a time he gained the wooden carved work above, and obtained a seat there just below the bowsprit, and hidden from the sight of those on deck a few feet above him. As he knew the vessels were drifting to leeward towards the shoals, he hoped to remain hidden until the vessel struck, and then to gain the shore.

Presently the shifting of the positions of the ships brought the vessel on which he was into the outside line. The shots now flew thickly about, and he could from time to time feel a jar as the vessel was struck.

So an hour went on. At the end of that time he heard a great shouting on deck, and the sound of men running to and fro. Happening to look down he saw that the sea was but a few feet below him, and knew that the great galleon was sinking. Another quarter of an hour she was so much lower that he was sure she could nor swim many minutes longer; and to avoid being drawn down with her he dropped into the water and swam off. He was but a short distance away when he heard a loud cry, and glancing over his shoulder saw the ship disappearing. He swam desperately, but was caught in the suck and carried under; but there was no great depth of water, and he soon came to the surface again. The sea was dotted with struggling men and pieces of wreckage. He swam to one of the latter, and held on until he saw some boats, which the next Spanish ship had lowered when she saw her consort disappearing, rowing towards them, and was soon afterwards hauled into one of them. He had closed his eyes as it came up, and assumed the appearance of insensibility, and he lay in the bottom of the boat immovable, until after a time he heard voices above, and then felt himself being carried up the ladder and laid down on the deck.

He remained quiet for some rime, thinking over what he had best do. He was certain that were it known he was English he would at once be stabbed and thrown overboard, for there was no hope of quarter; but he was for some time unable to devise any plan by which, even for a short rime, to conceal his nationality. He only knew a few words of Spanish, and would be detected the moment he opened his lips. He thought of leaping up suddenly and jumping overboard; but his chance of reaching the English ships to windward would be slight indeed. At last an idea struck him, and sitting up he opened his eyes and looked round. Several other Spaniards who had been picked up lay exhausted on the deck near him. A party of soldiers and sailors close by were working a cannon. The bulwarks were shot away in many places, dead and dying men lay scattered about, the decks were everywhere stained with blood, and no one paid any attention to him until presently the fire began to slacken. Shortly afterwards a Spanish officer came up and spoke to him.

Geoffrey rose to his feet, rubbed his eyes, yawned, and burst into an idiotic laugh. The officer spoke again but he paid no attention, and the Spaniard turned away, believing that the lad had lost his senses from fear and the horrors of the day.

As night came on he was several times addressed, but always with the same result. When after dark food and wine were served out, he seized the portion offered to him, and hurrying away crouched under the shelter of a gun, and devoured it as if fearing it would be taken from him again.

When he saw that the sailors were beginning to repair some of the most necessary ropes and stays that had been shot away, he pushed his way through them and took his share of the work, laughing idiotically from time to time. He had, when he saw that the galleon was sinking, taken off his doublet, the better to be able to swim, and in his shirt and trunks there was nothing to distinguish him from a Spaniard, and none suspected that he was other than he seemed to be — a ship's boy, who had lost his senses from fear. When the work was done, he threw himself on the deck with the weary sailors. His hopes were that the battle would be renewed in the morning, and that either the ship might be captured, or that an English vessel might pass so close alongside that he might leap over and swim to her.

Great was his disappointment next day when the sudden change of wind gave the Spanish fleet the weather gage, and enabled them to steer away for the north. He joined in the work of the crew, paying no attention whatever to what was passing around him, or heeding in the slightest the remarks made to him. Once or twice when an officer spoke to him sternly he gave a little cry, ran to the side, and crouched down as if in abject fear. In a very short time no attention was paid to him, and he was suffered to go about as he chose, being regarded as a harmless imbecile. He was in hopes that the next day the Spaniards would change their course and endeavour to beat back to the Channel, and was at once disappointed and surprised as they sped on before the southwesterly wind, which was hourly increasing in force. Some miles behind he could see the English squadron in pursuit; but these made no attempt to close up, being well contented to see the Armada sailing away, and being too straitened in ammunition to wish to bring on an engagement so long as the Spaniards were following their present course.

The wind blew with ever increasing force; the lightly ballasted ships made bad weather, rolling deep in the seas, straining heavily, and leaking badly through the opening seams and the hastily stopped shot holes. Water was extremely scarce, and at a signal from the admiral all the horses and mules were thrown overboard in order to husband the supply. Several of the masts, badly injured by the English shot, went by the board, and the vessels dropped behind crippled, to be picked up by the pursuing fleet.

Lord Howard followed as far as the mouth of the Forth; and seeing that the Spaniards made no effort to enter the estuary, and his provisions being now well nigh exhausted, he hove the fleet about and made back for the Channel, leaving two small vessels only to follow the Armada and watch its course, believing that it would make for Denmark, refit there, and then return to rejoin Parma.

It was a grievous disappointment to the English to be thus forced by want of provisions to relinquish the pursuit. Had they been properly supplied with provisions and ammunition they could have made an end of the Armada; whereas, they believed that by allowing them now to escape the whole work would have to be done over again. They had sore trouble to get back again off the Norfolk coast. The wind became so furious that the fleet was scattered. A few of the largest ships reached Margate; others were driven into Harwich, others with difficulty kept the sea until the storm broke.

It might have been thought that after such service as the fleet had rendered even Elizabeth might have been generous; but now that the danger was over, she became more niggardly than ever. No fresh provisions were supplied for the sick men, and though in the fight off the Dutch coast only some fifty or sixty had been killed, in the course of a very short time the crews were so weakened by deaths and disease that scarce a ship could have put to sea, however urgent the necessity. Drake and Howard spent every penny they could raise in buying fresh meat and vegetables, and in procuring some sort of shelter on shore for the sick. Had the men received the wages due to them they could have made a shift to have purchased what they so urgently required; but though the Treasury was full of money, not a penny was forthcoming until every item of the accounts had been investigated and squabbled over. Howard was compelled to pay from his private purse for everything that had been purchased at Plymouth, Sir John Hawkins was absolutely ruined by the demands made on him to pay for necessaries supplied to the fleet, and had the admirals and sailors of the fleet that saved England behaved like ignominious cowards, their treatment could not have been worse than that which they received at the hands of their sovereign.

But while the English seamen were dying like sheep from disease and neglect, their conquered foes were faring no better. They had breathed freely for the first time when they saw the English fleet bear up; an examination was made of the provisions that were left, and the crews were placed on rations of eight ounces of bread, half a pint of wine, and a pint of water a day. The fleet was still a great one, for of the hundred and fifty ships which had sailed from Corunna, a hundred and twenty still held together. The weather now turned bitterly cold, with fog and mist, squalls and driving showers; and the vessels, when they reached the north coast of Scotland, lost sight of each other, and each struggled for herself in the tempestuous sea.

119

By England's Aid: or The Freeing

A week later the weather cleared, and on the 9th of August Geoffrey looking round at daybreak saw fifteen other ships in sight. Among these were the galleons of Calderon and Ricaldo, the Rita, San Marcos, and eleven other vessels. Signals were flying from all of them, but the sea was so high that it was scarce possible to lower a boat. That night it again blew hard and the fog closed in, and in the morning Geoffrey found that the ship he was on, and all the others, with the exception of that of Calderon, were steering north; the intention of Ricaldo and De Leyva being to make for the Orkneys and refit there. Calderon had stood south, and had come upon Sidonia with fifty ships; and these, bearing well away to the west of Ireland, finally succeeded for the most part in reaching Spain, their crews reduced by sickness and want to a mere shadow of their original strength.

The cold became bitter as De Leyva's ships made their way towards the Orkneys. The storm was furious, and the sailors, unaccustomed to the cold and weakened by disease and famine, could no longer work their ships, and De Leyva was obliged at last to abandon his intention and make south. One galleon was driven on the Faroe Islands, a second on the Orkneys, and a third on the Isle of Mull, where it was attacked by the natives and burned with almost every one on board. The rest managed to make the west coast of Ireland, and the hope that they would find shelter in Galway Bay, or the mouth of the Shannon, began to spring up in the breasts of the exhausted crews.

The Irish were their co−religionists and allies, and had only been waiting for news of the success of the Armada to rise in arms against the English, who had but few troops there. Rumours of disaster had arrived, and a small frigate had been driven into Tralee Bay. The fears of the garrison at Tralee Castle overcame their feelings of humanity, and all on board were put to death. Two galleons put into Dingle, and landing begged for water; but the natives, deciding that the Spanish cause was a lost one, refused to give them a drop, seized the men who had landed in the boats, and the galleons had to put to sea again.

Another ship of a thousand tons, Our Lady of the Rosary, was driven into the furious straits between the Blasket Islands and the coast of Kerry. Of her crew of seven hundred, five hundred had died. Before she got halfway through she struck among the breakers, and all the survivors perished save the son of the pilot, who was washed ashore lashed to a plank. Six others who had reached the mouth of the Shannon sent their boats ashore for water; but although there were no English there the Irish feared to supply them, even though the Spaniards offered any sum of money for a few casks. One of the ships was abandoned and the others put to sea, only to be dashed ashore in the same gale that wrecked Our Lady of the Rosary, and of all their crews only one hundred and fifty men were cast ashore alive. Along the coast of Connemara, Mayo, and Sligo many other ships were wrecked. In almost every case the crews who reached the shore were at once murdered by the native savages for the sake of their clothes and jewellery.

Geoffrey had suffered as much as the rest of the crew on board the galleon in which he sailed. All were so absorbed by their own suffering and misery that none paid any attention to the idiot boy in their midst. He worked at such work as there was to do: assisted to haul on the ropes, to throw the dead overboard, and to do what could be done for the sick and wounded. Like all on board he was reduced almost to a skeleton, and was scarce able to stand.

As the surviving ships passed Galway Bay, one of them, which was leaking so badly that she could only have been kept afloat a few hours in any case, entered it, and brought up opposite the town. Don Lewis of Cordova, who commanded, sent a party on shore, believing that in Galway, between which town and Spain there had always been close connections, they would be well received. They were, however, at once taken prisoners. An attempt was made to get up the anchors again, but the crew were too feeble to be able to do so, and the natives coming out in their boats, all were taken prisoners and sent on shore. Sir Richard Bingham, the governor of Connaught, arrived in a few hours, and at once despatched search parties through Clare and Connemara to bring all Spaniards cast ashore alive to the town, and sent his son to Mayo to fetch down all who landed there. But young Bingham's mission proved useless; every Spaniard who had landed had been murdered by the natives, well nigh three thousand having been slain by the axes and knives of the savages who professed to be their co–religionists.

Sir Richard Bingham was regarded as a humane man, but he feared the consequences should the eleven hundred prisoners collected at Galway be restored to health and strength. He had but a handful of troops under him, and had had the greatest difficulty in keeping down the Irish alone. With eleven hundred Spanish soldiers to aid them the task would be impossible, and accordingly he gave orders that all, with the exception of Don Lewis himself, and three or four other nobles, should be executed. The order was carried out; Don Lewis, with those spared, was sent under an escort to Dublin, but the others being too feeble to walk were killed or died on the way, and Don Lewis himself was the sole survivor out of the crews of a dozen ships.

De Leyva, the most popular officer in the Armada, had with him in his ship two hundred and fifty young nobles of the oldest families in Spain. He was twice wrecked. The first time all reached the shore in safety, and were protected by O'Niel, who was virtually the sovereign of the north of Ulster. He treated them kindly for a time. They then took to sea again, but were finally wrecked off Dunluce, and all on board save five perished miserably. Over eight thousand Spaniards died on the Irish coast. Eleven hundred were put to death by Bingham, three thousand murdered by the Irish, the rest drowned; and of the whole Armada but fifty–four vessels, carrying between nine and ten thousand worn out men, reached Spain, and of the survivors a large proportion afterwards died from the effects of the sufferings they had endured.

CHAPTER X. THE WAR IN HOLLAND

In the confusion caused by the collision of the Active with the Spanish galleon no one had noticed the accident which had befallen Geoffrey Vickars, and his brother's distress was great when, on the ship getting free from among the Spaniards, he discovered that Geoffrey was missing. He had been by his side on the poop but a minute before the mast fell, and had no doubt that he had been carried overboard by its wreck. That he had survived he had not the least hope, and when a week later the Active on her way back towards the Thames was driven into Harwich, he at once landed and carried the sad news to his parents. England was wild with joy at its deliverance, but the household at Hedingham was plunged into deep sorrow.

Weeks passed and then Lionel received a letter from Francis Vere saying that Parma's army was advancing into Holland, and that as active work was at hand he had best, if his intentions remained unchanged, join him without delay.

He started two days later for Harwich, and thence took ship for Bergen op Zoom. Anchoring at Flushing, he learned that the Duke of Parma had already sat down in front of Bergen op Zoom, and had on the 7th attempted to capture Tholen on the opposite side of the channel, but had been repulsed by the regiment of Count Solms, with a loss of 400 men. He had then thrown up works against the water forts, and hot fighting had gone on, the garrison making frequent sallies upon the besiegers. The water forts still held out, and the captain therefore determined to continue his voyage into the town. The ship was fired at by the Spanish batteries, but passed safely between the water forts and dropped anchor in the port on the last day of September, Lionel having been absent from Holland just a year. He landed at once and made his way to the lodgings of Francis Vere, by whom he was received with great cordiality.

"I was greatly grieved," he said after the first greetings, "to hear of your brother's death. I felt it as if he had been a near relative of my own. I had hoped to see you both; and that affair concerning which my cousin wrote to me, telling me how cleverly you had discovered a plot against the queen's life, showed me that you would both be sure to make your way. Your father and mother must have felt the blow terribly?"

"They have indeed," Lionel said. "I do not think, however, that they altogether give up hope. They cling to the idea that he may have been picked up by some Spanish ship and may now be a prisoner in Spain."

Francis Vere shook his head.

"Of course, I know," Lionel went on, "their hope is altogether without foundation; for even had Geoffrey gained one of their ships, he would at once have been thrown overboard. Still I rather encouraged the idea, for it is better that hope should die out gradually than be extinguished at a blow; and slight though it was it enabled my father and mother to bear up better than they otherwise would have done. Had it not been for that I believe that my mother would have well nigh sunk beneath it. I was very glad when I got your letter, for active service will be a distraction to my sorrow. We have ever been together, Geoffrey and I, and I feel like one lost without him. You have not had much fighting here, I think, since I have been away?"

"No, indeed; you have been far more lucky than I have," Francis Vere said. "With the exception of the fight with the San Mateo I have been idle ever since I saw you, for not a shot has been fired here, while you have been taking part in the great fight for the very existence of our country. It is well that Parma has been wasting nine months at Dunkirk, for it would have gone hard with us had he marched hither instead of waiting there for the arrival of the Armada. Our force here has fallen away to well nigh nothing. The soldiers could get no pay, and were almost starved; their clothes were so ragged that it was pitiful to see them. Great numbers have died, and more gone back to England. As to the Dutch, they are more occupied in quarrelling with us than in preparing for defence, and they would right willingly see us go so that we did but deliver Flushing and Brill and this town back again to them. I was truly glad when I heard that Parma had broken up his camp at Dunkirk when the Armada sailed away, and was marching hither. Now that he has come, it may be that these wretched disputes will come to an end, and that something like peace and harmony will prevail in our councils. He could not have done better, as far as we are concerned, than in coming to knock his head against these walls; for Bergen is far too strong for him to take, and he will assuredly meet with no success here such as would counterbalance in any way the blow that Spanish pride has suffered in the defeat of the Armada. I think, Lionel, that you have outgrown your pageship, and since you have been fighting as a gentleman volunteer in Drake's fleet you had best take the same rank here."

The siege went on but slowly. Vigorous sorties were made, and the cavalry sometimes sallied out from the gates and made excursions as far as Wouw, a village three miles away, and took many prisoners. Among these were two commissaries of ordnance, who were intrusted to the safe keeping of the Deputy Provost Redhead. They were not strictly kept, and were allowed to converse with the provost's friends. One of these, William Grimeston, suspected that one of the commissaries, who pretended to be an Italian, was really an English deserter who had gone over with the traitor Stanley; and in order to see if his suspicions were correct, pretended that he was dissatisfied with his position and would far rather be fighting on the other side. The man at once fell into the trap, acknowledged that he was an Englishman, and said that if Grimeston and Redhead would but follow his advice they would soon become rich men, for that if they could arrange to give up one of the forts to Parma they would be magnificently rewarded.

Redhead and Grimeston pretended to agree, but at once informed Lord Willoughby, who was in command, of the offer that had been made to them. They were ordered to continue their negotiations with the traitor. The latter furnished them with letters to Stanley and Parma, and with these they made their way out of the town at night to the Spanish camp. They had an interview with the duke, and promised to deliver the north water fort over to him, for which service Redhead was to receive 1200 crowns and Grimeston 700 crowns, and a commission in Stanley's regiment of traitors.

Stanley himself entertained them in his tent, and Parma presented them with two gold chains. They then returned to Bergen and related all that had taken place to Lord Willoughby. The matter was kept a profound secret in the town, Francis Vere, who was in command of the north fort, and a few others only being made acquainted with what was going on.

124

On the appointed night, 22d of October, Grimeston went out alone, Redhead's supposed share of the business being to open the gates of the fort. When Grimeston arrived at Parma's camp he found that the Spaniards had become suspicious. He was bound and placed in charge of a Spanish captain, who was ordered to stab him at once if there was any sign of treachery. It was a dark night; the tide was out, for the land over which the Spaniards had to advance was flooded at other times. The attacking column consisted of three thousand men, including Stanley's regiment; and a number of knights and nobles accompanied it as volunteers.

As they approached the forts — Grimeston in front closely guarded by the Spanish captain — it was seen by the assailants that Redhead had kept his word: the drawbridge across the moat was down and the portcullis was up. Within the fort Lord Willoughby, Vere, and two thousand men were waiting for them. When about fifty had crossed the drawbridge the portcullis was suddenly let fall and the drawbridge hauled up. As the portcullis thundered down Grimeston tripped up the surprised Spaniard, and, leaping into the water, managed to make his way to the foot of the walls. A discharge of musketry and artillery from the fort killed a hundred and fifty of the attacking party, while those who had crossed the drawbridge were all either killed or taken prisoners. But the water in the moat was low. The Spaniards gallantly waded across and attacked the palisades, but were repulsed in their endeavour to climb them. While the fight was going on the water in the moat was rising, and scores were washed away and drowned as they attempted to return.

Parma continued the siege for some little time, but made no real attempt to take the place after having been repulsed at the north fort; and on the 12th of November broke up his camp and returned to Brussels.

After the siege was over Lord Willoughby knighted twelve of his principal officers, foremost among whom was Francis Vere, who was now sent home with despatches by his general, and remained in England until the end of January, when he was appointed sergeant major general of the forces, a post of great responsibility and much honour, by Lord Willoughby, with the full approval of the queen's government. He was accompanied on his return by his brother Robert.

A month after Sir Francis Vere's return Lord Willoughby left for England, and the whole burden of operations in the field fell upon Vere. His first trouble arose from the mutinous conduct of the garrison of Gertruydenberg. This was an important town on the banks of the old Maas, and was strongly fortified, one side being protected by the Maas while the river Douge swept round two other sides of its walls. Its governor, Count Hohenlohe, had been unpopular, the troops had received no pay, and there had been a partial mutiny before the siege of Bergen op Zoom began. This was appeased, by the appointment of Sir John Wingfield, Lord Willoughby's brother in law, as its governor.

In the winter the discontent broke out again. The soldiers had been most unjustly treated by the States, and there were long arrears of pay, and at first Sir John Wingfield espoused the cause of the men. Sir Francis Vere tried in vain to arrange matters. The Dutch authorities would not pay up the arrears, the men would not return to their duty until they did so, and at last became so exasperated that they ceased to obey their governor and opened communications with the enemy. Prince Maurice, who was now three and twenty years old, and devoted to martial pursuits and the cause of his countrymen, after consultation with Sir Francis Vere, laid siege to the town and made a furious assault upon it on the water aide. But the Dutch troops, although led by Count Solms and Count Philip of Nassau, were repulsed with great loss. The prince then promised nor only a pardon, but that the demands of the garrison should be complied with; but it was too late, and four days later Gertruydenberg was delivered up by the mutineers to the Duke of Parma, the soldiers being received into the Spanish service, while Wingfield and the officers were permitted to retire.

The States were furious, as this was the third city commanded by Englishmen that had been handed over to the enemy. The bad feeling excited by the treachery of Sir William Stanley and Roland Yorke at Deventer and Zutphen had died out after the gallant defence of the English at Sluys, but now broke out again afresh, and charges of treachery were brought not only against Wingfield but against many other English officers, including Sir Francis Vere. The queen, however, wrote so indignantly to the States that they had to withdraw their charges against most of the English officers.

In May Lord Willoughby, who was still in London, resigned his command. A number of old officers of distinction who might have laid claims to succeed him, among them Sir John Norris, Sir Roger Williams, Sir Thomas Wilford, Sir William Drury, Sir Thomas Baskerville, and Sir John Burrough, were withdrawn from the Netherlands to serve in France or Ireland, and no general in chief or lieutenant general was appointed, Sir Francis Vere as sergeant major receiving authority to command all soldiers already in the field or to be sent out during the absence of the general and lieutenant general. His official title was Her Majesty's Sergeant Major in the Field. The garrisons in the towns were under the command of their own governors, and those could supply troops for service in the field according to their discretion.

The appointment of so young a man as Sir Francis Vere to a post demanding not only military ability but great tact and diplomatic power, was abundant proof of the high estimate formed of him by the queen and her counsellors. The position was one of extreme difficulty. He had to keep on good terms with the queen and her government, with the government of the States, the English agent at the Hague, Prince Maurice in command of the army of the Netherlands, the English governors of the towns, and the officers or men of the force under his own command. Fortunately Barneveldt, who at that time was the most prominent man in the States, had a high opinion of Vere. Sir Thomas Bodley, the queen's agent, had much confidence in him, and acted with him most cordially, and Prince Maurice entertained a great respect for him, consulted him habitually in all military matters, and placed him in the position of marshal of the camp of the army of the Netherlands, in addition to his own command of the English portion of that army.

Vere's first undertaking was to lead a force of 12,000 men, of whom half were English, to prevent Count Mansfelt from crossing the Maas with an army of equal strength. Prince Maurice was present in person as general in chief. Intrenchments were thrown up and artillery planted; but just as Mansfelt was preparing to cross his troops mutinied, and he was obliged to fall back.

In October, with 900 of his own troops and twelve companies of Dutch horse, Sir Francis Vere succeeded in throwing a convoy of provisions into the town of Rheinberg, which was besieged by a large force of the enemy. As soon as he returned the States requested him to endeavour to throw in another convoy, as Count Mansfelt was marching to swell the force of the besiegers, and, after his arrival it would be well nigh impossible to send further aid into the town. Vere took with him 900 English and 900 Dutch infantry, and 800 Dutch cavalry. The enemy had possession of a fortified country house called Loo, close to which lay a thick wood traversed only by a narrow path, with close undergrowth and swampy ground on either side. The enemy were in great force around Loo, and came out to attack the expedition as it passed through the wood. Sending the Dutch troops on first, Vere attacked the enemy vigorously with his infantry and drove them back to the inclosure of Loo. As soon as his whole force had crossed the wood, he halted them and ordered them to form in line of battle facing the wood through which they had just passed, and from which the enemy were now pouring out in great force.

In order to give time to his troops to prepare for the action Vere took half his English infantry and advanced against them. They moved forward, and a stubborn fight took place between the pikemen. Vere's horse was killed, and fell on him so that he could not rise; but the English closed round him, and he was rescued with no other harm than a bruised leg and several pike thrusts through his clothes. While the conflict between the pikemen was going on the English arquebusiers opened fire on the flank of the enemy, and they began to fall back. Four times they rallied and charged the English, but were at last broken and scattered through the wood. The cavalry stationed there left their horses and fled through the undergrowth. Pressing forward the little English force next fell upon twenty-four companies of Neapolitan infantry, who were defeated without difficulty. The four hundred and fifty Englishmen then joined the main force, which marched triumphantly with their convoy of provisions into Rheinberg, and the next morning fortunately turning thick and foggy the force made its way back without interruption by the enemy.

CHAPTER XI. IN SPAIN

Alone among the survivors of the great Spanish Armada, Geoffrey Vickars saw the coast of Ireland fade away from sight without a feeling of satisfaction or relief. His hope had been that the ship would be wrecked on her progress down the coast. He knew not that the wild Irish were slaying all whom the sea spared, and that ignorant as they were of the English tongue, he would undoubtedly have shared the fate of his Spanish companions. He thought only of the risk of being drowned, and would have preferred taking this to the certainty of a captivity perhaps for life in the Spanish prisons. The part that he had played since he had been picked up off Gravelines could not be sustained indefinitely. He might as well spend his life in prison, where at least there would be some faint hope of being exchanged, as wander about Spain all his life as an imbecile beggar.

As soon, therefore, as he saw that the perils of the coast of Ireland were passed, and that the vessel was likely to reach Spain in safety, he determined that he would on reaching a port disclose his real identity. There were on board several Scotch and Irish volunteers, and he decided to throw himself upon the pity of one of these rather than on that of the

By England's Aid: or The Freeing

Spaniards. He did not think that in any case his life was in danger. Had he been detected when first picked up, or during the early part of the voyage, he would doubtless have been thrown overboard without mercy; but now that the passions of the combatants had subsided, and that he had been so long among them, and had, as he believed, won the goodwill of many by the assistance he had rendered to the sick and wounded, he thought that there was little fear of his life being taken in cold blood.

One of the Irish volunteers, Gerald Burke by name, had for a long time been seriously ill, and Geoffrey had in many small ways shown him kindness as he lay helpless on the deck, and he determined finally to confide in him. Although still very weak, Burke was now convalescent, and was sitting alone by the poop rail gazing upon the coast of Spain with eager eyes, when Geoffrey, under the pretext of coiling down a rope, approached him. The young man nodded kindly to him.

"Our voyage is nearly over, my poor lad," he said in Spanish, "and your troubles now will be worse than mine. You have given me many a drink of water from your scanty supply, and I wish that I could do something for you in return; but I know that you do not even understand what I say to you."

"Would you give me an opportunity of speaking to you after nightfall, Mr. Burke," Geoffrey said in English, "when no one will notice us speaking?"

The Irishman gave a start of astonishment at hearing himself addressed in English.

"My life is in your hands, sir; pray, do not betray me," Geoffrey said rapidly as he went on coiling down the rope.

"I will be at this place an hour after nightfall," the young Irishman replied when he recovered from his surprise. "Your secret will be safe with me."

At the appointed time Geoffrey returned to the spot. The decks were now deserted, for a drizzling rain was falling, and all save those on duty had retired below, happy in the thought that on the following morning they would be in port.

"Now, tell me who you are," the young Irishman began. "I thought you were a Spanish sailor, one of those we picked up when the Spanish galleon next to us foundered."

129

By England's Aid: or The Freeing

Geoffrey then told him how he had been knocked off an English ship by the fall of a mast, had swum to the galleon and taken refuge beneath her bowsprit until she sank, and how, when picked up and carried on to the Spanish ship, he feigned to have lost his senses in order to conceal his ignorance of Spanish.

"I knew," he said, "that were I recognized as English at the time I should at once be killed, but I thought that if I could conceal who I was for a time I should simply be sent to the galleys, where I have heard that there are many English prisoners working."

"I think death would have been preferable to that lot," Mr. Burke said.

"Yes, sir; but there is always the hope of escape or of exchange. When you spoke kindly to me this afternoon I partly understood what you said, for in this long time I have been on board I have come to understand a little Spanish, and I thought that maybe you would assist me in some way."

"I would gladly do so, though I regard Englishmen as the enemies of my country; but in what way can I help you? I could furnish you with a disguise, but your ignorance of Spanish would lead to your detection immediately."

"I have been thinking it over, sir, and it seemed to me that as there will be no objection to my landing tomorrow, thinking as they do that I have lost my senses, I might join you after you once got out of the town. I have some money in my waistbelt, and if you would purchase some clothes for me I might then join you as your servant as you ride along. At the next town you come to none would know but that I had been in your service during the voyage, and there would be nothing strange in you, an Irish gentleman, being accompanied by an Irish servant who spoke but little Spanish. I would serve you faithfully, sir, until perhaps some opportunity might occur for my making my escape to England."

"Yes, I think that might be managed," the young Irishman said. "When I land tomorrow I will buy some clothes suitable for a serving man. I do nor know the names of the hotels on shore, so you must watch me when I land and see where I put up. Come there in the evening at nine o'clock. I will issue out and give you the bundle of clothes, and tell you at what hour in the morning I have arranged to start. I will hire two horses; when they come round to the door, join me in front of the hotel and busy yourself in packing my trunks on

130

the baggage mules. When you have done that, mount the second horse and ride after me; the people who will go with us with the horses will naturally suppose that you have landed with me. Should any of our shipmates here see us start, it is not likely that they will recognize you. If they do so, I need simply say that as you had shown me such kindness on board ship I had resolved to take you with me to Madrid in order to see if anything could be done to restore you to reason. However, it is better that you should keep in the background as much as possible. I will arrange to start at so early an hour in the morning that none of those who may land with me from the ship, and may put up at the same inn, are likely to be about."

The next morning the vessel entered port. They were soon surrounded by boats full of people inquiring anxiously for news of other ships, and for friends and acquaintances on board. Presently large boats were sent off by the authorities, and the disembarkation of the sick and the helpless began. This indeed included the greater portion of the survivors, for there were but two or three score on board who were capable of dragging themselves about, the rest being completely prostrate by disease, exhaustion, hunger, and thirst. Geoffrey was about to descend into one of the boats, when the officer in command said roughly: "Remain on board and do your work, there is no need for your going into the hospital." One of the ship's officers, however, explained that the lad had altogether lost his senses, and was unable either to understand when spoken to or to reply to questions. Consequently he was permitted to take his place in the boat.

As soon as he stepped ashore he wandered away among the crowd of spectators. A woman, observing his wan face and feeble walk, called him into her house, and set food and wine before him. He made a hearty meal, but only shook his head when she addressed him, and laughed childishly and muttered his thanks in Spanish when she bestowed a dollar upon him as he left. He watched at the port while boat load after boat load of sick came ashore, until at last one containing the surviving officers and gentlemen with their baggage reached the land. Then he kept Gerald Burke in sight until he entered an inn, followed by two men carrying his baggage. Several times during the day food and money were offered him, the inhabitants being full of horror and pity at the sight of the famishing survivors of the crew of the galleon.

At nine o'clock in the evening Geoffrey took up his station near the door of the inn. A few minutes later Gerald Burke came out with a bundle. "Here are the clothes," he said. "I have hired horses for our journey to Madrid. They will be at the door at six o'clock in

131

the morning. I have arranged to travel by very short stages, for at first neither you nor I could sit very long upon a horse; however, I hope we shall soon gain strength as we go."

Taking the bundle, Geoffrey walked a short distance from the town and lay down upon the ground under some trees. The night was a warm one, and after the bitter cold they had suffered during the greater part of the voyage, it felt almost sultry to him. At daybreak in the morning he rose, put on the suit of clothes Gerald Burke had provided, washed his face in a little stream, and proceeded to the inn. He arrived there just as the clocks were striking six. A few minutes later two men with two horses and four mules came up to the door, and shortly afterwards Gerald Burke came our. Geoffrey at once joined him; the servants of the inn brought out the baggage, which was fastened by the muleteers on to two of the animals. Gerald Burke mounted one of the horses and Geoffrey the other, and at once rode on, the muleteers mounting the other two mules and following with those carrying the baggage.

"That was well managed," Gerald Burke said as they rode out of the town. "The muleteers can have no idea that you have but just joined me, and there is little chance of any of my comrades on board ship overtaking us, as all intend to stop for a few days to recruit themselves before going on. If they did they would not be likely to recognize you in your present attire, or to suspect that my Irish servant is the crazy boy of the ship."

After riding at an easy pace for two hours, they halted under the shade of some trees. Fruit, bread, and wine were produced from a wallet on one of the mules, and they sat down and breakfasted. After a halt of an hour they rode on until noon, when they again halted until four in the afternoon, for the sun was extremely hot, and both Gerald Burke and Geoffrey were so weak they scarce could sit their horses. Two hours further riding took them to a large village, where they put up at the inn. Geoffrey now fell into his place as Mr. Burke's servant — saw to the baggage being taken inside, and began for the first time to try his tongue at Spanish. He got on better than he had expected; and as Mr. Burke spoke with a good deal of foreign accent, it did not seem in any way singular to the people of the inn that his servant should speak but little of the language.

Quietly they journeyed on, doing but short distances for the first three or four days, but as they gained strength pushing on faster, and by the time they reached Madrid both were completely recovered from the effects of their voyage. Madrid was in mourning, for there was scarce a family but had lost relations in the Armada. Mr. Burke at once took lodgings and installed Geoffrey as his servant. He had many friends and acquaintances in the city, where he had been residing for upwards of a year previous to the sailing of the Armada.

For some weeks Geoffrey went out but little, spending his time in reading Spanish books and mastering the language as much as possible. He always conversed in that language with Mr. Burke, and at the end of six weeks was able to talk Spanish with some fluency. He now generally accompanied Mr. Burke if he went out, following him in the streets and standing behind his chair when he dined abroad. He was much amused at all he saw, making many acquaintances among the lackeys of Mr. Burke's friends, dining with them downstairs after the banquets were over, and often meeting them of an evening when he had nothing to do, and going with them to places of entertainment.

In this way his knowledge of Spanish improved rapidly, and although he still spoke with an accent he could pass well as one who had been for some years in the country. He was now perfectly at ease with the Spanish gentlemen of Mr. Burke's acquaintance. It was only when Irish and Scotch friends called upon his master that he feared awkward questions, and upon these occasions he showed himself as little as possible. When alone with Gerald Burke the latter always addressed Geoffrey as a friend rather than as a servant, and made no secret with him as to his position and means. He had been concerned in a rising in Ireland, and had fled the country, bringing with him a fair amount of resources. Believing that the Armada was certain to be crowned with success, and that he should ere long be restored to his estates in Ireland, he had, upon his first coming to Spain, spent his money freely. His outfit for the expedition had made a large inroad upon his store, and his resources were now nearly at an end.

"What is one to do, Geoffrey? I don't want to take a commission in Philip's army, though my friends could obtain one for me at once; but I have no desire to spend the rest of my life in the Netherlands storming the towns of the Dutch burghers."

"Or rather trying to storm them," Geoffrey said, smiling; "there have not been many towns taken of late years."

"Nor should I greatly prefer to be campaigning in France," Gerald went on, paying no attention to the interruption. "I have no love either for Dutch Calvinists or French Huguenots; but I have no desire either to be cutting their throats or for them to be cutting mine. I should like a snug berth under the crown here or at Cadiz, or at Seville; but I see

133

no chance whatever of my obtaining one. I cannot take up the trade of a footpad, though disbanded soldiers turned robbers are common enough in Spain. What is to be done?"

"If I am not mistaken," Geoffrey said with a smile, "your mind is already made up. It is not quite by accident that you are in the gardens of the Retiro every evening, and that a few words are always exchanged with a certain young lady as she passes with her duenna."

"Oh! you have observed that," Gerald Burke replied with a laugh. "Your eyes are sharper than I gave you credit for, Master Geoffrey. Yes, that would set me on my legs without doubt, for Donna Inez is the only daughter and heiress of the Marquis of Ribaldo; but you see there is a father in the case, and if that father had the slightest idea that plain Gerald Burke was lifting his eyes to his daughter it would not be many hours before Gerald Burke had several inches of steel in his body."

"That I can imagine," Geoffrey said, "since it is, as I learn from my acquaintances among the lackeys, a matter of common talk that the marquis intends to marry her to the son of the Duke of Sottomayor."

"Inez hates him," Gerald Burke said. "It is just like my ill luck, that instead of being drowned as most of the others were, he has had the luck to get safely back again. However, he is still ill, and likely to be so for some time. He was not so accustomed to starving as some of us, and he suffered accordingly. He is down at his estates near Seville."

"But what do you think of doing?" Geoffrey asked.

"That is just what I am asking you."

"It seems to me, certainly," Geoffrey went on, "that unless you really mean to run off with the young lady — for I suppose there is no chance in the world of your marrying her in any other way — it will be better both for you and her that you should avoid for the future these meetings in the gardens or elsewhere, and cast your thoughts in some other direction for the bettering of your fortunes."

By England's Aid: or The Freeing

"That is most sage advice, Geoffrey," the young Irishman laughed, "and worthy of my father confessor; but it is not so easy to follow. In the first place, I must tell you that I do not regard Inez as in any way a step to fortune, but rather as a step towards a dungeon. It would be vastly better for us both if she were the daughter of some poor hidalgo like myself. I could settle down then with her, and plant vines and make wine, and sell what I don't drink myself. As it is, I have the chance of being put out of the way if it is discovered that Inez and I are fond of each other; and in the next place, if we do marry I shall have to get her safely out of the kingdom, or else she will have to pass the rest of her life in a convent, and I the rest of mine in a prison or in the galleys; that is if I am not killed as soon as caught, which is by far the most likely result. Obnoxious sons in law do not live long in Spain. So you see, Geoffrey, the prospect is a bad one altogether; and if it were not that I dearly love Inez, and that I am sure she will be unhappy with Philip of Sottomayor, I would give the whole thing up, and make love to the daughter of some comfortable citizen who would give me a corner of his house and a seat at his table for the rest of my days."

"But, seriously —" Geoffrey began.

"Well, seriously, Geoffrey, my intention is to run away with Inez if it can be managed; but how it is to be managed at present I have not the faintest idea. To begin with, the daughter of a Spanish grandee is always kept in a very strong cage closely guarded, and it needs a very large golden key to open it. Now, as you are aware, gold is a very scarce commodity with me. Then, after getting her out, a lavish expenditure would be needed for our flight. We should have to make our way to the sea coast, to do all sorts of things to throw dust into the eyes of our pursuers, and to get a passage to some place beyond the domains of Philip, which means either to France, England, or the Netherlands. Beyond all this will be the question of future subsistence until, if ever, the marquis makes up his mind to forgive his daughter and take her to his heart again, a contingency, in my opinion, likely to be extremely remote."

"And what does the Lady Inez say to it all?" Geoffrey asked.

"The Lady Inez has had small opportunity of saying anything on the subject, Geoffrey. Here in Spain there are mighty few opportunities for courtship. With us at home these matters are easy enough, and there is no lack of opportunity for pleading your suit and winning a girl's heart if it is to be won; but here in Spain matters are altogether different,

135

and an unmarried girl is looked after as sharply as if she was certain to get into some mischief or other the instant she had an opportunity. She is never suffered to be for a moment alone with a man; out of doors or in she has always a duenna by her side; and as to a private chat, the thing is simply impossible."

"Then how do you manage to make love?" Geoffrey asked.

"Well, a very little goes a long way in Spain. The manner of a bow, the wave of a fan, the dropping of a glove or flower, the touch of a hand in a crowded room — each of these things go as far as a month's open love making in Ireland."

"Then how did you manage with the duenna so as to be able to speak to her in the gardens?"

"Well, in the first place, I made myself very attentive to the duenna; in the second place, the old lady is devout, and you know Ireland is the land of saints, and I presented her with an amulet containing a paring of the nail of St. Patrick."

Geoffrey burst into a laugh, in which the Irishman joined.

"Well, if it was not really St. Patrick's," the latter went on, "it came from Ireland anyhow, which is the next best thing. Then in the third place, the old lady is very fond of Inez; and although she is as strict as a dragon, Inez coaxed her into the belief that there could not be any harm in our exchanging a few words when she was close by all the time to hear what was said. Now, I think you know as much as I do about the matter, Geoffrey. You will understand that a few notes have been exchanged, and that Inez loves me. Beyond that everything is vague and uncertain, and I have not the slightest idea what will come of it."

Some weeks passed and nothing was done. The meetings between Gerald Burke and Inez in the Gardens of the Retiro had ceased a day or two afterwards, the duenna having positively refused to allow them to continue, threatening Inez to inform her father of them unless she gave them up.

Gerald Burke's funds dwindled rapidly, although he and Geoffrey lived in the very closest way.

"What in the world is to be done, Geoffrey? I have only got twenty dollars left, which at the outside will pay for our lodgings and food for another month. For the life of me I cannot see what is to be done when that is gone, unless we take to the road."

Geoffrey shook his head. "As far as I am concerned," he said, "as we are at war with Spain, it would be fair if I met a Spanish ship at sea to capture and plunder it, but I am afraid the laws of war do not justify private plunder. I should be perfectly ready to go out and take service in a vineyard, or to earn my living in any way if it could be managed."

"I would rob a cardinal if I had the chance," Gerald Burke said, "and if I ever got rich would restore his money four fold and so obtain absolution; only, unfortunately, I do not see my way to robbing a cardinal. As to digging in the fields, Geoffrey, I would rather hang myself at once. I am constitutionally averse to labour, and if one once took to that sort of thing there would be an end to everything."

"It is still open to you," Geoffrey said, "to get your friends to obtain a commission for you."

"I could do that," Gerald said moodily, "but of all things that is what I should most hate."

"You might make your peace with the English government and get some of your estates back again."

"That I will not do to feed myself," Gerald Burke said firmly. "I have thought that if I ever carry off Inez I might for her sake do so, for I own that now all hope of help from Spain is at an end, our cause in Ireland is lost, and it is no use going on struggling against the inevitable; but I am not going to sue the English government as a beggar for myself. No doubt I could borrow small sums from Irishmen and Scotchmen here, and hold on for a few months; but most of them are well nigh as poor as I am myself, and I would not ask them. Besides, there would be no chance of my repaying them; and, if I am to rob anyone, I would rather plunder these rich dons than my own countrymen."

"Of one thing I am resolved," Geoffrey said, "I will not live at your expense any longer, Gerald. I can speak Spanish very fairly now, and can either take service in some Spanish family or, as I said, get work in the field."

Gerald laughed. "My dear Geoffrey, the extra expenses caused by you last week were, as far as I can calculate, one penny for bread and as much for fruit; the rest of your living was obtained at the expense of my friends."

"At any rate," Geoffrey said smiling, "I insist that my money be now thrown into the common fund. I have offered it several times before, but you always said we had best keep it for emergency. I think the emergency has come now, and these ten English pounds in my belt will enable us to take some step or other. The question is, what step? They might last us, living as we do, for some three or four months, but at the end of that time we should be absolutely penniless; therefore now is the time, while we have still a small stock in hand, to decide upon something."

"But what are we to decide upon?" Gerald Burke asked helplessly.

"I have been thinking it over a great deal," Geoffrey said, "and my idea is that we had best go to Cadiz or some other large port. Although Spain is at war both with England and the Netherlands, trade still goes on in private ships, and both Dutch and English vessels carry on commerce with Spain; therefore it seems to me that there must be merchants in Cadiz who would be ready to give employment to men capable of speaking and writing both in Spanish and English, and in my case to a certain extent in Dutch. From there, too, there might be a chance of getting a passage to England or Holland. If we found that impossible owing to the vessels being too carefully searched before sailing, we might at the worst take passage as sailors on board a Spanish ship bound for the Indies, and take our chance of escape or capture there or on the voyage. That, at least, is what I planned for myself."

"I think your idea is a good one, Geoffrey. At any rate to Cadiz we will go. I don't know about the mercantile business or going as a sailor, but I could get a commission from the governor there as well as here in Madrid; but at any rate I will go. Donna Inez was taken last week by her father to some estates he has somewhere between Seville and Cadiz, in order, I suppose, that he may be nearer Don Philip, who is, I hear, at last recovering from his long illness. I do not know that there is the slightest use in seeing her again, but I will do so if it be possible; and if by a miracle I could succeed in carrying her off, Cadiz would be a more likely place to escape from than anywhere.

"Yes, I know. You think the idea is a mad one, but you have never been in love yet. When you are you will know that lovers do not believe in the word `impossible.' At any rate, I mean to give Inez the chance of determining her own fate. If she is ready to risk everything rather than marry Don Philip, I am ready to share the risk whatever it may be."

Accordingly on the following day Gerald Burke disposed of the greater part of his wardrobe and belongings, purchased two ponies for a few crowns, and he and Geoffrey, with a solitary suit of clothes in a wallet fastened behind the saddle, started for their journey to Cadiz. They mounted outside the city, for Gerald shrank from meeting any acquaintances upon such a sorry steed as he had purchased; but once on their way his spirits rose. He laughed and chatted gaily, and spoke of the future as if all difficulties were cleared away. The ponies, although rough animals, were strong and sturdy, and carried their riders at a good pace. Sometimes they travelled alone, sometimes jogged along with parties whom they overtook by the way, or who had slept in the same posadas or inns at which they had put up for the night.

Most of these inns were very rough, and, to Geoffrey, astonishingly dirty. The food consisted generally of bread and a miscellaneous olio or stew from a great pot constantly simmering over the fire, the flavour, whatever it might be, being entirely overpowered by that of the oil and garlic that were the most marked of its constituents. Beds were wholly unknown at these places, the guests simply wrapping themselves in their cloaks and lying down on the floor, although in a few exceptional cases bundles of rushes were strewn about to form a common bed.

But the travelling was delightful. It was now late in the autumn, and when they were once past the dreary district of La Mancha, and had descended to the rich plains of Cordova, the vintage was in full progress and the harvest everywhere being garnered in. Their midday meal consisted of bread and fruit, costing but the smallest coin, and eaten by the wayside in the shade of a clump of trees. They heard many tales on their way down of the bands of robbers who infested the road, but having taken the precaution of having the doubloons for which they had exchanged Geoffrey's English gold sewn up in their boots, they had no fear of encountering these gentry, having nothing to lose save their wallets and the few dollars they had kept out for the expenses of their journey. The few jewels that Gerald Burke retained were sewn up in the stuffing of his saddle.

By England's Aid: or The Freeing

After ten days' travel they reached Seville, where they stayed a couple of days, and where the wealth and splendour of the buildings surprised Geoffrey, who had not visited Antwerp or any of the great commercial centres of the Netherlands.

"It is a strange taste of the Spanish kings," he observed to Gerald Burke, "to plant their capital at Madrid in the centre of a barren country, when they might make such a splendid city as this their capital. I could see no charms whatever in Madrid. The climate was detestable, with its hot sun and bitter cold winds. Here the temperature is delightful; the air is soft and balmy, the country round is a garden, and there is a cathedral worthy of a capital."

"It seems a strange taste," Gerald agreed; "but I believe that when Madrid was first planted it stood in the midst of extensive forests, and that it was merely a hunting residence for the king."

"Then, when the forests went I would have gone too," Geoffrey said. "Madrid has not even a river worthy of the name, and has no single point to recommend it, as far as I can see, for the capital of a great empire. If I were a Spaniard I should certainly take up my residence in Seville."

Upon the following morning they again started, joining, before they had ridden many miles, a party of three merchants travelling with their servants to Cadiz. The merchants looked a little suspiciously at first at the two young men upon their tough steeds; but as soon as they discovered from their first salutations that they were foreigners, they became more cordial, and welcomed this accession of strength to their party, for the carrying of weapons was universal, and the portion of the road between Seville and Cadiz particularly unsafe, as it was traversed by so many merchants and wealthy people. The conversation speedily turned to the disturbed state of the roads.

"I do not think," one of the merchants said, "that any ordinary band of robbers would dare attack us," and he looked round with satisfaction at the six armed servants who rode behind them.

"It all depends," Gerald Burke said, with a sly wink at Geoffrey, "upon what value the robbers may place upon the valour of your servants. As a rule serving men are very chary of their skins, and I should imagine that the robbers must be pretty well aware of that

140

fact. Most of them are disbanded soldiers or deserters, and I should say that four of them are more than a match for your six servants. I would wager that your men would make but a very poor show of it if it came to fighting."

"But there are our three selves and you two gentlemen," the merchant said in a tone of disquiet.

"Well," Gerald rejoined, "I own that from your appearance I should not think, worshipful sir, that fighting was altogether in your line. Now, my servant, young as he is, has taken part in much fighting in the Netherlands, and I myself have had some experience with my sword; but if we were attacked by robbers we should naturally stand neutral. Having nothing to defend, and having no inclination whatever to get our throats cut in protecting the property of others, I think that you will see for yourselves that that is reasonable. We are soldiers of fortune, ready to venture our lives in a good service, and for good pay, but mightily disinclined to throw them away for the mere love of fighting."

CHAPTER XII. RECRUITING THEIR FUNDS

As soon as Gerald Burke began conversing with the merchants, Geoffrey fell back and took his place among their servants, with whom he at once entered into conversation. To amuse himself he continued in the same strain that he had heard Gerald adopt towards the merchants, and spoke in terms of apprehension of the dangers of the journey, and of the rough treatment that had befallen those who had ventured to offer opposition to the robbers. He was not long in discovering, by the anxious glances they cast round them, and by the manner of their questions, that some at least of the party were not to be relied upon in case of an encounter.

He was rather surprised at Gerald remaining so long in company with the merchants, for their pace was a slow one, as they were followed by eight heavily laden mules, driven by two muleteers, and it would have been much pleasanter, he thought, to have trotted on at their usual pace. About midday, as they were passing along the edge of a thick wood, a party of men suddenly sprang out and ordered them to halt. Geoffrey shouted to the men with him to come on, and drawing his sword dashed forward.

Two of the men only followed him. The others hesitated, until a shot from a musket knocked off one of their hats, whereupon the man and his comrades turned their horses' heads and rode off at full speed. The merchants had drawn their swords, and stood on the defensive, and Geoffrey on reaching them was surprised to find that Gerald Burke was sitting quietly on his horse without any apparent intention of taking part in the fight.

"Put up your sword, Geoffrey," he said calmly; "this affair is no business of ours. We have nothing to lose, and it is no business of ours to defend the money bags of these gentlemen."

The robbers, eight in number, now rushed up. One of the merchants, glancing round, saw that two of their men only had come up to their assistance. The muleteers, who were probably in league with the robbers, had fled, leaving their animals standing in the road. The prospect seemed desperate. One of the merchants was an elderly man, the others were well on middle age. The mules were laden with valuable goods, and they had with them a considerable sum of money for making purchases at Cadiz. It was no time for hesitation.

"We will give you five hundred crowns if you will both aid us to beat off these robbers."

"It is a bargain," Gerald replied. "Now, Geoffrey, have at these fellows!"

Leaping from their ponies they ranged themselves by the merchants just as the robbers attacked them. Had it not been for their aid the combat would have been a short one; for although determined to defend their property to the last, the traders had neither strength nor skill at arms. One was unhorsed at the first blow, and another wounded; but the two servants, who had also dismounted, fought sturdily, and Gerald and Geoffrey each disposed of a man before the robbers, who had not reckoned upon their interference, were prepared to resist their attack.

The fight did not last many minutes. The traders did their best, and although by no means formidable opponents, distracted the attention of the robbers, who were startled by the fall of two of their party. Geoffrey received a sharp cut on the head, but at the same moment ran his opponent through the body, while Gerald Burke cut down the man opposed to him. The other four robbers, seeing they were now outnumbered, at once took to their heels.

By England's Aid: or The Freeing

"By St. Jago!" one of the traders said, "you are stout fighters, young men, and have won your fee well. Methought we should have lost our lives as well as our goods, and I doubt not we should have done so had you not ranged yourselves with us. Now, let us bandage up our wounds, for we have all received more or less hurt."

When the wounds, some of which were serious, were attended to, the fallen robbers were examined. Three of them were dead; but the man last cut down by Gerald Burke seemed likely to recover.

"Shall we hang him upon a tree as a warning to these knaves, or shall we take him with us to the next town and give him in charge of the authorities there?" one of the traders asked.

"If I were you I would do neither," Gerald said, "but would let him go free if he will tell you the truth about this attack. It will be just as well for you to get to the bottom of this affair, and find out whether it is a chance meeting, or whether any of your own people have been in league with him."

"That is a good idea," the trader agreed, "and I will carry it out," and going up to the man, who had now recovered his senses, he said to him sternly: "We have made up our minds to hang you; but you may save your life if you will tell us how you came to set upon us. Speak the truth and you shall go free, otherwise we will finish with you without delay."

The robber, seeing an unexpected chance of escape from punishment, at once said that the captain of their band, who was the man Geoffrey had last run through, came out from Seville the evening before, and told him that one Juan Campos, with whom he had long had intimate relations, and who was clerk to a rich trader, had, upon promise that he should receive one fifth of the booty taken, informed him that his master with two other merchants was starting on the following morning for Cadiz with a very valuable lot of goods, and twenty–five thousand crowns, which they intended to lay out in the purchase of goods brought by some galleons that had just arrived from the Indies. He had arranged to bribe his master's two servants to ride away when they attacked the gang, and also to settle with the muleteers so that they should take no part in the affair. They had reckoned that the flight of two of the servants would probably affect the others, and had therefore expected the rich booty to fall into their hands without the trouble of striking a blow for it.

"It is well we followed your suggestion," one of the traders said to Gerald. "I had no suspicion of the honesty of my clerk, and had we not made this discovery he would doubtless have played me a similar trick upon some other occasion. I will ride back at once, friends, for if he hears of the failure of the attack he may take the alarm and make off with all he can lay his hands upon. Our venture was to be in common. I will leave it to you to carry it out, and return and dismiss Campos and the two rascally servants." The three traders went apart and consulted together. Presently the eldest of the party returned to the young men.

"We have another five days' journey before us," he said, "and but two servants upon whom we can place any reliance. We have evidence of the unsafety of the roads, and, as you have heard, we have a large sum of money with us. You have already more than earned the reward I offered you, and my friends have agreed with me that if you will continue to journey with us as far as Cadiz, and to give us the aid of your valour should we be again attacked, we will make the five hundred crowns a thousand. It is a large sum, but we have well nigh all our fortunes at stake, and we feel that we owe you our lives as well as the saving of our money."

"We could desire nothing better," Gerald replied, "and will answer with our lives that your goods and money shall arrive safely at Cadiz."

The traders then called up their two serving men, and told them that on their arrival at Cadiz they would present them each with a hundred crowns for having so stoutly done their duty. The employer of the treacherous clerk then turned his horse's head and rode back towards Seville, while the others prepared to proceed on their way. The two muleteers had now come out from among the bushes, and were busy refastening the bales on the mules, the ropes having become loosened in the struggles of the animals while the fight was going on. The merchants had decided to say nothing to the men as to the discovery that they were in league with the robbers.

"Half these fellows are in alliance with these bands, which are a scourge to the country," one of the traders said. "If we were to inform the authorities at the next town, we should, in the first place, be blamed for letting the wounded man escape, and secondly we might be detained for days while investigations are going on. In this country the next worse

144

thing to being a prisoner is to be a complainant. Law is a luxury in which the wealthy and idle can alone afford to indulge."

As soon, therefore, as the baggage was readjusted the party proceeded on their way.

"What do you think of that, Geoffrey?" Gerald Burke asked as he rode for a short distance by the side of his supposed servant.

"It is magnificent," Geoffrey replied; "and it seems to me that the real road to wealth in Spain is to hire yourself out as a guard to travellers."

"Ah, you would not get much if you made your bargain beforehand. It is only at a moment of urgent danger that fear will open purse strings widely. Had we bargained beforehand with these traders we might have thought ourselves lucky if we had got ten crowns apiece as the price of our escort to Cadiz, and indeed we should have been only too glad if last night such an offer had been made to us; but when a man sees that his property and life are really in danger he does not stop to haggle, but is content to give a handsome percentage of what is risked for aid to save the rest."

"Well, thank goodness, our money trouble is at an end," Geoffrey said; "and it will be a long time before we need have any anxiety on that score."

"Things certainly look better," Gerald said laughing; "and if Inez consents to make a runaway match of it with me I sha'n't have to ask her to pay the expenses."

Cadiz was reached without further adventure. The merchants kept their agreement honourably, and handed over a heavy bag containing a thousand crowns to Gerald on their arrival at that city. They had upon the road inquired of him the nature of his business there. He had told them that he was at present undecided whether to enter the army, in which some friends of his had offered to obtain him a commission, or to join in an adventure to the Indies. They had told him they were acquainted with several merchants at Cadiz who traded both with the east and west, and that they would introduce him to them as a gentleman of spirit and courage, whom they might employ with advantage upon such ventures; and this promise after their arrival there they carried out.

"Now, Geoffrey," Gerald said as they sat together that evening at a comfortable inn, "we must talk over matters here. We have five hundred crowns apiece, and need not trouble any longer as to how we are to support life. Your great object, of course, is to get out of this country somehow, and to make your way back to England. My first is to see Inez and find out whether she will follow my fortunes or remain to become some day Marchesa of Sottomayor. If she adopts the former alternative I have to arrange some plan to carry her off and to get out of the country, an operation in which I foresee no little difficulty. Of course if we are caught my life is forfeited, there is no question about that. The question for us to consider is how we are to set about to carry out our respective plans."

"We need only consider your plan as far as I can see," Geoffrey said. "Of course I shall do what I can to assist you, and if you manage to get off safely with the young lady I shall escape at the same time."

"Not at all," Burke said; "you have only to wait here quietly until you see an opportunity. I will go with you tomorrow to the merchants I was introduced to today, and say that I am going away for a time and shall be obliged if they will make you useful in any way until I return. In that way you will have a sort of established position here, and can wait until you see a chance of smuggling yourself on board some English or Dutch vessel. Mine is a very different affair. I may talk lightly of it, but I am perfectly aware that I run a tremendous risk, and that the chances are very strongly against me."

"Whatever the chances are," Geoffrey said quietly, "I shall share them with you. Your kindness has saved me from what at best might have been imprisonment for life, and not improbably would have been torture and death at the hands of the Inquisition, and I am certainly not going to withdraw myself from you now when you are entering upon what is undoubtedly a very dangerous adventure. If we escape from Spain we escape together; if not, whatever fate befalls you I am ready to risk."

"Very well; so be it, Geoffrey," Gerald Burke said, holding out his hand to him. "If your mind is made up I will not argue the question with you, and indeed I value your companionship and aid too highly to try to shake your determination. Let us then at once talk over what is now our joint enterprise. Ribaldo estate lies about halfway between this and Seville, and we passed within a few miles of it as we came hither. The first thing, of course, will be to procure some sort of disguise in which I can see Inez and have a talk with her. Now, it seems to me, for I have been thinking the matter over in every way as we rode, that the only disguise in which this would be possible would be that of a priest or monk."

Geoffrey laughed aloud. "You would in the first place have to shave off your moustachios, Gerald, and I fear that even after you had done so there would be nothing venerable in your appearance; and whatever the mission with which you might pretend to charge yourself, your chances of obtaining a private interview with the lady would be slight."

"I am afraid that I should lack the odour of sanctity, Geoffrey; but what else can one do? Think it over, man. The way in which you played the idiot when you were picked out of the water shows that you are quick at contriving a plan."

"That was a simple business in comparison to this," Geoffrey replied. "However, you are not pressed for time, and I will think it over tonight and may light upon some possible scheme, for I own that at present I have not the least idea how the matter is to be managed."

As in the morning there were several other travellers taking breakfast in the same room, the conversation was not renewed until Gerald Burke strolled out, followed at a respectful distance by Geoffrey, who still passed as his servant, and reached a quiet spot on the ramparts. Here Geoffrey joined him, and they stood for some minutes looking over the sea.

"What a magnificent position for a city!" Geoffrey said at last. "Standing on this rocky tongue of land jutting out at the entrance to this splendid bay it ought to be impregnable, since it can only be attacked on the side facing that sandy isthmus. What a number of ships are lying up the bay, and what a busy scene it is with the boats passing and repassing! Though they must be two miles away I fancy I can hear the shouts of the sailors."

"Yes, it is all very fine," Gerald said; "but I have seen it several times before. Still, I can make allowances for you. Do you see that group of small ships a mile beyond the others? Those are the English and Dutchmen. They are allowed to trade, but as you see they are kept apart, and there are three war galleys lying close to them. No one is allowed to land, and every boat going off is strictly examined, and all those who go on board have to show their permits from the governor to trade; so, you see, the chance of getting on board one of them is slight indeed. Higher up the bay lies Puerto de Santa Maria, where a great trade is carried on, and much wine shipped; though more comes from Jeres, which lies up the river. You know we passed through it on our way here.

"Yes, this is a splendid position for trade, and I suppose the commerce carried on here is larger than in any port in Europe; though Antwerp ranked as first until the troubles began in the Netherlands. But this ought to be first. It has all the trade of the Atlantic seaboard, and standing at the mouth of the Mediterranean commands that also; while all the wealth of the New World pours in here. That is great already; there is no saying what it will be in the future, while some day the trade from the far East should flow in here also by vessels trading round the south of Africa.

"Cadiz has but one fault: the space on which it stands is too small for a great city. You see how close the houses stand together, and how narrow are the streets. It cannot spread without extending beyond the rock over the sands, and then its strength would be gone, and it would be open to capture by an enterprising enemy having command of the sea. There now, having indulged your humour, let us return to more important matters. Have you thought over what we were talking about last night?"

"I have certainly thought it over," Geoffrey said; "but I do not know that thinking has resulted in much. The only plan that occurs to me as being at all possible is this. You were talking in joke at Madrid of turning robber. Would it be possible, think you, to get together a small band of men to aid you in carrying off the young lady, either from the grounds of her father's house or while journeying on the road? You could then have your talk with her. If you find her willing to fly with you, you could leave the men you have engaged and journey across the country in some sort of disguise to a port. If she objected, you could conduct her back to the neighbourhood of the house and allow her to return. There is one difficulty: you must, of course, be prepared with a priest, so that you can be married at once if she consents to accompany you."

Gerald Burke was silent for some time. "The scheme seems a possible one," he said at last; "it is the question of the priest that bothers me. You know, both in Seville and Cadiz there are Irish colleges, and at both places there are several priests whom I knew before they entered the Church, and who would, I am sure, perform the service for me on any ordinary occasion; but it is a different thing asking them to take a share in such a business

148

as this, for they would render themselves liable to all sorts of penalties and punishments from their superiors. However, the difficulty must be got over somehow, and at any rate the plan seems to promise better than anything I had thought of. The first difficulty is how to get the ruffians for such a business. I cannot go up to the first beetle browed knave I meet in the street and say to him, 'Are you disposed to aid me in the abduction of a lady?'"

"No," Geoffrey laughed; "but fortunately you have an intermediary ready at hand."

"How so?" Gerald exclaimed in surprise. "Why, how on earth can you have an acquaintance with any ruffians in Cadiz?"

"Not a very intimate acquaintance, Gerald; but if you take the trouble to go into the courtyard of the inn when we get back you will see one of those rascally muleteers who went in league with the robbers who attacked us on the way. He was in conversation when we came out with a man who breakfasted with us, and was probably bargaining for a load for his mules back to Seville. I have no doubt that through him you might put yourself into communication with half the cutthroats of the town."

"That is a capital idea, Geoffrey, and I will have a talk with the man as soon as we get back; for if he is not still there, I am sure to be able to learn from some of the men about the stables where to find him."

"You must go very carefully to work, Gerald," Geoffrey said. "It would never do to let any of the fellows know the exact object for which you engaged them, for they might be sure of getting a far larger sum from the marquis for divulging your plans to carry off his daughter than you could afford to pay them for their services."

"I quite see that, and will be careful."

On their return to the inn Gerald Burke at once made inquiries as to the muleteer, and learned that he would probably return in an hour to see if a bargain could be made with a trader for the hire of his mules back to Seville. Gerald waited about until the man came. "I want to have a talk with you, my friend," he said.

The muleteer looked at him with a suspicious eye. "I am busy," he said in a surly tone; "I have no time to waste."

"But it would not be wasting it if it were to lead to your putting a dozen crowns in your pocket."

"Oh, if it is to lead to that, senor, I can spare an hour, for I don't think that anything is likely to come out of the job I came here to try to arrange."

"We will walk away to a quieter place," Gerald said. "There are too many people about here for us to talk comfortably. The ramparts are but two or three minutes' walk; we can talk there without interruption."

When they arrived upon the ramparts Gerald commenced the conversation.

"I think you were foolish, my friend, not to have taken us into your confidence the other day before that little affair. You could have made an opportunity well enough. We stopped to luncheon; if you had drawn me aside, and told me frankly that some friends of yours were about to make an attack upon the traders, and that you would guarantee that they would make it worth my while —"

"What do you mean by saying my friends, or that I had any knowledge of the affair beforehand?" the man asked furiously.

"I say so," Gerald replied, "because I had it on excellent authority. The wounded robber made a clean breast of the whole affair, and of your share in it, as well as that of the rascally clerk of one of the traders. If it had not been for me the merchants would have handed you over to the magistrates at the place where we stopped that night; but I dissuaded them, upon the ground that they would have to attend as witnesses against you, and that it was not worth their while to lose valuable time merely for the pleasure of seeing you hung. However, all this is beside the question. What I was saying was, it is a pity you did not say to me frankly: 'Your presence here is inopportune; but if you will stand apart if any unexpected affair takes place, you will get say two thousand crowns out of the twenty–five thousand my friends are going to capture.' Had you done that, you see, things might have turned out differently."

"I did not know," the muleteer stammered.

"No, you did not know for certain, of course, that I was a soldier of fortune; but if you had been sharp you might have guessed it. However, it is too late for that now. Now, what I wanted to ask you was if you could get me half a dozen of your friends to take service under me in a little adventure I have to carry out. They will be well paid, and I do not suppose they will have much trouble over it."

"And what would you pay me, caballero?" the muleteer asked humbly; for he had been greatly impressed with the valour displayed by the young Irishman and his servant in the fray, and thought that he intended to get together a company for adventures on the road, in which case he might be able to have some profitable dealings with him in the future.

"I will give you twenty crowns," Gerald replied; "and considering that you owe your life to my interposition, I think that you ought not to haggle about terms."

"The party who attacked us," the muleteer said, "lost their captain and several of their comrades in that fray, and would I doubt not gladly enter into your service, seeing that they have received such proof of your worship's valour."

"Where could I see them?" Gerald asked.

"I think that they will be now in Jeres, if that would suit you, senor; but if not I could doubtless find a party of men in this town equally ready for your business."

"Jeres will do very well for me," Gerald said; "I shall be travelling that way and will put up at the Fonda where we stopped as we came through. When are you starting?"

"It depends whether I make my bargain with a man at your hotel," the muleteer replied; "and this I doubt not I shall do, for with the twenty crowns your honour is going to give me I shall not stand out for terms. He is travelling with clothes from Flanders, and if your worship thought —"

"No," Gerald said. "I do not wish to undertake any adventures of that sort until I have a band properly organized, and have arranged hiding places and methods of getting rid of the booty. I will go back with you to the inn, and if you strike your bargain you can tell

151

me as you pass out of the gate what evening you will meet me at Jeres."

On arriving at the inn Gerald lounged at the gate of the courtyard until the muleteer came out.

"I will meet your worship on the fifth night from this at Jeres."

"Very well; here are five crowns as an earnest on our bargain. If you carry it out well I shall very likely forget to deduct them from the twenty I promised you. Do not be surprised if you find me somewhat changed in appearance when you meet me there."

At the appointed time the muleteer with his train of animals entered the courtyards of the Fonda at Jeres. Gerald was standing on the steps of the inn. He had altered the fashion of his hair, had fastened on large bushy eyebrows which he had obtained from a skilful perruquier in Cadiz, and a moustache of imposing size turned up at the tips; he wore high buff leather boots, and there was an air of military swagger about him, and he was altogether so changed that at the first glance the muleteer failed to recognize him. As soon as the mules were unburdened, Gerald found an opportunity of speaking with him.

"I will go round at once," the man said, "to the place where I shall certainly obtain news of my friends if they are here. I told your honour that they might be here, but they may have gone away on some affair of business, and may be on the road or at Seville. They always work between this town and Seville."

"I understand that you may not meet them tonight; if not, I will meet you again in Seville. How long will you be finding out about them?"

"I shall know in half an hour, senor; if they are not here I shall be back here in less than an hour, but if I find them I shall be detained longer in order to talk over with them the offer your worship makes."

"Very well; in an hour you will find me in the street opposite the inn. I shall wait there until you come. If all is well make a sign and I will follow you. Do not mention to them that I have in any way disguised myself. Our acquaintance was so short that I don't fancy they had time to examine me closely; and I have my own reasons of wishing that they should not be acquainted with my ordinary appearance, and have therefore to some extent disguised myself."

"I will say nothing about it," the muleteer replied. "Your worship can depend upon my discretion."

"That is right," Gerald said. "We may have future dealings together, and I can reward handsomely those I find trustworthy and punish those who in the slightest degree disobey my orders."

In an hour and a half the muleteer returned, made a signal to Gerald and passed on. The latter joined him at a short distance from the hotel.

"It is all settled, senor. I found the men much dispirited at the loss of their captain and comrades; and when I proposed to them to take service under the caballero who wrought them such mischief the other day, they jumped at the idea, saying that under such a valiant leader there was no fear of the failure of any enterprise they might undertake."

A quarter of an hour's walking took them to a small inn of villainous appearance in one of the smallest lanes of the town. Gerald was wrapped from head to foot in his cloak, and only his face was visible. He had a brace of pistols in his belt, and was followed at a short distance, unnoticed by the muleteer, by Geoffrey, who had arranged to keep close to the door of any house he entered, and was to be in readiness to rush in and take part in the fray if he heard the sound of firearms within.

Gerald himself had not at first entertained any idea of treachery; but Geoffrey had pointed out that it was quite possible that the robbers and the muleteer had but feigned acquiescence in his proposals in order to get him into their power, and take revenge for the loss of their captain and comrades, and of the valuable booty which had so unexpectedly slipped through their fingers owing to his intervention.

The appearance of the six ruffians gathered in the low room, lighted by a wretched lamp, was not very assuring, and Gerald kept his hand on the butt of one of his pistols.

The four robbers who had been engaged in the fray, however, saluted him respectfully, and the other two members of the band, who had been absent on other business, followed their example. They had heard from those present of the extraordinary valour with which the two travelling companions of the trader had thrown themselves into the fray, and had alone disposed of their four comrades, and being without a leader, and greatly disheartened by their ill luck, they were quite ready to forgive the misfortunes Gerald had brought upon them, and to accept such a redoubtable swordsman as their leader.

Gerald began the conversation. "You have heard," he said, "from our friend here of the offer I make you. I desire a band of six men on whom I can rely for an adventure which promises large profit. Don't suppose that I am going to lead you to petty robberies on the road, in which, as you learned to your cost the other day, one sometimes gets more hard knocks than profit. Such adventures may do for petty knaves, but they are not suited to me. The way to get wealthy is to strike at the rich. My idea is to establish some place in an out of the way quarter where there is no fear of prying neighbours, and to carry off and hide there the sons and daughters of wealthy men and put them to ransom. In the first instance I am going to undertake a private affair of my own; and as you will really run no risk in the matter, for I shall separate myself from you after making my capture, I shall pay you only a earnest money of twenty crowns each. In future affairs we shall act upon the principle of shares. I shall take three shares, a friend who works with me will take two shares, and you shall take one share apiece. The risk will really be entirely mine, for I shall take charge of the captives we make at our rendezvous. You, after lending a hand in the capture, will return here and hold yourself in readiness to join me, and carry out another capture as soon as I have made all the necessary arrangements. Thus, if by any chance we are tracked, I alone and my friend will run the risk of capture and punishment. In that way we may, in the course of a few months, amass a much larger booty than we should in a lifetime spent in these wretched adventures upon travellers.

"Now, it is for you to say whether these terms will suit you, and whether you are ready to follow my orders and obey me implicitly. The whole task of making the necessary arrangements, or finding out the habits of the families one of whose members we intend carrying off, of bribing nurses or duennas, will be all my business. You will simply have to meet when you are summoned to aid in the actual enterprise, and then, when our captive is safely housed, to return here or scatter where you will and live at ease until again summoned. The utmost fidelity will be necessary. Large rewards will in many cases be offered for the discovery of the missing persons, and one traitor would bring ruin upon us all; therefore it will be absolutely necessary that you take an oath of fidelity to me, and swear one and all to punish the traitor with death. Do you agree to my proposal?"

154

There was a unanimous exclamation of assent. The plan seemed to offer probabilities of large booty with a minimum of trouble and risk. One or two suggested that they should like to join in the first capture on the same terms as the others, but Gerald at once pronounced this to be impossible.

"This is my own affair," he said, "and money is not now my object. As you will only be required to meet at a given hour some evening, and to carry off a captive who will not be altogether unwilling to come, there will be little or no risk in the matter, and twenty crowns will not be bad pay for an evening's work. After that you will, as I have said, share in the profits of all future captures we may undertake."

The band all agreed, and at once took solemn oaths of fidelity to their new leader, and swore to punish by death any one of their number who should betray the secrets of the body.

"That is well," Gerald said when the oaths had been taken. "It may be a week before you receive your first summons. Here are five crowns apiece for your expenses up to that time. Let one of you be in front of the great church as the clock strikes eight morning and evening. Do not wait above five minutes; if I am coming I shall be punctual. In the meantime take counsel among yourselves as to the best hiding place that can be selected. Between you you no doubt know every corner and hole in the country. I want a place which will be at once lonely and far removed from other habitations, but it must be at the same time moderately comfortable, as the captives we take must have no reason to complain of their treatment while in my hands. Think this matter over before I again see you."

Gerald then joined Geoffrey outside, and found that the latter was beginning to be anxious at his long absence. After a few words saying that everything had been successfully arranged, the two friends returned together to their inn.

CHAPTER XIII. THE FESTA AT SEVILLE

"And now, Gerald, that you have made your arrangements for the second half of the plan, how are you going to set about the first? because you said that you intended to give Donna Inez the option of flying with you or remaining with her father."

"So I do still. Before I make any attempt to carry her off I shall first learn whether she is willing to run the risks."

"But how are you going to set about it? You may be quite sure that she never goes outside the garden without having her duenna with her. If there is a chapel close by, doubtless she will go there once a day; and it seems to me that this would be the best chance of speaking to her, for I do not see how you can possibly introduce yourself into the grounds."

"That would be quite out of the question, in daylight at any rate, Geoffrey. I do not suppose she ever goes beyond the terrace by the house. But if I could communicate with her she might slip out for a few minutes after dark, when the old lady happened to be taking a nap. The question is how to get a letter into her hands."

"I think I might manage that, Gerald. It is not likely that the duenna ever happened to notice me. I might therefore put on any sort of disguise as a beggar and take my place on the road as she goes to chapel, and somehow or other get your note into her hand. I have heard Spanish girls are very quick at acting upon the smallest sign, and if I can manage to catch her eye for a moment she may probably be ingenious enough to afford me an opportunity of passing the note to her."

"That might be done," Gerald agreed. "We will at once get disguises. I will dress myself as an old soldier, with one arm in a sling and a patch over my eye; you dress up in somewhat the same fashion as a sailor boy. It is about twelve miles from here to Ribaldo's place. We can walk that easily enough, dress ourselves up within a mile or two of the place, and then go on and reconnoitre the ground."

"I should advise you to write your note before you start; it may be that some unexpected opportunity for handing it to her may present itself."

"I will do that; but let us sally out first and pick up two suits at some dealer in old clothes. There will be sure to be two or three of these in the poorer quarter."

The disguises were procured without difficulty, and putting them in a small wallet they started before noon on their walk. In four hours they reached the boundary of the Marquis of Ribaldo's estate. Going into a wood they assumed the disguises, packed their own clothes in a wallet, and hid this away in a clump of bushes. Then they again started — Gerald Burke with his arm in a sling and Geoffrey limping along with the aid of a thick stick he had cut in the wood.

On arriving at the village, a quarter of a mile from the gates of the mansion, they went into a small wine shop and called for two measures of the cheapest wine and a loaf of bread. Here they sat for some time, listening to the conversation of the peasants who frequented the wine shop. Sometimes a question was asked of the wayfarers. Gerald replied, for his companion's Spanish although fluent was not good enough to pass as that of a native. He replied to the question as to where they had received their hurts that they were survivors of the Armada, and grumbled that it was hard indeed that men who had fought in the Netherlands and had done their duty to their country should be turned adrift to starve.

"We have enough to pay for our supper and a night's lodging," he said, "but where we are going to take our meal tomorrow is more than I can say, unless we can meet with some charitable people."

"If you take your place by the roadside tomorrow morning," one of the peasants said, "you may obtain charity from Donna Inez de Ribaldo. She comes every morning to mass here; and they say she has a kind heart, which is more than men give her father the marquis the credit of possessing. We have not many poor round here, for at this time of year all hands are employed in the vineyards, therefore there is the more chance of your obtaining a little help."

"Thank you; I will take your advice," Gerald said. "I suppose she is sure to come?"

"She is sure enough; she never misses when she is staying here."

That night the friends slept on a bundle of straw in an outhouse behind the wine shop, and arranged everything; and upon the following morning took their seats by the roadside near the village. The bell of the chapel was already sounding, and in a few minutes they saw two ladies approaching, followed at a very short distance by a serving man. They had agreed that the great patch over Gerald's eye aided by the false moustachios, so completely disguised his appearance that they need have no fear of his being recognized; and it was therefore decided he should do the talking. As Donna Inez came up he commenced calling out: "Have pity, gracious ladies, upon two broken down soldiers. We have gone through all the dangers and hardships of the terrible voyage of the great Armada. We served in the ship San Josef and are now broken down, and have no means of earning our living."

Gerald had somewhat altered his natural voice while speaking, but Geoffrey was watching Donna Inez closely, and saw her start when he began to speak; and when he said they had been on board the San Josef a flush of colour came across her face.

"We must relieve these poor men," she said to the duenna; "it is pitiful to see them in such a state."

"We know not that their tale is true," the duenna replied sharply. "Every beggar in our days pretends to be a broken down soldier."

At this moment Donna Inez happened to glance at Geoffrey, who raised his hand to his face and permitted a corner of a letter to be momentarily seen.

"An impostor!" Gerald cried in a loud voice. "To think that I, suffering from my terrible wounds, should be taken as an impostor," and with a hideous yell he tumbled down as if in a fit, and rolled over and over on the ground towards the duenna.

Seized with alarm at his approach, she turned and ran a few paces backward. As she did so Geoffrey stepped up to Inez and held out the note, which she took and concealed instantly in her dress.

"There is nothing to be alarmed at," she cried to the duenna. "The poor man is doubtless in a fit. Here, my poor fellow, get aid for your comrade," and taking out her purse she handed a dollar to Geoffrey, and then joining the duenna proceeded on her way.

Geoffrey knelt beside his prostrate companion and appeared to be endeavouring to restore him, until the ladies and their servant were out of sight.

"That was well managed," Gerald Burke said, sitting up as soon as a turn of the road hid them from view. "Now we shall have our answer tomorrow. Thank goodness there is no occasion for us to remain any longer in these garments!"

By England's Aid: or The Freeing

They went to the wood and resumed their usual attire, and then walked to a large village some four miles away, and putting up at the principal inn remained there until early the next morning; then they walked back to the village they had left on the previous day and posted themselves in a thicket by the roadside, so that they could see passersby without being themselves observed.

"My fate will soon be decided now," Gerald said. "Will she wear a white flower or not?"

"I am pretty sure that she will," Geoffrey said. "She would not have started and coloured when she recognized your voice if she did not love you. I do not think you need be under much uneasiness on that score."

In half an hour the ladies again came along, followed as before by their servants. Donna Inez wore a bunch of white flowers in her dress.

"There is my answer," Gerald said. "Thank heaven! she loves me, and is ready to fly with me, and will steal out some time after dark to meet me in the garden."

As there was no occasion for him to stay longer, Geoffrey returned to the village where they slept the night before, and accounted for his companion's absence by saying that he had been detained on business and would probably not return until late at night, as he would not be able to see the person with whom he had affairs to transact until late. It was past ten o'clock when Gerald Burke returned.

"It is all arranged, Geoffrey. I hid in the garden close by the terrace as soon as it became dark. An hour later she came out and sauntered along the terrace until I softly called her name; then she came to me. She loves me with all her heart, and is ready to share my fate whatever it may be. Her father only two days ago had ordered her to prepare for her marriage with Don Philip, and she was in despair until she recognized my voice yesterday morning. She is going with her father to a grand festa at Seville next Wednesday. They will stop there two nights — the one before the festa and the one after. I told her that I could not say yet whether I should make the attempt to carry her off on her journey or after her return here, as that must depend upon circumstances. At any rate, that gives us plenty of time to prepare our plans. Tomorrow we will hire horses and ride to Seville, and I will there arrange with one of my friends at the Irish College to perform the ceremony. However, we will talk it all over tomorrow as we ride. I feel as sleepy as a dog now after the day's excitement."

Upon the road next day they agreed that if possible they would manage to get Inez away in Seville itself Owing to the large number of people who would be attracted there to witness the grand procession and high mass at the cathedral, the streets would be crowded, and it might be possible for Inez to slip away from those with her. If this could be managed it would be greatly preferable to the employment of the men to carry her off by force. Therefore they agreed that the band should be posted so that the party could be intercepted on its way back; but that this should be a last resource, and that if possible Inez should be carried off in Seville itself.

On reaching Seville they put up at an inn. Gerald at once proceeded to the Irish College. Here he inquired for a young priest, who had been a near neighbour of his in Ireland and a great friend of his boyhood. He was, he knew, about to return home. He found that he was at the moment away from Seville, having gone to supply the place of a village cure who had been taken suddenly ill. This village was situated, he was told, some six miles southeast of the town. It was already late in the afternoon, but time was precious; and Gerald, hiring a fresh horse, rode out at once to the village. His friend was delighted to see him, for they had not met since Gerald passed through Seville on his way to join the Armada at Cadiz, and the young priest had not heard whether he had escaped the perils of the voyage.

"It is lucky you have come, Gerald," he said when the first greetings were over, "for I am going to return to Ireland in a fortnight's time. I am already appointed to a charge near Cork, and am to sail in a Bristol ship which is expected in Cadiz about that time. Is there any chance of my meeting you there?"

"An excellent chance, Denis, though my route is not as clearly marked out as yours is. I wish to heaven that I could go by the same ship. And that leads to what I have come to see you about," and he then told his friend the service he wished him to render.

"It is rather a serious business, Gerald; and a nice scrape I should get in if it were found out that I had solemnized the marriage of a young lady under age without the consent of her father, and that father a powerful nobleman. However, I am not the man to fail you at a pinch, and if matters are well managed there is not much risk of its being found out that I had a hand in it until I am well away, and once in Ireland no one is likely to make any great fuss over my having united a runaway pair in Spain. Besides, if you and the young lady have made up your minds to run away, it is evidently necessary that you should be married at once; so my conscience is perfectly clear in the business. And now, what is your plan?"

"The only part of my plan that is settled is to bring her here and marry her. After that I shall have horses ready, and we will ride by unfrequented roads to Malaga or some other port and take a passage in a ship sailing say to Italy, for there is no chance of getting a vessel hence to England. Once in Italy there will be no difficulty in getting a passage to England. I have with me a young Englishman, as staunch a friend as one can need. I need not tell you all about how I became acquainted with him; but he is as anxious to get out of Spain as I am, and that is saying no little."

"It seems rather a vague plan, Gerald. There is sure to be a great hue and cry as soon as the young lady is found to be missing. The marquis is a man of great influence, and the authorities will use every effort to enable him to discover her."

"You see, Denis, they will have no reason for supposing that I have had any hand in the matter, and therefore no special watch will be set at the ports. The duenna for her own sake is not likely to say a word about any passages she may have observed between us at Madrid, and she is unaware that there have been any communications with her since."

"I suppose you will at once put on disguises, Gerald."

"Yes, that will of course be the first thing."

"If you dress her as a young peasant woman of the better class and yourself as a small cultivator, I will mention to my servant that I am expecting my newly married niece and her husband to stay with me for a few days. The old woman will have no idea that I, an Irishman, would not have a Spanish niece, and indeed I do not suppose that she has any idea that I am not a Spaniard. I will open the church myself and perform the service late in the evening, so that no one will be aware of what is going on. Of course I can put up your friend too. Then you can stay quietly here as long as you like."

"That will do admirably, Denis; but I think we had best go on the next morning," Gerald said, "although it will be a day or two before there is anything like an organized pursuit.

It will be supposed that she is in Seville, and inquiries will at first be confined to that town. If she leaves a note behind saying that she is determined even to take the veil rather than marry the man her father has chosen for her, that will cause additional delay. It will be supposed that she is concealed in the house of some friend, or that she has sought a refuge in a nunnery, and at any rate there is not likely to be any search over the country for some days, especially as her father will naturally be anxious that what he will consider an act of rebellion on the part of his daughter shall not become publicly known."

"All this, of course, is if we succeed in getting her clear away during the fete. If we have to fall back on the other plan I was talking of and carry her off by force on the way home, the search will be immediate and general. In that case nothing could be better than your plan that we should stop here quietly for a few days with you. They will be searching for a band of robbers and will not dream of making inquiry for the missing girl in a quiet village like this."

"Well, we will leave that open, Gerald. I shall let it be known that you are expected, and whenever you arrive you will be welcome."

As soon as the point was arranged Gerald again mounted his horse and returned to Seville. There upon the following morning he engaged a lodging for the three days of the festa in a quiet house in the outskirts of the town, and they then proceeded to purchase the various articles necessary for their disguise and that of Inez. The next morning they started on their return to Jeres. Here Gerald made arrangements with the band to meet him in a wood on the road to Cadiz at eight in the morning on the day following the termination of the festa at Seville. One of the party was to proceed on that day to the house among the hills they had fixed upon as their hiding place, and to get provisions and everything requisite for the reception of their captive. They received another five crowns each, the remaining fifteen was to be paid them as soon as they arrived with their captive at the house.

The party remained in ignorance as to the age and sex of the person they were to carry off, and had little curiosity as to the point, as they regarded this but a small adventure in comparison to the lucrative schemes in which they were afterwards to be sharers.

These arrangements made, Gerald and Geoffrey returned to Seville, and reached that city on the eve of the commencement of the festa, and took up their abode at the lodging they had hired. On the following morning they posted themselves in the street by which the party they expected would arrive. Both were attired in quiet citizen dress, and Gerald retained his formidable moustachios and bushy eyebrows.

In two or three hours a coach accompanied by four lackeys on horseback came up the street, and they saw that it contained the Marquis of Ribaldo, his daughter, and her duenna. They followed a short distance behind it until it entered the courtyard of a stately mansion, which they learnt on inquiry from a passerby belonged to the Duke of Sottomayor. The streets were already crowded with people in holiday attire, the church bells were ringing, and flags and decorations of all kinds waved along the route that was to be followed by the great procession. The house did not stand on this line, and it was necessary therefore for its inmates to pass through the crowd either to the cathedral or to the balcony of the house from which they might intend to view the procession pass.

Half an hour after the arrival of the coach, the marquis and his daughter, accompanied by Don Philip de Sottomayor, sallied out, escorted by six armed lackeys, and took their way towards the cathedral. They had, however, arrived very late, and the crowd had already gathered so densely that even the efforts of the lackeys and the angry commands of the marquis and Don Philip failed to enable them to make a passage. Very slowly indeed they advanced some distance into the crowd, but each moment their progress became slower. Gerald and Geoffrey had fallen in behind them and advanced with them as they worked themselves in the crowd.

Angry at what they considered the impertinence of the people for refusing to make way for them, the nobles pressed forward and engaged in an angry controversy with those in front, who urged, and truly, that it was simply impossible for them to make way, so wedged in were they by the people on all sides. The crowd, neither knowing nor caring who were those who thus wished to take precedence of the first comers, began to jeer and laugh at the angry nobles, and when these threatened to use force threatened in return.

As soon as her father had left her side, Gerald, who was immediately behind Inez, whispered in her ear, "Now is the time, Inez. Go with my friend; I will occupy the old woman."

"Keep close to me, senora, and pretend that you are ill," Geoffrey said, to her, and without hesitation Inez turned and followed him, drawing her mantilla more closely over her face.

"Let us pass, friends," Geoffrey said as he elbowed his way through those standing behind them, "the lady needs air," and by vigorous efforts he presently arrived at the outskirts of the crowd, and struck off with his charge in the direction of their lodging. "Gerald Burke will follow us as soon as he can get out," he said. "Everything is prepared for you, senora, and all arrangements made."

"Who are you, sir?" the girl asked. "I do not recall your face, and yet I seem to have seen it before."

"I am English, senora, and am a friend of Gerald Burke's. When in Madrid I was disguised as his servant; for as an Englishman and a heretic it would have gone hard with me had I been detected."

There were but few people in the streets through which they passed, the whole population having flocked either to the streets through which the procession was to pass, or to the cathedral or churches it was to visit on its way. Gerald had told Inez at their interview that, although he had made arrangements for carrying her off by force on the journey to or from Seville, he should, if possible, take advantage of the crowd at the function to draw her away from her companions. She had, therefore, put on her thickest lace mantilla, and this now completely covered her face from the view of passersby. Several times she glanced back.

"Do nor be uneasy about him, senora," Geoffrey said. "He will not try to extricate himself from the crowd until you are discovered to be missing, as to do so would be to attract attention. As soon as your loss is discovered he will make his way out, and will then come on at the top of his speed to the place whither I am conducting you, and I expect that we shall find him at the door awaiting us."

A quarter of an hour's walk took them to the lodging, and Inez gave a little cry of joy as the door was opened to them by Gerald himself.

"The people of the house are all out," he said, after their first greeting. "In that room you will find a peasant girl's dress. Dress yourself as quickly as you can; we shall be ready for you in attire to match. You had best do up your own things into a bundle, which I will carry. If they were left here they might, when the news of your being missing gets abroad, afford a clue to the manner of your escape. I will tell you all about the arrangements we have made as we go along."

"Have you arranged —" and she hesitated.

"Yes, an Irish priest, who is an old friend of mine, will perform the ceremony this evening."

A few minutes later two seeming peasants and a peasant girl issued out from the lodging. The two men carried stout sticks with bundles slung over them.

"Be careful of that bundle," Inez said, "for there are all my jewels in it. After what you had said I concealed them all about me. They are my fortune, you know. Now, tell me how you got on in the crowd."

"I first pushed rather roughly against the duenna, and then made the most profuse apologies, saying that it was shameful people should crowd so, and that they ought at once to make way for a lady who was evidently of high rank. This mollified her, and we talked for three or four minutes; and in the meantime the row in front, caused by your father and the lackeys quarrelling with the people, grew louder and louder. The old lady became much alarmed, and indeed the crowd swayed about so that she clung to my arm. Suddenly she thought of you, and turning round gave a scream when she found you were missing. 'What is the matter?' I asked anxiously. 'The young lady with me! She was here but an instant ago!' (She had forgotten you for fully five minutes.) 'What can have become of her?'

"I suggested that no doubt you were close by, but had got separated from her by the pressure of the crowd. However, she began to squall so loudly that the marquis looked round. He was already in a towering rage, and he asked angrily, 'What are you making all this noise about?' and then looking round exclaimed, 'Where is Inez?' 'She was here a moment since!' the old lady exclaimed, 'and now she has got separated from me.' Your father looked in vain among the crowd, and demanded whether anyone had seen you. Someone said that a lady who was fainting had made her way out five minutes before. The marquis used some strong language to the old lady, and then informed Don Philip what had happened, and made his way back out of the crowd with the aid of the lackeys,

165

and is no doubt inquiring for you in all the houses near; but, as you may imagine, I did not wait. I followed close behind them until they were out of the crowd, and then slipped away, and once round the corner took to my heels and made my way back, and got in two or three minutes before you arrived."

The two young men talked almost continuously during their walk to the village in order to keep up the spirits of Donna Inez, and to prevent her from thinking of the strangeness of her position and the perils that lay before them before safety could be obtained. Only once she spoke of the future.

"Is it true, Gerald, that there are always storms and rain in your country, and that you never see the sun, for so some of those who were in the Armada have told me?"

"It rains there sometimes, Inez, I am bound to admit; but it is often fine, and the sun never burns one up as it does here. I promise you you will like it, dear, when you once become accustomed to it."

"I do not think I shall," she said, shaking her head; "I am accustomed to the sun, you know. But I would rather be with you even in such an island as they told me of than in Spain with Don Philip."

The village seemed absolutely deserted when they arrived there, the whole population having gone over to Seville to take part in the great fete. Father Denis received his fair visitor with the greatest kindness. "Here, Catherine," he cried to his old servant, "here are the visitors I told you I expected. It is well that we have the chambers prepared, and that we killed that capon this morning."

That evening Gerald Burke and Inez de Ribaldo were married in the little church, Geoffrey Vickars being the only witness. The next morning there was a long consultation over their plans. "I could buy you a cart in the village and a pair of oxen, and you could drive to Malaga," the priest said, "but there would be a difficulty about changing your disguises after you had entered the town. I think that the boldest plan will be the safest one. I should propose that you should ride as a well to do trader to Malaga, with your wife behind you on a pillion, and your friend here as your servant. Lost as your wife was in the crowd at the fete, it will be a long time before the fact that she has fled will be realized. For a day or two the search will be conducted secretly, and only when the house

166

of every friend whom she might have visited has been searched will the aid of the authorities be called in, and the poorer quarters, where she might have been carried by two or three ruffians who may have met her as she emerged in a fainting condition, as is supposed, from the crowd, be ransacked. I do not imagine that any search will be made throughout the country round for a week at least, by which time you will have reached Malaga, and, if you have good fortune, be on board a ship."

This plan was finally agreed to. Gerald and his friend at once went over to Seville and purchased the necessary dresses, together with two strong horses and equipments. It was evening before their return to the village. Instead of entering it at once they rode on a mile further, and fastened the horses up in a wood. Gerald would have left them there alone, but Geoffrey insisted on staying with them for the night.

"I care nothing about sleeping in the open air, Gerald, and it would be folly to risk the success of our enterprise upon the chance of no one happening to come through the wood, and finding the animals before you return in the morning. We had a hearty meal at Seville, and I shall do very well until morning."

Gerald and his wife took leave of the friendly priest at daybreak the next morning, with the hope that they would very shortly meet in Ireland. They left the village before anyone was stirring.

The peasant clothes had been left behind them. Gerald carried two valises, the one containing the garments in which Inez had fled, the other his own attire — Geoffrey having resumed the dress he had formerly worn as his servant.

On arriving at the wood the party mounted, and at once proceeded on their journey. Four days' travel took them to Malaga, where they arrived without any adventure whatever. Once or twice they met parties of rough looking men; but travelling as they did without baggage animals, they did not appear promising subjects for robbery, and the determined appearance of master and man, each armed with sword and pistols, deterred the fellows from an attempt which promised more hard knocks than plunder.

After putting up at an inn in Malaga, Gerald went down at once to the port to inquire for a vessel bound for Italy. There were three or four such vessels in the harbour, and he had no difficulty in arranging for a passage to Naples for himself, his wife, and servant. The

167

vessel was to sail on the following morning, and it was with a deep feeling of satisfaction and relief that they went on board her, and an hour later were outside the port.

"It seems marvellous to me," Gerald said, as he looked back upon the slowly receding town, "that I have managed to carry off my prize with so little difficulty. I had expected to meet with all sorts of dangers, and had I been the peaceful trader I looked, our journey could not be more uneventful."

"Perhaps you are beginning to think that the prize is not so very valuable after all," Inez said, "since you have won it so easily."

"I have not begun to think so yet," Gerald laughed happily. "At any rate I shall wait until I get you home before such ideas begin to occur to me."

"Directly I get to Ireland," Inez said, "I shall write to my father and tell him that I am married to you, and that I should never have run away had he not insisted on my marrying a man I hated. I shall, of course, beg him to forgive me; but I fear he never will."

"We must hope that he will, Inez, and that he will ask you to come back to Spain sometimes. I do not care for myself, you know, for as I have told you my estate in Ireland is amply large enough for my wants; but I shall be glad, for your sake, that you should be reconciled to him."

Inez shook her head.

"You do not know my father, Gerald. I would never go back to Spain again — not if he promised to give me his whole fortune. My father never forgives; and were he to entice me back to Spain, it would be only to shut me up and to obtain a dispensation from Rome annulling the marriage, which he would have no difficulty in doing. No, you have got me, and will have to keep me for good. I shall never return to Spain, never. Possibly when my father hears from me he may send me over money to make me think he has forgiven me, and to induce me some day or other to come back to visit him, and so get me into his power again; but that, Gerald, he shall never do."

CHAPTER XIV. THE SURPRISE OF BREDA

Lionel Vickars had, by the beginning of 1590, come to speak the Dutch language well and fluently. Including his first stay in Holland he had now been there eighteen months, and as he was in constant communications with the Dutch officers and with the population, he had constant occasion for speaking Dutch, a language much more akin to English than any other continental tongue, and indeed so closely allied to the dialect of the eastern counties of England, that the fishermen of our eastern ports had in those days little difficulty in conversing with the Hollanders.

He was one day supping with Sir Francis Vere when Prince Maurice and several of his officers were also there. The conversation turned upon the prospects of the campaign of the ensuing spring. Lionel, of course, took no part in it, but listened attentively to what was being said and was very pleased to find that the period of inactivity was drawing to an end, and that their commanders considered that they had now gathered a force of sufficient strength to assume the offensive.

"I would," Prince Maurice said, "that we could gain Breda. The city stands like a great sentinel against every movement towards Flanders, and enables the Spaniards to penetrate at all times towards the heart of our country; but I fear that it is altogether beyond our means. It is one of the strongest cities in the Netherlands, and my ancestors, who were its lords, little thought that they were fortifying and strengthening it in order that it might be a thorn in the side of their country. I would give much, indeed, to be able to wrest it from the enemy; but I fear it will be long before we can even hope for that. It could withstand a regular siege by a well provided army for months; and as to surprise, it is out of the question, for I hear that the utmost vigilance is unceasingly maintained."

A few days after this Lionel was talking with Captain de Heraugiere, who had also been at the supper. He had taken part in the defence of Sluys and was one of the officers with whom Lionel was most intimate.

"It would be a rare enterprise to surprise Breda," Captain de Heraugiere said; "but I fear it is hopeless to think of such a thing."

"I do not see why it should be," Lionel said. "I was reading when I was last at home

169

about our wars with the Scotch, and there were several cases in which very strong places that could not have been carried by assault were captured suddenly by small parties of men who disguised themselves as waggoners, and hiding a score or two of their comrades in a wagon covered with firewood, or sacks of grain, boldly went up to the gates. When there they cut the traces of their horses so that the gates could not be closed, or the portcullis lowered, and then falling upon the guards, kept them at bay until a force, hidden near the gates, ran up and entered the town. I see not why a similar enterprise should not be attempted at Breda."

"Nor do I," Captain Heraugiere said; "the question is how to set about such a scheme."

"That one could not say without seeing the place," Lionel remarked. "I should say that a plan of this sort could only be successful after those who attempted it had made themselves masters of all particulars of the place and its ways. Everything would depend upon all going smoothly and without hitches of any kind. If you really think of undertaking such an adventure, Captain Heraugiere, I should be very glad to act under you if Sir Francis Vere will give me leave to do so; but I would suggest that the first step should be for us to go into Breda in disguise. We might take in a wagon load of grain for sale, or merely carry on our backs baskets with country produce, or we could row up in a boat with fish."

"The plan is certainly worth thinking of," Captain Heraugiere said. "I will turn it over in my mind for a day, and will then talk to you again. It would be a grand stroke, and there would be great honour to be obtained; but it will not do for me to go to Prince Maurice and lay it before him until we have a plan completely worked out, otherwise we are more likely to meet with ridicule than praise."

The following day Captain Heraugiere called at Lionel's lodgings. "I have lain awake all night thinking of our scheme," he said, "and have resolved to carry out at least the first part of it — to enter Breda and see what are the prospects of success, and the manner in which the matter had best be set about. I propose that we two disguise ourselves as fishermen, and going down to the river between Breda and Willemstad bargain with some fishermen going up to Breda with their catch for the use of their boat. While they are selling the fish we can survey the town and see what is the best method of introducing a force into it. When our plan is completed we will go to Voorne, whither Prince Maurice starts tomorrow, and lay the matter before him."

By England's Aid: or The Freeing

"I will gladly go with you to Breda," Lionel said, "and, as far as I can, aid you there; but I think that it would be best that you only should appear in the matter afterwards. I am but a young volunteer, and it would be well that I did not appear at all in the matter, which you had best make entirely your own. But I hope, Captain Heraugiere, that should the prince decide to adopt any plan you may form, and intrust the matter to you, that you will take me with you in your following."

"That I will assuredly," Captain Heraugiere said, "and will take care that if it should turn out successful your share in the enterprise shall be known."

"When do you think of setting about it?" Lionel asked.

"Instantly. My company is at Voorne, and I should return thither with the prince today. I will at once go to him and ask for leave to be absent on urgent affairs for a week. Do you go to Sir Francis Vere and ask for a similar time. Do not tell him, if you can help it, the exact nature of your enterprise. But if you cannot obtain leave otherwise, of course you must do so. I will be back here in two hours' time. We can then at once get our disguises, and hire a craft to take us to Willemstad."

Lionel at once went across to the quarters of Sir Francis Vere.

"I have come, Sir Francis, to ask for a week's leave of absence."

"That you can have, Lionel. Where are you going —shooting ducks on the frozen meres?"

"No, Sir Francis. I am going on a little expedition with Captain Heraugiere, who has invited me to accompany him. We have an idea in our heads that may perhaps be altogether useless, but may possibly bear fruit. In the first case we would say nothing about it, in the second we will lay it before you on our return."

"Very well," Sir Francis said with a smile. "You showed that you could think at Sluys, and I hope something may come of this idea of yours, whatever it may be."

At the appointed time Captain Heraugiere returned, having obtained leave of absence from the prince. They at once went out into the town and bought the clothes necessary for their disguise. They returned with these to their lodgings, and having put them on went down to the wharf, where they had no difficulty in bargaining with the master of a small craft to take them to Willemstad, as the Spaniards had no ships whatever on the water between Rotterdam and Bergen op Zoom. The boat was to wait three days for them at that town, and to bring them back to Rotterdam. As there was no reason for delay they at once went on board and cast off. The distance was but thirty miles, and just at nightfall they stepped ashore at the town of Willemstad.

The next morning they had no difficulty in arranging with a fisherman who was going up to Breda with a cargo of fish to take the place of two of his boatmen at the oars.

"We want to spend a few hours there," Captain Heraugiere said, "and will give you five crowns if you will leave two of your men here and let us take their places."

"That is a bargain," the man said at once; "that is, if you can row, for we shall scarce take the tide up to the town, and must keep on rowing to get there before the ebb begins."

"We can row, though perhaps not so well as your own men. You are, I suppose, in the habit of going there, and are known to the guards at the port? They are not likely, I should think, to notice that you haven't got the same crew as usual?"

"There is no fear of that, and if they did I could easily say that two of my men were unable to accompany me today, and that I have hired fresh hands in their places."

Two of the men got out. Captain Heraugiere and Lionel Vickars took their places, and the boat proceeded up the river. The oars were heavy and clumsy, and the newcomers were by no means sorry when, after a row of twelve miles, they neared Breda.

"What are the regulations for entering Breda?" Captain Heraugiere asked as they approached the town.

"There are no particular regulations," the master of the boat said, "save that on entering the port the boat is searched to see that it contains nothing but fish. None are allowed to enter the gates of the town without giving their names, and satisfying the officer on guard that they have business in the place."

An officer came on board as the boat ran up alongside the quay and asked a few questions. After assisting in getting the basket of fish on shore Captain Heraugiere and Lionel sauntered away along the quay, leaving the fishermen to dispose of their catch to the townspeople, who had already begun to bargain for them.

The river Mark flowed through the town, supplying its moats with water. Where it left the town on the western side was the old castle, with a moat of its own and strong fortified lines. Within was the quay, with an open place called the fish market leading to the gates of the new castle. There were 600 Spanish infantry in the town and 100 in the castle, and 100 cavalry. The governor of Breda, Edward Lanzavecchia, was absent superintending the erection of new fortifications at Gertruydenberg, and in his absence the town was under the command of his son Paolo.

Great vigilance was exercised. All vessels entering port were strictly examined, and there was a guard house on the quay. Lying by one of the wharves was a large boat laden with peat, which was being rapidly unloaded, the peat being sold as soon as landed, as fuel was very short in the city.

"It seems to me," Lionel said as they stood for a minute looking on, "that this would be just the thing for us. If we could make an arrangement with the captain of one of these peat boats we might hide a number of men in the hold and cover them with peat. A place might be built large enough, I should think, to hold seventy or eighty men, and yet be room for a quantity of peat to be stowed over them."

"A capital idea," Captain Heraugiere said. "The peat comes from above the town. We must find out where the barges are loaded, and try to get at one of the captains."

After a short walk through the town they returned to the boat. The fisherman had already sold out his stock, and was glad at seeing his passengers return earlier than he expected; but as the guard was standing by he rated them severely for keeping him waiting so long, and with a muttered excuse they took their places in the boat and rowed down the river.

"I want you to put us ashore on the left bank as soon as we are our of sight of the town," Captain Heraugiere said. "As it will be heavy work getting your boat back with only two of you, I will give you a couple of crowns beyond the amount I bargained with you for."

"That will do well enough," the man said. "We have got the tide with us, and can drop down at our leisure."

As soon as they were landed they made a wide detour to avoid the town, and coming down again upon the river above it, followed its banks for three miles, when they put up at a little inn in the small village of Leur on its bank. They had scarcely sat down to a meal when a man came in and called for supper. The landlord placed another plate at the table near them, and the man at once got into conversation with them, and they learnt that he was master of a peat boat that had that morning left Breda empty.

"We were in Breda ourselves this morning," Captain Heraugiere said, "and saw a peat boat unloading there. There seemed to be a brisk demand for the fuel."

"Yes; it is a good trade at present," the man said. "There are only six of us who have permits to enter the port, and it is as much as we can do to keep the town supplied with fuel; for, you see, at any moment the river may be frozen up, so the citizens need to keep a good stock in hand. I ought not to grumble, since I reap the benefit of the Spanish regulations; but all these restrictions on trade come mighty hard upon the people of Breda. It was not so in the old time."

After supper was over Captain Heraugiere ordered a couple of flasks of spirits, and presently learned from the boatman that his name was Adrian Van de Berg, and that he had been at one time a servant in the household of William of Orange. Little by little Captain Heraugiere felt his way, and soon found that the boatman was an enthusiastic patriot. He then confided to him that he himself was an officer in the State's service, and had come to Breda to ascertain whether there was any possibility of capturing the town by surprise.

"We hit on a plan today," he said, "which promises a chance of success; but it needs the assistance of one ready to risk his life."

"I am ready to risk my life in any enterprise that has a fair chance of success," the boatman said, "but I do not see how I can be of much assistance."

"You can be of the greatest assistance if you will, and will render the greatest service to your country if you will join in our plan. What we propose is, that we should construct a shelter of boards four feet high in the bottom of your boat, leading from your little cabin aft right up to the bow. In this I calculate we could stow seventy men; then the peat could be piled over it, and if you entered the port somewhat late in the afternoon you could manage that it was not unladen so as to uncover the roof of our shelter before work ceased for the night. Then we could sally out, overpower the guard on the quay, make for one of the gates, master the guard there, and open it to our friends without."

"It is a bold plan and a good one," Van de Berg said, "and I am ready to run my share of the risk with you. I am so well known in Breda that they do not search the cargo very closely when I arrive, and I see no reason why the party hidden below should not escape observation. I will undertake my share of the business if you decide to carry it out. I served the prince for fifteen years, and am ready to serve his son. There are plenty of planks to be obtained at a place three miles above here, and it would not take many hours to construct the false deck. If you send a messenger here giving me two days' notice, it shall be built and the peat stowed on it by the time you arrive."

It was late at night before the conversation was concluded, and the next morning Captain Heraugiere and Lionel started on their return, struck the river some miles below Breda, obtained a passage over the river in a passing boat late in the afternoon, and, sleeping at Willemstad, went on board their boat next morning and returned to Rotterdam. It was arranged that Lionel should say nothing about their journey until Captain Heraugiere had opened the subject to Prince Maurice.

"You are back before your time," Sir Francis Vere said when Lionel reported himself for duty. "Has anything come of this project of yours, whatever it may be?"

"We hope so, sir, Captain Heraugiere will make his report to Prince Maurice. He is the leader of the party, and therefore he thought it best that he should report to Prince Maurice, who, if he thinks well of it, will of course communicate with you."

The next day a message arrived from Voorne requesting Sir Francis Vere to proceed thither to discuss with the prince a matter of importance. He returned after two days' absence, and presently sent for Lionel.

"This is a rare enterprise that Captain Heraugiere has proposed to the prince," he said, "and promises well for success. It is to be kept a profound secret, and a few only will know aught of it until it is executed. Heraugiere is of course to have command of the party which is to be hidden in the barge, and is to pick out eighty men from the garrisons of Gorcum and Lowesteyn. He has begged that you shall be of the party, as he says that the whole matter was in the first case suggested to him by you. The rest of the men and officers will be Dutch."

A fortnight later, on the 22nd of February, Sir Francis Vere on his return from the Hague, where Prince Maurice now was, told Lionel that all was arranged. The message had come down from Van de Berg that the hiding place was constructed. They were to join Heraugiere the next day.

On the 24th of February the little party starred. Heraugiere had chosen young, active, and daring men. With him were Captains Logier and Fervet, and Lieutenant Held. They embarked on board a vessel, and were landed near the mouth of the Mark, as De Berg was this time going to carry the peat up the river instead of down, fearing that the passage of seventy men through the country would attract attention. The same night Prince Maurice, Sir Francis Vere, Count Hohenlohe, and other officers sailed to Willemstad, their destination having been kept a strict secret from all but those engaged in the enterprise. Six hundred English troops, eight hundred Dutch, and three hundred cavalry had been drawn from different garrisons, and were also to land at Willemstad.

When Heraugiere's party arrived at the point agreed on at eleven o'clock at night, Van de Berg was not there, nor was the barge; and angry and alarmed at his absence they searched about for him for hours, and at last found him in the village of Terheyde. He made the excuse that he had overslept himself, and that he was afraid the plot had been discovered. As everything depended upon his cooperation, Heraugiere abstained from the angry reproaches which the strange conduct of the man had excited; and as it was now too late to do anything that night, a meeting was arranged for the following evening, and a message was despatched to the prince telling him that the expedition was postponed for a day. On their return, the men all gave free vent to their indignation.

"I have no doubt," Heraugiere said, "that the fellow has turned coward now that the time has come to face the danger. It is one thing to talk about a matter as long as it is far distant, but another to look it in the face when it is close at hand. I do not believe that he will come tomorrow.

By England's Aid: or The Freeing

"If he does not he will deserve hanging," Captain Logier said; "after all the trouble he has given in getting the troops together, and after bringing the prince himself over."

"It will go very near hanging if not quite," Heraugiere muttered. "If he thinks that he is going to fool us with impunity, he is mightily mistaken. If he is a wise man he will start at daybreak, and get as far away as he can before nightfall if he does not mean to come."

The next day the party remained in hiding in a barn, and in the evening again went down to the river. There was a barge lying there laden high with turf. A general exclamation of satisfaction broke from all when they saw it. There were two men on it. One landed and came to meet them.

"Where is Van de Berg?" Captain Heraugiere asked as he came up.

"He is ill and unable to come, but has sent you this letter. My brother and myself have undertaken the business."

The letter merely said that the writer was too ill to come, but had sent in his place his two nephews, one or other of whom always accompanied him, and who could be trusted thoroughly to carry out the plan. The party at once went on board the vessel, descended into the little cabin aft, and then passed through a hole made by the removal of two planks into the hold that had been prepared for them. Heraugiere remained on deck, and from time to time descended to inform those below of the progress being made. It was slow indeed, for a strong wind laden with sleet blew directly down the river. Huge blocks of ice floated down, and the two boatmen with their poles had the greatest difficulty in keeping the boat's head up the stream.

At last the wind so increased that navigation became impossible, and the barge was made fast against the bank. From Monday night until Thursday morning the gale continued. Progress was impossible, and the party cramped up in the hold suffered greatly from hunger and thirst. On Thursday evening they could sustain it no longer and landed. They were for a time scarce able to walk, so cramped were their limbs by their long confinement, and made their way up painfully to a fortified building called Nordand, standing far from any other habitations. Here they obtained food and drink, and remained until eleven at night. One of the boatmen came to them with news that the wind had changed, and was now blowing in from the sea. They again took their places on board,

177

but the water was low in the river, and it was difficult work passing the shallows, and it was not until Saturday afternoon that they passed the boom below the town and entered the inner harbour.

An officer of the guard came off in a boat and boarded the barge. The weather was so bitterly cold that he at once went into the little cabin and there chatted with the two boatmen. Those in the hold could hear every word that was said, and they almost held their breath, for the slightest noise would betray them. After a while the officer got into his boat again, saying he would send some men off to warp the vessel into the castle dock, as the fuel was required by the garrison there. As the barge was making its way towards the watergate, it struck upon a hidden obstruction in the river and began to leak rapidly. The situation of those in the hold was now terrible, for in a few minutes the water rose to their knees, and the choice seemed to be presented to them of being drowned like rats there, or leaping overboard, in which case they would be captured and hung without mercy. The boatmen plied the pumps vigorously, and in a short time a party of Italian soldiers arrived from the shore and towed the vessel into the inner harbour, and made her fast close to the guard house of the castle. A party of labourers at once came on board and began to unload the turf; the need of fuel both in the town and castle being great, for the weather had been for some time bitterly cold.

A fresh danger now arose. The sudden immersion in the icy water in the close cabin brought on a sudden inclination to sneeze and cough. Lieutenant Held, finding himself unable to repress his cough, handed his dagger to Lionel Vickars, who happened to be sitting next to him, and implored him to stab him to the heart lest his cough might betray the whole party; but one of the boatmen who was standing close to the cabin heard the sounds, and bade his companion go on pumping with as much noise and clatter as possible, while he himself did the same, telling those standing on the wharf alongside that the boat was almost full of water. The boatmen behaved with admirable calmness and coolness, exchanging jokes with acquaintances on the quay, keeping up a lively talk, asking high prices for their peat, and engaging in long and animated bargains so as to prevent the turf from being taken too rapidly ashore.

At last, when but a few layers of turf remained over the roof of the hold, the elder brother told the men unloading that it was getting too dark, and he himself was too tired and worn out to attend to things any longer. He therefore gave the man some money and told them to go to the nearest public house to drink his health, and to return the first thing in the morning to finish unloading. The younger of the two brothers had already left the boat. He made his way through the town, and started at full speed to carry the news to Prince Maurice that the barge had arrived safely in the town, and the attempt would be made at midnight; also of the fact they had learned from those on the wharf, that the governor had heard a rumour that a force had landed somewhere on the coast, and had gone off again to Gertruydenberg in all haste, believing that some design was on foot against that town. His son Paolo was again in command of the garrison.

A little before midnight Captain Heraugiere told his comrades that the hour had arrived, and that only by the most desperate bravery could they hope to succeed, while death was the certain consequence of failure. The band were divided into two companies. He himself with one was to attack the main guard house; the other, under Fervet, was to seize the arsenal of the fortress. Noiselessly they stole out from their hiding place, and formed upon the wharf within the inclosure of the castle. Heraugiere moved straight upon the guard house. The sentry was secured instantly; but the slight noise was heard, and the captain of the watch ran out, but was instantly cut down.

Others came our with torches, but after a brief fight were driven into the guard house; when all were shot down through the doors and windows. Captain Ferver and his band had done equally well. The magazine of the castle was seized, and its defenders slain. Paolo Lanzavecchia made a sally from the palace with a few of his adherents, but was wounded and driven back; and the rest of the garrison of the castle, ignorant of the strength of the force that had thus risen as it were from the earth upon them, fled panic stricken, not even pausing to destroy the bridge between the castle and the town.

Young Paolo Lanzavecchia now began a parley with the assailants; but while the negotiations were going on Hohenlohe with his cavalry came up — having been apprised by the boatman that the attempt was about to be made — battered down the palisade near the watergate, and entered the castle. A short time afterwards Prince Maurice, Sir Francis Vere, and other officers arrived with the main body of the troops. But the fight was over before even Hohenlohe arrived; forty of the garrison being killed, and not a single man of the seventy assailants. The burgomaster, finding that the castle had fallen, and that a strong force had arrived, then sent a trumpeter to the castle to arrange for the capitulation of the town, which was settled on the following terms:— All plundering was commuted for the payment of two months' pay to every soldier engaged in the affair. All who chose might leave the city, with full protection to life and property. Those who were willing to remain were not to be molested in their consciences or households with regard to religion.

The news of the capture of Breda was received with immense enthusiasm throughout Holland. It was the first offensive operation that had been successfully undertaken, and gave new hope to the patriots.

Parma was furious at the cowardice with which five companies of foot and one of horse — all picked troops — had fled before the attack of seventy Hollanders. Three captains were publicly beheaded in Brussels and a fourth degraded to the ranks, while Lanzavecchia was deprived of the command of Gertruydenberg.

For some months before the assault upon Breda the army of Holland had been gaining vastly in strength and organization. Prince Maurice, aided by his cousin Lewis William, stadholder of Friesland, had been hard at work getting it into a state of efficiency. Lewis William, a man of great energy and military talent, saw that the use of solid masses of men in the field was no longer fitted to a state of things when the improvements in firearms of all sorts had entirely changed the condition of war. He therefore reverted to the old Roman methods, and drilled his soldiers in small bodies; teaching them to turn and wheel, advance or retreat, and perform all sorts of manoeuvres with regularity and order. Prince Maurice adopted the same plan in Holland, and the tactics so introduced proved so efficient that they were sooner or later adopted by all civilized nations.

At the time when William of Orange tried to relieve the hard pressed city of Haarlem, he could with the greatest difficulty muster three or four thousand men for the purpose. The army of the Netherlands was now 22,000 strong, of whom 2000 were cavalry. It was well disciplined, well equipped, and regularly paid, and was soon to prove that the pains bestowed upon it had not been thrown away. In the course of eighteen years that had followed the capture of Brill and the commencement of the struggle with Spain, the wealth and prosperity of Holland had enormously increased. The Dutch were masters of the sea coast, the ships of the Zeelanders closed every avenue to the interior, and while the commerce of Antwerp, Ghent, Bruges, and the other cities of the provinces that remained in the hands of the Spaniards was for the time destroyed, and their population fell off by a half, Holland benefited in proportion.

From all the Spanish provinces men of energy and wealth passed over in immense numbers to Holland, where they could pursue their commerce and industries — free from the exactions and cruelty under which they had for so many years groaned. The result was that the cities of Holland increased vastly in wealth and population, and the resources at the disposal of Prince Maurice enormously exceeded those with which his father had for so many years sustained the struggle.

For a while after the capture of Breda there was breathing time in Holland, and Maurice was busy in increasing and improving his army. Parma was fettered by the imperious commands of Philip, who had completely crippled him by withdrawing a considerable number of his troops for service in the war which he was waging with France. But above all, the destruction of the Armada, and with it of the naval supremacy of Spain, had changed the situation.

Holland was free to carry on her enterprises by sea, and had free communication and commerce with her English ally; while communication between Spain and the Netherlands was difficult. Reinforcements could no longer be sent by sea, and had to be sent across Europe from Italy. Parma was worn out by exertions, disappointment, and annoyance, and his health was seriously failing; while opposed to him were three young commanders — Maurice, Lewis William, and Francis Vere — all men of military genius and full of confidence and energy.

CHAPTER XV. A SLAVE IN BARBARY

The Terifa had left port but a few hours when a strong wind rose from the north, and rapidly increased in violence until it was blowing a gale. "Inez is terribly ill," Gerald said when he met Geoffrey on deck the following morning.

"I believe at the present moment she would face her father and risk everything if she could but be put on shore."

"I can well imagine that. However, she will think otherwise tomorrow or next day. I believe these Mediterranean storms do not last long. There is no fear of six weeks of bad weather such as we had when we were last afloat together."

"No. I have just been speaking to the captain. He says they generally blow themselves out in two or three days; but still, even that is not a pleasant lookout. These vessels are not like your English craft, which seem to be able to sail almost in the eye of the wind. They are lubberly craft, and badly handled; and if this gale lasts for three days we shall be down on the Barbary coast, and I would rather risk another journey through Spain than get down so near the country of the Moors."

"I can understand that," Geoffrey agreed. "However, I see there are some thirty soldiers forward on their way to join one of the regiments in Naples, so we ought to be able to beat off any corsair that might come near us."

"Yes; but if we got down on their coast we might be attacked by half a dozen of them," Gerald said. "However, one need not begin to worry one's self at present; the gale may abate within a few hours."

At the end of the second day the wind went down suddenly; and through the night the vessel rolled heavily, for the sea was still high, and there was not a breath of wind to fill her sails and steady her. By the morning the sea had gone down, but there was still an absence of wind.

"We have had a horrible night," Gerald remarked, "but we may think ourselves fortunate indeed," and he pointed to the south, where the land was plainly visible at a distance of nine or ten miles. "If the gale had continued to blow until now we should have been on shore long before this."

"We are too near to be pleasant," Geoffrey said, "for they can see us as plainly as we can see the land. It is to be hoped that a breeze may spring up from the south before long and enable us to creep off the land. Unless I am greatly mistaken I can see the masts of some craft or other in a line with those white houses over there."

"I don't see them," Gerald replied, gazing intently in the direction in which Geoffrey pointed.

"Let us go up to the top, Gerald; we shall see her hull from there plainly enough."

On reaching the top Gerald saw at once that his friend's eyes had not deceived him.

"Yes, there is a vessel there sure enough, Geoffrey. I cannot see whether she has one or two masts, for her head is in this direction."

"That is not the worst of it," Geoffrey said, shading his eyes and gazing intently on the distant object. "She is rowing; I can see the light flash on her oars every stroke. That is a Moorish galley, and she is coming out towards us."

"I believe you are right," Gerald replied after gazing earnestly for some time. "Yes, I saw the flash of the oars then distinctly."

They at once descended to the deck and informed the captain of what they had seen. He hastily mounted to the top.

"There is no mistake about it," he said after looking intently for a short time; "it is one of the Barbary corsairs, and she is making out towards us. The holy saints preserve us from these bloodthirsty infidels."

"The saints will do their work if we do ours," Gerald remarked; "and we had best do as large a share as possible. What is the number of your crew, captain?"

"Nineteen men altogether."

"And there are thirty soldiers, and six male passengers in the cabin," Gerald said; "so we muster fifty–four. That ought to be enough to beat off the corsair."

On returning to the deck the captain informed the officer in charge of the troops on board that a Moorish pirate was putting off towards them, and that unless the wind came to their aid there was no chance of escaping a conflict with her.

"Then we must fight her, captain," the officer, who was still a youth, said cheerfully. "I have thirty men, of whom at least half are veterans. You have four cannon on board, and there are the crew and passengers."

"Fifty–four in all," Gerald said. "We ought to be able to make a good fight of it."

Orders were at once given, soldiers and crew were mustered and informed of the approaching danger.

"We have got to fight, men, and to fight hard," the young officer said; "for if we are beaten you know the result — either our throats will be cut or we shall have to row in their galleys for the rest of our lives. So there is not much choice."

In an hour the corsair was halfway between the coast and the vessel. By this time every preparation had been made for her reception. Arms had been distributed among the crew and such of the passengers as were not already provided, the guns had been cast loose and ammunition brought up, cauldrons of pitch were ranged along the bulwarks and fires lighted on slabs of stone placed beneath them. The coppers in the galley were already boiling.

"Now, captain," the young officer said, "do you and your sailors work the guns and ladle out the pitch and boiling water, and be in readiness to catch up their pikes and axes and aid in the defence if the villains gain a footing on the deck. I and my men and the passengers will do our best to keep them from climbing up."

The vessel was provided with sweeps, and the captain had in the first place proposed to man them; but Gerald pointed out that the corsair would row three feet to their one, and that it was important that all should be fresh and vigorous when the pirates came alongside. The idea had consequently been abandoned, and the vessel lay motionless in the water while the corsair was approaching. Inez, who felt better now that the motion had subsided, came on deck as the preparations were being made. Gerald told her of the danger that was approaching. She turned pale.

"This is dreadful, Gerald, I would rather face death a thousand times than be captured by the Moors."

"We shall beat them off, dear, never fear. They will not reckon upon the soldiers we have on board, and will expect an easy prize. I do not suppose that, apart from the galley slaves, they have more men on board than we have, and fighting as we do for liberty, each of us ought to be equal to a couple of these Moorish dogs. When the conflict begins you must go below."

"I shall not do that," Inez said firmly. "We will share the same fate whatever it may be, Gerald; and remember that whatever happens I will not live to be carried captive among them, I will stab myself to the heart if I see that all is lost."

"You shall come on deck if you will, Inez, when they get close alongside. I do not suppose there will be many shots fired — they will be in too great a hurry to board; but as long as they are shooting you must keep below. After that come up if you will. It would make a coward of me did I know that a chance shot might strike you."

"Very well, then, Gerald, to please you I will go down until they come alongside, then come what will I shall be on deck."

As the general opinion on board was that the corsairs would not greatly outnumber them, while they would be at a great disadvantage from the lowness of their vessel in the water, there was a general feeling of confidence, and the approach of the enemy was watched with calmness. When half a mile distant two puffs of smoke burst out from the corsair's bows. A moment later a shot struck the ship, and another threw up the water close to her stern. The four guns of the Tarifa had been brought over to the side on which the enemy was approaching, and these were now discharged. One of the shots carried away some oars on the starboard side of the galley, another struck her in the bow. There was a slight confusion on board; two or three oars were shifted over from the port to the starboard side, and, she continued her way.

The guns were loaded again, bags of bullets being this time inserted instead of balls. The corsairs fired once more, but their shots were unanswered; and with wild yells and shouts they approached the motionless Spanish vessel.

"She is crowded with men," Gerald remarked to Geoffrey. "She has far more on board than we reckoned on."

"We have not given them a close volley yet," Geoffrey replied. "If the guns are well aimed they will make matters equal."

The corsair was little more than her own length away when the captain gave the order, and the four guns poured their contents upon her crowded decks. The effect was terrible. The mass of men gathered in her bow in readiness to board as soon as she touched the

By England's Aid: or The Freeing

Tarifa were literally swept away. Another half minute she was alongside the Spaniard, and the Moors with wild shouts of vengeance tried to clamber on board.

But they had not reckoned upon meeting with more than the ordinary crew of a merchant ship. The soldiers discharged their arquebuses, and then with pike and sword opposed an impenetrable barrier to the assailants, while the sailors from behind ladled over the boiling pitch and water through intervals purposely left in the line of the defenders. The conflict lasted but a few minutes. Well nigh half the Moors had been swept away by the discharge of the cannon, and the rest, but little superior in numbers to the Spaniards, were not long before they lost heart, their efforts relaxed, and shouts arose to the galley slaves to row astern.

"Now, it is our turn!" the young officer cried. "Follow me, my men; we will teach the dogs a lesson." As he spoke he sprang from the bulwark down upon the deck of the corsair. Geoffrey, who was standing next to him, followed his example, as did five or six soldiers. They were instantly engaged in a hand to hand fight with the Moors. In the din and confusion they heard not the shouts of their comrades. After a minute's fierce fighting, Geoffrey, finding that he and his companions were being pressed back, glanced round to see why support did not arrive, and saw that there were already thirty feet of water between the two vessels. He was about to spring overboard, when the Moors made a desperate rush, his guard was beaten down, a blow from a Moorish scimitar fell on his head, and he lost consciousness.

It was a long time before he recovered. The first sound he was aware of was the creaking of the oars. He lay dreamily listening to this, and wondering what it meant until the truth suddenly flashed across him. He opened his eyes and looked round. A heavy weight lay across his legs, and he saw the young Spanish officer lying dead there. Several other Spaniards lay close by, while the deck was strewn with the corpses of the Moors. He understood at once what had happened. The vessels had drifted apart just as he sprang on board, cutting off those who had boarded the corsair from all assistance from their friends, and as soon as they had been overpowered the galley had started on her return to the port from which she had come out.

"At any rate," he said to himself, "Gerald and Inez are safe; that is a comfort, whatever comes of it."

186

By England's Aid: or The Freeing

It was not until the corsair dropped anchor near the shore that the dispirited Moors paid any attention to those by whom their deck was cumbered. Then the Spaniards were first examined. Four, who were dead, were at once tossed overboard. Geoffrey and two others who showed signs of life were left for the present, a bucket of water being thrown over each to revive them. The Moorish wounded and the dead were then lowered into boats and taken on shore for care or burial. Then Geoffrey and the two Spaniards were ordered to rise.

All three were able to do so with some difficulty, and were rowed ashore. They were received when they landed by the curses and execrations of the people of the little town, who would have torn them to pieces had not their captors marched them to the prison occupied by the galley slaves when on shore, and left them there. Most of the galley slaves were far too exhausted by their long row, and too indifferent to aught but their own sufferings, to pay any attention to the newcomers. Two or three, however, came up to them and offered to assist in bandaging their wounds. Their doublets had already been taken by their captors; but they now tore strips off their shirts, and with these staunched the bleeding of their wounds.

"It was lucky for you that five or six of our number were killed by that discharge of grape you gave us," one of them said, "or they would have thrown you overboard at once. Although, after all, death is almost preferable to such a life as ours."

"How long have you been here?" Geoffrey asked.

"I hardly know," the other replied; "one almost loses count of time here. But it is somewhere about ten years. I am sturdy, you see. Three years at most is the average of our life in the galleys, though there are plenty die before as many months have passed. I come of a hardy race. I am not a Spaniard. I was captured in an attack on a town in the West Indies, and had three years on board one of your galleys at Cadiz. Then she was captured by the Moors, and here I have been ever since."

"Then you must be an Englishman!" Geoffrey exclaimed in that language.

The man stared at him stupidly for a minute, and then burst into tears. "I have never thought to hear my own tongue again, lad," he said, holding out his hand. "Aye, I am English, and was one of Hawkins' men. But how come you to be in a Spanish ship? I have heard our masters say, when talking together, that there is war now between the English and Spaniards; that is, war at home. There has always been war out on the Spanish Main, but they know nothing of that."

"I was made prisoner in a fight we had with the great Spanish Armada off Gravelines," Geoffrey said.

"We heard a year ago from some Spaniards they captured that a great fleet was being prepared to conquer England; but no news has come to us since. We are the only galley here, and as our benches were full, the prisoners they have taken since were sent off at once to Algiers or other ports, so we have heard nothing. But I told the Spaniards that if Drake and Hawkins were in England when their great fleet got there, they were not likely to have it all their own way. Tell me all about it, lad. You do nor know how hungry I am for news from home."

Geoffrey related to the sailor the tale of the overthrow and destruction of the Armada, which threw him into an ecstasy of satisfaction.

"These fellows," he said, pointing to the other galley slaves, "have for the last year been telling me that I need not call myself an Englishman any more, for that England was only a part of Spain now. I will open their eyes a bit in the morning. But I won't ask you any more questions now; it is a shame to have made you talk so much after such a clip as you have had on the head."

Geoffrey turned round on the sand that formed their only bed, and was soon asleep, the last sound he heard being the chuckling of his companion over the discomfiture of the Armada.

In the morning the guard came in with a great dish filled with a sort of porridge of coarsely ground grain, boiled with water. In a corner of the yard were a number of calabashes, each composed of half a gourd. The slaves each dipped one of these into the vessel, and so ate their breakfast. Before beginning Geoffrey went to a trough, into which a jet of water was constantly falling from a small pipe, bathed his head and face, and took a long drink.

By England's Aid: or The Freeing

"We may be thankful," the sailor, who had already told him that his name was Stephen Boldero, said, "that someone in the old times laid on that water. If it had not been for that I do not know what we should have done, and a drink of muddy stuff once or twice a day is all we should have got. That there pure water is just the saving of us."

"What are we going to do now?" Geoffrey asked. "Does the galley go out every day?"

"Bless you, no; sometimes not once a month; only when a sail is made out in sight, and the wind is light enough to give us the chance of capturing her. Sometimes we go out on a cruise for a month at a time; but that is not often. At other times we do the work of the town, mend the roads, sweep up the filth, repair the quays; do anything, in fact, that wants doing. The work, except in the galleys, is not above a man's strength. Some men die under it, because the Spaniards lose heart and turn sullen, and then down comes the whip on their backs, and they break their hearts over it; but a man as does his best, and is cheerful and willing, gets on well enough except in the galleys.

"That is work that is. There is a chap walks up and down with a whip, and when they are chasing he lets it fall promiscuous, and even if you are rowing fit to kill yourself you do not escape it; but on shore here if you keep up your spirits things ain't altogether so bad. Now I have got you here to talk to in my own lingo I feel quite a different man. For although I have been here ten years, and can jabber in Spanish, I have never got on with these fellows; as is only natural, seeing that I am an Englishman and know all about their doings in the Spanish Main, and hate them worse than poison. Well, our time is up, so I am off. I do nor expect they will make you work till your wounds are healed a bit."

This supposition turned out correct, and for the next week Geoffrey was allowed to remain quietly in the yard when the gang went out to their work. At the end of that time his wound had closed, and being heartily sick of the monotony of his life, he voluntarily fell in by the side of Boldero when the gang was called to work. The overseer was apparently pleased at this evidence of willingness on the part of the young captive, and said something to him in his own tongue. This his companion translated as being an order that he was not to work too hard for the present.

"I am bound to say, mate, that these Moors are, as a rule, much better masters than the Spaniards. I have tried them both, and I would rather be in a Moorish galley than a Spanish one by a long way; except just when they are chasing a ship, and are half wild

189

with excitement. These Moors are not half bad fellows, while it don't seem to me that a Spaniard has got a heart in him. Then again, I do not think they are quite so hard on Englishmen as they are on Spaniards; for they hate the Spaniards because they drove them out of their country. Once or twice I have had a talk with the overseer when he has been in a special good humour, and he knows we hate the Spaniards as much as they do, and that though they call us all Christian dogs, our Christianity ain't a bit like that of the Spaniards. I shall let him know the first chance I have that you are English too, and I shall ask him to let you always work by the side of me."

As Stephen Boldero had foretold, Geoffrey did not find his work on shore oppressively hard. He did his best, and, as he and his companion always performed a far larger share of work than that done by any two of the Spaniards, they gained the goodwill of their overlooker, who, when a fortnight later the principal bey of the place sent down a request for two slaves to do some rough work in his garden, selected them for the work.

"Now we will just buckle to, lad," Stephen Boldero said. "This bey is the captain of the corsair, and he can make things a deal easier for us if he chooses; so we will not spare ourselves. He had one of the men up there two years ago, and kept him for some months, and the fellow found it so hard when he came back here again that he pined and died off in no time."

A guard took them to the bey's house, which stood on high ground behind the town. The bey came out to examine the men chosen for his work.

"I hear," he said, "that you are both English, and hate the Spaniards as much as we do. Well, if I find you work well, you will be well treated; if not, you will be sent back at once. Now, come with me, and I shall show you what you have to do."

The high wall at the back of the garden had been pulled down, and the bey intended to enlarge the inclosure considerably.

"You are first," he said, "to dig a foundation for the new wall along that line marked out by stakes. When that is done you will supply the masons with stone and mortar. When the wall is finished the new ground will all have to be dug deeply and planted with shrubs, under the superintendence of my gardener. While you are working here you will not return to the prison, but will sleep in that out house in the garden."

By England's Aid: or The Freeing

"You shall have no reason to complain of our work," Boldero said. "We Englishmen are no sluggards, and we do not want a man always looking after us as those lazy Spaniards do."

As soon as they were supplied with tools Geoffrey and his companion set to work. The trench for the foundations had to be dug three feet deep; and though the sun blazed fiercely down upon them, they worked unflinchingly. From time to time the bey's head servant came down to examine their progress, and occasionally watched them from among the trees. At noon he bade them lay aside their tools and come into the shed, and a slave boy brought them out a large dish of vegetables, with small pieces of meat in it.

"This is something like food," Stephen said as he sat down to it. "It is ten years since such a mess as this has passed my lips. I do not wonder that chap fell ill when he got back to prison if this is the sort of way they fed him here."

That evening the Moorish overseer reported to the bey that the two slaves had done in the course of the day as much work as six of the best native labourers could have performed, and that without his standing over them or paying them any attention whatever. Moved by the report, the bey himself went down to the end of the garden.

"It is wonderful," he said, stroking his beard. "Truly these Englishmen are men of sinews. Never have I seen so much work done by two men in a day. Take care of them, Mahmoud, and see that they are well fed; the willing servant should be well cared for."

The work went steadily on until the wall was raised, the ground dug, and the shrubs planted. It was some months before all this was done, and the two slaves continued to attract the observation and goodwill of the bey by their steady and cheerful labour. Their work began soon after sunrise, and continued until noon. Then they had three hours to themselves to eat their midday meal and doze in the shed, and then worked again until sunset. The bey often strolled down to the edge of the trees to watch them, and sometimes even took guests to admire the way in which these two Englishmen, although ignorant that any eyes were upon them, performed their work.

His satisfaction was evinced by the abundance of food supplied them, their meal being frequently supplemented by fruit and other little luxuries. Severely as they laboured, Geoffrey and his companion were comparatively happy. Short as was the time that the former had worked with the gang, he appreciated the liberty he now enjoyed, and especially congratulated himself upon being spared the painful life of a galley slave at sea. As to Boldero, the change from the prison with the companions he hated, its degrading work, and coarse and scanty food, made a new man of him.

He had been but two–and–twenty when captured by the Spaniards, and was now in the prime of life and strength. The work, which had seemed very hard to Geoffrey at first, was to him but as play, while the companionship of his countryman, his freedom from constant surveillance, the absence of all care, and the abundance and excellence of his food, filled him with new life; and the ladies of the bey's household often sat and listened to the strange songs that rose from the slaves toiling in the garden.

As the work approached its conclusion Geoffrey and his companion had many a talk over what would next befall them. There was one reason only that weighed in favour of the life with the slave gang. In their present position there was no possibility whatever, so far as they could discern, of effecting their escape; whereas, as slaves, should the galley in which they rowed be overpowered by any ship it attacked, they would obtain their freedom. The chance of this, however, was remote, as the fast–rowing galleys could almost always make their escape should the vessel they attacked prove too strong to be captured.

When the last bed had been levelled and the last shrub planted the superintendent told them to follow him into the house, as the bey was desirous of speaking with them. They found him seated on a divan.

"Christians," he said, "I have watched you while you have been at work, and truly you have not spared yourselves in my service, but have laboured for me with all your strength, well and willingly. I see now that it is true that the people of your nation differ much from the Spaniards, who are dogs.

"I see that trust is to be placed in you, and were you but true believers I would appoint you to a position where you could win credit and honour. As it is, I cannot place you over believers in the prophet; but neither am I willing that you should return to the gang from which I took you. I will, therefore, leave you free to work for yourselves. There are many of my friends who have seen you labouring, and will give you employment. It will be known in the place that you are under my protection, and that any who insult or ill treat you will be severely punished. Should you have any complaint to make, come freely to me and I will see that justice is done you.

"This evening a crier will go through the place proclaiming that the two English galley slaves have been given their freedom by me, and will henceforth live in the town without molestation from anyone, carrying on their work and selling their labour like true believers. The crier will inform the people that the nation to which you belong is at war with our enemies the Spaniards, and that, save as to the matter of your religion, you are worthy of being regarded as friends by all good Moslems. My superintendent will go down with you in the morning. I have ordered him to hire a little house for you and furnish it with what is needful, to recommend you to your neighbours, and to give you a purse of piastres with which to maintain yourselves until work comes to you."

Stephen Boldero expressed the warmest gratitude, on the part of his companion and himself, to the bey for his kindness.

"I have done but simple justice," the bey said, "and no thanks are necessary. Faithful work should have its reward, and as you have done to me so I do to you."

The next morning as they were leaving, a female slave presented them with a purse of silver, the gift of the bey's wife and daughters, who had often derived much pleasure from the songs of the two captives. The superintendent conducted them to a small hut facing the sea. It was furnished with the few articles that were, according to native ideas, necessary for comfort. There were cushions on the divan of baked clay raised about a foot above the floor, which served as a sofa during the day and as a bed at night. There was a small piece of carpet on the floor and a few cooking utensils on a shelf, and some dishes of burnt clay; and nothing more was required. There was, however, a small chest, in which, after the superintendent had left, they found two sets of garments as worn by the natives.

"This is a comfort indeed," Geoffrey said. "My clothes are all in rags, and as for yours the less we say about them the better. I shall feel like a new man in these things."

"I shall be glad myself," Stephen agreed, "for the clothes they give the galley slaves are scarce decent for a Christian man to wear. My consolation has been that if they had been shocked by our appearance they would have given us more clothes; but as they did not mind it there was no reason why I should. Still it would be a comfort to be clean and decent again."

For the first few days the natives of the place looked askance at these Christians in their midst, but the bey's orders had been peremptory that no insults should be offered to them. Two days after their liberation one of the principal men of the place sent for them and employed them in digging the foundations for a fountain, and a deep trench of some hundred yards in length for the pipe bringing water to it. After that they had many similar jobs, receiving always the wages paid to regular workmen, and giving great satisfaction by their steady toil. Sometimes when not otherwise engaged they went out in boats with fishermen, receiving a portion of the catch in payment for their labours.

So some months passed away. Very frequently they talked over methods of escape. The only plan that seemed at all possible was to take a boat and make out to sea; but they knew that they would be pursued, and if overtaken would revert to their former life at the galleys, a change which would be a terrible one indeed after the present life of freedom and independence. They knew, too, that they might be days before meeting with a ship, for all traders in the Mediterranean hugged the northern shores as much as possible in order to avoid the dreaded corsairs, and there would be a far greater chance of their being recaptured by one of the Moorish cruisers than of lighting upon a Christian trader.

"It is a question of chance," Stephen said, "and when the chance comes we will seize it; but it is no use our giving up a life against which there is not much to be said, unless some fair prospect of escape offers itself to us."

CHAPTER XVI. THE ESCAPE

"In one respect," Geoffrey said, as they were talking over their chance of escape, "I am sorry that the bey has behaved so kindly to us."

"What is that?" Stephen Boldero asked in surprise.

"Well, I was thinking that were it not for that we might manage to contrive some plan of escape in concert with the galley slaves, get them down to the shore here, row off to the galley, overpower the three or four men who live on board her, and make off with her. Of course we should have had to accumulate beforehand a quantity of food and some barrels of water, for I have noticed that when they go out they always take their stores on board with them, and bring on shore on their return what has nor been consumed. Still, I suppose that could be managed. However, it seems to me that our hands are tied in that direction by the kindness of the bey. After his conduct to us it would be ungrateful in the extreme for us to carry off his galley."

"So it would, Geoffrey. Besides I doubt whether the plan would succeed. You may be sure the Spaniards are as jealous as can be of the good fortune that we have met with, and were we to propose such a scheme to them the chances are strongly in favour of one of them trying to better his own position by denouncing us. I would only trust them as far as I can see them. No, if we ever do anything it must be done by ourselves. There is no doubt that if some night when there is a strong wind blowing from the southeast we were to get on board one of these fishing boats, hoist a sail, and run before it, we should not be far off from the coast of Spain before they started to look for us. But what better should we be there? We can both talk Spanish well enough, but we could not pass as Spaniards. Besides, they would find out soon enough that we were not Catholics, and where should we be then? Either sent to row in their galleys or clapped into the dungeons of the Inquisition, and like enough burnt alive at the stake. That would be out of the frying pan into the fire with vengeance."

"I think we might pass as Spaniards," Geoffrey said; "for there is a great deal of difference between the dialects of the different provinces, and confined as you have been for the last ten years with Spanish sailors you must have caught their way of talking. Still, I agree with you it will be better to wait for a bit longer for any chance that may occur rather than risk landing in Spain again, where even if we passed as natives we should have as hard work to get our living as we have here, and with no greater chance of making our way home again."

During the time that they had been captives some three or four vessels had been brought in by the corsair. The men composing the crews had been either sold as slaves to Moors or Arabs in the interior or sent to Algiers, which town lay over a hundred miles to the east. They were of various nationalities, Spanish, French, and Italian, as the two friends learned from the talk of the natives, for they always abstained from going near the point where the prisoners were landed, as they were powerless to assist the unfortunate captives in any way, and the sight of their distress was very painful to them.

195

By England's Aid: or The Freeing

One day, however, they learned from the people who were running down to the shore to see the captives landed from a ship that had been brought in by the corsair during the night, that there were two or three women among the captives. This was the first time that any females had been captured since their arrival at the place, for women seldom travelled far from their homes in those days, except the wives of high officials journeying in great ships that were safe from the attack of the Moorish corsairs.

"Let us go down and see them," Boldero said. "I have not seen the face of a white woman for nine years."

"I will go if you like," Geoffrey said. "They will not guess that we are Europeans, for we are burnt as dark as the Moors."

They went down to the landing place. Eight men and two women were landed from the boat. These were the sole survivors of the crew.

"They are Spaniards," Boldero said. "I pity that poor girl. I suppose the other woman is her servant."

The girl, who was about sixteen years of age, was very pale, and had evidently been crying terribly. She did not seem to heed the cries and threats with which the townspeople as usual assailed the newly arrived captives, but kept her eyes fixed upon one of the captives who walked before her.

"That is her father, no doubt," Geoffrey said. "It is probably her last look at him. Come away, Stephen; I am awfully sorry we came here. I shall not be able to get that girl's face out of my mind for I don't know how long."

Without a word they went back to their hut. They had no particular work that day. Geoffrey went restlessly in and out, sometimes pacing along the strand, sometimes coming in and throwing himself on the divan. Stephen Boldero went on quietly mending a net that had been damaged the night before, saying nothing, but glancing occasionally with an amused look at his companion's restless movements. Late in the afternoon Geoffrey burst our suddenly: "Stephen, we must try and rescue that girl somehow from her fate."

By England's Aid: or The Freeing

"I supposed that was what it was coming to," Boldero said quietly. "Well, let me hear all about it. I know you have been thinking it over ever since morning. What are your ideas?"

"I do not know that I have any ideas beyond getting her and her father down to a boat and making off."

"Well, you certainly have not done much if you haven't got farther than that," Stephen said drily. "Now, if you had spent the day talking it over with me instead of wandering about like one out of his mind, we should have got a great deal further than that by this time. However, I have been thinking for you. I know what you young fellows are. As soon as I saw that girl's face and looked at you I was dead certain there was an end of peace and quietness, and that you would be bent upon some plan of getting her off. It did not need five minutes to show that I was right; and I have been spending my time thinking, while you have thrown yours away in fidgeting.

"Well, I think it is worth trying. Of course it will be a vastly more difficult job getting the girl and her father away than just taking a boat and sailing off as we have often talked of doing. Then, on the other hand, it would altogether alter our position afterwards. By his appearance and hers I have no doubt he is a well to do trader, perhaps a wealthy one. He walked with his head upright when the crowd were yelling and cursing, and is evidently a man of courage and determination. Now, if we had reached the Spanish coast by ourselves we should have been questioned right and left, and, as I have said all along, they would soon have found that we were not Spaniards, for we could not have said where we came from, or given our past history, or said where our families lived. But it would be altogether different if we landed with them. Every one would be interested about them. We should only be two poor devils of sailors who had escaped with them, and he would help to pass it off and get us employment; so that the difficulty that has hitherto prevented us from trying to escape is very greatly diminished. Now, as to getting them away. Of course she has been taken up to the bey's, and no doubt he will send her as a present to the bey of Algiers. I know that is what has been done several times before when young women have been captured.

"I have been thinking it over, and I do not see a possibility of getting to speak to her as long as she is at the bey's. I do not see that it can be done anyhow. She will be indoors most of the time, and if she should go into the garden there would be other women with

197

her. Our only plan, as far as I can see at present, would be to carry her off from her escort on the journey. I do not suppose she will have more than two, or at most three, mounted men with her, and we ought to be able to dispose of them. As to her father, the matter is comparatively easy. We know the ways of the prison, and I have no doubt we can get him out somehow; only there is the trouble of the question of time. She has got to be rescued and brought back and hidden somewhere till nightfall, he has got to be set free the same evening, and we have to embark early enough to be well out of sight before daylight; and maybe there will not be a breath of wind stirring. It is a tough job, Geoffrey, look at it which way you will."

"It is a tough job," Geoffrey agreed. "I am afraid the escort would be stronger than you think. A present of this kind to the bey is regarded as important, and I should say half a dozen horsemen at least will be sent with her. In that case an attempt at rescue would be hopeless. We have no arms, and if we had we could not kill six mounted men; and if even one escaped, our plans would be all defeated. The question is, would they send her by land? It seems to me quite as likely that they might send her by water."

"Yes, that is likely enough, Geoffrey. In that case everything would depend upon the vessel he sent her in. If it is the great galley there is an end of it; if it is one of their little coasters it might be managed. We are sure to learn that before long. The bey might keep her for a fortnight or so, perhaps longer, for her to recover somewhat from the trouble and get up her good looks again, so as to add to the value of the present. If she were well and bright she would be pretty enough for anything. In the meantime we can arrange our plans for getting her father away. Of course if she goes with a big escort on horseback, or if she goes in the galley, there is an end of our plans. I am ready to help you, Geoffrey, if there is a chance of success; but I am not going to throw away my life if there is not, and unless she goes down in a coaster there is an end of the scheme."

"I quite agree to that," Geoffrey replied; "we cannot accomplish impossibilities."

They learned upon the following day that three of the newly arrived captives were to take the places of the galley slaves who had been killed in the capture of the Spanish ship, which had defended itself stoutly, and that the others were to be sold for work in the interior.

By England's Aid: or The Freeing

"It is pretty certain," Boldero said, "that the trader will not be one of the three chosen for the galley. The work would break him down in a month. That makes that part of the business easier, for we can get him away on the journey inland, and hide him up here until his daughter is sent off."

Geoffrey looked round the bare room.

"Well, I do not say as how we could hide him here," Boldero said in answer to the look, "but we might hide him somewhere among the sand hills outside the place, and take him food at night."

"Yes, we might do that," Geoffrey agreed. "That could be managed easily enough, I should think, for there are clumps of bushes scattered all over the sand hills half a mile back from the sea. The trouble will be if we get him here, and find after all that we cannot rescue his daughter."

"That will make no difference," Boldero said. "In that case we will make off with him alone. Everything else will go on just the same. Of course, I should be very sorry not to save the girl; but, as far as we are concerned, if we save the father it will answer our purpose."

Geoffrey made no reply. Just at that moment his own future was a very secondary matter, in comparison, to the rescue of this unhappy Spanish girl.

Geoffrey and his companion had been in the habit of going up occasionally to the prison. They had won over the guard by small presents, and were permitted to go in and out with fruit and other little luxuries for the galley slaves. They now abstained from going near the place, in order that no suspicion might fall upon them after his escape of having had any communication with the Spanish trader.

Shortly after the arrival of the captives two merchants from the interior came down, and Geoffrey learned that they had visited the prison, and had made a bargain with the bey for all the captives except those transferred to the galley. The two companions had talked the matter over frequently, and had concluded it was best that only one of them should be engaged in the adventure, for the absence of both might be noticed. After some discussion it was agreed that Geoffrey should undertake the task, and that Boldero should go alone to the house where they were now at work, and should mention that his friend was unwell, and was obliged to remain at home for the day.

As they knew the direction in which the captives would be taken Geoffrey started before daybreak, and kept steadily along until he reached a spot where it was probable they would halt for the night. It was twenty miles away, and there was here a well of water and a grove of trees. Late in the afternoon he saw the party approaching. It consisted of the merchants, two armed Arabs, and the five captives, all of whom were carrying burdens. They were crawling painfully along, overpowered by the heat of the sun, by the length of the journey, and by the weight they carried. Several times the Arabs struck them heavily with their sticks to force them to keep up.

Geoffrey retired from the other side of the clump of trees, and lay down in a depression of the sand hills until darkness came on, when he again entered the grove, and crawling cautiously forward made his way close up to the party. A fire was blazing, and a meal had been already cooked and eaten. The traders and the two Arabs were sitting by the fire; the captives were lying extended on the ground. Presently, at the command of one of the Arabs, they rose to their feet and proceeded to collect some more pieces of wood for the fire. As they returned the light fell on the gray hair of the man upon whom Geoffrey had noticed that the girl's eyes were fixed.

He noted the place where he lay down, and had nothing to do now but to wait until the party were asleep. He felt sure that no guard would be set, for any attempt on the part of the captives to escape would be nothing short of madness. There was nowhere for them to go, and they would simply wander about until they died of hunger and exhaustion, or until they were recaptured, in which case they would be almost beaten to death. In an hour's time the traders and their men lay down by the fire, and all was quiet. Geoffrey crawled round until he was close to the Spaniard. He waited until he felt sure that the Arabs were asleep, and then crawled up to him. The man started as he touched him.

"Silence, senor," Geoffrey whispered in Spanish; "I am a friend, and have come to rescue you."

"I care not for life; a few days of this work will kill me, and the sooner the better. I have nothing to live for. They killed my wife the other day, and my daughter is a captive in their hands. I thank you, whoever you are, but I will not go."

"We are going to try to save your daughter too," Geoffrey whispered; "we have a plan for carrying you both off."

The words gave new life to the Spaniard. "In that case, sir, I am ready. Whoever you are whom God has sent to my aid I will follow you blindly, whatever comes of it."

Geoffrey crawled away a short distance, followed by the Spaniard. As soon as they were well beyond the faint light now given out by the expiring fire they rose to their feet, and gaining the track took their way on the backward road. As soon as they were fairly away, Geoffrey explained to the Spaniard who he was, and how he had undertaken to endeavour to rescue him. The joy and gratitude of the Spaniard were too deep for words, and he uttered his thanks in broken tones. When they had walked about a mile Geoffrey halted.

"Sit down here," he said. "I have some meat and fruit here and a small skin of water. We have a long journey before us, for we must get near the town you left this morning before daybreak, and you must eat to keep up your strength."

"I did not think," the Spaniard said, "when we arrived at the well, that I could have walked another mile had my life depended upon it. Now I feel a new man, after the fresh hope you have given me. I no longer feel the pain of my bare feet or the blisters the sun has raised on my naked back. I am struggling now for more than life — for my daughter. You shall not find me to fail, sir."

All night they toiled on. The Spaniard kept his promise, and utterly exhausted as he was, and great as was the pain in his limbs, held on bravely. With the first dawn of morning they saw the line of the sea before them. They now turned off from the track, and in another half hour the Spaniard took shelter in a clump of bushes in a hollow, while Geoffrey, having left with him the remainder of the supply of provisions and water, pursued his way and reached the hut just as the sun was shining in the east, and without having encountered a single person.

"Well, have you succeeded?" Boldero asked eagerly, as he entered.

"Yes; I have got him away. He is in hiding within a mile of this place. He kept on like a hero. I was utterly tired myself, and how he managed to walk the distance after what he had gone through in the day is more than I can tell. His name is Mendez. He is a trader in

Cadiz, and owns many vessels. He was on his way to Italy, with his wife and daughter, in one of his own ships, in order to gratify the desire of his wife to visit the holy places at Rome. She was killed by a cannon shot during the fight, and his whole heart is now wrapped up in his daughter. And now, Stephen, I must lie down and sleep. You will have to go to work alone today again, and can truly say that I am still unfit for labour."

Four days later it became known in the little town that a messenger had arrived from the merchant who bought the slaves from the bey, saying that one of them had made his escape from their first halting place.

"The dog will doubtless die in the desert," the merchant wrote; "but if he should find his way down, or you should hear of him as arriving at any of the villages, I pray you to send him up to me with a guard. I will so treat him that it will be a lesson to my other slaves not to follow his example."

Every evening after dark Geoffrey went out with a supply of food and water to the fugitive. For a week he had no news to give him as to his daughter; but on the eighth night he said that he and his companion had that morning been sent by the bey on board the largest of the coasting vessels in the port, with orders to paint the cabins and put them in a fit state for the reception of a personage of importance.

"This is fortunate, indeed," Geoffrey went on. "No doubt she is intended for the transport of your daughter. Her crew consists of a captain and five men, but at present they are living ashore; and as we shall be going backwards and forwards to her, we ought to have little difficulty in getting on board and hiding away in the hold before she starts. I think everything promises well for the success of our scheme."

The bey's superintendent came down the next day to see how matters were going on on board the vessel. The painting was finished that evening, and the next day two slaves brought down a quantity of hangings and cushions, which Geoffrey and his companion assisted the superintendent to hang up and place in order. Provisions and water had already been taken on board, and they learnt that the party who were to sail in her would come off early the next morning.

At midnight Geoffrey, Boldero, and the Spaniard came down to the little port, embarked in a fisherman's boat moored at the stairs, and noiselessly rowed off to the vessel. They mounted on to her deck barefooted. Boldero was the last to leave the boat, giving her a vigorous push with his foot in the direction of the shore, from which the vessel was but some forty yards away. They descended into the hold, where they remained perfectly quiet until the first light of dawn enabled them to see what they were doing, and then moved some baskets full of vegetables, and concealed themselves behind them.

A quarter of an hour later they heard a boat come alongside, and the voices of the sailors. Then they heard the creaking of cordage as the sails were let fall in readiness for a start. Half an hour later another boat came alongside. There was a trampling of feet on the deck above them, and the bey's voice giving orders. A few minutes later the anchor was raised, there was more talking on deck, and then they heard a boat push off, and knew by the rustle of water against the planks beside them that the vessel was under way.

The wind was light and the sea perfectly calm, and beyond the slight murmur of the water, those below would not have known that the ship was in motion. It was very hot down in the hold, but fortunately the crew had nor taken the trouble to put on the hatches, and at times a faint breath of air could be felt below. Geoffrey and his companion talked occasionally in low tones; but the Spaniard was so absorbed by his anxiety as to the approaching struggle, and the thought that he might soon clasp his daughter to his arms, that he seldom spoke.

No plans could be formed as to the course they were to take, for they could not tell whether those of the crew off duty would retire to sleep in the little forecastle or would lie down on deck. Then, too, they were ignorant as to the number of men who had come on board with the captive. The overseer had mentioned the day before that he was going, and it was probable that three or four others would accompany him. Therefore they had to reckon upon ten opponents. Their only weapons were three heavy iron bolts, some two feet long. These Boldero had purchased in exchange for a few fish, when a prize brought in was broken up as being useless for the purposes of the Moors.

"What I reckon is," he said, "that you and I ought to be able to settle two apiece of these fellows before they fairly know what is happening. The Don ought very well to account for another. So that only leaves five of them; and five against three are no odds worth speaking of, especially when the five are woke up by a sudden attack, and ain't sure how many there are against them. I don't expect much trouble over the affair."

By England's Aid: or The Freeing

"I don't want to kill more of the poor fellows than I can help," Geoffrey said.

"No more do I; but you see it's got to be either killing or being killed, and I am perfectly certain which I prefer. Still, as you say, if the beggars are at all reasonable I ain't for hurting them, but the first few we have got to hit hard. When we get matters a little even, we can speak them fair."

The day passed slowly, and in spite of their bent and cramped position Geoffrey and Stephen Boldero dozed frequently. The Spaniard never closed an eye. He was quite prepared to take his part in the struggle; and as he was not yet fifty years of age, his assistance was not to be despised. But the light hearted carelessness of his companions, who joked under their breath, and laughed and ate unconcernedly with a life and death struggle against heavy odds before them, surprised him much.

As darkness came on the party below became wakeful. Their time was coming now, and they had no doubt whatever as to the result. Their most formidable opponents would be the men who had come on board with the bey's superintendent, as these, no doubt, would be fully armed. As for the sailors, they might have arms on board, but these would nor be ready to hand, and it was really only with the guards they would have to deal.

"I tell you what I think would be a good plan, Stephen," Geoffrey said suddenly. "You see, there is plenty of spare line down here; if we wait until they are all asleep we can go round and tie their legs together, or put ropes round their ankles and fasten them to ring bolts. If we could manage that without waking them, we might capture the craft without shedding any blood, and might get them down into the hold one after the other."

"I think that is a very good plan," Stephen agreed. "I do not like the thought of knocking sleeping men on the head any more than you do; and if we are careful, we might get them all tied up before an alarm is given. There, the anchor has gone down. I thought very likely they would not sail at night. That is capital. You may be sure that they will be pretty close inshore, and they probably will have only one man on watch; and as likely as not even one, for they will nor dream of any possible danger."

For another two hours the sound of talk on deck went on, but at last all became perfectly quiet. The party below waited for another half hour, and then noiselessly ascended the ladder to the deck, holding in one hand a cudgel, in the other a number of lengths of line cut about six feet long. Each as he reached the deck lay down flat. The Spaniard had been told to remain perfectly quiet while the other two went about their task.

First they crawled aft, for the bey's guards would, they knew, be sleeping at that end, and working together they tied the legs of these men without rousing them. The ropes could not be tightly pulled, as this would at once have disturbed them. They were therefore fastened somewhat in the fashion of manacles, so that although the men might rise to their feet they would fall headlong the moment they tried to walk. In addition other ropes were fastened to these and taken from one man to another. Then their swords were drawn from the sheaths and their knives from their sashes.

The operation was a long one, as it had to be conducted with the greatest care and caution. They then crept back to the hatchway and told the Spaniard that the most formidable enemies had been made safe.

"Here are a sword and a knife for you, senor; and now as we are all armed I consider the ship as good as won, for the sailors are not likely to make much resistance by themselves. However, we will secure some of them. The moon will be up in half an hour, and that will be an advantage to us.

The captain and three of the sailors were soon tied up like the others. Two men were standing in the bow of the vessel leaning against the bulwarks, and when the moon rose it could be seen by their attitude that both were asleep.

"Now, we may as well begin," Geoffrey said. "Let us take those two fellows in the bow by surprise. Hold a knife to their throats, and tell them if they utter the least sound we will kill them. Then we will make them go down into the forecastle and fasten them there."

"I am ready," Stephen said, and they stole forward to the two sleeping men. They grasped them suddenly by the throat and held a knife before their eyes, Boldero telling them in a stern whisper that if they uttered a cry they would be stabbed to the heart. Paralysed by the sudden attack they did not make the slightest struggle, but accompanied their unknown assailants to the forecastle and were there fastened in. Joined now by the Spaniard, Geoffrey and his companion went aft and roused one of the sleepers there with a threat similar to that which had silenced the sailors.

He was, however, a man of different stuff He gave a loud shout and grappled with Boldero, who struck him a heavy blow with his fist in the face, and this for a moment silenced him; but the alarm being given, the superintendent and the two men struggled to their feet, only however to fall prostrate as soon as they tried to walk.

"Lie quiet and keep silence!" Boldero shouted in a threatening voice.

"You are unarmed and at our mercy. Your feet are bound and you are perfectly helpless. We do not wish to take your lives, but unless you are quiet we shall be compelled to do so."

The men had discovered by this time that their arms had gone, and were utterly disconcerted by the heavy and unexpected fall they had just had. Feeling that they were indeed at the mercy of their captors, they lay quiet.

"Now then," Boldero went on, "one at a time. Keep quiet, you rascals there!" he broke off shouting to the sailors who were rolling and tumbling on the deck forward, "or I will cut all your throats for you. Now then, Geoffrey, do you and the senor cut the rope that fastens that man on the port side to his comrades. March him to the hatchway and make him go down into the hold. Keep your knives ready and kill him at once if he offers the slightest resistance."

One by one the superintendent, the three guards, the captain and sailors were all made to descend into the hold, and the hatches were put over it and fastened down.

"Now, senor," Geoffrey said, "we can spare you."

The Spaniard hurried to the cabin, opened the door, and called out his daughter's name. There was a scream of delight within as Dolores Mendez, who had been awakened by the tumult, recognized her father's voice, and leaping up from her couch threw herself into his arms. Geoffrey and his companion now opened the door of the forecastle and called the two sailors out.

"Now," Boldero said, "if you want to save your lives you have got to obey our orders. First of all fall to work and get up the anchor, and then shake out the sails again. I will take the helm, Geoffrey, and do you keep your eye on these two fellows. There is no fear of their playing any tricks now that they see they are alone on deck, but they might, if your back were turned, unfasten the hatches. However, I do not think we need fear trouble that way, as for aught they know we may have cut the throats of all the others."

A few minutes later the vessel was moving slowly through the water with her head to the northwest.

"We must be out of sight of land if we can by the morning," Stephen said, when Geoffrey two hours later came to take his place at the helm; "at any rate until we have passed the place we started from. Once beyond that it does not matter much; but it will be best either to keep out of sight of land altogether, or else to sail pretty close to it, so that they can see the boat is one of their own craft. We can choose which we will do when we see which way the breeze sets in in the morning."

It came strongly from the south, and they therefore determined to sail direct for Carthagena.

CHAPTER XVII. A SPANISH MERCHANT

As soon as the sails had been set, and the vessel was under way, the Spaniard came out from the cabin.

"My daughter is attiring herself, senor," he said to Stephen Boldero, for Geoffrey was at the time at the helm. "She is longing to see you, and to thank you for the inestimable services you have rendered to us both. But for you I should now be dying or dead, my daughter a slave for life in the palace of the bey. What astonishes us both is that such noble service should have been rendered to us by two absolute strangers, and not strangers only, but by Englishmen — a people with whom Spain is at war — and who assuredly can have no reason to love us. How came you first to think of interesting yourself on our behalf?"

"To tell you the truth, senor," Stephen Boldero said bluntly, "it was the sight of your daughter and not of yourself that made us resolve to save you if possible, or rather, I should say, made my friend Geoffrey do so. After ten years in the galleys one's heart gets pretty rough, and although even I felt a deep pity for your daughter, I own it would never have entered my mind to risk my neck in order to save her. But Geoffrey is younger and more easily touched, and when he saw her as she landed pale and white and grief stricken, and yet looking as if her own fate touched her less than the parting from you, my good friend Geoffrey Vickars was well nigh mad, and declared that in some way or other, and at whatever risk to ourselves, you must both be saved. In this matter I have been but a passive instrument in his hands; as indeed it was only right that I should be, seeing that he is of gentle blood and an esquire serving under Captain Vere in the army of the queen, while I am but a rough sailor. What I have done I have done partly because his heart was in the matter, partly because the adventure promised, if successful, to restore me to freedom, and partly also, senor, for the sake of your brave young daughter."

"You are modest, sir," the Spaniard said. "You are one of those who belittle your own good deeds. I feel indeed more grateful than I can express to you as well as to your friend."

The merchant's daughter now appeared at the door of the cabin. Her father took her hand and led her up to Boldero. "This, Dolores, is one of the two Englishmen who have at the risk of their lives saved me from death and you from worse than death. Thank him, my child, and to the end of your life never cease to remember him in your prayers."

"I am glad to have been of assistance, senora," Boldero said as the girl began to speak; "but as I have just been telling your father, I have played but a small part in the business, it is my friend Don Geoffrey Vickars who has been the leader in the matter. He saw you as you landed at the boat, and then and there swore to save you, and all that has been done has been under his direction. It was he who followed and rescued your father, and I have really had nothing to do with the affair beyond hiding myself in the hole and helping to tie up your Moors."

"Ah, sir," the girl said, laying her hands earnestly upon the sailor's shoulder, "it is useless for you to try to lessen the services you have rendered us. Think of what I was but an hour since — a captive with the most horrible of all fates before me, and with the belief that my father was dying by inches in the hands of some cruel taskmaster, and now he is beside me and I am free. This has been done by two strangers, men of a nation which I have been taught to regard as an enemy. It seems to me that no words that I can speak could tell you even faintly what I feel, and it is God alone who can reward you for what you have done."

Leaving Boldero the Spaniard and his daughter went to the stern, where Geoffrey was standing at the helm.

"My daughter and I have come to thank you, senor, for having saved us from the worst of fates and restored us to each other. Your friend tells me that it is to you it is chiefly due that this has come about, for that you were so moved to pity at the sight of my daughter when we first landed, that you declared at once that you would save her from her fate at whatever risk to yourself, and that since then he has been but following your directions."

"Then if he says that, senor, he belies himself. I was, it is true, the first to declare that we must save your daughter at any cost if it were possible to do so; but had I not said so, I doubt not he would have announced the same resolution. Since then we have planned everything together; and as he is older and more experienced than I am, it was upon his opinion that we principally acted. We had long made up our minds to escape when the opportunity came. Had it nor been that we were stirred into action by seeing your daughter in the hands of the Moors, it might have been years before we decided to run the risks. Therefore if you owe your freedom to us, to some extent we owe ours to you; and if we have been your protectors so far, we hope that when we arrive in Spain you will be our protectors there, for to us Spain is as much an enemy's country as Barbary."

"That you can assuredly rely upon," the trader replied. "All that I have is at your disposal."

For an hour they stood talking. Dolores said but little. She had felt no shyness with the stalwart sailor, but to this youth who had done her such signal service she felt unable so frankly to express her feelings of thankfulness.

By morning the coast of Africa was but a faint line on the horizon, and the ship was headed west. Except when any alteration of the sails was required, the two Moors who acted as the crew were made to retire into the forecastle, and were there fastened in, Geoffrey and Boldero sleeping by turns.

After breakfast the little party gathered round the helm, and at the request of Juan Mendez, Geoffrey and Stephen both related how it befell that they had become slaves to the Moors.

By England's Aid: or The Freeing

"Your adventures are both singular," the trader said when they had finished. "Yours, Don Geoffrey, are extraordinary. It is marvellous that you should have been picked up in that terrible fight, and should have shared in all the perils of that awful voyage back to Spain without its being ever suspected that you were English. Once landed in the service as you say of Senor Burke, it is not so surprising that you should have gone freely about Spain. But your other adventures are wonderful, and you and your friend were fortunate indeed in succeeding as you did in carrying off the lady he loved; and deeply they must have mourned your supposed death on the deck of the Moorish galley. And now tell me what are your plans when you arrive in Spain?"

"We have no fixed plans, save that we hope some day to be able to return home," Geoffrey said. "Stephen here could pass well enough as a Spaniard when once ashore without being questioned, and his idea is, if there is no possibility of getting on board an English or Dutch ship at Cadiz, to ship on board a Spaniard, and to take his chance of leaving her at some port at which she may touch. As for myself, although I speak Spanish fluently, my accent would at once betray me to be a foreigner. But if you will take me into your house for a time until I can see a chance of escaping, my past need not be inquired into. You could of course mention, were it asked, that I was English by birth, but had sailed in the Armada with my patron, Mr. Burke, and it would be naturally supposed that I was an exile from England."

"That can certainly be managed," the trader said. "I fear that it will be difficult to get you on board a ship either of your countrymen or of the Hollanders; these are most closely watched lest fugitives from the law or from the Inquisition should escape on board them. Still, some opportunity may sooner or later occur; and the later the better pleased shall I be, for it will indeed be a pleasure to me to have you with me."

In the afternoon Geoffrey said to Stephen, "I have been thinking, Stephen, about the men in the hold, and I should be glad for them to return to their homes. If they go with us to Spain they will be made galley slaves, and this I should not like, especially in the case of the bey's superintendent. The bey was most kind to us, and this man himself always spoke in our favour to him, and behaved well to us. I think, therefore, that out of gratitude to the bey we should let them go. The wind is fair, and there are, so far as I can see, no signs of any change of weather. By tomorrow night the coast of Spain will be in sight. I see no reason, therefore, why we should not be able to navigate her until we get near the land, when Mendez can engage the crew of some fishing boat to take us into a port. If we put them into the boat with plenty of water and provisions, they will make the coast by morning; and as I should guess that we must at present be somewhere abreast of the port from which we started, they will nor be very far from home when they land."

"I have no objection whatever, Geoffrey. As you say we were not treated badly, at any rate from the day when the bey had us up to his house; and after ten years in the galleys, I do not wish my worst enemies such a fate. We must, of course, be careful how we get them into the boat."

"There will be three of us with swords and pistols, and they will be unarmed," Geoffrey said. "We will put the two men now in the forecastle into the boat first, and let the others come up one by one and take their places. We will have a talk with the superintendent first, and give him a message to the bey, saying that we are not ungrateful for his kindness to us, but that of course we seized the opportunity that presented itself of making our escape, as he would himself have done in similar circumstances; nevertheless that as a proof of our gratitude to him, we for his sake release the whole party on board, and give them the means of safely returning."

An hour later the boat, pulled by four oars, left the side of the ship with the crew, the superintendent and guards, and the two women who had come on board to attend upon Dolores upon the voyage.

The next morning the vessel was within a few miles of the Spanish coast. An hour later a fishing–boat was hailed, and an arrangement made with the crew to take the vessel down to Carthagena, which was, they learned, some fifty miles distant. The wind was now very light, and it was not until the following day that they entered the port. As it was at once perceived that the little vessel was Moorish in rigging and appearance, a boat immediately came alongside to inquire whence she came.

Juan Mendez had no difficulty in satisfying the officer as to his identity, he being well known to several traders in the town. His story of the attack upon his ship by Barbary pirates, its capture, and his own escape and that of his daughter by the aid of two Christian captives, excited great interest as soon as it became known in the town; for it was rare, indeed, that a captive ever succeeded in making his escape from the hands of the Moors. It had already been arranged that, in telling his story, the trader should make as little as possible of his companions' share in the business, so that public attention should not be attracted towards them. He himself with Dolores at once disembarked, but his companions did not come ashore until after nightfall.

Stephen Boldero took a Spanish name, but Geoffrey retained his own, as the story that he was travelling as servant with Mr. Burke, a well known Irish gentleman who had accompanied the Armada, was sufficient to account for his nationality. Under the plea that he was anxious to return to Cadiz as soon as possible, Senor Mendez arranged for horses and mules to start the next morning. He had sent out two trunks of clothes to the ship an hour after he landed, and the two Englishmen therefore escaped all observation, as they wandered about for an hour or two after landing, and did not go to the inn where Mendez was staying until it was time to retire to bed.

The next morning the party started. The clothes that Geoffrey was wearing were those suited to an employee in a house of business, while those of Boldero were such as would be worn by the captain or mate of a merchant vessel on shore. Both were supplied with arms, for although the party had nothing to attract the cupidity of robbers beyond the trunks containing the clothes purchased on the preceding day, and the small amount of money necessary for their travel on the road, the country was so infested by bands of robbers that no one travelled unarmed. The journey to Cadiz was, however, accomplished without adventure.

The house of Senor Mendez was a large and comfortable one. Upon the ground floor were his offices and store rooms. He himself and his family occupied the two next floors, while in those above his clerks and employees lived. His unexpected return caused great surprise, and in a few hours a number of acquaintances called to hear the story of the adventures through which he had passed, and to condole with him on the loss of his wife. At his own request Stephen Boldero had been given in charge of the principal clerk, and a room assigned to him in the upper story.

"I shall be much more comfortable," he said, "among your people, Don Mendez. I am a rough sailor, and ten years in the galleys don't improve any manners a man may have had. If I were among your friends I would be out of place and uncomfortable, and should always have to be bowing and scraping and exchanging compliments, and besides they would soon find out that my Spanish was doubtful. I talk a sailor's slang, but I doubt if I should understand pure Spanish. Altogether, I should be very uncomfortable, and should make you uncomfortable, and I would very much rather take my place among the men that work for you until I can get on board a ship again."

Geoffrey was installed in the portion of the house occupied by the merchant, and was introduced by him to his friends simply as the English gentleman who had rescued him and his daughter from the hands of the Moors, it being incidentally mentioned that he had sailed in the Armada, and that he had fallen into the hands of the corsairs in the course of a voyage made with his friend Mr. Burke to Italy. He at once took his place as a friend and assistant of the merchant; and as the latter had many dealings with Dutch and English merchants, Geoffrey was able to be of considerable use to him in his written communications to the captains of the various vessels of those nationalities in the port.

"I think," the merchant said to him a fortnight after his arrival in Cadiz, "that, if it would not go against your conscience, it would be most advisable that you should accompany me sometimes to church. Unless you do this, sooner or later suspicion is sure to be roused, and you know that if you were once suspected of being a heretic, the Inquisition would lay its hands upon you in no time."

"I have no objection whatever," Geoffrey said. "Were I questioned I should at once acknowledge that I was a Protestant; but I see no harm in going to a house of God to say my prayers there, while others are saying theirs in a different manner. There is no church of my own religion here, and I can see no harm whatever in doing as you suggest."

"I am glad to hear that that is your opinion," Senor Mendez said, "for it is the one point concerning which I was uneasy. I have ordered a special mass at the church of St. Dominic tomorrow, in thanksgiving for our safe escape from the hands of the Moors, and it would be well that you should accompany us there."

"I will do so most willingly," Geoffrey said. "I have returned thanks many times, but shall be glad to do so again in a house dedicated to God's service."

Accordingly the next day Geoffrey accompanied Don Mendez and his daughter to the church of St. Dominic, and as he knelt by them wondered why men should hate each other because they differed as to the ways and methods in which they should worship God. From that time on he occasionally accompanied Senor Mendez to the church, saying his prayers earnestly in his own fashion, and praying that he might some day be restored to his home and friends.

He and the merchant had frequently talked over all possible plans for his escape, but the extreme vigilance of the Spanish authorities with reference to the English and Dutch trading ships seemed to preclude any possibility of his being smuggled on board. Every bale and package was closely examined on the quay before being sent off. Spanish officials were on board from the arrival to the departure of each ship, and no communication whatever was allowed between the shore and these vessels, except in boats belonging to the authorities, every paper and document passing first through their hands for examination before being sent on board. The trade carried on between England, Holland, and Spain at the time when these nations were engaged in war was a singular one; but it was permitted by all three countries, because the products of each were urgently required by the others. It was kept within narrow limits, and there were frequent angry complaints exchanged between the English government and that of Holland, when either considered the other to be going beyond that limit.

Geoffrey admitted to himself that he might again make the attempt to return to England, by taking passage as before in a ship bound for Italy, but he knew that Elizabeth was negotiating with Philip for peace, and thought that he might as well await the result. He was, indeed, very happy at Cadiz, and shrank from the thought of leaving it.

Stephen Boldero soon became restless, and at his urgent request Juan Mendez appointed him second mate on board one of his ships sailing for the West Indies, his intention being to make his escape if an opportunity offered; but if not, he preferred a life of activity to wandering aimlessly about the streets of Cadiz. He was greatly grieved to part from Geoffrey, and promised that, should he ever reach England, he would at once journey down to Hedingham, and report his safety to his father and mother.

"You will do very well here, Master Geoffrey," he said. "You are quite at home with all the Spaniards, and it will not be very long before you speak the language so well that, except for your name, none would take you for a foreigner. You have found work to do, and are really better off here than you would be starving and fighting in Holland. Besides," he said with a sly wink, "there are other attractions for you. Juan Mendez treats you as a son, and the senorita knows that she owes everything to you. You might do worse than settle here for life. Like enough you will see me back again in six months' time, for if I see no chance of slipping off and reaching one of the islands held by the buccaneers, I shall perforce return in the ship I go out in."

By England's Aid: or The Freeing

At parting Senor Mendez bestowed a bag containing five hundred gold pieces upon Stephen Boldero as a reward for the service he had rendered him.

Geoffrey missed him greatly. For eighteen months they had been constantly together, and it was the sailor's companionship and cheerfulness that had lightened the first days of his captivity; and had it not been for his advice and support he might now have been tugging at an oar in the bey's corsair galley. Ever since they had been at Cadiz he had daily spent an hour or two in his society; for when work was done they generally went for a walk together on the fortifications, and talked of England and discussed the possibility of escape. After his departure he was thrown more than before into the society of the merchant and his daughter. The feeling that Dolores had, when he first saw her, excited within him had changed its character. She was very pretty now that she had recovered her life and spirits, and she made no secret of the deep feeling of gratitude she entertained towards him. One day, three months after Stephen's departure, Senor Mendez, when they were alone together, broached the subject on which his thoughts had been turned so much of late.

"Friend Geoffrey," he said, "I think that I am not mistaken in supposing that you have an affection for Dolores. I have marked its growth, and although I would naturally have rather bestowed her upon a countryman, yet I feel that you have a right to her as having saved her from the horrible fate that would have undoubtedly befallen her, and that it is not for me, to whom you have restored her, besides saving my own life, to offer any objection. As to her feelings, I have no doubt whatever. Were you of my religion and race, such a match would afford me the greatest happiness. As it is I regret it only because I feel that some day or other it will lead to a separation from me. It is natural that you should wish to return to your own country, and as this war cannot go on for ever, doubtless in time some opportunity for doing so will arrive. This I foresee and must submit to, but if there is peace I shall be able occasionally to visit her in her home in England. I naturally hope that it will be long before I shall thus lose her. She is my only child, and I shall give as her dower the half of my business, and you will join me as an equal partner. When the war is over you can, if you wish, establish yourself in London, and thence carry on and enlarge the English and Dutch trade of our house. I may even myself settle there. I have not thought this over at present, nor is there any occasion to do so. I am a wealthy man and there is no need for me to continue in business, and I am not sure when the time comes I shall not prefer to abandon my country rather than be separated from my daughter. At any rate for the present I offer you her hand and a share in my business."

Geoffrey expressed in suitable terms the gratitude and delight he felt at the offer. It was contrary to Spanish notions that he should receive from Dolores in private any assurance that the proposal in which she was so largely concerned was one to which she assented willingly, but her father at once fetched her in and formally presented her to Geoffrey as his promised wife, and a month later the marriage was solemnized at the church of St. Dominic.

CHAPTER XVIII. IVRY

The day after the capture of Breda Sir Francis Vere sent for Lionel Vickars to his quarters. Prince Maurice and several of his principal officers were there, and the prince thanked him warmly for the share he had taken in the capture of the town.

"Captain Heraugiere has told me," he said, "that the invention of the scheme that has ended so well is due as much to you as to him, that you accompanied him on the reconnoitring expedition and shared in the dangers of the party in the barge. I trust Sir Francis Vere will appoint you to the first ensigncy vacant in his companies, but should there be likely to be any delay in this I will gladly give you a commission in one of my own regiments."

"I have forestalled your wish, prince," Sir Francis said, "and have this morning given orders that his appointment shall be made out as ensign in one of my companies, but at present I do not intend him to join. I have been ordered by the queen to send further aid to help the King of France against the League. I have already despatched several companies to Brittany, and will now send two others. I would that my duties permitted me personally to take part in the enterprise, for the battle of the Netherlands is at present being fought on the soil of France; but this is impossible. Several of my friends, however, volunteers and others, will journey with the two companies, being desirous of fighting under the banner of Henry of Navarre. Sir Ralph Pimpernel, who is married to a French Huguenot lady and has connections at the French court, will lead them. I have spoken to him this morning, and he will gladly allow my young friend here to accompany him. I think that it is the highest reward I can give him, to afford him thus an opportunity of seeing stirring service; for I doubt not that in a very short time a great battle will be fought. We know that Alva has sent eighteen hundred of the best cavalry of Flanders to aid the League, and he is sure to have given orders that they are to be back again as soon as possible. How do you like the prospect, Lionel?"

Lionel warmly expressed his thanks to Sir Francis Vere for his kindness, and said that nothing could delight him more than to take part in such an enterprise.

"I must do something at any rate to prove my gratitude for your share in the capture of this city," Prince Maurice said; "and will send you presently two of the best horses of those we have found in the governor's stables, together with arms and armour suitable to your rank as an officer of Sir Francis Vere."

Upon the following morning a party of ten knights and gentlemen including Lionel Vickars, rode to Bergen op Zoom. The two companies, which were drawn from the garrison of that town, had embarked the evening before in ships that had come from England to transport them to France. Sir Ralph Pimpernel and his party at once went on board, and as soon as their horses were embarked the sails were hoisted. Four days' voyage took them to the mouth of the Seine, and they landed at Honfleur on the south bank of the river. There was a large number of ships in port, for the Protestant princes of Germany were, as well as England, sending aid to Henry of Navarre, and numbers of gentlemen and volunteers were flocking to his banners.

For the moment Henry IV represented in the eyes of Europe the Protestant cause. He was supported by the Huguenots of France and by some of the Catholic noblemen and gentry. Against him were arrayed the greater portion of the Catholic nobles, the whole faction of the Guises and the Holy League, supported by Philip of Spain.

The party from Holland disembarked at midday on the 9th of March. Hearing rumours that a battle was expected very shortly to take place, Sir Ralph Pimpernel started at once with his mounted party for Dreux, which town was being besieged by Henry, leaving the two companies of foot to press on at their best speed behind him. The distance to be ridden was about sixty miles, and late at night on the 10th they rode into a village eight miles from Dreux. Here they heard that the Duke of Mayenne, who commanded the force of the League, was approaching the Seine at Mantes with an army of ten thousand foot and four thousand horse.

By England's Aid: or The Freeing

"We must mount at daybreak, gentlemen," Sir Ralph Pimpernel said, "or the forces of the League will get between us and the king. It is evident that we have but just arrived in time, and it is well we did not wait for our footmen."

The next morning they mounted early and rode on to the royal camp near Dreux. Here Sir Ralph Pimpernel found Marshal Biron, a relation of his wife, who at once took him to the king.

"You have just arrived in time, Sir Ralph," the king said when Marshal Biron introduced him, "for tomorrow, or at latest the day after, we are likely to try our strength with Mayenne. You will find many of your compatriots here. I can offer you but poor hospitality at present, but hope to entertain you rarely some day when the good city of Paris opens its gates to us."

"Thanks, sire," Sir Ralph replied; "but we have come to fight and not to feast."

"I think I can promise you plenty of that at any rate," the king said. "You have ten gentlemen with you, I hear, and also that there are two companies of foot from Holland now on their way up from Honfleur."

"They landed at noon the day before yesterday, sire, and will probably be up tomorrow."

"They will be heartily welcome, Sir Ralph. Since Parma has sent so large a force to help Mayenne it is but right that Holland, which is relieved of the presence of these troops, should lend me a helping hand."

Quarters were found for the party in a village near the camp; for the force was badly provided with tents, the king's resources being at a very low ebb; he maintained the war, indeed, chiefly by the loans he received from England and Germany. The next day several bodies of troops were seen approaching the camp. A quarter of an hour later the trumpets blew; officers rode about, ordering the tents to be levelled and the troops to prepare to march. A messenger from Marshal Biron rode at full speed into the village, where many of the volunteers from England and Germany, besides the party of Sir Ralph Pimpernel, were lodged.

"The marshal bids me tell you, gentlemen, that the army moves at once. Marshal D'Aumont has fallen back from Ivry; Mayenne is advancing. The siege will be abandoned at present, and we march towards Nonancourt, where we shall give battle tomorrow if Mayenne is disposed for it."

The camps were struck and the wagons loaded, and the army marched to St. Andre, a village situated on an elevated plain commanding a view of all the approaches from the country between the Seine and Eure.

"This is a fine field for a battle," Sir Ralph said, as the troops halted on the ground indicated by the camp marshals. "It is splendid ground for cavalry to act, and it is upon them the brunt of the fighting will fall. We are a little stronger in foot; for several companies from Honfleur, our own among them, have come up this morning, and I hear we muster twelve thousand, which is a thousand more than they say Mayenne has with him. But then he has four thousand cavalry to our three thousand; and Parma's regiments of Spaniards, Walloons, and Italian veterans are far superior troops to Henry's bands of riders, who are mostly Huguenot noblemen and gentlemen with their armed retainers, tough and hardy men to fight, as they have shown themselves on many a field, but without any of the discipline of Parma's troopers.

"If Parma himself commanded yonder army I should not feel confident of the result; but Mayenne, though a skilful general, is slow and cautious, while Henry of Navarre is full of fire and energy, and brave almost to rashness. We are in muster under the command of the king himself. He will have eight hundred horse, formed into six squadrons, behind him, and upon these will, I fancy, come the chief shock of the battle. He will be covered on each side by the English and Swiss infantry; in all four thousand strong.

"Marshal Biron will be on the right with five troops of horse and four regiments of French infantry; while on the left will be the troops of D'Aumont, Montpensier, Biron the younger, D'Angouleme, and De Givry, supported in all by two regiments of French infantry, one of Swiss, and one of German. The marshal showed us the plan of battle last night in his tent. It is well balanced and devised."

It was late in the evening before the whole of the force had reached the position and the tents were erected. One of these had been placed at the disposal of Sir Ralph's party. Sir Ralph and four of his companions had been followed by their mounted squires, and these collected firewood, and supplied the horses with forage from the sacks they carried slung from their saddles, while the knights and gentlemen themselves polished their arms and armour, so as to make as brave a show as possible in the ranks of the king's cavalry.

When they had eaten their supper Lionel Vickars strolled through the camp, and was amused at the contrast presented by the various groups. The troops of cavalry of the French nobles were gaily attired; the tents of the officers large and commodious, with rich hangings and appointments. The sound of light hearted laughter came from the groups round the campfires, squires and pages moved about thickly, and it was evident that comfort, and indeed luxury, were considered by the commanders as essential even upon a campaign. The encampments of the German, Swiss, and English infantry were of far humbler design. The tents of the officers were few in number, and of the simplest form and make. A considerable portion of the English infantry had been drawn from Holland, for the little army there was still the only body of trained troops at Elizabeth's disposal.

The Swiss and Germans were for the most part mercenaries. Some had been raised at the expense of the Protestant princes, others were paid from the sums supplied from England. The great proportion of the men were hardy veterans who had fought under many banners, and cared but little for the cause in which they were fighting, provided they obtained their pay regularly and that the rations were abundant and of good quality.

The French infantry regiments contained men influenced by a variety of motives. Some were professional soldiers who had fought in many a field during the long wars that had for so many years agitated France, others were the retainers of the nobles who had thrown in their cause with Henry, while others again were Huguenot peasants who were fighting, not for pay, but in the cause of their religion.

The cavalry were for the most part composed of men of good family, relations, connections, or the superior vassals of the nobles who commanded or officered them. The king's own squadrons were chiefly composed of Huguenot gentlemen and their mounted retainers; but with these rode many foreign volunteers like Sir Ralph Pimpernel's party, attracted to Henry's banner either from a desire to aid the Protestant cause or to gain military knowledge and fame under so brave and able a monarch, or simply from the love of excitement and military ardour.

The camp of this main body of cavalry or "battalia" as the body on whom the commander of our army chiefly relied for victory was called, was comparatively still and silent. The Huguenot gentlemen, after the long years of persecution to which those of their religion had been exposed, were for the most part poor. Their appointments were simple, and they fought for conscience' sake, and went into battle with the stern enthusiasm that afterwards animated Cromwell's Ironsides.

It was not long before the camp quieted down; for the march had been a long one, and they would be on their feet by daybreak. The king himself, attended by Marshals D'Aumont and Biron, had gone through the whole extent of the camp, seen that all was in order, that the troops had everywhere received their rations, and that the officers were acquainted with the orders for the morrow. He stayed a short time in the camp of each regiment and troop, saying a few words of encouragement to the soldiers, and laughing and joking with the officers. He paused a short time and chatted with Sir Ralph Pimpernel, who, at his request, introduced each of his companions to him.

Lionel looked with interest and admiration at the man who was regarded as the champion of Protestantism against Popery, and who combined in himself a remarkable mixture of qualities seldom found existing in one person. He was brave to excess and apparently reckless in action, and yet astute, prudent, and calculating in council. With a manner frank, open, and winning, he was yet able to match the craftiest of opponents at their own weapons of scheming and duplicity. The idol of the Huguenots of France, he was ready to purchase the crown of France at the price of accepting the Catholic doctrines, for he saw that it was hopeless for him in the long run to maintain himself against the hostility of almost all the great nobles of France, backed by the great proportion of the people and aided by the pope and the Catholic powers, so long as he remained a Protestant. But this change of creed was scarcely even foreseen by those who followed him, and it was the apparent hopelessness of his cause, and the gallantry with which he maintained it, that attracted the admiration of Europe.

Henry's capital was at the time garrisoned by the troops of the pope and Spain. The great nobles of France, who had long maintained a sort of semi independence of the crown, were all against him, and were calculating on founding independent kingdoms. He himself was excommunicated. The League were masters of almost the whole of France, and were well supplied with funds by the pope and the Catholic powers while Henry was entirely dependent for money upon what he could borrow from Queen Elizabeth and the

States of Holland. But no one who listened to the merry laugh of the king as he chatted with the little group of English gentlemen would have thought that he was engaged in a desperate and well nigh hopeless struggle, and that the following day was to be a decisive one as to his future fortunes.

"Well, gentlemen," he said as he turned his horse to ride away, "I must ask you to lie down as soon as possible. As long as the officers are awake and talking the men cannot sleep; and I want all to have a good night's rest. The enemy's camp is close at hand and the battle is sure to take place at early dawn."

As the same orders were given everywhere, the camp was quiet early, and before daylight the troops were called under arms and ranged in the order appointed for them to fight in.

The army of the League was astir in equally good time. In its centre was the battalia composed of six hundred splendid cavalry, all noblemen of France, supported by a column of three hundred Swiss and two thousand French infantry. On the left were six hundred French cuirassiers and the eighteen hundred troops of Parma, commanded by Count Egmont. They were supported by six regiments of French and Lorrainers, and two thousand Germans. The right wing was composed of three regiments of Spanish lancers, two troops of Germans, four hundred cuirassiers, and four regiments of infantry.

When the sun rose and lighted up the contending armies, the difference between their appearance was very marked. That of the League was gay with the gilded armour, waving plumes, and silken scarfs of the French nobles, whose banners fluttered brightly in the air, while the Walloons and Flemish rivalled their French comrades in the splendour of their appointments. In the opposite ranks there was neither gaiety nor show. The Huguenot nobles and gentlemen, who had for so many years been fighting for life and religion, were clad in armour dinted in a hundred battlefields; and while the nobles of the League were confident of victory and loud in demanding to be led against the foe, Henry of Navarre and his soldiers were kneeling, praying to the God of battles to enable them to bear themselves well in the coming fight. Henry of Navarre wore in his helmet a snow white plume, which he ordered his troops to keep in view, and to follow wherever they should see it waving, in case his banner went down.

Artillery still played but a small part in battles on the field and there were but twelve pieces on the ground, equally divided between the two armies. These opened the battle, and Count Egmont, whose cavalry had suffered from the fire of the Huguenot cannon, ordered a charge, and the splendid cavalry of Parma swept down upon the right wing of Henry. The cavalry under Marshal Biron were unable to withstand the shock and were swept before them, and Egmont rode on right up to the guns and sabred the artillerymen. Almost at the same moment the German riders under Eric of Brunswick, the Spanish and French lancers, charged down upon the centre of the Royal Army. The rout of the right wing shook the cavalry in the centre. They wavered, and the infantry on their flanks fell back but the king and his officers rode among them, shouting and entreating them to stand firm. The ground in their front was soft and checked the impetuosity of the charge of the Leaguers, and by the time they reached the ranks of the Huguenots they were broken and disordered, and could make no impression whatever upon them.

As soon as the charge was repulsed, Henry set his troops in motion, and the battalia charged down upon the disordered cavalry of the League. The lancers and cuirassiers were borne down by the impetuosity of the charge, and Marshal Biron, rallying his troops, followed the king's white plume into the heart of the battle. Egmont brought up the cavalry of Flanders to the scene, and was charging at their head when he fell dead with a musketball through the heart.

Brunswick went down in the fight, and the shattered German and Walloon horse were completely overthrown and cut to pieces by the furious charges of the Huguenot cavalry.

At one time the victorious onset was checked by the disappearance of the king's snow white plumes, and a report ran through the army that the king was killed. They wavered irresolutely. The enemy, regaining courage from the cessation of their attacks, were again advancing, when the king reappeared bareheaded and covered with dust and blood, but entirely unhurt. He addressed a few cheerful words to his soldiers, and again led the charge. It was irresistible; the enemy broke and fled in the wildest confusion hotly pursued by the royalist cavalry, while the infantry of the League, who had so far taken no part whatever in the battle, were seized with a panic, threw away their arms, and sought refuge in the woods in their rear.

Thus the battle was decided only by the cavalry, the infantry taking no part in the fight on either side. Eight hundred of the Leaguers either fell on the battlefield or were drowned in crossing the river in their rear. The loss of the royalists was but one fourth in number. Had the king pushed forward upon Paris immediately after the battle, the city would probably have surrendered without a blow; and the Huguenot leaders urged this course upon him. Biron and the other Catholics, however, argued that it was better to undertake a regular siege, and the king yielded to this advice, although the bolder course would have been far more in accordance with his own disposition.

He was probably influenced by a variety of motives. In the first place his Swiss mercenaries were in a mutinous condition, and refused to advance a single foot unless they received their arrears of pay, and this Henry, whose chests were entirely empty, had no means of providing. In the second place he was at the time secretly in negotiation with the pope for his conversion, and may have feared to give so heavy a blow to the Catholic cause as would have been effected by the capture of Paris following closely after the victory of Ivry. At any rate he determined upon a regular siege. Moving forward he seized the towns of Lagny on the Maine, and Corbeil on the Seine, thus entirely cutting off the food supply of Paris.

Lionel Vickars had borne his part in the charges of the Huguenot cavalry, but as the company to which he belonged was in the rear of the battalia, he had no personal encounters with the enemy.

After the advance towards Paris the duties of the cavalry consisted entirely in scouting the country, sweeping in provisions for their own army, and preventing supplies from entering Paris. No siege operations were undertaken, the king relying upon famine alone to reduce the city. Its population at the time the siege commenced was estimated at 400,000, and the supply of provisions to be sufficient for a month. It was calculated therefore that before the League could bring up another army to its relief, it must fall by famine.

But no allowance had been made for the religious enthusiasm and devotion to the cause of the League that animated the population of Paris. Its governor, the Duke of Nemours, brother of Mayenne, aided by the three Spanish delegates, the Cardinal Gaetano, and by an army of priests and monks, sustained the spirits of the population; and though the people starved by thousands, the city resisted until towards the end of August. In that month the army of the League, united with twelve thousand foot and three thousand horse from the Netherlands under Parma himself, advanced to its assistance; while Maurice of Holland, with a small body of Dutch troops and reinforcements from England, had strengthened the army of the king.

The numbers of the two armies were not unequal. Many of the French nobles had rallied round Henry after his victory, and of his cavalry four thousand were nobles and their retainers who served at their own expense, and were eager for a battle. Parma himself had doubts as to the result of the conflict. He could rely upon the troops he himself had brought, but had no confidence in those of the League; and when Henry sent him a formal challenge to a general engagement, Parma replied that it was his custom to refuse combat when a refusal seemed advantageous for himself, and to offer battle whenever it suited his purpose to fight.

For seven days the two armies, each some twenty–five thousand strong, lay within a mile or two of each other. Then the splendid cavalry of Parma moved out in order of battle, with banners flying, and the pennons of the lances fluttering in the wind. The king was delighted when he saw that the enemy were at last advancing to the fight. He put his troops at once under arms, but waited until the plan of the enemy's battle developed itself before making his dispositions. But while the imposing array of cavalry was attracting the king's attention, Parma moved off with the main body of his army, threw a division across the river on a pontoon bridge, and attacked Lagny on both sides.

When Lagny was first occupied some of Sir Ralph Pimpernel's party were appointed to take up their quarters there, half a company of the English, who had come with them from Holland, were also stationed in the town, the garrison being altogether 1200 strong. Lionel's horse had received a bullet wound at Ivry and although it carried him for the next day or two, it was evident that it needed rest and attention and would be unfit to carry his rider for some time. Lionel had no liking for the work of driving off the cattle of the unfortunate land owners and peasants, however necessary it might be to keep the army supplied with food, and was glad of the excuse that his wounded horse afforded him for remaining quietly in the town when his comrades rode our with the troop of cavalry stationed there. It happened that the officer in command of the little body of English infantry was taken ill with fever, and Sir Ralph Pimpernel requested Lionel to take his place. This he was glad to do, as he was more at home at infantry work than with cavalry. The time went slowly, but Lionel, who had comfortable quarters in the house of a citizen, did not find it long. The burgher's family consisted of his wife and two daughters, and these congratulated themselves greatly upon having an officer quartered upon them who not only acted as a protection to them against the insolence of the rough soldiery, but was courteous and pleasant in his manner, and tried in every way to show that he regarded himself as a guest and not a master.

After the first week's stay he requested that instead of having his meals served to him in a room apart he might take them with the family. The girls were about Lionel's age, and after the first constraint wore off he became great friends with them; and although at first he had difficulty in making himself understood, he readily picked up a little French, the girls acting as his teachers.

"What do you English do here?" the eldest of them asked him when six weeks after his arrival they were able to converse fairly in a mixture of French and Spanish. "Why do you not leave us French people to fight out our quarrels by ourselves?"

"I should put it the other way," Lionel laughed. "Why don't you French people fight out your quarrels among yourselves instead of calling in foreigners to help you? It is because the Guises and the League have called in the Spaniards to fight on the Catholic side that the English and Dutch have come to help the Huguenots. We are fighting the battle of our own religion here, not the battle of Henry of Navarre."

"I hate these wars of religion," the girl said. "Why can we not all worship in our own way?"

"Ah, that is what we Protestants want to know, Mademoiselle Claire; that is just what your people won't allow. Did you not massacre the Protestants in France on the eve of St. Bartholomew? and have not the Spaniards been for the last twenty years trying to stamp out with fire and sword the new religion in the Low Countries? We only want to be left alone."

"But your queen of England kills the Catholics."

"Not at all," Lionel said warmly; "that is only one of the stories they spread to excuse their own doings. It is true that Catholics in England have been put to death, and so have people of the sect that call themselves Anabaptists; but this has been because they had been engaged in plots against the queen, and not because of their religion. The Catholics of England for the most part joined as heartily as the Protestants in the preparations for the defence of England in the time of the Armada. For my part, I cannot understand why people should quarrel with each other because they worship God in different ways."

"It is all very bad, I am sure," the girl said; "France has been torn to pieces by these religious wars for years and years. It is dreadful to think what they must be suffering in Paris now."

"Then why don't they open their gates to King Henry instead of starving themselves at the orders of the legate of the pope and the agent of Philip of Spain? I could understand if there was another French prince whom they wanted as king instead of Henry of Navarre. We fought for years in England as to whether we would have a king from the house of York or the house of Lancaster, but when it comes to choosing between a king of your own race and a king named for you by Philip of Spain, I can't understand it."

"Never mind, Master Vickars. You know what you are fighting for, don't you?"

"I do; I am fighting here to aid Holland. Parma is bringing all his troops to aid the Guise here, and while they are away the Dutch will take town after town, and will make themselves so strong that when Parma goes back he will find the nut harder than ever to crack."

"How long will Paris hold out, think you, Master Vickars? They say that provisions are well nigh spent."

"Judging from the way in which the Dutch towns held on for weeks and weeks after, as it seemed, all supplies were exhausted, I should say that if the people of Paris are as ready to suffer rather than yield as were the Dutch burghers, they may hold on for a long time yet. It is certain that no provisions can come to them as long as we hold possession of this town, and so block the river."

"But if the armies of Parma and the League come they may drive you away, Master Vickars."

"It is quite possible, mademoiselle; we do not pretend to be invincible, but I think there will be some tough fighting first."

As the weeks went on Lionel Vickars came to be on very intimate terms with the family. The two maidservants shared in the general liking for the young officer. He gave no more trouble than if he were one of the family, and on one or two occasions when disturbances

227

were caused by the ill conduct of the miscellaneous bands which constituted the garrison, he brought his half company of English soldiers at once into the house, and by his resolute attitude prevented the marauders from entering.

When Parma's army approached Sir Ralph Pimpernel with the cavalry joined the king, but Lionel shared in the disappointment felt by all the infantry of the garrison of Lagny that they could take no share in the great battle that was expected. Their excitement rose high while the armies lay watching each other. From the position of the town down by the river neither army was visible from its walls, and they only learned when occasional messengers rode in how matters were going on. One morning Lionel was awoke by a loud knocking at his door. "What is it?" he shouted, as he sat up in bed.

"It is I — Timothy Short, Master Vickars. The sergeant has sent me to wake you in all haste. The Spaniards have stolen a march upon us. They have thrown a bridge across the river somewhere in the night, and most all their army stands between us and the king while a division are preparing to besiege the town on the other side." Lionel was hastily throwing on his clothes and arming himself while the man was speaking.

"Tell the sergeant," he said, "to get the men under arms. I will be with him in a few minutes."

When Lionel went out he found that the household was already astir.

"Go not out fasting," his host said. "Take a cup of wine and some food before you start. You may be some time before you get an opportunity of eating again if what they say is true."

"Thank you heartily," Lionel replied as he sat down to the table, on which some food had already been placed; "it is always better to fight full than fasting."

"Hark you!" the bourgeois said in his ear; "if things go badly with you make your way here. I have a snug hiding place, and I shall take refuge there with my family if the Spaniards capture the town. I have heard of their doings in Holland, and that when they capture a town they spare neither age nor sex, and slay Catholics as well as Protestants; therefore I shall take refuge till matters have quieted down and order is restored. I shall set to work at once to carry my valuables there, and a goodly store of provisions. My warehouse man will remain in charge above. He is faithful and can be trusted, and he will tell the Spaniards that I am a good Catholic, and lead them to believe that I fled with my family before the Huguenots entered the town."

"Thank you greatly," Lionel replied; "should the need arise I will take advantage of your kind offer. But it should not do so. We have twelve hundred men here, and half that number of citizens have kept the Spaniards at bay for months before towns no stronger than this in Holland. We ought to be able to defend ourselves here for weeks, and the king will assuredly come to our relief in two or three days at the outside."

Upon Lionel sallying out he found the utmost confusion and disorder reigning. The commandant was hurriedly assigning to the various companies composing the garrison their places upon the walls. Many of the soldiers were exclaiming that they had been betrayed, and that it were best to make terms with the Spaniards at once. The difference between the air of a quiet resolution that marked the conduct of the people and troops at Sluys and the excitement manifested here struck Lionel unpleasantly. The citizens all remained in their houses, afraid lest the exultation they felt at the prospect of deliverance would be so marked as to enrage the soldiery. Lionel's own company was standing quietly and in good order in the marketplace, and as soon as he received orders as to the point that he should occupy on the walls Lionel marched them away.

In half an hour the Spanish batteries, which had been erected during the night, opened fire upon several points of the walls. The town was ill provided with artillery, and the answer was feeble, and before evening several breaches had been effected, two of the gates blown in, and the Spaniards, advanced to the assault. Lionel and his company, with one composed of Huguenot gentlemen and their retainers and another of Germans defended the gate at which they were posted with great bravery, and succeeded in repulsing the attacks of the Spaniards time after time. The latter pressed forward in heavy column, only to recoil broken and shattered from the archway, which was filled high with their dead. The defenders had just succeeded in repulsing the last of these attacks, when some soldiers ran by shouting "All is lost, the Spaniards have entered the town at three points!"

The German company at once disbanded and scattered. The Huguenot noble said to Lionel: "I fear that the news is true; listen to the shouts and cries in the town behind us. I will march with my men and see if there is any chance of beating back the Spaniards; if not it were best to lay down our arms and ask for quarter. Will you try to hold this gate until I return?"

"I will do so," Lionel said; "but I have only about thirty men left, and if the Spaniards come on again we cannot hope to repulse them."

"If I am not back in ten minutes it will be because all is lost," the Huguenot said; "and you had then best save yourself as you can."

But long before the ten minutes passed crowds of fugitives ran past, and Lionel learned that great numbers of the enemy had entered, and that they were refusing quarter and slaying all they met.

"It is useless to stay here longer to be massacred," he said to his men. "I should advise you to take refuge in the churches, leaving your arms behind you as you enter. It is evident that further resistance is useless, and would only cost us our lives. The Spaniards are twenty to one, and it is evident that all hope of resistance is at an end." The men were only too glad to accept the advice, and throwing down their arms, hurried away. Lionel sheathed his sword, and with the greatest difficulty made his way through the scene of wild confusion to the house where he had lodged. The doors of most of the houses were fast closed and the inhabitants were hurling down missiles of all kinds from the upper windows upon their late masters. The triumphant shouts of the Spaniards rose loud in the air, mingled with despairing cries and the crack of firearms. Lionel had several narrow escapes from the missiles thrown from the windows and roofs, but reached the house of the merchant safely. The door was half opened.

"Thanks be to heaven that you have come. I had well nigh given you up, and in another minute should have closed the door. The women are all below, but I waited until the last minute for you."

Barring the door Lionel's host led the way downstairs into a great cellar, which served as a warehouse, and extended under the whole house. He made his way through the boxes and bales to the darkest corner of the great cellar. Here he pulled up a flag and showed another narrow stair, at the bottom of which a torch was burning. Bidding Lionel descend he followed him, lowered the flag behind him, and then led the way along a narrow passage, at the end of which was a door. Opening it Lionel found himself in an arched chamber. Two torches were burning, and the merchant's wife and daughters and the two female domestics were assembled. There was a general exclamation of gladness as Lionel entered.

"We have been greatly alarmed," the mercer's wife said, "lest you should not be able to gain the house, Master Vickars; for we heard that the Spaniards are broken in at several points."

"It was fortunately at the other end of the town to that which I was stationed," Lionel said; "and I was just in time. You have a grand hiding place here. It looks like the crypt of a church."

"That is just what it is," the mercer said. "It was the church of a monastery that stood here a hundred years ago. The monks then moved into a grander place in Paris, and the monastery and church which adjoined our house were pulled down and houses erected upon the site. My grandfather, knowing of the existence of the crypt, thought that it might afford a rare hiding place in case of danger, and had the passage driven from his cellar into it. Its existence could never be suspected; for as our cellar extends over the whole of our house, as can easily be seen, none would suspect that there was a hiding place without our walls. There are three or four chambers as large as this. One of them is stored with all my choicest silks and velvets, another will serve as a chamber for you and me. I have enough provisions for a couple of months, and even should they burn the house down we are safe enough here."

CHAPTER XIX. STEENWYK

Three days passed, and then a slight noise was heard as of the trap door being raised. Lionel drew his sword.

"It is my servant, no doubt," the merchant said; "he promised to come and tell me how things went as soon as he could get an opportunity to come down unobserved. We should hear more noise if it were the Spaniards." Taking a light he went along the passage, and returned immediately afterwards followed by his man; the latter had his head bound up, and carried his arm in a sling. An exclamation of pity broke from the ladies.

"You are badly hurt, Jacques. What has happened?"

"It is well it is no worse, mistress," he replied. "The Spaniards are fiends, and behaved as if they were sacking a city of Dutch Huguenots instead of entering a town inhabited by friends. For an hour or two they cut and slashed, pillaged and robbed. They came rushing into the shop, and before I could say a word one ran me through the shoulder and another laid my head open. It was an hour or two before I came to my senses. I found the house turned topsy turvy; everything worth taking had gone, and what was not taken was damaged. I tied up my head and arm as best I could, and then sat quiet in a corner till the din outside began to subside. The officers did their best, I hear, and at last got the men into order. Numbers of the townsfolk have been killed, and every one of the garrison was butchered. I tell you, mistress, it is better to have ten Huguenot armies in possession one after another than one Spanish force, though the latter come as friends and co-religionists. Well, as soon as things quieted down the soldiers were divided among the houses of the townsfolk, and we have a sergeant and ten men quartered above; but half an hour ago they were called away on some duty, and I took the opportunity to steal down here."

"Have you told them that we were away, Jacques?"

"No, monsieur; no one has asked me about it. They saw by the pictures and shrines that you were good Catholics, and after the first outburst they have left things alone. But if it is not too dreary for the ladies here, I should advise you to wait for a time and see how things go before you show yourselves."

"That is my opinion too, Jacques. We can wait here for another two months if need be. Doubtless, unless the Huguenots show signs of an intention to attack the town, only a small garrison will be left here, and it may be that those in our house will be withdrawn."

"Do you think it will be possible for me to make my escape, Jacques?" Lionel asked.

"I should think so, sir. Ever since the Spaniards entered the town boats with provisions for Paris have been coming along in great numbers. From what I hear the soldiers say there is no chance of a battle at present, for the Huguenot army have drawn off to a distance, seeing that Paris is revictualled and that there is no chance of taking it. They say that numbers of the French lords with the Huguenot army have drawn off and are making

232

for their homes. At any rate there is no fear of an attack here, and the gates stand open all day. Numbers of the townsfolk have been to Paris to see friends there, and I should say that if you had a disguise you could pass out easily enough."

The question was discussed for some time. Lionel was very anxious to rejoin the army, and it was finally settled that Jacques should the next night bring him down a suit of his own clothes, and the first time the soldiers were all away should fetch him out, accompany him through the gates of the town, and act as his guide as far as he could.

The next night Lionel received the clothes. Two days later Jacques came down early in the morning to say that the soldiers above had just gone out on duty. Lionel at once assumed his disguise, and with the heartiest thanks for the great service they had rendered him took his leave of the kind merchant and his family. Jacques was charged to accompany him as far as possible, and to set him well on his way towards the Huguenot army, for Lionel's small knowledge of French would be detected by the first person who accosted him. On going out into the street Lionel found that there were many peasants who had come in to sell fowls, eggs, and vegetables in the town, and he and Jacques passed without a question through the gates.

Jacques had, the evening before, ascertained from the soldiers the position of Parma's army. A long detour had to be made, and it was two days before they came in sight of the tents of Henry's camp. They had observed the greatest precautions on their way, and had only once fallen in with a troop of Parma's cavalry. These had asked no questions, supposing that Jacques and his companion were making their way from Paris to visit their friends after the siege, there being nothing in their attire to attract attention, still less suspicion. The peasants they met on their way eagerly demanded news from Paris, but Jacques easily satisfied them by saying that they had had a terrible time, and that many had died of hunger, but that now that the river was open again better times had come. When within a couple of miles of the army Jacques said good–bye to Lionel, who would have rewarded him handsomely for his guidance, but Jacques would not accept money.

"You are the master's guest," he said, "and you saved his house from plunder when your people were in possession. He and my mistress would never forgive me if I took money from you. I am well content in having been able to assist so kind a young gentleman."

When Lionel arrived at the camp he soon found his way to Sir Ralph Pimpernel's tent, where he was received as one from the dead. There was no difficulty in providing himself again with armour and arms, for of these there were abundance — the spoils of Ivry — in the camp. When he was reclothed and rearmed Sir Ralph took him to the king's tent, and from him Henry learned for the first time the circumstances that had attended the capture of Lagny.

"And so they put the whole garrison to the sword," the king said with indignation. "I will make any Spaniards that fall in my hands pay dearly for it!"

Henry had indeed been completely out generalled by his opponent. While he had been waiting with his army for a pitched battle Parma had invested Lagny, and there were no means of relieving it except by crossing the river in the face of the whole army of the enemy, an enterprise impossible of execution. As soon as Lagny had fallen provisions and ammunition were at once poured into Paris, two thousand boat loads arriving in a single day.

King Henry's army immediately fell to pieces. The cavalry having neither food nor forage rode off by hundreds every day, and in a week but two thousand out of his six thousand horse remained with him. The infantry also, seeing now no hope of receiving their arrears of pay, disbanded in large numbers, and after an unsuccessful attempt to carry Paris by a night attack, the king fell back with the remnant of his force. Corbeil was assaulted and captured by Parma, and the two great rivers of Paris were now open.

If Parma could have remained with his army in France, the cause of Henry of Navarre would have been lost. But sickness was making ravages among his troops. Dissensions broke our between the Spaniards, Italians, and Netherlanders of his army and their French allies, who hated the foreigners, though they had come to their assistance. Lastly, his presence was urgently required in the Netherlands, where his work was as far from being done as ever. Therefore to the dismay of the Leaguers he started early in November on his march back.

No sooner did he retire than the king took the field again, recaptured Lagny and Corbeil, and recommenced the siege of Paris, while his cavalry hung upon the rear and flanks of Parma's army and harassed them continually, until they crossed the frontier, where the duke found that affairs had not improved during his absence.

Lionel had obtained permission to accompany the force which captured Lagny, and as soon as they entered the town hurried to the mercer's house. He found Jacques in possession, and learned that the family had weeks before left the crypt and reoccupied the house, but had again taken refuge there when the Huguenots attacked the town. Lionel at once went below, and was received with delight. He was now able to repay to some extent the obligations he had received from them, by protecting them from all interference by the new captors of the town, from whom the majority of the citizens received harsh treatment for the part they had taken in attacking the garrison when the Spaniards first entered.

Prince Maurice's visit to the camp of Henry had been but a short one; and as soon as Parma had effected the relief of Paris, and there was no longer a chance of a great battle being fought, he returned to Holland, followed after the recapture of Lagny by Sir Ralph Pimpernel and the few survivors of his party, who were all heartily weary of the long period of inaction that had followed the victory at Ivry.

They found that during their absence there had been little doing in the Netherlands, save that Sir Francis Vere, with a small body of English infantry and cavalry, had stormed some formidable works the Spaniards had thrown up to prevent relief being given to Recklinghausen, which they were besieging. He effected the relief of the town and drove off the besiegers. He then attacked and captured a fort on the bank of the Rhine, opposite the town of Wesel.

At the end of the year 1590 there were, including the garrisons, some eight thousand English infantry and cavalry in Holland, and the year that followed was to see a great change in the nature of the war. The efforts of Prince Maurice to improve his army were to bear effect, and with the assistance of his English allies he was to commence an active offensive war, to astonish his foes by the rapidity with which he manoeuvred the new fighting machine he had created, and to commence a new departure in the tactics of war.

In May he took the field, requesting Vere to cooperate with him in the siege of Zutphen. But Sir Francis determined in the first place to capture on his own account the Zutphen forts on the opposite side of the river, since these had been lost by the treachery of Roland Yorke. He dressed up a score of soldiers, some as peasants, others as countrywomen, and provided them with baskets of eggs and other provisions. At daybreak these went down by twos and threes to the Zutphen ferry, as if waiting to be taken across to the town; and while waiting for the boat to come across for them, they sat down near the gate of the fort.

A few minutes later a party of English cavalry were seen riding rapidly towards the fort. The pretended country people sprang to their feet, and with cries of alarm ran towards it for shelter. The gates were thrown open to allow them to enter. As they ran in they drew out the arms concealed under their clothes and overpowered the guard. The cavalry dashed up and entered the gate before the garrison could assemble, and the fort was captured.

Vere at once began to throw up his batteries for the attack upon the town across the river, and the prince invested the city on the other side. So diligently did the besiegers work that before a week had passed after the surprise of the fort the batteries were completed, thirty–two guns placed in position, and the garrison, seeing there was no hope of relief, surrendered.

On the very day of taking possession of the town, the allies, leaving a garrison there, marched against Deventer, seven miles down the river, and within five days had invested the place, and opened their batteries upon the weakest part of the town. A breach was effected, and a storm was ordered. A dispute arose between the English, Scotch, and Dutch troops as to who should have the honour of leading the assault. Prince Maurice decided in favour of the English, in order that they might have an opportunity of wiping out the stigma on the national honour caused by the betrayal of Deventer by the traitor Sir William Stanley.

To reach the breach it was necessary to cross a piece of water called the Haven. Sir Francis Vere led the English across the bridge of boats which had been thrown over the water; but the bridge was too short. Some of the troops sprang over and pushed boldly for the breach, others were pushed over and drowned. Many of those behind stripped off their armour and swam across the Haven, supported by some Dutch troops who had been told off to follow the assaulting party. But at the breach they were met by Van der Berg, the governor, with seven companies of soldiers, and these fought so courageously that the assailants were unable to win their way up the breach, and fell back at last with a loss of two hundred and twenty–five men killed and wounded.

While the assault was going on, the artillery of the besiegers continued to play upon other parts of the town, and effected great damage. On the following night the garrison endeavoured to capture the bridge across the Haven, but were repulsed with loss, and in the morning the place surrendered. The success of the patriots was due in no slight degree to the fact that Parma with the greatest part of his army was again absent in France, and the besieged towns had therefore no hope of assistance from without. The States now determined to seize the opportunity of capturing the towns held by the Spaniards in Friesland.

The three principal towns in the possession of the Spaniards were Groningen, Steenwyk, and Coevorden. After capturing several less important places and forts Prince Maurice advanced against Steenwyk. But just as he was about to commence the siege he received pressing letters from the States to hurry south, as Parma was marching with his whole army to capture the fort of Knodsenburg, which had been raised in the previous autumn as a preparation for the siege of the important city of Nymegen.

The Duke of Parma considered that he had ample time to reduce Knodsenburg before Prince Maurice could return to its assistance. Two great rivers barred the prince's return, and he would have to traverse the dangerous district called the Foul Meadow, and the great quagmire known as the Rouvenian Morass. But Prince Maurice had now an opportunity of showing the excellence of the army he had raised and trained. He received the news of Parma's advance on the 15th of July; two days later he was on the march south, and in five days had thrown bridges of boats across the two rivers, had crossed morass and swamp, and appeared in front of the Spanish army.

One assault had already been delivered by the Spaniards against Knodsenburg, but this had been repulsed with heavy loss. As soon as the patriot army approached the neighbourhood, Parma's cavalry went out to drive in its skirmishers. Vere at once proposed to Prince Maurice to inflict a sharp blow upon the enemy, and with the approval of the prince marched with 1200 foot and 500 horse along the dyke which ran across the low country. Marching to a spot where a bridge crossed a narrow river he placed half his infantry in ambush there; the other half a quarter of a mile further back.

Two hundred light cavalry were sent forward to beat up the enemy's outposts, and then retreat; the rest of the cavalry were posted in the rear of the infantry. Another dyke ran nearly parallel with the first, falling into it at some distance in the rear of Vere's position, and here Prince Maurice stationed himself with a body of horse and foot to cover Vere's retreat should he be obliged to fall back. About noon the light cavalry skirmished with the enemy and fell back, but were not followed. About half an hour later the scouts brought word that the Spaniards were at hand.

Suddenly and without orders 800 of Maurice's cavalry galloped off to meet the enemy; but they soon came back again at full speed, with a strong force of Spanish cavalry in pursuit. Vere's infantry at once sallied out from their ambush among the trees, poured their fire into the enemy, and charged them with their pikes. The Spaniards turned to fly, when Vere's cavalry charged them furiously and drove them back in headlong rout to their own camp, taking a great number of prisoners, among them many officers of rank, and 500 horses. Parma finding himself thus suddenly in face of a superior army, with a rapid river in his rear, fell back across the Waal, and then proceeded to Spa to recruit his shattered health, leaving Verdugo, an experienced officer, in command.

Instead of proceeding to besiege Nymegen, Maurice marched away as suddenly and quickly as before, and captured Hulst, on the borders of Zeeland and Brabant, a dozen miles only from Antwerp, and then turning again was, in three days, back at Nymegen, and had placed sixty−eight pieces of artillery in position. He opened fire on the 20th of October, and the next day the important city of Nymegen surrendered. This series of brilliant successes greatly raised the spirits of the Netherlanders, and proportionately depressed those of the Spaniards and their adherents.

Parma himself was ill from annoyance and disappointment. The army with which he might have completed the conquest of the Netherlands had, in opposition to his entreaties and prayers, been frittered away by Philip's orders in useless expeditions in France, while the young and active generals of the Dutch and English armies were snatching town after town from his grasp, and consolidating the Netherlands, so recently broken up by Spanish strongholds, into a compact body, whose increasing wealth and importance rendered it every day a more formidable opponent. It is true that Parma had saved first Paris and afterwards Rouen for the League, but it was at the cost of loosening Philip's hold over the most important outpost of the Spanish dominions.

In the following spring Parma was again forced to march into France with 20,000 men, and Maurice, as soon as the force started, prepared to take advantage of its absence. With 6000 foot and 2000 horse he again appeared at the end of May before Steenwyk. This town was the key to the province of Drenthe, and one of the safeguards of Friesland; it was considered one of the strongest fortresses of the time. Its garrison consisted of sixteen companies of foot and some cavalry, and 1200 Walloon infantry, commanded by Lewis, the youngest of the Counts de Berg, a brave lad of eighteen years of age.

In this siege, for the first time, the spade was used by soldiers in the field. Hitherto the work had been considered derogatory to troops, and peasants and miners had been engaged for the work; but Prince Maurice had taught his soldiers that their duty was to work as well as fight, and they now proved the value of his teaching.

The besieged made several successful sorties, and Sir Francis Vere had been severely wounded in the leg. The cannonade effected but little damage on the strong walls; but the soldiers, working night and day, drove mines under two of the principal bastions, and constructed two great chambers there; these were charged, one with five thousand pounds of powder, the other with half that quantity. On the 3d of July the mines were sprung. The bastion of the east gate was blown to pieces and the other bastion greatly injured, but many of the Dutch troops standing ready for the assault were also killed by the explosion.

The storming parties, however, rushed forward, and the two bastions were captured. This left the town at the mercy of the besiegers. The next day the garrison surrendered, and were permitted to march away. Three hundred and fifty had been killed, among them young Count Lewis Van der Berg, and two hundred had been left behind, severely wounded, in the town. Between five and six hundred of the besiegers were killed during the course of the siege. The very day after the surrender of Steenwyk Maurice marched away and laid siege to Coevorden. This city, which was most strongly fortified, lay between two great swamps, between which there was a passage of about half a mile in width.

Another of the Van der Bergs, Count Frederick, commanded the garrison of a thousand veterans. Verdugo sent to Parma and Mondragon for aid, but none could be sent to him, and the prince worked at his fortifications undisturbed. His force was weakened by the withdrawal of Sir Francis Vere with three of the English regiments, Elizabeth having sent peremptory orders that this force should follow those already withdrawn to aid Henry of Navarre in Brittany. Very unwillingly Vere obeyed, and marched to Doesburg on the Yssel. But a fortnight after he arrived there, while he was waiting for ships to transport him to Brittany the news came to him that Verdugo, having gathered a large force together, was about to attack Prince Maurice in his camp, and Vere at once started to the prince's aid.

On the night of the 6th of September, Verdugo, with 4000 foot and 1800 cavalry, wearing their shirts outside their armour to enable them to distinguish each other in the dark, fell upon Maurice's camp. Fortunately the prince was prepared, having intercepted a letter from Verdugo to the governor of the town. A desperate battle took place, but at break of day, while its issue was still uncertain, Vere, who had marched all night, came up and threw himself into the battle. His arrival was decisive. Verdugo drew off with a loss of 300 killed, and five days later Coevorden surrendered, and Prince Maurice's army went into winter quarters.

A few weeks later Parma died, killed by the burden Philip threw upon him, broken down by the constant disappointment of his hopes of carrying his work to a successful end, by the incessant interference of Philip with his plans, and by the anxiety caused by the mutinies arising from his inability to pay his troops, although he had borrowed to the utmost on his own possessions, and pawned even his jewels to keep them from starvation. He was undoubtedly the greatest commander of his age, and had he been left to carry out his own plans would have crushed out the last ember of resistance in the Netherlands and consolidated the power of Spain there.

He was succeeded in his post by the Archduke Albert, but for a time Ernest Mansfeldt continued to command the army, and to manage the affairs in the Netherlands. In March, 1593, Prince Maurice appeared with his army in front of Gertruydenberg. The city itself was an important one, and its position on the Maas rendered it of the greatest use to the Spaniards, as through it they were at any moment enabled to penetrate into the heart of Holland. Gertruydenberg and Groningen, the capital of Friesland, were now, indeed, the only important places in the republic that remained in possession of the Spaniards. Hohenlohe with a portion of the army established himself to the east of the city, Maurice with its main body to the west.

Two bridges constructed across the river Douge afforded a means of communication between two armies, and plank roads were laid across the swamps for the passage of baggage wagons. Three thousand soldiers laboured incessantly at the works, which were intended not only to isolate the city, but to defend the besiegers from any attack that might be made upon them by a relieving army. The better to protect themselves, miles of country were laid under water, and palisade work erected to render the country impregnable by cavalry.

Ernest Mansfeldt did his best to relieve the town. His son, Count Charles, with five thousand troops, had been sent into France, but by sweeping up all the garrisons, he moved with a considerable army towards Gertruydenberg and challenged Maurice to issue out from his lines to fight him. But the prince had no idea of risking a certain success upon the issue of a battle.

A hundred pieces of artillery on the batteries played incessantly on the town, while a blockading squadron of Zeeland ships assisted in the bombardment, and so terrible was the fire, that when the town was finally taken only four houses were found to have escaped injury.

Two commandants of the place were killed one after the other, and the garrison of a thousand veterans, besides the burgher militia, was greatly reduced in strength. At last, after ninety days' siege, the town suddenly fell. Upon the 24th of June three Dutch captains were relieving guard in the trenches near the great north bastion of the town, when it occurred to them to scale the wall of the fort and see what was going on inside. They threw some planks across the ditch, and taking half a company of soldiers, climbed cautiously up. They obtained a foothold before the alarm was given. There was a fierce hand to hand struggle, and sixteen of the party fell, and nine of the garrison. The rest fled into the city. The Governor Gysant, rushing to the rescue without staying to put on his armour, was killed.

Count Solms came from the besieging camp to investigate the sudden uproar, and to his profound astonishment was met by a deputation from the city asking for terms of surrender. Prince Maurice soon afterwards came up, and the terms of capitulation were agreed upon. The garrison were allowed to retire with side arms and baggage, and fifty wagons were lent to them to carry off their wounded.

In the following spring Coevorden, which had been invested by Verdugo, was relieved, and Groningen, the last great city of the Netherlands in the hands of the Spaniards, was besieged. Mines were driven under its principal bastion, and when these were sprung, after sixty–five days' siege, the city was forced to surrender. Thus for the first time, after years of warfare, Holland, Zeeland, and Friesland became truly united, and free from the grasp of the hated invader.

Throughout the last three years of warfare Sir Francis Vere had proved an able assistant to the prince, and the English troops had fought bravely side by side with the Dutch; but their contingent had been but a small one, for the majority of Vere's force had, like that of the Spaniards, been withdrawn for service in France. The struggle in that country was nearly at an end. The conversion of Henry of Navarre for the second time to the Catholic religion had ranged many Catholics, who had hitherto been opposed to him, under his banner, while many had fallen away from the ranks of the League in disgust, when Philip of Spain at last threw off the mask of disinterestedness, and proposed his nephew the Archduke Ernest as king of France.

In July, 1595, a serious misfortune befell the allied army. They had laid siege to Crolle, and had made considerable progress with the siege, when the Spanish army, under command of Mondragon, the aged governor of Antwerp, marched to its relief. As the army of Maurice was inferior in numbers, the States would nor consent to a general action. The siege was consequently raised; and Mondragon having attained his object, fell back to a position on the Rhine at Orsoy, above Rheinberg, whence he could watch the movements of the allied army encamped on the opposite bank at Bislich, a few miles below Wesel.

The Spanish army occupied both sides of the river, the wing on the right bank being protected from attack by the river Lippe, which falls into the Rhine at Wesel, and by a range of moorland hills called the Testerburg. The Dutch cavalry saw that the slopes of this hill were occupied by the Spaniards, but believed that their force consisted only of a few troops of horse. Young Count Philip of Nassau proposed that a body of cavalry should swim the Lippe, and attack and cut them off. Prince Maurice and Sir Francis Vere gave a very reluctant consent to the enterprise, but finally allowed him to take a force of five hundred men.

With him were his brothers Ernest and Louis, his nephew Ernest de Solms, and many other nobles of Holland. Sir Marcellus Bacx was in command of them. The English contingent was commanded by Sir Nicholas Parker and Robert Vere. On August 22d they swam the Lippe and galloped in the direction where they expected to find two or three troops of Spanish horse; but Mondragon had received news of their intentions, and they suddenly saw before them half the Spanish army. Without hesitation the five hundred

English and Dutch horsemen charged desperately into the enemy's ranks, and fought with extraordinary valour, until, altogether overpowered by numbers, Philip of Nassau and his nephew Ernest were both mortally wounded and taken prisoners.

Robert Vere was slain by a lance thrust in the face, and many other nobles and gentlemen fell. Thus died one of the three brave brothers, for the youngest, Horace, had also joined the army in 1590. The survivors of the band under Sir Nicholas Parker and Marcellus Bacx managed to effect their retreat, covered by a reserve Prince Maurice had posted on the opposite side of the river.

CHAPTER XX. CADIZ

In March, 1596, Sir Francis Vere returned to Holland. He had during his absence in England been largely taken into the counsels of Queen Elizabeth, and it had been decided that the war should be carried into the enemy's country, and a heavy blow struck at the power of Spain. Vere had been appointed to an important command in the proposed expedition, and had now come out charged with the mission of persuading the States General to cooperate heartily with England, and to contribute both money and men. There was much discussion in the States; but they finally agreed to comply with the queen's wishes, considering that there was no surer way of bringing the war to a termination than to transport it nearer to the heart of the enemy.

As soon as the matter was arranged, Sir Francis Vere left the Hague and went to Middleburg, where the preparations for the Dutch portion of the expedition were carried out. It consisted of twenty– two Dutch ships, under Count William of Nassau, and a thousand of the English troops in the pay of the States. The company commanded by Lionel Vickars was one of those chosen to accompany the expedition; and on the 22d of April it started from Flushing and joined the British fleet assembled at Dover. This was under the command of Lord Howard as lord admiral, the Earl of Essex as general, Lord Thomas Howard as vice admiral, and Sir Walter Raleigh as rear admiral.

Sir Francis Vere was lieutenant general and lord marshal. He was to be the chief adviser of the Earl of Essex, and to have the command of operations on shore. The ships of war consisted of the Ark Royal, the Repulse, Mere Honour, War Sprite, Rainbow, Mary Rose, Dreadnought, Vanguard, Nonpareil, Lion, Swiftsure, Quittance, and Tremontaine. There were also twelve ships belonging to London, and the twenty–two Dutch vessels. The fleet, which was largely fitted out at the private expense of Lord Howard and the Earl of Essex, sailed from Dover to Plymouth. Sir Francis Vere went by land, and set to work at the organization of the army.

A month was thus spent, and on the 1st of June the fleet set sail. It carried 6860 soldiers and 1000 volunteers, and was manned by nearly 7000 sailors. There had been some dispute as to the relative ranks of Sir Francis Vere and Sir Walter Raleigh, and it was settled that Sir Francis should have precedence on shore, and Sir Walter Raleigh at sea.

All on board the fleet were full of enthusiasm at the enterprise upon which they were embarked. It was eight years since the Spanish Armada had sailed to invade England; now an English fleet was sailing to attack Spain on her own ground. Things had changed indeed in that time. Spain, which had been deemed invincible, had suffered many reverses; while England had made great strides in power, and was now mistress of the seas, on which Spain had formerly considered herself to be supreme.

A favourable wind from the northeast carried the fleet rapidly across the Bay of Biscay, and it proceeded on its way, keeping well out of sight of the coast of Portugal. The three fastest sailers of the fleet were sent on ahead as soon as they rounded Cape St. Vincent, with orders to capture all small vessels which might carry to Cadiz the tidings of the approach of the fleet.

Early on the morning of the 20th June the fleet anchored off the spit of San Sebastian on the southern side of the city.

Cadiz was defended by the fort of San Sebastian on one side and that of San Felipe on the other; while the fort of Puntales, on the long spit of sand connecting the city with the mainland, defended the channel leading up to Puerto Real, and covered by its guns the Spanish galleys and ships of war anchored there. Lying off the town when the English fleet came in sight were forty richly laden merchant ships about to sail for Mexico, under the convoy of four great men of war, two Lisbon galleons, two argosies, and three frigates.

As soon as the English were seen, the merchant ships were ordered up the channel to Puerto Real, and the men of war and the fleet of seventeen war galleys were ranged under the guns of Fort Puntales to prevent the English passing up. It had first been decided to attempt a landing in the harbour of Galeta, on the south side of the city; but a heavy sea was setting in, and although the troops had been got into the boats they were re–embarked, and the fleet sailed round and anchored at the mouth of the channel leading up the bay. A council of war was held that night, and it was decided that the fleet should move up the bay with the tide next morning, and attack the Spanish fleet.

The next morning at daybreak the ships got up their anchors and sailed up the channel, each commander vying with the rest in his eagerness to be first in the fray. They were soon hotly engaged with the enemy; the fort, men of war, and galleys opening a heavy fire upon them, to which, anchoring as close as they could get to the foe, the English ships hotly responded. The galleys were driven closer in under the shelter of the fire of the fort, and the fire was kept up without intermission from six o'clock in the morning until four in the afternoon.

By that time the Spaniards had had enough of it. The galleys slipped their cables and made sail for a narrow channel across the spit, covered by the guns of the fort. Three of them were captured by Sir John Wingfield in the vanguard, but the rest got through the channel and escaped. The men of war endeavoured to run ashore, but boarding parties in boats from the Ark Royal and Repulse captured two of them. The Spaniards set fire to the other two. The argosies and galleons were also captured. Sir Francis Vere at once took the command of the land operations. The boats were all lowered, and the regiments of Essex, Vere, Blount, Gerard, and Clifford told off as a landing party. They were formed in line. The Earl of Essex and Sir Francis Vere took their place in a boat in advance of the line, and were followed by smaller boats crowded with gentlemen volunteers.

They landed between the fort of Puntales and the town. The regiments of Blount, Gerard, and Clifford were sent to the narrowest part of the spit to prevent reinforcements being thrown into the place; while those of Essex and Vere and the gentlemen volunteers turned towards Cadiz. Each of these parties consisted of about a thousand men.

The walls of Cadiz were so strong that it had been intended to land guns from the fleet, raise batteries, and make a breach in the walls. Vere, however, perceiving some Spanish cavalry and infantry drawn up outside the walls, suggested to Essex that an attempt should be made to take the place by surprise. The earl at once agreed to the plan.

Vere marched the force across to the west side of the spit, his movements being concealed by the sand hills from the Spanish. Sir John Wingfield with two hundred men was ordered to march rapidly on against the enemy, driving in their skirmishers, and then to retreat hastily when the main body advanced against him. Three hundred men under Sir Matthew Morgan were posted as supports to Wingfield, and as soon as the latter's flying force joined them the whole were to fall upon the Spaniards and in turn chase them back to the walls, against which the main body under Essex and Vere were to advance.

The orders were ably carried out. The Spaniards in hot chase of Wingfield found themselves suddenly confronted by Morgan's force, who fell upon them so furiously that they fled back to the town closely followed by the English. Some of the fugitives made their way in at the gates, which were hurriedly closed, while others climbed up at the bastions, which sloped sufficiently to afford foothold. Vere's troops from the Netherlands, led by Essex, also scaled the bastions and then an inner wall behind it. As soon as they had captured this they rushed through the streets, shooting and cutting down any who opposed them.

Sir Francis Vere, who had also scaled the ramparts, knew that cities captured by assaults had often been lost again by the soldiers scattering. He therefore directed the rest of the troops to burst open the gate. This was with some difficulty effected, and he then marched them in good order to the marketplace, where the Spaniards had rallied and were hotly engaged with Essex. The opposition was soon beaten down, and those defending the town hall were forced to surrender. The troops were then marched through the town, and the garrison driven either into the convent of San Francisco or into the castle of Felipe. The convent surrendered on the same evening and the castle on the following day. The loss upon the part of the assailants was very small, but Sir John Wingfield was mortally wounded.

The English behaved with the greatest courtesy to their captives, their conduct presenting an extraordinary contrast to that of the Spaniards under similar circumstance in the Netherlands. The women were treated with the greatest courtesy, and five thousand inhabitants, including women and priests, were allowed to leave the town with their clothes. The terms were that the city should pay a ransom of 520,000 ducats, and that some of the chief citizens should remain as hostages for payment. As soon as the fighting ceased, Lionel Vickars accompanied Sir Francis Vere through the streets to set guards, and see that no insult was offered to any of the inhabitants. As they passed along, the

246

door of one of the mansions was thrown open. A gentleman hurried out; he paused for a moment, exclaiming, "Sir Francis Vere!" and then looking at Lionel rushed forward towards him with a cry of delight. Sir Francis Vere and Lionel stared in astonishment as the former's name was called; but at the sound of his own name Lionel fell back a step as if stupefied, and then with a cry of "Geoffrey!" fell into his brother's arms.

"It is indeed Geoffrey Vickars!" Sir Francis Vere exclaimed. "Why, Geoffrey, what miracle is this? We have thought you dead these six years, and now we find you transmuted into a Spanish don."

"I may look like one, Sir Francis," Geoffrey said as he shook his old commander's hand, "but I am English to the backbone still. But my story is too long to tell now. You will be doubtless too busy tonight to spare time to listen to it, but I pray you to breakfast with me in the morning, when I will briefly relate to you the outline of my adventures. Can you spare my brother for tonight, Sir Francis?"

"I would do so were there ten times the work to be got through," Sir Francis replied. "Assuredly I would not keep asunder for a minute two brothers who have so long been separated. I will breakfast with you in the morning and hear this strange story of yours; for strange it must assuredly be, since it has changed my young page of the Netherlands into a Spanish hidalgo."

"I am no hidalgo, Sir Francis, but a trader of Cadiz, and I own that although I have been in some way a prisoner, seeing that I could not effect my escape, I have not fared badly. Now, Lionel, come in. I have another surprise for you." Lionel, still confused and wonder stricken at this apparent resurrection of his brother from the dead, followed him upstairs. Geoffrey led the way into a handsomely furnished apartment, where a young lady was sitting with a boy two years old in her lap.

"Dolores, this is my brother Lionel, of whom you have so often heard me speak. Lionel, this is my wife and my eldest boy, who is named after you."

It was some time before Lionel could completely realize the position, and it was not until Dolores in somewhat broken English bade him welcome that he found his tongue.

By England's Aid: or The Freeing

"But I cannot understand it all!" he exclaimed, after responding to the words of Dolores. "I saw my brother in the middle of the battle with the Armada. We came into collision with a great galleon, we lost one of our masts, and I never saw Geoffrey afterwards; and we all thought that he had either been shot by the musketeers on the galleon, or had been knocked overboard and killed by the falling mast."

"I had hoped that long before this you would have heard of my safety, Lionel, for a sailor friend of mine promised if he reached England to go down at once to Hedingham to tell them there. He left the ship he was in out in the West Indies, and I hoped had reached home safely."

"We have heard nothing, Geoffrey. The man has never come with your message. But now tell me how you were saved."

"I was knocked over by the mast, Lionel, but as you see I was not killed. I climbed up into a passing Spanish ship, and concealed myself in the chains until she was sunk, when I was, with many of the crew, picked up by the boats of other ships. I pretended to have lost my senses and my speech, and none suspected that I was English. The ship I was on board was one of those which succeeded after terrible hardships in returning to Spain. An Irish gentleman on board her, to whom I confided my secret, took me as a servant. After many adventures I sailed with him for Italy, where we hoped to get a ship for England. On the way we were attacked by Barbary pirates. We beat them off, but I was taken prisoner. I remained a captive among them for nearly two years, and then with a fellow prisoner escaped, together with Dolores and her father, who had also been captured by the pirates. We reached Spain in safety, and I have since passed as one of the many exiles from England and Ireland who have taken refuge here; and Senor Mendez, my wife's father, was good enough to bestow her hand upon me, partly in gratitude for the services I had rendered him in his escape, partly because he saw she would break her heart if he refused."

"You know that is not true, Geoffrey," Dolores interrupted.

"Never mind, Dolores, it is near enough. And with his daughter," he continued, "he gave me a share in his business. I have been a fortunate man indeed, Lionel; but I have always longed for a chance to return home; until now none has ever offered itself, and I have grieved continually at the thought that my father and mother and you were mourning for

248

me as dead. Now you have the outline of my story; tell me about all at home."

"Our father and mother are both well, Geoffrey, though your supposed loss was a great blow for them. But is it still home for you, Geoffrey? Do you really mean to return with us?"

"Of course I do, Lionel. At the time I married I arranged with Senor Mendez that whenever an opportunity occurred I was to return home, taking, of course, Dolores with me. She has been learning English ever since, and although naturally she would rather that we remained here she is quite prepared to make her home in England. We have two boys, this youngster, and a baby three months old, so, you see, you have all at once acquired nephews as well as a brother and sister. Here is Senor Mendez. This is my brother, senor, the Lionel after whom I named my boy, though I never dreamed that our next meeting would take place within the walls of Cadiz."

"You have astounded us, senor," the merchant said courteously. "We thought that Cadiz was safe from an attack; and though we were aware you had defeated our fleet we were astonished indeed when two hours since we heard by the din and firing in the streets that you had captured the city. Truly you English do not suffer the grass to grow under your feet. When we woke this morning no one dreamed of danger, and now in the course of one day you have destroyed our fleet, captured our town, and have our lives and properties at your disposal."

"Your lives are in no danger, senor, and all who choose are free to depart without harm or hindrance. But as to your property — I don't mean yours, of course, because as Geoffrey's father in law I am sure that Sir Francis Vere will inflict no fine upon you — but the city generally will have to pay, I hear, some half million ducats as ransom.

"That is as nothing," the Spaniard said, "to the loss the city will suffer in the loss of the forty merchant ships which you will doubtless capture or burn. Right glad am I that no cargo of mine is on board any of them, for I do not trade with Mexico; but I am sure the value of the ships with their cargoes cannot be less than twenty millions of ducats. This will fall upon the traders of this town and of Seville. Still, I own that the ransom of half a million for a city like Cadiz seems to me to be very moderate, and the tranquillity that already prevails in the town is beyond all praise. Would that such had been the behaviour of my countrymen in the Netherlands!"

Don Mendez spoke in a tone of deep depression. Geoffrey made a sign to his brother to come out on to the balcony, while the merchant took a seat beside his daughter.

"'Tis best to leave them alone," he said as they looked down into the street, where the English and their Dutch allies, many of whom had now landed, were wandering about examining the public buildings and churches, while the inhabitants looked with timid curiosity from their windows and balconies at the men who had, as if by magic, suddenly become their masters. "I can see that the old gentleman is terribly cut up. Of course, nothing has been said between us yet, for it was not until we heard the sound of firing in the streets that anyone thought there was the smallest risk of your capturing the city. Nevertheless, he must be sure that I shall take this opportunity of returning home.

"It has always been understood between us that I should do so as soon as any safe method of making a passage could be discovered; but after being here with him more than three years he had doubtless come to believe that such a chance would never come during his lifetime, and the thought of an early separation from his daughter, and the break up of our household here, must be painful to him in the extreme. It has been settled that I should still remain partner in the firm, and should manage our affairs in England and Holland; but this will, of course, be a comparatively small business until peace is restored, and ships are free to come and go on both sides as they please. But I think it is likely he will himself come to live with us in England, and that we shall make that the headquarters of the firm, employing our ships in traffic with Holland, France, and the Mediterranean until peace is restored with Spain, and having only an agent here to conduct such business as we may be able to carry on under the present stringent regulations.

"In point of fact, even if we wound up our affairs and disposed of our ships, it would matter little to us, for Mendez is a very rich man, and as Dolores is his only child he has no great motive beyond the occupation it gives him for continuing in business.

"So you are a captain now, Lionel! Have you had a great deal of fighting?"

"Not a great deal. The Spaniards have been too much occupied with their affairs in France to give us much work to do. In Holland I took part in the adventure that led to the capture of Breda, did some fighting in France with the army of Henry of Navarre, and have been concerned in a good many sieges and skirmishes. I do not know whether you heard of the death of Robert Vere. He came out just after the business of the Armada, and fell in the fight the other day near Wesel — a mad business of Count Philip of Nassau. Horace is serving with his troop. We have recovered all the cities in the three provinces, and Holland is now virtually rid of the Spaniards.

"Things have greatly changed since the days of Sluys and Bergen op Zoom. Holland has increased marvellously in strength and wealth. We have now a splendidly organized army, and should not fear meeting the Spaniards in the open field if they would but give the chance to do so in anything like equal numbers. Sir Francis is marshal of our army here, and is now considered the ablest of our generals; and he and Prince Maurice have never yet met with a serious disaster. But how have you escaped the Inquisition here, Geoffrey? I thought they laid hands on every heretic?"

"So they do," Geoffrey replied; "but you see they have never dreamed that I was a heretic. The English, Irish, and Scotchmen here, either serving in the army or living quietly as exiles, are, of course, all Catholics, and as they suppose me to be one of them, it does not seem to have entered their minds that I was a Protestant. Since I have been here I have gone with my wife and father in law to church, and have said my prayers in my own way while they have said theirs. I cannot say I have liked it, but as there was no church of my own it did not go against my conscience to kneel in theirs. I can tell you that, after being for nearly a couple of years a slave among the Moors, one thinks less of these distinctions than one used to do. Had the Inquisition laid hands on me and questioned me, I should at once have declared myself a Protestant; but as long as I was not questioned I thought it no harm to go quietly and pay my devotions in a church, even though there were many things in that church with which I wholly disagreed.

"Dolores and I have talked the matter over often, and have arrived at the conclusion long since that there is no such great difference between us as would lead us to hate each other."

Lionel laughed.

"I suppose we generally see matters as we want to, Geoffrey; but it will be rather a shock to our good father and mother when you bring them home a Catholic daughter."

"I daresay when she has once settled in England among us, Lionel, she will turn round to our views on the subject; not that I should ever try to convert her, but it will likely enough come of itself. Of course, she has been brought up with the belief that heretics are very terrible people. She has naturally grown out of that belief now, and is ready to admit that there may be good heretics as well as good Catholics, which is a long step for a Spanish woman to take. I have no fear but that the rest will come in time. At present I have most carefully abstained from talking with her on the subject. When she is once in England I shall be able to talk to her freely without endangering her life by doing so."

Upon the following morning Sir Francis Vere breakfasted with Geoffrey, and then he and Lionel heard the full account of his adventures, and the manner in which it came about that he was found established as a merchant in Cadiz.

They then talked over the situation. Sir Francis was much vexed that the lord admiral had not complied with the earnest request the Earl of Essex had sent him, as soon as he landed, to take prompt measures for the pursuit and capture of the merchant ships. Instead of doing this, the admiral, considering the force that had landed to be dangerously weak, had sent large reinforcements on shore as soon as the boats came off, and the consequence was that at dawn that morning masses of smoke rising from the Puerto Real showed that the Duke of Medina Sidonia had set the merchant ships on fire rather than that they should fall into the hands of the English.

For a fortnight the captors of Cadiz remained in possession. Senor Mendez had, upon the day after their entry, discussed the future with Geoffrey. To the latter's great satisfaction he took it for granted that his son in law would sail with Dolores and the children in the English fleet, and he at once entered into arrangements with him for his undertaking the management of the business of the firm in England and Holland.

"Had I wound up my affairs I should accompany you at once, for Dolores is everything to me, and you, Geoffrey, have also a large share of my affection; but this is impossible. We have at present all our fifteen ships at sea, and these on their return to port would be confiscated at once were I to leave. Besides, there are large transactions open with the merchants at Seville and elsewhere. Therefore I must, for the present at any rate, remain here. I shall incur no odium by your departure. It will be supposed that you have reconciled yourself with your government, and your going home will therefore seem only natural; and it will be seen that I could not, however much I were inclined, interfere to prevent the departure of Dolores and the children with you.

By England's Aid: or The Freeing

"I propose to send on board your ships the greater portion of my goods here suitable for your market. This, again, will not excite bad feelings, as I shall say that you as my partner insisted upon your right to take your share of our merchandise back to England with you, leaving me as my portion our fleet of vessels. Therefore all will go on here as before. I shall gradually reduce my business and dispose of the ships, transmitting my fortune to a banker in Brussels, who will be able to send it to England through merchants in Antwerp, and you can purchase vessels to replace those I sell.

"I calculate that it will take me a year to complete all my arrangements. After that I shall again sail for Italy, and shall come to England either by sea or by travelling through Germany, as circumstances may dictate. On arriving in London I shall know where to find you, for by that time you will be well known there; and at any rate the bankers to whom my money is sent will be able to inform me of your address."

These arrangements were carried out, and at the departure of the fleet, Geoffrey, with Dolores and the children, sailed in Sir Francis Vere's ship the Rainbow, Sir Francis having insisted on giving up his own cabin for the use of Dolores. On leaving Cadiz the town was fired, and the cathedral, the church of the Jesuits, the nunneries of Santa Maria and Candelaria, two hundred and ninety houses, and, greatest loss of all, the library of the Jesuits, containing invaluable manuscripts respecting the Incas of Peru, were destroyed.

The destruction of the Spanish fleet, and the enormous loss caused by the burning of Cadiz and the loss of the rich merchant fleet, struck a terrible blow at the power and resources of Spain. Her trade never recovered from its effects, and her prestige suffered very greatly in the eyes of Europe. Philip never rallied from the blow to his pride inflicted by this humiliation.

Lionel had at first been almost shocked to find that Geoffrey had married a Spanish woman and a Catholic; but the charming manner of Dolores, her evident desire to please, and the deep affection with which she regarded her husband, soon won his heart. He, Sir Francis Vere, and the other officers and volunteers on board, vied with each other in attention to her during the voyage; and Dolores, who had hitherto been convinced that Geoffrey was a strange exception to the rule that all Englishmen were rough and savage animals, and who looked forward with much secret dread to taking up her residence among them, was quite delighted, and assured Geoffrey she was at last convinced that all she had heard to the disadvantage of his countrymen was wholly untrue.

The fleet touched at Plymouth, where the news of the immense success they had gained was received with great rejoicing; and after taking in fresh water and stores, they proceeded along the coast and anchored in the mouth of the Thames. Here the greater part of the fleet was disbanded, the Rainbow and a few other vessels sailing up to Greenwich, where the captains and officers were received with great honour by the queen, and were feasted and made much of by the city.

The brothers, the day after the ship cast anchor, proceeded to town, and there hired horses for their journey down into Essex. This was accomplished in two days, Geoffrey riding with Dolores on a pillion behind him with her baby in her lap, while young Lionel was on the saddle before his uncle.

When they approached Hedingham Lionel said, "I had best ride forward Geoffrey to break the news to them of your coming. Although our mother has always declared that she would not give up hope that you would some day be restored to us, they have now really mourned you as dead."

"Very well, Lionel. It is but a mile or so; I will dismount and put the boy up in the saddle and walk beside him, and we shall be in a quarter of an hour after you."

The delight of Mr. and Mrs. Vickars on hearing Geoffrey was alive and close at hand was so great that the fact he brought home a Spanish wife, which would under other circumstances have been a great shock to them, was now scarcely felt, and when the rapturous greeting with which he was received on his arrival was over, they welcomed his pretty young wife with a degree of warmth which fully satisfied him. Her welcome was, of course, in the first place as Geoffrey's wife, but in a very short time his father and mother both came to love her for herself, and Dolores very quickly found herself far happier at Hedingham Rectory than she had thought she could be away from her native Spain.

The announcement Geoffrey made shortly after his arrival, that he had altogether abandoned the trade of soldiering, and should in future make his home in London, trading in conjunction with his father in law, assisted to reconcile them to his marriage. After a fortnight's stay at Hedingham Geoffrey went up to London, and there took a house in the city, purchased several vessels, and entered upon business, being enabled to take at once a good position among the merchants of London, thanks to the ample funds with which he was provided.

Two months later he went down to Essex and brought up Dolores and the children, and established them in his new abode.

The apprenticeship he had served in trade at Cadiz enabled Geoffrey to start with confidence in his business. He at once notified all the correspondents of the firm in the different ports of Europe, that in future the business carried on by Signor Juan Mendez at Cadiz would have its headquarters in London, and that the firm would trade with all ports with the exception of those of Spain. The result was that before many months had elapsed there were few houses in London doing a larger trade with the Continent than that of Mendez and Vickars, under which title they had traded from the time of Geoffrey's marriage with Dolores.

CHAPTER XXI. THE BATTLE OF NIEUPORT

The year after the capture of Cadiz, Lionel Vickars sailed under Sir Francis Vere with the expedition designed to attack the fleet which Philip of Spain had gathered in Ferrol, with the intention, it was believed, of invading Ireland in retaliation for the disaster at Cadiz. The expedition met with terrible weather in the Bay of Biscay, and put back scattered and disabled to Plymouth and Falmouth. In August they again sailed, but were so battered by another storm that the expedition against Ferrol was abandoned, and they sailed to the Azores. There, after a skirmish with the Spaniards, they scattered among the islands, but missed the great Spanish fleet laden with silver from the west, and finally returned to England without having accomplished anything, while they suffered from another tempest on their way home, and reached Plymouth with difficulty.

Fortunately the same storm scattered and destroyed the great Spanish fleet at Ferrol, and the weather thus for the second time saved England from invasion. Late in the autumn, after his return from the expedition, Sir Francis Vere went over to Holland, and by his advice Prince Maurice prepared in December to attack a force of 4000 Spanish infantry and 600 cavalry, which, under the command of the Count of Varras, had gathered at the village of Turnhout, twenty miles from Breda.

A force of 5000 foot and 800 horse were secretly assembled at Gertruydenberg. Sir

By England's Aid: or The Freeing

Francis Vere brought an English regiment, and personally commanded one of the two troops into which the English cavalry was divided. Sir Robert Sidney came with 300 of the English garrison at Flushing, and Sir Alexander Murray with a Scotch regiment. The expedition started on the 23d of January, 1598, and after marching twenty–four miles reached the village of Rivels, three miles from Turnhout, two hours after dark.

The night was bitter cold, and after cooking supper the men wrapt themselves up in their cloaks, and lay down on the frozen ground until daybreak. The delay, although necessary, enabled the enemy to make their escape. The news that the allies had arrived close at hand reached Count Varras at midnight, and a retreat was at once ordered. Baggage wagons were packed and despatched, escorted by the cavalry, and before dawn the whole force was well on its road. Prince Maurice had set off an hour before daybreak, and on reaching Turnhout found that the rear guard of the enemy had just left the village. They had broken down the wooden bridge across the River Aa, only one plank being left standing, and had stationed a party to defend it.

Maurice held a hasty council of war. All, with the exception of Sir Francis Vere and Sir Marcellus Bacx, were against pursuit, but Maurice took the advice of the minority. Vere. with two hundred Dutch musketeers advanced against the bridge; his musketry fire drove off the guard, and with a few mounted officers and the two hundred musketeers he set out in pursuit. He saw that the enemy's infantry were marching but slowly, and guessed that they were delayed by the baggage wagons in front.

The country was wooded, and he threw the musketeers among the trees with orders to keep up a dropping fire, while he himself with sixteen horsemen followed closely upon the enemy along the road. Their rear guard kept up a skirmishing fire, slightly wounding Vere in the leg; but all this caused delay, and it was three hours before they emerged on an open heath, three miles from the bridge. Vere placed his musketeers among some woods and inclosed fields on the left of the heath, and ordered them to keep up a brisk fire and to show themselves as if advancing to the attack. He himself, reinforced by some more horsemen who had come up, continued to follow in the open.

The heath was three miles across, and Vere, constantly skirmishing with the Spanish infantry, who were formed in four solid squares, kept watching for the appearance of Maurice and the cavalry. At length these came in sight. Vere galloped up to the prince, and urged that a charge should be made at once. The prince assented. Vere, with the

By England's Aid: or The Freeing

English cavalry, charged down upon the rear of the squares, while Hohenlohe swept down with the Dutch cavalry upon their flanks. The Spanish musketeers fired and at once fled, and the cavalry dashed in among the squares of pikemen and broke them.

Several of the companies of horse galloped on in pursuit of the enemy's horse and baggage. Vere saw that these would be repulsed, and formed up the English cavalry to cover their retreat. In a short time the disordered horse came back at full gallop, pursued by the Spanish cavalry, but these, seeing Vere's troops ready to receive them, retreated at once. Count Varras was slain, together with three hundred of the Spanish infantry. Six hundred prisoners were taken, and thirty-eight colours fell into the victor's hands.

The success was gained entirely by the eight hundred allied horse, the infantry never arriving upon the field. The brilliant little victory, which was one of the first gained by the allies in the open field, was the cause of great rejoicings. Not only were the Spaniards no longer invincible, but they had been routed by a force but one-sixth of their own number, and the battle showed how greatly the individual prowess of the two peoples had changed during the progress of the war.

The Archduke Ernest had died in 1595, and had been succeeded by the Archduke Albert in the government of the Netherlands. He had with him no generals comparable with Parma, or even with Alva. His troops had lost their faith in themselves and their contempt for their foes. Holland was grown rich and prosperous, while the enormous expenses of carrying on the war both in the Netherlands and in France, together with the loss of the Armada, the destruction of the great fleet at Ferrol, and the capture of Cadiz and the ships there, had exhausted the resources of Spain, and Philip was driven to make advances for peace to France and England. Henry IV, knowing that peace with Spain meant an end of the civil war that had so long exhausted France, at once accepted the terms of Philip, and made a separate peace, in spite of the remonstrances of the ambassadors of England and Holland, to both of which countries he owed it in no small degree that he had been enabled to support himself against the faction of the Guises backed by the power of Spain.

A fresh treaty was made between England and the Netherlands, Sir Francis Vere being sent out as special ambassador to negotiate. England was anxious for peace, but would not desert the Netherlands if they on their part would relieve her to some extent of the heavy expenses caused by the war. This the States consented to do, and the treaty was

257

duly signed on both sides. A few days before its conclusion Lord Burleigh, who had been Queen Elizabeth's chief adviser for forty years, died, and within a month of its signature Philip of Spain, whose schemes he had so long opposed, followed him to the grave.

On the 6th of the previous May Philip had formally ceded the Netherlands to his daughter Isabella, between whom and the Archduke Albert a marriage had been arranged. This took place on the 18th of April following, shortly after his death. It was celebrated at Valencia, and at the same time King Philip III was united to Margaret of Austria.

In the course of 1599 there was severe fighting on the swampy island between the rivers Waal and Maas, known as the Bommel Waat, and a fresh attempt at invasion by the Spaniards was repulsed with heavy loss, Sir Francis Vere and the English troops taking a leading part in the operations.

The success thus gained decided the States General to undertake an offensive campaign in the following year. The plan they decided upon was opposed both by Prince Maurice and Sir Francis Vere as being altogether too hazardous; but the States, who upon most occasions were averse to anything like bold action, upon the present occasion stood firm to their decision. Their plan was to land an army near Ostend, which was held by the English, and to besiege the town of Nieuport, west of Ostend, and after that to attack Dunkirk. In the opinion of the two generals an offensive operation direct from Holland would have been far preferable, as in case of disaster the army could fall back upon one of their fortified towns, whereas, if beaten upon the coast, they might be cut off from Ostend and entirely destroyed. However, their opinions were overruled, and the expedition prepared. It consisted of 12,000 infantry, 1600 cavalry, and 10 guns. It was formed into three divisions. The van, 4500 strong, including 1600 English veterans, was commanded by Sir Francis Vere; the second division by Count Everard Solms; the rear division by Count Ernest of Nassau; while Count Louis Gunther of Nassau was in command of the cavalry. The army embarked at Flushing, and landed at Philippine, a town at the head of the Braakeman inlet.

There was at the time only a small body of Spaniards in the neighbourhood, but as soon as the news reached the Archduke Albert at Brussels he concentrated his army round Ghent. The troops had for some time been in a mutinous state, but, as was always the case with them, they returned to their habits of military obedience the moment danger threatened.

By England's Aid: or The Freeing

The Dutch army advanced by rapid marches to the neighbourhood of Ostend, and captured the fort and redoubts which the Spaniards had raised to prevent its garrison from undertaking offensive operations.

Two thousand men were left to garrison these important positions, which lay on the line of march which the Spaniards must take coming from Bruges to Nieuport. The rest of the army then made their way across the country, intersected with ditches, and upon the following day arrived before Nieuport and prepared to besiege it. The Dutch fleet had arrived off the town, and co–operated with the army in building a bridge across the little river, and preparing for the siege.

Towards the evening, however, the news arrived from Ostend, nine miles away, that a large force of the enemy had appeared before one of the forts just captured. Most of the officers were of opinion that the Spanish force was not a large one, and that it was a mere feint to induce the Dutch to abandon the siege of Nieuport and return to Ostend. Sir Francis Vere maintained that it was the main body of the archduke's army, and advised Maurice to march back at once with his whole force to attack the enemy before they had time to take the forts.

Later on in the evening, however, two of the messengers arrived with the news that the forts had surrendered. Prince Maurice then, in opposition to Vere's advice, sent off 2500 infantry, 500 horse, and 2 guns, under the command of Ernest of Nassau, to prevent the enemy from crossing the low ground between Ostend and the sand hills, Vere insisting that the whole army ought to move. It fell out exactly as he predicted; the detachment met the whole Spanish army, and broke and fled at the first fire, and thus 2500 men were lost in addition to the 2000 who had been left to garrison the forts.

At break of day the army marched down to the creek, and as soon as the water had ebbed sufficiently waded across and took up their position among the sand hills on the seashore. The enemy's army was already in sight, marching along on the narrow strip of land between the foot of the dunes and the sea. A few hundred yards towards Ostend the sand hills narrowed, and here Sir Francis Vere took up his position with his division. He placed a thousand picked men, consisting of 250 English, 250 of Prince Maurice's guard, and 500 musketeers, partly upon two sand hills called the East and West Hill, and partly in the bottom between them, where they were covered by a low ridge connecting the two hills.

The five hundred musketeers were placed so that their fire swept the ground on the south, by which alone the enemy's cavalry could pass on that side. On the other ridge, facing the sea, were seven hundred English pikemen and musketeers; two hundred and fifty English and fifty of the guard held the position of East Hill, which was most exposed to the attack. The rest of the division, which consisted of six hundred and fifty English and two thousand Dutch, were placed in readiness to reinforce the advanced party. Half the cavalry, under Count Louis, were on the right of the dunes, and the other half, under Marcellus Bacx, on the left by the sea.

The divisions of Count Solms and Count Ernest of Nassau were also on the seashore in the rear of West Hill. A council of war was held to decide whether the army should advance to the attack or await it. Vere advised the latter course, and his advice was adopted.

The archduke's army consisted of ten thousand infantry, sixteen hundred horse, and six guns. Marshal Zapena was in command, while the cavalry were led by the Admiral of Arragon. They rested for two hours before advancing — waiting until the rise of the tide should render the sands unserviceable for cavalry, their main reliance being upon their infantry. Their cavalry led the advance, but the two guns Vere had placed on West Hill plied them so hotly with shot that they fell back in confusion.

It was now high tide, and there were but thirty yards between the sea and the sand hills. The Spaniards therefore marched their infantry into the dunes, while the cavalry prepared to advance between the sand hills and the cultivated fields inland. The second and third divisions of Maurice's army also moved away from the shore inland. They now numbered but three thousand men, as the four thousand five hundred who had been lost belonged entirely to these divisions, Sir Francis Vere's division having been left intact. It was upon the first division that the whole brunt of the battle fell, they receiving some assistance from the thousand men remaining under Count Solms that were posted next to them; while the rear division was never engaged at all.

At half past two o'clock on the afternoon of the 2d of June, 1600, the battle began. Vere's plan was to hold his advanced position as long as possible, bring the reserves up as required until he had worn out the Spaniards, then to send for the other two divisions and to fall upon them. The company of Lionel Vickars formed part of the three hundred men stationed on the East Hill, where Vere also had taken up his position. After an exchange of fire for some time five hundred picked Spanish infantry rushed across the hollow between the two armies, and charged the hill. For half an hour a desperate struggle took place; the Spaniards were then obliged to fall back behind some low ridges at its foot.

In the meantime the enemy's cavalry had advanced along the grass grown tract, a hundred and fifty yards wide, between the foot of the dunes and the cultivated country inland. They were received, however, by so hot a fire by the five hundred musketeers posted by Vere in the sand hills on their flank, and by the two cannon on West Hill, that they fell back upon their infantry just as the Dutch horse, under Count Louis, advanced to charge them.

Vere sent orders to a hundred Englishmen to move round from the ridge and to attack the Spaniards who had fallen back from the attack of East Hill, on their flank, while sixty men charged down the hill and engaged them in front. The Spaniards broke and fled back to their main body. Then, being largely reinforced, they advanced and seized a sandy knoll near West Hill. Here they were attacked by the English, and after a long and obstinate fight forced to retire. The whole of the Spanish force now advanced, and tried to drive the English back from their position on the low ridge across the bottom connecting the two hills. The seven hundred men were drawn from the north ridge, and as the fight grew hotter the whole of the sixteen hundred English were brought up.

Vere sent for reinforcements, but none came up, and for hours the sixteen hundred Englishmen alone checked the advance of the whole of the Spanish army. Sir Francis Vere was fighting like a private soldier in the midst of his troops. He received two balls in the leg, but still kept his seat and encouraged his men. At last the little band, receiving no aid or reinforcements from the Dutch, were forced to fall back. As they did so, Vere's horse fell dead under him and partly upon him, and it was with great difficulty that those around him extricated him. On reaching the battery on the sands Vere found the thousand Dutch of his division, who asserted that they had received no orders to advance. There were also three hundred foot under Sir Horace Vere and some cavalry under Captain Ball. These and Horace's infantry at once charged the Spaniards, who were pouting out from the sand hills near to the beach, and drove them back.

The Spaniards had now captured East Hill, and two thousand of their infantry advanced into the valley beyond, and drove back the musketeers from the south ridge, and a large force advanced along the green way; but their movements were slow, for they were worn out by their long struggle, and the English officers had time to rally their men again. Horace Vere returned from his charge on the beach, and other companies rallied and joined him, and charged furiously down upon the two thousand Spaniards. The whole of the Dutch and English cavalry also advanced. Solms' thousand men came up and took part in the action, and the batteries plied the Spaniards with their shot. The latter had done all they could, and were confounded by this fresh attack when they had considered the victory as won. In spite of the efforts of their officers they broke and fled in all directions. The archduke headed their flight, and never drew rein until he reached Brussels.

Zapena and the Admiral of Arragon were both taken prisoners, and about a third of the Spanish army killed and wounded. Of the sixteen hundred English half were killed or wounded; while the rest of the Dutch army suffered scarcely any loss — a fact that shows clearly to whom the honour of the victory belongs. Prince Maurice, in his letter to the queen, attributed his success entirely to the good order and directions of Sir Francis Vere. Thus, in a pitched battle the English troops met and defeated an army of six times their strength of the veterans of Spain, and showed conclusively that the English fighting man had in no way deteriorated since the days of Agincourt, the last great battle they had fought upon the Continent.

The battle at Nieuport may be considered to have set the final seal upon the independence of Holland. The lesson first taught at Turnhout had now been impressed with crushing force. The Spaniards were no longer invincible; they had been twice signally defeated in an open field by greatly inferior forces. Their prestige was annihilated; and although a war continued, there was no longer the slightest chance that the result of the long and bloody struggle would be reversed, or that Spain would ever again recover her grip of the lost provinces.

Sir Francis Vere was laid up for some months with his wounds. Among the officers who fought under him at Nieuport were several whose names were to become famous for the part they afterwards bore in the civil struggle in England. Among others were Fairfax, Ogle, Lambart, and Parker. Among those who received the honour of knighthood for their behaviour at the battle was Lionel Vickars. He had been severely wounded in the fight at East Hill, and was sent home to be cured there. It was some months before he again took the field, which he did upon the receipt of a letter from Sir Francis Vere, telling him that the Spaniards were closing in in great force round Ostend, and that his company was one of those that had been sent off to aid in the defence of that town.

During his stay in England he had spent some time with Geoffrey in London. Juan Mendez had now arrived there, and the business carried on by him and Geoffrey was flourishing greatly. Dolores had much missed the outdoor life to which she was accustomed, and her father had bought a large house with a fine garden in Chelsea; and she and Geoffrey were now installed there with him, Geoffrey going to and fro from the city by boat. They had now replaced the Spanish trading vessels by an equal number of English craft; and at the suggestion of Juan Mendez himself his name now stood second to that of Geoffrey, for the prejudice against foreigners was still strong in England.

CHAPTER XXII. OLD FRIENDS

The succession of blows that had been given to the power and commerce of Spain had immensely benefited the trade of England and Holland. France, devastated by civil war, had been in no position to take advantage of the falling off in Spanish commerce, and had indeed herself suffered enormously by the emigration of tens of thousands of the most intelligent of her population owing to her persecution of the Protestants. Her traders and manufacturers largely belonged to the new religion, and these had carried their industry and knowledge to England and Holland. Thus the religious bigotry of the kings of Spain and France had resulted in enormous loss to the trade and commerce of those countries, and in corresponding advantage to their Protestant rivals.

Geoffrey Vickars and his partner reaped the full benefit of the change, and the extensive acquaintance of the Spanish trader with merchants in all the Mediterranean ports enabled him to turn a large share of the new current of trade into the hands of Geoffrey and himself. The capital which he transferred from Spain to England was very much larger than that employed by the majority of English merchants, whose wealth had been small indeed in comparison to that of the merchant princes of the great centres of trade such as Antwerp, Amsterdam, Genoa, and Cadiz, and Geoffrey Vickars soon came to be looked upon as one of the leading merchants in the city of London.

"There can be no doubt, Geoffrey," his brother said as he lay on a couch in the garden in the early days of his convalescence, and looked at the river dotted with boats that flowed past it, "the falling of that mast was a fortunate thing for you. One never can tell how things will turn our. It would have seemed as if, were you not drowned at once, your lot would have been either a life's work in the Spanish galleys, or death in the dungeons of the Inquisition. Instead of this, here you are a wealthy merchant in the city, with a charming wife, and a father in law who is, although a Spaniard, one of the kindest and best men I ever met. All this time I, who was not knocked over by that mast, have been drilling recruits, making long marches, and occasionally fighting battles, and am no richer now than the day when we started together as Francis Vere's pages. It is true I have received the honour of knighthood, and that of course I prize much; but I have only my captain's pay to support my dignity, and as I hardly think Spain will continue this useless struggle much longer, in which case our army in Holland will be speedily disbanded, the prospect before me is not altogether an advantageous one."

"You must marry an heiress, Lionel," Geoffrey laughed. "Surely Sir Lionel Vickars, one of the heroes of Nieuport, and many another field, should be able to win the heart of some fair English damsel, with broad acres as her dower. But seriously, Lionel," he went on, changing his tone, "if peace come, and with it lack of employment, the best thing for you will be to join me. Mendez is getting on in years; and although he is working hard at present, in order, as he says, to set everything going smoothly and well here, he is looking forward to taking matters more easily, and to spending his time in tranquil pleasure with Dolores and her children. Therefore, whensoever it pleases you, there is a place for you here. We always contemplated our lines running in the same groove, and I should be glad that they should do so still. When the time comes we can discuss what share you shall have of the business; but at any rate I can promise you that it shall be sufficient to make you a rich man."

"Thank you, with all my heart, Geoffrey. It may be that some day I will accept your offer, though I fear you will find me but a sorry assistant. It seems to me that after twelve years of campaigning I am little fitted for life as a city merchant."

"I went through plenty of adventure for six years, Lionel, but my father in law has from the first been well satisfied with my capacity for business. You are not seven-and-twenty yet. You have had enough rough campaigning to satisfy anyone, and should be glad now of an easier and more sober method of life. Well, there is no occasion to settle anything at present, and I can well understand that you should prefer remaining in the army until the war comes to an end. When it does so, we can talk the matter over again; only be well assured that the offer will be always open to you, and that I shall be glad indeed to have you with me."

By England's Aid: or The Freeing

A few days after Lionel left him Geoffrey was passing along Chepe, when he stopped suddenly, stared hard at a gentleman who was approaching him, and then rushed towards him with outstretched hand.

"My dear Gerald!" he exclaimed, "I am glad to see you."

The gentleman started back with an expression of the profoundest astonishment.

"Is it possible?" he cried. "Is it really Geoffrey Vickars?"

"Myself, and no other, Gerald."

"The saints be praised! Why, I have been thinking of you all these years as either dead or labouring at an oar in the Moorish galleys. By what good fortune did you escape? and how is it I find you here, looking for all the world like a merchant of the city?"

"It is too long a story to tell now, Gerald. Where are you staying?"

"I have lodgings at Westminster, being at present a suitor at court."

"Is your wife with you?"

"She is. I have left my four children at home in Ireland."

"Then bring her to sup with me this evening. I have a wife to introduce to yours, and as she is also a Spaniard it will doubtless be a pleasure to them both."

"You astound me, Geoffrey. However, you shall tell me all about it this evening, for be assured that we shall come. Inez has so often talked about you, and lamented the ill fortune that befell you owing to your ardour."

"At six o'clock, then," Geoffrey said. "I generally dwell with my father in law at Chelsea, but am just at present at home. My house is in St. Mary Ave; anyone there will tell you which it is."

That evening the two friends had a long talk together. Geoffrey learnt that Gerald Burke reached Italy without further adventure, and thence took ship to Bristol, and so crossed over to Ireland. On his petition, and solemn promise of good behaviour in future, he was pardoned and a small portion of his estate restored to him. He was now in London endeavouring to obtain a remission of the forfeiture of the rest.

"I may be able to help you in that," Geoffrey said. "Sir Francis Vere is high in favour at court, and he will, at my prayer, I feel sure, use his influence in your favour when I tell him how you acted my friend on my landing in Spain from the Armada."

Geoffrey then gave an account of his various adventures from the time when he was struck down from the deck of the Barbary corsair until the present time.

"How was it," he asked when he concluded, "that you did not write to my parents, Gerald, on your return home? You knew where they lived."

"I talked the matter over with Inez," Gerald replied, "and we agreed that it was kinder to them to be silent. Of course they had mourned you as killed in the fight with the Armada. A year had passed, and the wound must have somewhat healed. Had I told them that you had escaped death at that time, had been months with me in Spain, and had, on your way home, been either killed by the Moors or were a prisoner in their galleys, it would have opened the wound afresh, and caused them renewed pain and sorrow."

"No doubt you were right, Gerald, and that it was, as you say, the kindest thing to leave them in ignorance of my fate."

Upon the next visit Sir Francis Vere paid to England, Geoffrey spoke to him with regard to Gerald Burke's affairs. Sir Francis took the matter up warmly, and his influence sufficed in a very short time to obtain an order for the restoration to Gerald of all his estates. Inez and Dolores became as fast friends as were their husbands; and when the Burkes came to England Geoffrey's house was their home.

The meeting with Gerald was followed by a still greater surprise, for not many days after, when Geoffrey was sitting with his wife and Don Mendez under the shade of a broad cypress in the garden of the merchant's house at Chelsea, they saw a servant coming across towards them, followed by a man in seafaring attire.

By England's Aid: or The Freeing

"Here is a person who would speak to you, Master Vickars," the servant said. "I told him it was not your custom to see any here, and that if he had aught to say he should call at your house in St. Mary Axe; but he said that he had but just arrived from Hedingham, and that your honour would excuse his intrusion when you saw him."

"Bring him up; he may be the bearer of a message from my father," Geoffrey said; and the servant went back to the man, whom he had left a short distance off.

"Master Vickars will speak with you."

The sailor approached the party. He stood for a minute before Geoffrey without speaking. Geoffrey looked at him with some surprise, and saw that the muscles of his face were twitching, and that he was much agitated. As he looked at him remembrance suddenly flashed upon him, and he sprang to his feet. "Stephen Boldero!" he exclaimed.

"Ay, ay, Geoffrey, it is me."

For a time the men stood with their right hands clasped and the left on each other's shoulders. Tears fell down the sailor's weather beaten cheeks, and Geoffrey himself was too moved to speak. For two years they had lived as brothers, had shared each other's toils and dangers, had talked over their plans and hopes together; and it was to Stephen that Geoffrey owed it that he was not now a galley slave in Barbary.

"Old friend, where have you been all this time?" he said at last, "I had thought you dead, and have grieved sorely for you."

"I have had some narrow escapes," Stephen said; "but you know I am tough. I am worth a good many dead men yet."

"Delores, Senor Mendez, you both remember Stephen Boldero?" Geoffrey said, turning to them.

"We have never forgotten you," the Spaniard said, shaking hands with the sailor, "nor how much we owe to you. I sent out instructions by every ship that sailed to the Indies that inquiries should be made for you; and moreover had letters sent by influential friends to the governors of most of the islands saying that you had done great service to me and

mine, and praying that if you were in any need or trouble you might be sent back to
Cadiz, and that any moneys you required might be given to you at my charge. But we
have heard nought of you from the day when the news came that you had left the ship in
which you went out.”

“I have had a rough time of it these five years,” Stephen said. “But I care not now that I
am home again and have found my friend Geoffrey. I arrived in Bristol but last week, and
started for London on the day I landed, mindful of my promise to let his people know that
he was safe and well, and with some faint hope that the capture of Cadiz had set him at
liberty. I got to Hedingham last night, and if I had been a prince Mr. Vickars and his
dame and Sir Lionel could not have made more of me. They were fain that I should stop
with them a day or two; but when I heard that you were in London and had married
Senora Dolores, and that Senor Mendez was with you — all of which in no way surprised
me, for methought I saw it coming before I left Cadiz — I could not rest, but was up at
daylight this morning. Your brother offered to procure me a horse, but I should have
made bad weather on the craft, and after walking from Bristol the tramp up to London
was nothing. I got to your house in the city at four; and, finding that you were here, took
a boat at once, for I could not rest until I saw my friend again.”

Geoffrey at once took him into the house and set him down to a meal; and when the party
were gathered later on in the sitting room, and the candles were lighted, Stephen told his
story.

“As you will have heard, we made a good voyage to the Indies. We discharged our cargo,
and took in another. I learned that there were two English ships cruising near San
Domingo, and the Dons were in great fear of them. I thought that my chance lay in
joining them, so when we were at our nearest port to that island I one night borrowed one
of the ship's boats without asking leave, and made off. I knew the direction in which San
Domingo lay, but no more. My hope was that I should either fall in with our ships at sea,
or, when I made the island, should be able to gather such information as might guide me
to them. When I made the land, after being four days out, I cruised about till the
provisions and water I had put on board were exhausted, and I could hold out no longer.
Then I made for the island and landed.

“You may be sure I did not make for a port, where I should be questioned, but ran ashore
in a wooded bay that looked as if no one had ever set foot there before. I dragged the boat

up beyond, as I thought, the reach of the sea, and started to hunt for food and water. I found enough berries and things to keep me alive, but not enough to stock my boat for another cruise. A week after I landed there was a tornado, and when it cleared off and I had recovered from my fright — for the trees were blown down like rushes, and I thought my last day was come — I found that the boat was washed away.

"I was mightily disheartened at this, and after much thinking made up my mind that there was nought for it but to keep along the shore until I arrived at a port, and then to give out that I was a shipwrecked sailor, and either try to get hold of another boat, or take passage back to Spain and make a fresh start. However, the next morning, just as I was starting, a number of natives ran out of the bush and seized me, and carried me away up into the hills.

"It was not pleasant at first, for they lit a big fire and were going to set me on the top of it, taking me for a Spaniard. Seeing their intentions, I took to arguing with them, and told them in Spanish that I was no Spaniard, but an Englishman, and that I had been a slave to the Spaniards and had escaped. Most of them understood some Spanish, having themselves been made to work as slaves in their plantations, and being all runaways from the tyranny of their masters. They knew, of course, that we were the enemies of the Spaniards, and had heard of places being sacked and ships taken by us. But they doubted my story for a long time, till at last one of them brought a crucifix that had somehow fallen into their hands, and held it up before me. When I struck it down, as a good Protestant should do, they saw that I was not of the Spanish religion, and so loosed my bonds and made much of me.

"They could tell me nothing of the whereabouts of our ships, for though they had seen vessels at times sail by, the poor creatures knew nothing of the difference of rig between an English craft and a Spaniard. I abode with them for two years, and aided them in their fights whenever the Spaniards sent out parties, which they did many times, to capture them. They were poor, timorous creatures, their spirits being altogether broken by the tyranny of the Dons; but when they saw that I feared them not, and was ready at any time to match myself against two or, if need be, three of the Spaniards, they plucked up heart, and in time came to fight so stoutly that the Spaniards thought it best to leave them alone, seeing that we had the advantage of knowing every foot of the woods, and were able to pounce down upon them when they were in straitened places and forced to fight at great disadvantage.

By England's Aid: or The Freeing

"I was regarded as a great chief by the natives, and could have gone on living with them comfortably enough had not my thoughts been always turning homeward, and a great desire to be among my own people, from whom I had been so long separated, devoured me. At last a Spanish ship was driven ashore in a gale; she went to pieces, and every soul was drowned. When the gale abated the natives went down to collect the stores driven ashore, and I found on the beach one of her boats washed up almost uninjured, so nothing would do but I must sail away in her. The natives tried their hardest to persuade me to stay with them, but finding that my mind was fixed beyond recall they gave way and did their best to aid me. The boat was well stored with provisions; we made a sail for her out of one belonging to the ship, and I set off, promising them that if I could not alight upon an English ship I would return to them.

"I had intended to keep my promise, but things turned out otherwise. I had not been two days at sea when there was another storm, for at one time of the year they have tornadoes very frequently. I had nothing to do but to run for it, casting much of my provisions overboard to lighten the boat, and baling without ceasing to keep out the water she took in. After running for many hours I was, somewhere about midnight, cast on shore. I made a shift to save myself, and in the morning found that I was on a low key. Here I lived for three weeks. Fortunately there was water in some of the hollows of the rocks, and as turtles came ashore to lay their eggs I managed pretty well for a time; but the water dried up, and for the last week I had nought to drink but the blood of the turtles.

One morning I saw a ship passing not far off; and making a signal with the mast of the boat that had been washed ashore with me I attracted their attention. I saw that she was a Spaniard, but I could not help that, for I had no choice but to hail her. They took me to Porto Rico and there reported me as a shipwrecked sailor they had picked up. The governor questioned me closely as to what vessel I had been lost from, and although I made up a good story he had his doubts. Fortunately it did not enter his mind that I was not a Spaniard; but he said he believed I was some bad character who had been marooned by my comrades for murder or some other crime, and so put me in prison until he could learn something that would verify my story.

"After three months I was taken out of prison, but was set to work on the fortifications, and there for another two years I had to stop. Then I managed to slip away one day, and, hiding till nightfall, made my way down through the town to the quays and swam out to a vessel at anchor. I climbed on board without notice, and hid myself below, where I lay for two days until she got up sail. When I judged she was well away from the land I went on deck and told my story, that I was a shipwrecked sailor who had been forced by the governor to work at the fortifications. They did not believe me, saying that I must be some criminal who had escaped from justice, and the captain said he should give me up at the next port the ship touched. Fortunately four days afterwards a sail hove in sight and gave chase, and before it was dark was near enough to fire a gun and make us heave to, and a quarter of an hour later a boat came alongside, and I again heard English spoken for the first time since I had left you at Cadiz.

"It was an English buccaneer, who, being short of water and fresh vegetables, had chased us, though seeing we were but a petty trader and not likely to have aught else worth taking on board. They wondered much when I discovered myself to them and told them who I was and how I had come there; and when, on their rowing me on board their ship, I told the captain my story he told me that he thought I was the greatest liar he had ever met. To be a galley slave among the Spaniards, a galley slave among the Moors, a consorter with Indians for two years, and again a prisoner with the Spaniards for as much more than fell to the lot of any one man, and he, like the Spanish governor, believed that I was some rascal who had been marooned, only he thought that it was from an English ship. However, he said that as I was a stout fellow he would give me another chance; and when, a fortnight later, we fell in with a great Spanish galleon and captured her with a great store of prize money after a hard fight for six hours, the last of which was passed on the deck of the Spaniard cutting and slashing — for, being laden with silver, she had a company of troops on board in addition to her crew — the captain said, that though an astonishing liar there was no better fellow on board a ship, and, putting it to the crew, they agreed I had well earned my share of the prize money. When we had got the silver on board, which was a heavy job I can tell you, though not an unpleasant one, we put what Spaniards remained alive into the boats, fired the galleon, and set sail for England, where we arrived without adventure.

"The silver was divided on the day before we cast anchor, the owner's share being first set aside, every man his share, and the officers theirs in proportion. Mine came to over a thousand pounds, and it needed two strong men to carry the chest up to the office of the owners, who gave me a receipt for it, which, as soon as I got, I started for London; and here, as you see, I am."

"And now, what do you propose to do with yourself, Stephen?" Geoffrey asked.

"I shall first travel down again to Devonshire and see what friends I have remaining there. I do not expect to find many alive, for fifteen years make many changes. My father and mother were both dead before I started, and my uncle, with whom I lived for a time, is scarce like to be alive now. Still I may find some cousins and friends I knew as a boy."

"I should think you have had enough of the sea, Stephen, and you have now ample to live ashore in comfort for the rest of your life."

"Yes, I shall go no more to sea," Stephen said. "Except for this last stroke of luck fortune has always been against me. What I should like, Master Geoffrey, most of all, would be to come up and work under you. I could be of advantage in seeing to the loading and unloading of vessels and the storage of cargo. As for pay, I should not want it, having, as you say, enough to live comfortably upon. Still I should like to be with you."

"And I should like to have you with me, Stephen. Nothing would give me greater pleasure. If you are still of that mind when you return from Devonshire we can again talk the matter over, and as our wishes are both the same way we can have no difficulty in coming to an agreement."

Stephen Boldero remained for a week in London and then journeyed down to Devonshire. His idea of entering Geoffrey's service was never carried out, for after he had been gone two months Geoffrey received a letter from him saying that one of his cousins, who had been but a little girl when he went away, had laid her orders upon him to buy a small estate and settle down there, and that as she was willing to marry him on no other terms he had nothing to do but to assent.

Once a year, however, regularly to the end of his life Stephen Boldero came up to London to stay for a fortnight with Geoffrey, always coming by road, for he declared that he was convinced if he set foot on board a ship again she would infallibly be wrecked on her voyage to London.

CHAPTER XXIII. THE SIEGE OF OSTEND

On the 5th of July, 1601, the Archduke Albert began the siege of Ostend with 20,000 men and 50 siege guns. Ostend had been completely rebuilt and fortified eighteen years previously, and was defended by ramparts, counterscarps, and two broad ditches. The sand hills between it and the sea were cut through, and the water filled the ditches and surrounded the town. To the south the country was intersected by a network of canals. The river Yper Leet came in at the back of the town, and after mingling with the salt water in the ditches found its way to the sea through the channels known as the Old Haven and the Geule, the first on the west, the second on the east of the town.

On either side of these channels the land rose slightly, enabling the besiegers to plant their batteries in very advantageous positions. The garrison at first consisted of but 2000 men under Governor Vander Nood. The States General considered the defence of Ostend to be of extreme importance to the cause, and appointed Sir Francis Vere general of the army in and about Ostend, and sent with him 600 Dutch troops and eight companies of English under the command of his brother, Sir Horace. This raised the garrison to the strength of 3600 men. Sir Francis landed with these reinforcements on the sands opposite the old town, which stood near the seashore between the Old Haven and the Geule, and was separated from the new town by a broad channel. He was forced to land here, as the Spanish guns on the sand hills commanded the entrances of the two channels.

Sixteen thousand of the Spanish troops under the order of the archduke were encamped to the west of the town, and had 30 of their siege guns in position there, while 4000 men were stationed on the east of the town under Count Bucquoy. Ten guns were in position on that side. Ostend had no natural advantages for defence beyond the facility of letting the sea into the numerous channels and ditches which intersected the city, and protected it from any operations on the south side. On the east the Geule was broad and deep, and an assault from this side was very difficult. The Old Haven, on the west side, was fast filling up, and was fordable for four hours every tide.

This, therefore, was the weak side of the town. The portion especially exposed to attack was the low sandy flat on which the old town stood, to the north of Ostend. It was against this point, separated only from the enemy's position by the shallow Old Haven, that the Spaniards concentrated their efforts. The defence here consisted of a work called the Porc Espic, and a bastion in its rear called the Helmond. Three works lay to the north of the ditch dividing the old from the new town, while on the opposite side of this ditch was a fort called the Sand Hill, from which along the sea face of the town ran strong palisades and bastions.

The three principal bastions were named the Schottenburg, Moses' Table, and the Flamenburg, the last named defending the entrance to the Geule on the eastern side. There was a strong wall with three bastions, the North Bulwark, the East Bulwark or Pekell, and the Spanish Bulwark at the southeast angle, with an outwork called the Spanish Half Moon on the other side of the Geule. The south side was similarly defended by a wall with four strong bastions, while beyond these at the southwest corner lay a field called the Polder, extending to the point where the Yper Leer ran into the ditches.

Sir Francis Vere's first step after his arrival was to throw up three redoubts to strengthen the wall round this field, as had the enemy taken possession of it they might have set the windmills upon it to work and have drained out many of the ditches. Having secured this point he cut a passage to the sea between the Northwest Bulwark and the Flamenburg Fort, so that shipping might enter the port without having to ascend the Geule, exposed to the fire of the Spanish guns. To annoy the enemy and draw them away from the vital point near the sea, he then stationed 200 men on some rising ground surrounded by swamps and ditches at some distance to the south of the city, and from here they were able to open fire on the enemy's boats coming with supplies from Bruges.

The operation was successful. The Spaniards, finding their line of communication threatened, advanced in force from their position by the sea, and their forts opened a heavy fire on the little work thrown up. Other similar attempts would have been made to harass the Spaniards and divert them from their main work, had not Sir Francis Vere been severely wounded in the head on the 4th of August by a shot from the Spanish batteries, which continued to keep up a tremendous fire upon the town. So serious was the wound that the surgeons were of opinion that the only chance of saving his life was to send him away from the din and turmoil of the siege; and on the 10th he was taken to Middelburg, where he remained for a month, returning to Ostend long before his wound was properly healed.

On the 1st of August a batch of recruits had arrived from England, and on the 8th 1200 more were landed. The fire of the besiegers was now so heavy that the soldiers were forced to dig underground quarters to shelter themselves. Sir Horace Vere led out several sorties; but the besiegers, no longer distracted by the feints contrived by Sir Horace Vere, succeeded in erecting a battery on the margin of the Old Haven, and opened fire on the Sand Hill Fort.

On the 19th of September Sir Francis Vere returned to the town, to the great joy of the garrison. Reinforcements continued to arrive, and at this time the garrison numbered 4480. There were, too, a large number of noblemen and gentlemen from England, France, and Holland, who had come to learn the art of war under the man who was regarded as the greatest general of the time. All who were willing to work and learn were heartily welcomed; those who were unwilling to do so were soon made to feel that a besieged city was no place for them.

While the fighting was going on the archduke had attempted to capture the place by treason. He engaged a traitor named Coningsby; who crossed to England, obtained letters of introduction to Vere, and then went to Ostend. Thence he sent intelligence to the besiegers of all that took place in the town, placing his letters at night in an old boat sunk in the mud on the bank of the Old Haven, a Spaniard wading across at low tide and fetching them away. He then attempted to bribe a sergeant to blow up the powder magazine. The sergeant revealed the plot. Coningsby was seized and confessed everything, and by an act of extraordinary clemency was only sentenced to be whipped out of town.

This act of treachery on the part of the archduke justified the otherwise dishonourable stratagem afterwards played by Vere upon him. All through October and November the Spaniards were hard at work advancing their batteries, sinking great baskets filled with sand in the Old Haven to facilitate the passage of the troops, and building floating batteries in the Geule. On the night of the 4th of December they advanced suddenly to the attack. Vere and his officers leapt from their beds and rushed to the walls, and after a fierce struggle the besiegers were driven back. Straw was lighted to enable the musketeers and gunners to fire upon them as they retreated, and the assault cost them five hundred lives.

On the 12th a hard frost set in, and until Christmas a strong gale from the southeast blew. No succour could reach the town. The garrison were dwindling fast, and ammunition falling short. It required fully 4000 men to guard the walls and forts, while but 2500 remained capable of bearing arms. It was known that the archduke soon intended to make an assault with his whole force, and Vere knew that he could scarcely hope to repel it. He called a council of his chief officers, and asked their opinion whether with the present numbers all parts of the works could be manned in case of assault, and if not whether it was advisable to withdraw the guards from all the outlying positions and to hold only the town.

They were unanimously of opinion that the force was too small to defend the whole, but Sir Horace Vere and Sir John Ogle alone gave their advice to abandon the outlying forts rather than endanger the loss of the town. The other officers were of opinion that all the works should be held, although they acknowledged that the disposable force was incapable of doing so. Some days elapsed, and Vere learned that the Spanish preparations were all complete, and that they were only waiting for a low tide to attack. Time was everything, for a change of wind would bring speedy succour, so without taking council with anyone he sent Sir John Ogle with a drummer to the side of the Old Haven.

Don Mateo Serrano came forward, and Ogle gave his message, which was that General Vere wished to have some qualified person to speak to him. This was reported to the archduke, who agreed that Serrano and another Spanish officer should go into the town, and that Ogle and a comrade should come as hostages into the Spanish camp. Sir John Ogle took his friend Sir Charles Fairfax with him, and Serrano and Colonel Antonio crossed into Ostend. The two Englishmen were conducted to the archduke, who asked Sir John Ogle to tell him if there was any deceit in the matter. Ogle answered if there were it was more than he knew, for Vere had simply charged him to carry the message, and that he and Fairfax had merely come as hostages for the safe return of the Spanish officers.

Ogle was next asked whether he thought the general intended sincerely or not, and could only reply that he was altogether unacquainted with the general's purpose.

The next morning Serrano and Antonio returned without having seen Vere. The pretext on which they had been sent back was that there was some irregularity in their coming across; but instead of their being sent back across the Old Haven they were sent across the Geule, and had to make a long round to regain the archduke's camp.

Thus a day and a night were gained. The next day, towards evening, the two Spanish officers were admitted into Ostend, and received very hospitably by Sir Francis. After supper many healths were drunk, and then Sir Francis informed them to their astonishment that his proposal was not that he should surrender Ostend, but that the archduke should raise the siege. But it was now far too late for them to return, and they went to bed in the general's quarters. During the two nights thus gained the defenders had worked incessantly in repairing the palisades facing the point at which the attack would take place, a work that they had hitherto been unable to perform owing to the tremendous fire that the Spaniards kept up night and day upon it.

At break of day five men of war from Zeeland came to anchor off the town. They brought four hundred men, and provisions and materials of war of all kinds. They were immediately landed under a heavy fire from the enemy's batteries on both sides. The firing awoke the two Spanish envoys, who inquired what was taking place. They were politely informed by Sir Francis Vere that succour had arrived, and the negotiations were of course broken off; and they were accordingly sent back, while Ogle and Fairfax returned to Ostend.

Vere's account of the transaction was that he had simply asked for two Spanish officers to speak with him. He had offered no terms, and there was therefore no breach of faith. The commander of a besieged town, he insisted, is always at liberty to propose a parley, which the enemy can accept or not as he chooses. At any rate, it was not for the archduke, who had hired a traitor to corrupt the garrison, to make a complaint of treachery. Twelve hundred men were employed for the next eight days in strengthening the works, Sir Francis being always with them at night, when the water was low, encouraging them by his presence and example.

Early in January he learned that the enemy were preparing for the assault, and on the 7th a crushing fire was kept up on the Porc Espic, Helmond, and Sand Hill forts. The Spaniards had by this time fired 163,200 cannon shot into the town, and scarcely a whole house was left standing. Towards evening they were seen bringing scaling ladders to the opposite bank of the Haven. Two thousand Italian and Spanish troops had been told off to attack the sand hill, two thousand were to assault Helmond and the Porc Espic, two parties of five hundred men each were to attack other works, while on the east side Count Bucquoy was to deliver a general assault.

The English general watched all these preparations with the greatest vigilance. At high water he closed the west sluice, which let the water into the town ditch from the Old Haven, in the rear of Helmond, in order to retain as much water as possible, and stationed his troops at the various points most threatened. Sir Horace Vere and Sir Charles Fairfax, with twelve weak companies, some of them reduced to ten or twelve men, were stationed on the sand hill.

By England's Aid: or The Freeing

Four of the strongest companies garrisoned the Porc Espic; ten weak companies and nine cannon loaded with musket bullets defended the Helmond. These posts were commanded by Sergeant Major Carpenter and Captain Meetkerk; the rest of the force were disposed at the other threatened points. Sir Francis himself, with Sir Lionel Vickars as his right hand, took his post on the wall of the old town, between the sand hill and the Schottenburg, which had been much damaged by the action of the waves during the gales and by the enemy's shot. Barrels of ashes, heaps of stones and bricks, hoops bound with squibs and fireworks, ropes of pitch, hand grenades, and barrels of nails were collected in readiness to hurl down upon the assailants.

At dusk the besiegers ceased firing, to allow the guns to cool. Two engineer officers with fifty stout sappers, who each had a rose noble for every quarter of an hour's work, got on to the breach in front of the sand hill, and threw up a small breastwork, strengthened by palisades, across it. An officer crept down towards the Old Haven, and presently returned with the news that two thousand of the enemy were wading across, and forming up in battalions on the Ostend side.

Suddenly a gun boomed out from the archduke's camp as a signal to Bucquoy, and just as the night had fairly set in the besiegers rushed to the assault from all points. They were received by a tremendous fire from the guns of the forts and the muskets of the soldiers; but, although the effect was serious, they did not hesitate a moment, but dashed forwards towards the foot of the sand hill and the wall of the old town, halted for a moment, poured in a volley, and then rushed into the breach and against the walls. The volley had been harmless, for Vere had ordered the men to lie flat until it was given. As the Spaniards climbed up barrels of ashes were emptied upon them, stones and heavy timbers hurled down, and flaming hoops cast over their necks. Three times they climbed to the crest of the sand hill, and as many times gained a footing on the Schottenburg; but each time they were beaten back with great slaughter. As fiercely did they attack at the other points, but were everywhere repulsed.

On the east side three strong battalions of the enemy attacked the outwork across the Geule, known as the Spanish Half Moon. Vere, who was everywhere supervising the defence, ordered the weak garrison there to withdraw, and sent a soldier out to give himself up, and to tell them that the Half Moon was slenderly manned, and to offer to lead them in. The offer was accepted, and the Spaniards took possession of the work.

278

The general's object was to occupy them, and prevent their supporting their comrades in the western attack. The Half Moon, indeed, was quite open towards the town. Tide was rising, and a heavy fire was opened upon the captors of the work from the batteries across the Geule, and they were driven out with the loss of three hundred men. At length the assault was repulsed at all points, and the assailants began to retire across the Old Haven. No sooner did they begin to ford it than Vere opened the west sluice, and the water in the town ditch rushed down in a torrent, carrying numbers of the Spaniards away into the sea.

Altogether, the assault cost the Spaniards two thousand men. An enormous amount of plunder in arms, gold chains, jewels, and rich garments were obtained by the defenders from the bodies of the fallen. The loss of the garrison was only thirty killed and a hundred wounded.

The repulse of the grand attack upon Ostend by no means put an end to the siege. Sir Francis Vere, his brother Horace, Sir John Ogle, and Sir Lionel Vickars left, the general being summoned to assume command in the field; but the siege continued for two years and a half longer. Many assaults were repulsed during that time, and the town only surrendered on the 20th September, 1604, when the sand hill, which was the key of the whole position, was at last captured by the Spaniards.

It was but a heap of ruins that they had become possessed of after their three years' siege, and its capture had not only cost them an immense number of men and a vast amount of money, but the long and gallant defence had secured upon a firm basis the independence of Holland. While the whole available force of Spain had been so occupied Prince Maurice and his English allies had captured town after town, and had beaten the enemy whenever they attempted to show themselves in the open field. They had more than counterbalanced the loss of Ostend by the recapture of Sluys, and had so lowered the Spanish pride that not long afterwards a twelve years truce was concluded, which virtually brought the war to an end, and secured for ever the independence of Holland.

During the last year or two of the war Sir Francis Vere, worn out by his fatigues and the countless wounds he had received in the service of the Netherlands, had resigned his command and retired to England, being succeeded in his position by Sir Horace. Lionel Vickars fought no more after he had borne his part in the repulse of the great assault against Ostend. He had barely recovered from the effect of the wound he had received at the battle of Nieuport, and the fatigues and anxiety of the siege, together with the damp air from the marshes, brought on a serious attack of fever, which completely prostrated him as soon as the necessity for exertion had passed. He remained some weeks at the Hague, and then, being somewhat recovered, returned home.

While throughout all England the greatest enthusiasm had been aroused by the victory of Nieuport and the repulse of the Spaniards at Ostend, the feeling was naturally higher in the Vere's county of Essex than elsewhere. As soon as Lionel Vickars was well enough to take any share in gaieties he received many invitations to stay at the great houses of the county, where most of the gentry were more or less closely connected with the Veres; and before he had been home many months he married Dorothy Windhurst, one of the richest heiresses in the county, and a cousin of the Veres. Thus Geoffrey had, after Juan Mendez retired from taking any active part in the business, to work alone until his sons were old enough to join him in the business. As soon as they were able to undertake its active management, Geoffrey bought an estate near Hedingham, and there settled down, journeying occasionally to London to see how the affairs of the house went on, and to give advice to his sons. Dolores had, two or three years after her arrival in England, embraced the faith of her husband; and although she complained a little at times of the English climate, she never once regretted the step she had taken in leaving her native Spain.

THE END

Printed in the United States
30004LVS00003B/44